The Infusion
of
Archie Lambert

Books by Thom Reese

The Empty
A Savage Distance
The Demon Baqash
Chasing Kelvin
Dead Man's Fire
13 Bodies
The Crimson Soul of Nathan Greene

COMING SOON!

The Dracula Journals

The Infusion
of
Archie Lambert

Thom Reese

SPEAKING VOLUMES, LLC
NAPLES, FLORIDA
2016

The Infusion of Archie Lambert

Copyright © 2016 by Thom Reese

ISBN 978-1-62815-492-4

For my three amazing daughters,

Trista, Amy and Brittany.

You've grown and spread your wings, but you are each in my heart and thoughts every hour, every minute, every breath.

Acknowledgements

A book manuscript is like clay. It begins with the vague shape of what it will become and with each draft, with each revision and refinement, continues to transform until at some point the author must relinquish it and send it to the publisher and then into the world.

But while this is an oftentimes solitary process with hundreds of hours spent alone with the imagination, the computer, and sometimes the cat for company, no manuscript comes to fruition without the help and encouragement of others. As always, special thanks to my amazing wife Kathy. You always find those little things that make the book better and you're always there to give me a kick or a hug, depending on the need. You breathe life into my soul. My girls Trista, Amy, and Brittany are both inspirations and encouragers. I love you each beyond words. A special thank you to Jeff Granstrom for his continued insightful input on all of my manuscripts. Thank you also to Shane Sather for his feedback and suggestions on this manuscript. I'd also like to thank Kurt and Erica Mueller, Jonathan Maberry, Ray Garton, Amy Densham, Travis Szynski, and Kym Low.

Chapter One

Death, it seemed, had become quite noisy. There were shouts, screams, roars of outrage, the sounds of crashing furniture—and commercial interruptions. Death had offered no dreams. The patient had not been taken to heaven; nor had he been subjected to its much less inviting counterpart. But his death was really not a death—not in the traditional sense. He'd been offered the economy package. Darkness. Pure, simple, ink-black darkness. By this point, though, it was no longer death at all, but merely a coma, and even this faded in lingering wisps of green and gray, the only remaining remnant of his demise being the peculiar impression that his very soul was subject to an unsettling scrutiny.

The patient's first conscious sensation of the physical world was not of sound or of sight, but rather that something was sticking out of his right forearm, an I.V. It made the arm feel stiff, sore. There was a tingling, not unpleasant, but still rather more intense than anything considered comfortable. It was akin to a mild electrical current racing up his arm, then down through his torso, into his legs, and once reaching the very tips of each of his ten toes, reversing to retrace its way through his now living body, eventually reaching his head where it settled into a dull and slightly uneven buzz. He was still only emerging from the blackest depths, his mind had yet to fully engage, and yet still he managed to wonder why. Why this sensation? What did it mean? He hadn't yet stopped to ponder where he was—or even who he was—but this question, at least, clawed its way to the surface.

Then came taste. Lavender, of all things. He'd never tasted lavender, but if he could taste the smell of lavender, this would have been that taste: sweet, slightly exotic, yet powdery and dry. It made his nose tickle, and his tongue move about his mouth seeking saliva to rehydrate his system. Again, peculiar. Why any taste at all? Nothing was right. None of this. He was not right. Somehow he knew this and yet could not fathom what the thought might mean. He thought to scream, to voice his mounting fear, his growing terror at his situation, but was not yet sure how that might be done.

Next came sound. At first it was very far off, and small, as if cascading down a long hollow tunnel, bounding off metallic walls, surging, swelling. But then abruptly it was upon him, surrounding, nettling, pressing yet not penetrating. Initially it was the subtly annoying sound of the bleeping heart monitor beside his bed, and then the chaotic turbulence of the daytime television world.

He gasped.

A sharp intake of breath.

His eyes fluttered open.

Just barely, the eyelids at first moving independently of one another, causing a strobe-like effect. The light hurt them, and initially sights and sounds were indistinct, shadows floating about, voices and music warbling in and out of phase. He could make out the flickering television mounted before him on the wall. He wanted to leave, to flee back into the welcoming darkness, his sweet and silent oblivion, but he was as a fossil, petrified, immobile.

To his left, a frumpy middle-aged nurse puttered about, straightening a potted plant, sliding a tissue box to the rear right corner of an end table, and generally trying to appear busy. Her features and form seemed fluid, as if her body stretched and contorted in some insane elastic waltz. But soon she settled into a satisfactorily human configuration.

The patient allowed a subtle sigh to flee his lungs. There was a normalcy about this person, and yet…

A name. At the forefront in his mind. Paramount. All important.

"Jill?" he said in a tiny voice, still not fully understanding where he was or what had happened to him. "Jill?" he repeated, though at some level he must have known the nurse could not be Jill. Of course, this could not be Jill.

She had not heard him and so he summoned what little strength he could muster and spoke a bit louder. "I need a drink," he said, his voice weak, dry, the vocal cords tight and unaccustomed to use. It felt like his voice hadn't been used in weeks. He barely knew how to form these few words or to project them once he'd willed his mouth and tongue into reluctant compliance. It was almost as if he'd never spoken before, as if he was an infant just learning how to control his own body. And the tone of the voice. It was high. Too high. Unfamiliar. Almost like a woman's voice, not like his normal gravely baritone, or even like the weakened gasps of the past few months.

Why had he thought that? The past few months. What did he mean by that thought?

The nurse moved hesitantly, as if she'd encountered some formerly unknown life form. "We didn't think you'd ever come out of it," she exclaimed in a voice that was both hushed and urgent.

"Beer," he said, his voice still barely above a gasping croak.

There was another voice now, feminine, from his right. "Joey?" she said. "Joey, is that you?"

He let his head lull in the direction of the sound. There was a young woman seated on a loveseat, a laptop computer on her thighs. Her cobalt blue eyes narrowed, and her slim lips quivered as she said the name again. "Joey?" Three feet to her left, in a separate seat, was a man, not tall, maybe five-eight, mid-thirties, with a three-day beard, flannel shirt, and blue jeans. He was just coming into consciousness. "Joey?" asked the woman again, her voice tight and anxious as if she had to keep saying the name in order to believe whatever it was that she believed.

"It's him," said the nurse. "He's awake." The nurse leaned over the patient, testing his pulse with two cold fingers, gazing at the monitors to his left. "How are you feeling, honey?"

"Beer," he said in a soprano croak. He now understood that he was in a hospital room, bland, sterile, utilitarian. Why was he here? Who were these people? None of this seemed as it should.

The nurse's face twisted into an exasperated crumple as she snorted and patted his shoulder gently. "Beer isn't on your chart, honey. Let me get Dr. Lambert. I'm sure he'll want to see you right away."

Dr. Lambert.

Dr. Lambert…

Giving him one more pat for good measure, the nurse turned and moved out of the room, leaving the patient with the young couple. The woman now stood beside his bed, gazing down at him, a curious expression on her face.

She was in her mid-thirties, bore little makeup, and wore a functional black top, designer jeans, and a cautious expression on her pallid face. The woman certainly could be attractive, but now appeared only tired and strained.

"Joey," she said almost hesitantly. "Mommy thought we'd never see you again." Her words were nearly garbled as she nibbled her thumb knuckle unconsciously.

"Mommy?" he asked, his voice tight and high.

"Yes, Joey. It's me." Her fingers seemed to tremble as her lips grew taut. "Do you remember?"

"Remember?" asked the patient.

"Esther?" said the man, now fully emerging from his listless sleep, massaging his eyes with his palms, then blinking several times with the shake of his head causing his shoulder length hair to tumble wildly. "Esther, what's going on?"

"He's awake," said the woman as she eyed the patient. Her tone was even and controlled, suppressing obvious emotion.

The man squinted and then rose with a stretch and a groan, his light green eyes curious and hopeful. "Joey?" smiled the man as he drew closer, still wiping crust from his eyes. "Joey. You made it, champ." There was no repression here. The man nearly screamed the words, his easy grin stretching from cheek to cheek.

The woman gazed at the patient as the man patted his shoulder, giving it an earnest squeeze. "We were so worried about you," said the man.

The patient remained silent. This was not right. None of this was right.

"Do you remember anything?" asked the woman who fought some internal struggle, her knuckles rising to her lips before pulling away only to return seconds later.

"I don't remember you," he said in a flat, emotionless tone. He couldn't allow his confusion or unease to become apparent. Not until he cleared his head of the lingering mist. Not until it came together. Everything was still jumbled, cascading fragments of memory, quick snatches of meaning, but nothing solid, nothing he could cling to.

The woman's eyes narrowed, her jaw clenched, her lips slid into a tight grin. "Oh," she said. "Are you certain?"

The patient had no idea who this woman was, or what she was doing in his hospital room. Obviously she and the man believed themselves to be his parents, but that was ludicrous. He was in his mid-forties—he knew this now, though moments before he couldn't have said for sure. These two had to be ten years his juniors. How could they possibly think him their son?

There was commotion in the hallway, voices rising and falling, questions barked and then answered. The familiar form of Dr. Colin Lambert marched through the doorway, clipboard in hand, lab coat rumpled and stained, a determined and possibly even worried expression on his taut, angular face. He was trailed closely by the jabbering middle-aged nurse.

"It's true," said Colin with a nearly suppressed grin as he stepped to beside the bed, pulled a penlight from his breast pocket, and examined each of the patient's eyes. His gaze was intense, curious, even bemused, but not overly familiar or friendly as he felt about the temples, squeezing the patient's head as he might a ripe melon. He lifted the patient slightly, tapping at the base of his skull and then a foot or so down the spine. He moved to the feet, tickling each one, apparently seeking to learn if there was sensation. He nodded and snorted, making notes on his clipboard. He told the nurse to order something called a "SPECT," then studied the nearby monitors.

Colin leaned over him, once again inspecting his eyes. "Say something for me," he said.

"Who are these people?" asked the patient. His voice, though still sore, was becoming less raspy with use.

The woman answered before Colin could respond. "I'm your mother."

"Not my mother," he began to say, but Colin cut him off mid-sentence.

"He's disoriented, Mrs. Burke. He's been through an ordeal, suffered trauma.

The woman appeared extremely fragile yet determined. It seemed she fought some internal turmoil. The man, though silent, was perplexed, standing opposite his wife and gazing at the patient with a curious and worrisome expression.

"Joey," repeated the woman. "Do you know me? Do you remember anything?" Her tone was even and nearly controlled, cracking only at the very last syllable.

Colin straightened, strolled around the bed, and led the couple toward the door. "The boy," he said. "He may not be the same as the boy you remember." At this, the woman glared at Colin, her eyes somehow both intense and confused, her hands wriggling before her, grappling with one another in some bizarre bout for control.

"What should we expect, Doctor?" asked the man, who, though visibly shaken, was obviously attempting to remain strong.

"That, Greg, is yet to be seen," said Colin. "He will need time to adjust. I'll run tests, keep him for observation. We're at the beginning of a very long road." Colin placed his hand on the man's shoulder. "Now, I suggest you and Esther go to the cafeteria, get some food, allow me to do a more thorough examination. Come back to my office, in say, an hour. We'll discuss matters at that time."

"No," said the woman. "He just woke up. He needs me beside him." There was conviction in the voice, a stout proclamation verging on hysteria.

Colin nodded, but stated firmly, "Right now he needs me, his doctor. Your presence will only aggravate and confuse him."

"And why would you think that?" she nearly barked. The trepidation was gone. This was the lioness protecting her cub.

"Because he's already showing signs of agitation and disorientation." Colin paused, studying the woman. "Mrs. Burke, Esther, at this moment, for this first hour or so at least, he should not be forced into emotionally charged scenarios. Questioning by a concerned and well-meaning parent could be detrimental."

Greg, the husband, glanced nervously at his wife and then allowed his gaze to rest on Colin, obviously attempting to decide whether or not to comply with the doctor's orders. "Alright," he said, again glancing at Esther. "I get it. We'll go find some food. But, we won't stay gone for long. We've waited for this for..." Here he broke off, unable to complete the thought as finally, tears pushed through to the surface.

"No," said Esther, glaring venom at her spouse. "I'll stay."

"Eventually, yes, but not now," said Colin in his most authoritative tone.

Esther seemed as though she might speak, but Greg said, "We don't want to cause a stir, Esther. Let the man do his job." Wiping his eyes with a sleeve, he put his opposite hand on Esther's shoulder.

She jerked away. "I won't be kept from my boy."

Colin nodded. "There is no need for concern. You will have regular access."

Greg nodded. Esther gazed at the patient. Their eyes met. And there was something in the woman's stare. Was it scrutiny, fear, perhaps anger that the encounter had not gone as she'd hoped? And then they were gone, Esther marching from the room with a loud huff, Greg trailing behind with a backward glance and a cautious wink, leaving the patient confused and unsettled.

Colin sighed, clicked his pen twice, and crossed to the patient, his cool gray eyes intent and focused.

"Colin," asked the patient. "What's happened to me?"

The patient's father set his clipboard at the foot of the bed and leaned closer, his lips nearly to the boy's ear. The patient could smell the familiar aroma of peanuts on his breath. "Remember," whispered Colin. "Archie, you must remember."

Chapter Two

Archie did remember. Not right then, not on Colin's command. But perhaps a day or two later, after much prodding and enough stimulants to make a Starbucks addict leap and scream, he came around. And when the memories came, they came not in little pieces of vague remembrances, or in half dreams or mystic riddles. The whole thing was there, like a movie to be viewed in vivid high definition.

He remembered the phone call. The voice had been familiar, almost painfully so. It was a masculine voice, older, but maybe a bit stronger than the last time he'd heard it. Still, there was tentativeness, hesitation. "Archie? Archie, are you there?"

"Hello, Colin," said Archie. He'd not called Colin "Dad" or "Daddy" since he'd been twelve or thirteen years old. The title just didn't fit. In truth, Archie suspected that Colin had been somewhat relieved when his son had begun addressing him by his given name, as if this act relieved him of responsibility, freeing him to go about his life with even less regard for his two children and their mother.

There was a pause on the line, a sigh, a swallow. "Archie, I heard… Cancer."

"Yeah," said Archie. What else was there to say?

Another swallow, another sigh. "How long?"

"They say I have three months. That's a stretch."

"Archie… When were you going to tell me?"

Archie clenched his fist. "Colin, I don't mean to be insensitive, but it's been what? Five, six years? Not even a Christmas card. I wasn't."

Colin hesitated, perhaps pondering his next response. There was a rustle on the line as if he'd stood up and begun to pace. "What about your wife?" he finally asked.

"Ex-wife," corrected Archie. "Marcie. She doesn't know. All I have to pass on are bills and memories. She'd prefer the bills."

"Archie… I'm a physician."

"I know what my father does for a living, Colin. You're a neurologist—one of the best. You do research. But the cancer's not in my brain, or in my nervous system, it's in my lungs, and my stomach, and my intestines. It's…" He trailed off without completing the thought. It was one thing to hear about the illness, to understand its severity, to even come to grips with its ramifications, but it was another thing to verbalize it, to force it out into the open where all of the well-meaning vultures could pick and prod. It was almost as if it was still all just a dream, some sick, twisted nightmare until it was shared with another human being. Then it became real. It became ugly, dangerous. A tear escaped Archie's eye and raced down his left cheek. His nose dripped, but he refused to sniffle and let Colin in on his misery.

Archie heard footsteps through the receiver, heels on a hardwood floor, then a door closing. When Colin spoke again, it was in a low quiet tone, almost a whisper. "Listen, Archie. There's a procedure—experimental. I've been involved in its development for nearly seven years."

"Don't give me false hope, Colin. You and I both know this body's shot."

"That's the thing," he said in his low hushed tone. "This procedure would have very little to do with your body."

*****

On the fifth day in what was to be Archie Lambert's last hospital stay, he was pulled early from bed, shuffled into a wheelchair, and wheeled into an elevator. At first he hated the things—the wheelchairs. He despised being pushed around like some infant incapable of tending to even insignificant needs. But eventually he'd become weak enough, and movement became painful enough, that he longed to have a nurse at his side twenty-four/seven, just so she could give him a cup of water or scratch an itch, so that she could turn the television to the Bulls game or readjust his pillows. The wheelchair became his friend and his nemesis. It was a means to escape the monotonous existence within any one of the many small rooms he'd occupied recently. But it was also a painful and exhausting process just to take the few steps from bed to chair.

9

Archie shared the elevator with an elderly man who lay on a gurney. I.V. solutions dripped steadily into the man's veins. He was coughing, pale, staring at Archie through yellow pleading eyes, and mumbling something about someone named Betsy. Archie looked down and away. There was nothing he could say to the man, no hope he could give. They were both racing toward the grave, and no one could predict which would get there first. The man reached for Archie, his fingertips lightly brushing his right arm. Archie jerked away, longing to get off on the next floor. "Betsy," said the man. "Betsy."

The elevator door opened and Archie was wheeled into a long richly carpeted hallway lined with offices. The man called to Betsy again and Archie prayed he'd find her at least one last time before he was gone.

Archie was taken to an office. It was spacious and finely furnished with a large mahogany desk, several tall bookcases, subtle yet elegant lamps, and a plush wool rug that undoubtedly came from somewhere outside of the continental United States. Numerous awards and degrees adorned the darkly paneled walls and a brain-shaped trophy sat on a shelf beside a photograph of Colin and a chubby gray-haired man in a tuxedo. No pictures indicating family or hobbies were evident, but journals and medical tomes filled all of Colin's available space.

In striking contrast to his sickeningly spotless and uncluttered office, the man, Dr. Colin Lambert, appeared as a rumpled academic: dark brown hair slightly askew and laced with silver, pale yellow cardigan sweater wrinkled and stained with what appeared to be orange jelly, and thick plastic glasses which he continually pushed at with his narrow and delicate index finger. Strangers thought him peculiar, the way he dressed, his inattention to his appearance, but Archie understood all too well. Colin was a man driven by his research and little else mattered—least of all the fashion foibles of strangers. Those who knew him were aware of his brilliance; those unconnected to his goals were of no import. Colin was brilliant, obsessed, and socially inept. A widower since age fifty-one, nearly seventeen years now, he sat behind his expansive desk scanning some unquestionably critical reports and speaking to a severe, yet illogically attractive woman of about forty, who sat before him.

"Colin," she said in a tone of both butter and spice. "We're not questioning the science. It's brilliant. But…"

"Ethics," interrupted Colin. "You're concerned about ethics, morality, right, wrong, and," he added with a grin and a nod. "Public perception. I get it, Diana. I don't believe you really give a damn about it, but I do get it. Would you like some peanuts?" Colin extended a carnival glass bowl of his favorite snack.

The woman declined the peanuts and sighed, inclining her head just slightly in Archie's direction, revealing clear, chocolate brown eyes, nearly black, intelligent and knowing. She smoothed her dark straight hair with a whisk of a narrow hand and said, "There is a question of ethics, yes. But, the true concern is the science."

"I'm quite aware of your concerns," said Colin as he withdrew the bowl and snatched a handful of nuts. "It's just that your concerns are not my greatest concern."

The woman allowed her lips to curl just slightly, yet her eyes remained firm and fixed. "Colin, we are dear friends, yes, but not lovers. You can push me only so far."

Colin grinned. "I presume no relationship beyond that of close, professional, admiration," he said.

"Fair enough," nodded the woman with perhaps a hint of melancholy in her tone. "Then I trust I will see your report by the end of the day."

It seemed it was then that Colin remembered Archie's presence. He turned, his gray eyes narrowing and his sloping brows furrowing just slightly above his near triangular nose. The thin line of his mouth curled with the hint of annoyance until, only a moment later, his eyes widened as he examined his renegade son.

"Diana," he said, while still eying Archie. "Another day, I suppose. As you see, a patient has arrived." The woman said nothing, but rose, giving Colin a narrow gaze. "Yes, yes," said Colin. "I will consider your concerns. Nothing will be done without your consent. Fair enough?"

She nodded. "Very well. I'll take that as a promise to be kept. Good day, Colin." And with that she turned, eyed Archie with a curious stare, one eyebrow rising as if in contemplation, and then proceeded past him and through the door. It seemed the woman might be interested in Colin—romantically—and that perhaps the feeling was mutual. But Archie knew Colin would never pursue a relationship. His mother had essentially lived the life of a widow for two decades before she finally passed and freed Colin to devote his life completely and wholly to his work. Besides, this woman had to be twenty-five years his junior; younger even than Archie. Still, something had been there, some connection. And if not romantic, then what?

Even though Archie and Colin had seen each other several times since their initial phone conversation, Colin's gaze still lingered on his son with a dreary sadness. It may have been Archie's bald head or his slight one hundred and ten pound frame—the last time they'd seen one another prior to Archie's illness he'd been a beefy 260 pounds with curly locks and a full mustache. Being on the research end of things, Colin was separated from day-to-day contact with the sick and dying. He'd never had to develop a bedside manner or a stomach for that lingering odor that often accompanied the nearly dead.

Colin regained his composer with a nod and a blink, inviting Archie into the room. The nurse rolled his chair to before Colin's desk, locked the wheels, and then, with a quick pat to her patient's shoulder, nodded and retreated.

Colin popped two nuts into his mouth and leaned forward on his elbows, examining his son with a practiced physician's eye. "How bad is it today?"

Archie allowed himself a soft chuckle. "Bad," he said.

Colin nodded. Blinked. His Adam's apple bobbed.

Archie remained still. He might have even appeared glassy-eyed, for he focused on nothing but his own inner turmoil. There was so much to consider. Colin's procedure—his potential "cure"—sounded insane, ridiculous even. A rational man would have scoffed and stomped from the room shaking his head and muttering curses under his breath. And that was exactly why Archie *was* considering it. To a desperate man, the insane sometimes seemed the most plausible solution to life's cascading dramas.

"Your color is good," lied Colin.

"Yeah," said Archie with a forced grin. "Me and Dracula, we go to the same tanning salon."

Colin picked up a pen and then placed it to the right side of his desk. There was something he wanted to say, but was having a hard time getting around to it. "Listen, Archie," he said. "We've got some news. Good news. Exciting, even." He stared at his son expectantly. Archie gave him a nod, inviting him to proceed. "You see," he continued. "A twelve year-old boy nearly drown in his family's swimming pool." Colin smiled and shifted.

Archie shook his head. "This is your idea of exciting news? No wonder Mom never took you anywhere public."

Colin cleared his throat and grinned. "Actually, I believe that had more to do with my lagging sense of humor." He picked up the pen again, this time holding it with the thumb and index finger of both hands and twirling it like a rolling log. "The boy's been in a coma for nearly six weeks. There's absolutely no cognitive activity."

Archie's stomach took a swan dive into the deep end of his bowels. "Are you saying this is our guy?"

"Yes, that is what I'm saying. The parents are likely to terminate life support. That is, if we don't proceed."

"Twelve years old?" asked Archie, his voice weaker even than it had been a moment before.

Colin nodded and slipped his pen into the breast pocket of his crinkled and spotted cardigan. "Yes, twelve," he said in a soothing tone that Archie had thought him incapable of producing. "Listen, Archie, I know this could be problematic, as… Well, I suppose it should be. But we're running out of time. If I thought there was another way. If I'd learned about your cancer sooner, if we had more time to be selective, well maybe…"

Colin trailed off, avoiding eye contact with his dying son. Archie should have thought Colin a monster for even broaching the subject. And once again, a sane man, a man with other options, a man with any faith or with any hope for the future, would rightly have slapped Colin hard in the face and gone directly to whatever governing board held him accountable. But Archie was not sane, not in the traditional sense. Oh, he had his wits about him. He hadn't lost touch with reality or run screaming in terror of some imagined conspiracy. But he was desperate. He knew his time was measured in weeks, maybe even in days. If Colin was a monster, well then so was Archie. It was amazing what a human being would agree to when all hope was lost, when all alternatives were sealed tightly away from frantic clutching fingers. Humans are born with an internal selfishness, a capacity to rationalize anything, even the most horrendous acts, if no other options remain.

Archie leaned forward, gazing at Colin, trying to make contact with his evasive eyes as he spoke in a slow steady voice. "I want to live, Colin. Now tell me, is this what it's going to take to make that happen?"

Colin looked up. His eyes were wet and his lips taut. Archie swallowed, drawing his mouth into a tight grimace. He believed it was the first time he'd seen his father produce a tear. "Yes, Archie," said Colin. "I believe it is. We just don't have much in the way of options. This... Well, it's a tragedy, isn't it? This tragic event is really what we've been waiting for—a young, healthy body with a dormant, yet intact, brain." Colin scooted his chair back and then rose, strolling over to the coffee maker situated on a small cabinet to the left of his desk. He didn't speak again till he'd poured the deep brown liquid into a pea-green mug, scooped in three spoonfuls of sugar, a dash of creamer, stirred the mixture, and returned to his seat. "Archie, you must understand that we're actually transferring the electrical energies from your brain, your thought patterns, your personality..."

"My soul," added Archie.

Colin sighed, took a tentative sip of his coffee, and gazed at Archie. There were crow's feet in the corners of his eyes, lines running down each side of his face encircling his mouth. His hairline, though always high, seemed to have slipped just a little further toward the crown of his head. He set the mug on the desk beside his pen. "Yes, if you choose to call it a soul, I suppose that's what it is. We'll be infusing your consciousness onto the neocortex and hippocampus of this boy."

"And this will be me?" asked Archie. "I mean really me, not just my memories, but me? It won't be this kid running around with my autobiography on file, but I'll still exist?"

Colin nodded and stared purposefully into his son's eyes. "Yes, it should really be you."

"And this spookville sci-fi nightmare has never been done before?"

Colin took another sip of coffee and shifted subtly in his seat. A thin line of the liquid slipped down his chin and he wiped it with his knitted sleeve. "It worked on rodents. They were able to remember a maze that another rodent had run."

"Rodents. Can I use your phone? I need to put in an order for a coffin."

"As well," added Colin. "Some higher primates. A chimp that had never been taught American Sign Language used it quite proficiently after receiving the infusion of one which had. He even responded to the name of the other chimp, developed the same tastes in meals."

"No humans?"

Colin took another sip of coffee, paused, and then downed the rest of the mug. He rose, crossed to the coffee maker, and while pouring another cup said, "You're the first."

Archie remembered when he was a child, Colin had leant his bicycle—a brand new Schwinn Continental—to Chucky Gates, one of the neighborhood's many bullies. Chucky had run the bike into the back of a parked truck, bending the rim of the front tire. He'd scrambled away, leaving the bike behind. Colin had lied about what had happened. He'd turned away, avoided eye contact as he'd claimed to have never let the infamous Chucky use his son's bike.

"Colin," said Archie. "I need the truth. Have there been other humans to receive the procedure?"

Colin turned from the coffeemaker and stared at Archie, his gaze firm and strong, almost frightening in its intensity. "No, Archie. I have never performed this procedure on human subjects." Colin stood firm, but there was a slight quiver to his hand as he held his steaming coffee mug. "I'm serious," he said.

Archie rose from his wheelchair, weak, shaking. He had meant the gesture to appear dramatic, but it only emphasized how feeble he'd become. Still, he needed to make his point, needed for Colin to understand the gravity of his proposal. "You're serious?" Archie spat with what little energy he had to give. "Well, so am I. Colin, if I understand you correctly, this procedure will kill my body. If my soul, consciousness, whatever you want to call it, if that doesn't make the trip—I'm day-old meat. No offense, *Dad*, but I'm not all that sure it's worth the risk."

Colin stepped forward, his eyes narrow. Any hesitation, any nervousness, had evaporated. "You just told me that you want to live. I don't see where the risk lies."

"Excuse me—I could die."

Colin seated himself on the corner of his desk. He set the mug down and folded his hands in his lap. His expression was gentle, yet firm, his lips twitching subtly at the right corner. "Archie," he said. "You are about to die. Period. You've got weeks at best. That's all you're risking is a couple of weeks, not a lifetime. And the boy, he's already gone. Anything that he'd been, any consciousness or soul, as you call it, has already evaporated. There is no neural activity. So, dismiss your guilt. This is no different than taking a liver from an accident victim and giving it to a patient in need of that organ."

Archie lowered himself into the wheelchair, winded and defeated. This time it wasn't Colin who had a hard time maintaining eye contact. "Run this thing by me again," said Archie.

Chapter Three

Archie had pain—real pain. Deep down in the gut, eat a man from the inside out pain. It was the kind everyone knew existed, but could never begin to understand until it snatched a man in its cold diseased fingers and gnawed away at his very being. Then all a person could think about was alleviating it, diminishing it just a little, even if it took dying—or worse—to beat the brat.

But there was an upside—if it could be called such. It was amazing how knowing that life was at its end could cause a person to revel in the things of the living, to reminisce of even the painful memories of life, that in those dying days suddenly seem precious and so very worth holding onto.

Archie wasn't the brightest star on the planet, but neither was he the dimmest. He'd never finished college, but likely had enough credits scattered about various institutions to warrant a bachelor's degree and half of a master's. The problem was he'd never figured out just what to major in. His father, Colin, had refused to fund him if he majored in art, stating that this was a fool's degree and of no use to anyone. But this had left Archie directionless. Every time he'd head three semesters in one direction, he'd get discouraged and do an about-face, rushing off toward another of Colin's suggested career paths.

After three colleges, five majors, and a trade school, Archie had finally left the academic world behind and tentatively crept into the work force. Once there, he'd found that he was no more focused. He sold cars, then computers, then insurance, and then slipped back into cars. He delivered and then repossessed televisions and mattresses for one of those rent-to-own outfits. He ran pizzas for a local ma and pa shop that went under without giving him his final paycheck. He dabbled in telemarketing and even took a stab at a particularly tempting multi-level marketing deal.

His true passion had been cartooning, the Sunday paper variety. And though this seemed to be a fading art form, he'd rushed after it passionately. He had several characters and three different strip ideas that he alternately pulled out, reworked, and submitted to all of the fashionable syndicates, each time, sure that he held the next "Peanuts" or "Calvin and Hobbes." But mostly, he'd simply show his work to the guys and gals at the bar. They'd laughed and encouraged him and he'd felt just a little bit better about himself and his dream.

Several times he'd nearly given up, realizing that this was just another unrealistic phantom. But inevitably, just as he'd sworn to walk away, he'd sell an individual cartoon, maybe to a local paper or to a literary magazine, and find renewed hope. And because of this dream, he'd treated every new job not as a career, but as something to get him by until he "made it."

He did make it.

Oh, it took until he was forty-three years-old and nearly bankrupt, but even as the number of daily newspapers was diminishing nationwide due to the strength of online news outlets, he'd finally sold his Gilly Baskerville strip to a major syndicate. The strip did okay. Not great, but okay; each month adding six or seven new newspapers and/or websites to its roster, building a fan base, and slowly edging Archie toward the rim of an acceptable income. If it hadn't been for the emergence of cancer, the strip just might have truly broken into the major markets instead of hovering mostly in small town papers and little known websites with Anchorage and Atlanta being its only metropolitan conquests. But none of this really mattered, for by the time Gilly Baskerville first saw the light of day, Archie had been dealing with other issues. He'd immersed himself in Gilly Baskerville's world, pouring all of his emotion into those three daily frames, but it didn't make up for what he'd lost or for what he was about to face. Gilly Baskerville seemed almost to laugh at his creator, haunting him with the emptiness of his dreams.

Marrying Marcie Briggs and then dutifully producing their amazing daughter Jill had been, in Archie's eyes, his greatest life accomplishment. But even this, he'd ruined. Marcie had been patient with his revolving door employment routine, and quietly tolerated his comic strip fantasy. It had been his drinking that concerned her, his gambling that exasperated her, and his flirtations that she just refused to tolerate. Marcie was bright, pretty, and forgiving. She'd come from an upper middle class family, her dad being a bank executive and her mother a school librarian. Marcie had been on the road to a nursing career when Archie snatched her for his own, wooing her away from Chad Phillips, a walking ego in desperate need of a bad toupee. It seemed his self-effacing humor and easy laugh had been a nice change at the time; though Chad eventually launched a chain of golf shops and soon owned homes in Florida, Hawaii, and Cancun.

Obviously, he'd done slightly better than had Archie.

Marcie's father, Marvin Briggs, had liked Archie and Marcie had realized this was a plus. Their first date had been nerve-racking. Archie had asked Marcie to a movie. It had been one of the *Star Wars* films, or maybe *Star Trek*, Archie couldn't really remember which. Sci-fi wasn't his thing. Marcie had cancelled a date with Chad in order to go with him. Marvin, a big man with a quiet and intimidating voice, had answered the door, looked Archie up and down, snorted at the yellow roses he'd held, and said, "Well, you're not that prissy Chad fellow, so I sure don't know who you are or what you're doing here."

The man had intended to throw Archie off balance—and he had—but somehow Archie managed to laugh and say, "Oh, I'm sorry to bother you, sir. But I'm taking a survey. I was wondering if you could tell me how a florist can charge twenty-five dollars for a handful of dead flowers."

Marvin chuckled and waved Archie in. Marcie peered out from the kitchen, her large blue eyes twinkling in the lamplight and her smallish mouth curled into an impish grin, but Marvin directed Archie to the living room, a spacious area with early American furniture, country-style wallpaper, and a red brick fireplace that looked as if it had never been used. The whole room, in fact, seemed to be more a museum than a home. There was no dust, no smudges, no magazines or newspapers littering the coffee table. No coasters awaited use on the end tables, and the indentions from their trek into the room were the only evidences of foot traffic on the plush blue carpeting.

"How do you know my daughter?" asked Marvin as he seated himself in his leather recliner, indicating that Archie should sit on the couch opposite him.

"Um, from college, sir. We've got a class together."

"My name's not 'sir.' It's Marvin."

"Okay," said Archie, not really thinking he should venture calling the man by his first name. It seemed maybe Marvin had laid a trap for Archie, and was now waiting for the jaws to snap shut.

"My daughter's got a boyfriend, you know."

"Prissy Chad," responded Archie, borrowing Marvin's assessment of his competition.

Marvin chuckled, and then leaned forward resting his forearms on his lap just above the knees. "Yes, he is. But, how do I know you're any better?"

Every young man has a natural fear of a girl's father. Most of the time, though, the father does nothing more than to shake the boy's hand, ask him about school or work, and then tell him to respect the girl and get her home at a decent hour. It's an obligatory ritual, a little uncomfortable, but incurs no consequence beyond what a can of Right Guard and a stiff shot of whiskey can fix. This man was different. He purposely kept Archie off guard. He asked questions that had no well defined and over rehearsed responses. As odd as it may seem, Archie rather liked the guy.

"Well," said Archie in response to the man's question. "I guess you'll have to figure that out for yourself."

His heart nearly beat through his chest, but Archie opened and closed his hands, working them, attempting to relieve stress. Marvin nodded and said, "It sounds like you're planning to stick around long enough for me to find out."

"Well, I…"

Marvin cut Archie off before he could respond. "Marcie and Chad are serious. Marrying serious. What is it she sees in you to make her risk losing that?"

"Dad!" squealed Marcie as she stepped from her hiding place behind the door and into the room. "You're going to scare him away."

Marvin chuckled. "No. I don't think I can scare this one that easily."

He was wrong of course. Archie was the type that masked his inner feelings with a laugh and a shrug and then dove face first into a three night drinking binge. But Marcie ushered him out before her dad could do much damage. And when he returned for the next date, and the next, and the next, he knew he would be drawn into the living room with Marvin, and that he had better hold his own, or he'd be labeled prissy, and thus, unworthy of Marvin's daughter.

Maybe it was that Archie actually held his own with her father, or maybe—and more likely—he was a convenient excuse for her to distance herself from Chad and his looming proposal, but Marcie grabbed Archie's arm and laughed as they walked down the driveway toward his car, a mid eighties Chevy Impala, blue with a vinyl top. "What did my dad say to you?" she giggled. "You looked so nervous."

"You heard every word," responded Archie. "You were hiding behind the door the whole time."

She laughed, "Well, I had to make sure my dad wasn't abusing you."

"Then why weren't you in the room as soon as he opened his mouth?"

The couple made their way to the movie, ate popcorn, and sipped from separate cups of Coke. Twice, Archie tried to put his arm around her, but Marcie shrugged him off with a giggle and an elbow. Afterward they went to a little place called "Louie's Pub" for burgers and beer. Their conversation centered on her relationship with her younger siblings, three of them, all boys, all high school football stars. She laughed about their immaturity, but Archie saw that she loved them dearly with an almost motherly affection. He was also keenly aware of the unspoken message that if he hurt her in any way, he might well be subjected to their wrath.

They drove home in near silence. Maybe they'd just talked themselves out, or maybe they were both contemplating where the relationship might go. Archie was nervous. Marcie had been so easy to talk with, so quick to laugh and joke, her silence seemed unnatural and dangerous. He found himself playing over the date in his mind, reconstructing the conversations, searching for some fatal slip he might have made.

He parked in the driveway, and walked her to the back door. Then she began talking again. Not about anything important, not about inner feelings or aspirations, just about music and bands, about her friend Lilly who was dating such a loser. Archie relaxed some, realizing, as all young men must come to realize, that he would never fully understand any woman.

They laughed and joked some more. Archie showed her one of his cartoons, it was folded into quarters and bent as a result of having been in his pocket. The drawing was of a man pointing at a sleeping bull and saying, "Bulldozer." She laughed at the stupid pun and complimented him on his artwork. He told her she could keep it and she refolded it, slipping it into the pocket of her jeans.

She stared up at him, seemingly peering into his soul, and asked, "Are you happy, Archie?"

Like her father, she had a knack for asking difficult questions. "Well, yeah," he said. "We had a good time. I still have over five dollars in my wallet."

"No," she said. "Really happy. Happy with you're life?"

Archie stared down at her, paused for a single breath, and lied a lie that at the time he thought to be a truth. "Yeah, Marcie. Yeah, I think I am."

Marcie nodded, grinned, and said, "Good. It's important to be happy." She gave him a quick peck on the cheek and opened the door to go inside.

"Wait," he said. "Is it true?"

"What?"

"About you and Chad. Your dad said the two of you might be getting married."

Marcie cocked her head and grinned. "No," she said. "I think I'm going to marry you." Then she disappeared into the house without another word.

Chapter Four

Colin's procedure went something like this. Long term memory is stored in the cerebral cortex. The cortex is filled with ten billion nerve cells. These cells, or neurons, get activated every time a new memory arrives. As more memories are added, similar memories become connected, creating a net of memories similar in concept to internet connections. You get to the NBA home page and then click into the Bulls, the Jazz, the Lakers from there.

Not all memories make it to the cortex. There's a gatekeeper called the hippocampus, which basically determines if a memory is worthy of long-term storage, or should simply hang out in short-term memory before slipping off into oblivion. Think Saint Peter at the Pearly Gates.

What Colin proposed to do was to inject twenty microliters of preprogrammed nanofibers, consisting of a special ionic peptide, and carrying the coding of Archie's neural net, onto the kid's brain. These tiny amino acids would then create a duplicate net and allow the child's hippocampus to then recognize and welcome any matching data received. Colin then planned to transfer the electrical energies from Archie's living brain through the boy's hippocampus, and into his dormant cortex. These energies should naturally seek the now-familiar net, and attach within.

*****

Archie was given an I.V. drip and his vitals were taken at least twice. Sensors were placed near his heart, in various spots about his head, and along the back of his neck on the spine. He was pulled and prodded, and a jell-like substance was spread across his bald head. A technician made a small incision toward the base of his skull and something warm and pulsating was implanted.

Somewhere in the midst of it all, another gurney was rolled in. On it was Joey Burke, the twelve year-old whose body Archie was somehow intended to inhabit. He was pale, still, and attached to a ventilator. And as Archie looked at this boy, so tranquil, so far removed from the careless joys of youth, he thought of his precious little Jill. She would be a couple of years older than this boy by now, but she had been about Joey's age the last time he'd seen her. Still, being a father—even, and maybe especially, if one happened to be of the absentee variety—meant never quite admitting that your baby girl was growing up.

And Archie wept. For at that moment, in that brightly lit and sickeningly sterile operating room, he knew in his heart that he would never again see his little girl, that all the things of his life, both good and bad, were going to die with his body, no matter what route his soul chose to take.

Archie's contemplations were gratefully interrupted as Colin entered the room. He was wearing a surgical gown, his eyes brooding below his sloping brows. Without addressing Archie, he supervised as his staff connected the boy and Archie to the same equipment. Archie could hear the dialogue and feel the tugs and pulls, but he could see none of what these professionals did.

Colin and two of his associates eventually crossed the room and stood contemplating two monitors. One featured a jagged and active line, the second, a flat impassive line. Archie guessed these were their brain waves, Joey's and his own. He also assumed that his was the one that appeared active, though certainly his life contained sufficient evidence to the contrary.

Finally Archie's father approached, patting him on the shoulder and saying, "Good evening, Archie." It wasn't really evening, at least not unless evening extended to twelve o'clock. For some reason, the procedure had been done quite late in the day.

Archie angled his head as best he could to meet Colin's gaze, and attempted a weak smile. "Hey, Colin, ready to play Doc. Frankenstein?" He pointed to his chest, where he'd clipped one of his cartoons, a drawing of Doctor Frankenstein trying to force an oversized brain into the open top of the monster's head.

Colin's demeanor remained calm, firm, humorless. This was the professional Colin, not the socially awkward father that Archie knew so well. "Yes, Archie. We're prepared to begin. The nanofibers were injected into the boy several days ago. A single photon emission computed tomography was performed, as well as magnetic resonance imaging. Our instruments indicate that the nanofibers have created an acceptable duplicate of your neural net upon the boy's cerebral cortex." He moved around to where Archie could see him better. His gray eyes were liquid, but steady. "You'll be conscious through much of the procedure. I want to avoid dampening your neural energies with depressants. You shouldn't feel anything in terms of pain, but it's possible that you may pass out on your own. That's permissible."

Archie smiled. "It's permissible for me to pass out? Colin, you never told me you'd flunked a class your freshman year of college."

"Well, I... What class?" Archie's father looked perplexed. In Colin's world, an A- would have been considered a failure.

"Bedside manner 101," said Archie.

Colin offered him a quick professional nod. This was Archie's doctor, not his father. "It's time, Archie. Please stay calm."

It suddenly occurred to Archie that this was it. Colin was ready to proceed. These were to be his last few moments alive as Archie Lambert. If somehow, some crazy way, this procedure actually worked, he would be waking up in little Joey Burke's body. And if it didn't work—and that really was the most probable outcome—well, he wouldn't be waking up at all. At least not on the physical plane. He'd never given religion much thought, hadn't really wanted to be bothered with it. To Archie it seemed nothing more than a crutch for the weak, or maybe a place to go where people could either feel really good or really bad about themselves, depending on their taste in denominations. But in the past weeks he'd sometimes wondered if God was real, if maybe all of that hocus-pocus had something to it. He thought he might have tried to pray just then. But he knew that even if he did, it was hollow. For here he was, trying to cheat God of his due. What right did he have to pray?

Archie forced his thoughts elsewhere, off of the supernatural, away from the probabilities of heaven or hell. His mind returned to Jill. He'd brought something with him into the operating room, something special, something precious. He'd held it crumpled in his right hand through all of the preparations. "Take this," he said, handing his father a small crumpled photograph. It was of Archie and Jill, back when he still lived at home with her and her mother. Back when she still loved him.

"Hmmm," said Colin. "Your daughter?"

"Your granddaughter—Jill. She doesn't know. Not even that I'm sick. I haven't seen her in maybe a year—almost two. Her mother, Marcie, she didn't like my influence. I stayed away."

Colin stared at the photograph, his eyes moist, his hand offering a subtle quiver. Archie had broken his calm professional exterior. He'd crossed the line from patient back to son. "What should I do with this?" asked Colin.

"Give it to me. After." He paused. "And if I don't… You know. If I'm not here after, give it to Jill. I've written something on the back for her."

Colin nodded and slid the photograph into his breast pocket. "It's time," he said, his voice tight, his eyes focused on the floor.

Archie grabbed his arm as he turned. "Colin?"

"Yes, Archie."

"Tell me this is going to work."

Colin paused, nodded, and then moved beyond Archie's field of vision.

*****

Archie was staring toward the ceiling. Bright lights shone down upon him. He could hear Colin's voice and those of the other medical personnel, but these were distant and indistinct, almost as if the things of this life no longer mattered. There was a low hum in the background, the room was cool, even chilly, and began to shift from side to side. Archie closed his eyes, squinting and then opening them. He was determined to remain conscious throughout the procedure no matter how "permissible" it was for him to pass out. These might be his last few moments; he wanted every one of them.

Everything was wavy and indistinct. The ceiling—for that was all he could really see—faded to blue and then to a deep uncompromising red. There was an opening, a wavering black gap, circular in shape, smacking shut and then open, twisting and oozing, with dozens of wavering tendrils snaking out in all directions. White appeared, from the center of the opening, a white so pure as to defy description. No snowdrift was ever so white, no ray of light so undefiled. The white was all and it was nothing. A tentacle of this white slipped toward Archie, embracing him, and then squeezing. The air shot from his lungs like water from a fire hose. He couldn't breathe, couldn't move. He tried to scream, but no sound would come forward. Tighter and tighter, it squeezed. A rib broke and then another. He could feel his organs bursting. So agonized was he that he couldn't even form the question, "What is this thing? How is this possible?" He wept. He cursed. He begged to be released back into his glorious cancer, but no god heard his pleas, no angel plucked him from his misery.

Abruptly, he was pulled forward toward the ceiling that was not a ceiling. He heard his spine crack at the sudden uneven jolt, but was now beyond screaming. He moved up, up, away from his present reality. He could feel nothing. There was no physical sensation; it was more that he simply moved forward, like a camera lens zooming in on a distant object. Of course he could feel nothing. His spine had been snapped. Strange that he would think of these things at such a time.

Up, up he went. Through the gaping, slurping aperture, beyond the realm of the physical.

Archie was deposited in a yard with a chain-link fence and freshly-mowed grass. A dog ran across, passing before the wavering portal, a large furry beast, a Saint Bernard named Ace. Archie knew this because this was his dog, though Ace had been put down when Archie was nine.

The scene was dark, nearly black, but highlighted with varying hues of pulsating scarlet, nearly glowing, casting odd shadows in places where shadows should not have been. The images were sharp, clear, but slightly malformed, the proportions askew, as if Archie was viewing them through a damaged lens. The white tentacle slid along behind him, ever-present, but not in his direct line of vision.

He moved forward, though not of his own volition. He saw himself as a young boy of perhaps seven or eight years old, wearing an over-sized pair of cut-off shorts, a dirty red T-shirt, and a crew cut. He was throwing a ball for Ace to chase. But the dog missed the ball and it soared through the open kitchen window.

Gliding past his younger self, Archie found himself following the ball through the windowpane. But instead of arriving in the kitchen of his childhood home, Archie was now in a church sanctuary. It was a small place, sparsely furnished with wooden pews and worn carpeting, capable of seating perhaps eighty people. There were roughly fifty present now, all dressed in their Sunday best.

The ball rolled across the shiny wooden floor and came to rest beside a bride—Marcie. A young and relatively trim Archie stood beside her, his curly hair longer than the current Archie would ever care to admit having worn it. This youthful Archie was in a black tux with tails, and the loopy expression on his face reminded Archie that he'd gone into the ceremony slightly buzzed.

Marcie and Archie kissed, turned to face the small congregation, and moved forward down the aisle as everyone rose and clapped.

There was movement to the left. A shadowy object, round and rotating, yet indistinct. Its numerous eyes stared at Archie, though he could see none of them. How did he know they existed, these eyes? Archie wasn't sure that he really possessed any true physical form at this time, yet still a chill cascaded over his being in thunderous waves. This thing should not be.

And Archie was on the move, sweeping past the mysterious form, through the open window of the small church and into a bar. A place called Curly Jake's. A middle-aged Archie was at the far right end of the bar, seated with two men, Dennis and Scott. A couple of his old telemarketing buddies. The three men were laughing, shouting jokes across to a table where three young women—easily fifteen years their juniors—were seated. The expressions on the women's faces were ones of amused disdain.

Archie's focus landed on another figure: the shadowy form. Vaguely round, undulating, indistinct, nearly invisible. Archie tried his best to avoid its gaze, but again, he had no control over the situation. They stared at one another. Archie and the shadowy form. It was turning clockwise and counterclockwise simultaneously. And still they stared at one another. Stared and pondered. The thing was malevolent. This he knew as a certainty. Surely this was the death of him. He didn't know how or even what the thing might be, but of this inevitable end he was certain. And Archie wanted so very much to scream, but screaming required lungs and he didn't have those just then, which made him want to scream all the more.

And then Archie was swept away on the creeping scarlet wave, through another door, and then another, and another. Scene after scene appeared before him, accelerating, as if his soul was gaining momentum with each successive memory. He was no longer able to see expressions on faces, or even to identify the participants. Some of the events were painfully clear, things that he had always remembered, others, events he didn't recognize, places he couldn't recall ever having been.

Eventually his speed reached the point where he could no longer distinguish anything at all. The strange semi-world around him became a rush of color, an artist's brush, flashing with vengeance: scarlet, violet, topaz, they swished and merged, till finally Archie could distinguish no color at all.

Something changed.

A tug, back in the direction from which he'd come. Then a surge forward. Then another retreat. The scenes before him jumped and collided one into another. The thirty year-old Archie standing beside his toddler self, his adult home compacted to within his childhood living room.

Two twirling forms, fluid and indistinct, elastic, yet vaguely round, raced about him, both emerald in color, though one was brighter, nearly translucent, while the other was dark and murky, almost mud-like. The two figures danced and dodged, sometimes colliding before retreating to then approach again from another angle. A fight to the death. It might as well have been two Rottweilers biting and clawing, ripping and gnashing in a pit while excited men shouted bets over the din.

An echoing thud invaded Archie's fragile reality. Louder, louder. *Thud! Thud! Thud!* It was a deep, resonating tone, but was echoed by what could only be described as a chirp. The sound had an odor. Lavender. With each *thud* the smell increased until it became entirely overwhelming. Archie feared he might drown in the fragrance. For the thousandth time he tried to scream, but the flowery aroma filled his nonexistent lungs. He couldn't breathe. He couldn't breathe!

The ever-present white tentacle slithered forward, growing, growing, surrounding the scene, blotting out the landscape. And with it came dread and fear unparalleled in life. The white was all-encompassing, wrapping around Archie, squeezing, pressing, killing.

Chapter Five

Archie died with the ailing body of a forty-five year old cancer victim and awoke in the young healthy body of a twelve year-old boy. He couldn't help but to stare at his hands and arms. How short the limbs, how soft and white the skin. And the eyes. How clearly these young eyes viewed the limbs before them. As an adult, he hadn't given his vision much thought. True, he'd recently found it necessary to hold a pill bottle at arm's length just to read the tiny print on the label, but aside from that, he hadn't considered his eyesight bad. But now, viewing the world through Joey's eyes, it became clear just how unclear his vision had become. Even the colors were more vibrant. Not that there was much color to see in his little vanilla hospital room: a few flowers, a blue and pink love seat, and whatever happened to be on the television at the time. But it was all brilliant, sharp, clear. He could see a tiny crack on the baseboard, a smudge on a curtain, the discoloration of the paint just beside the door.

Another thing that had become clear was that Greg and Esther Burke, Joey's parents, weren't going anywhere. At least one of them stayed at his bedside nearly every hour of every day, and most of the time they were both present, Greg flipping through television channels, seeking, but never finding, something of even minor interest, and Esther alternately staring through the window onto the wooded landscape, or tapping away on her laptop while placing a series of high-pressure sales calls. Apparently she was in sales, something to do with telecommunications, but Archie hadn't yet figured out the specifics. As to Greg, Archie wondered if he was employed. Shoulder length hair, perpetually scruffy three-day beard, unbuttoned flannel shirts over classic rock band T-shirts. Maybe he cleaned up well, but, if he was employed, how could he spend all of his time in this room? Esther at least brought her work along for the ride.

Their behavior confused him. Yes, this was their son's body, still breathing, still active and functioning. But Archie was not their son. Joey was gone. Still they acted as if Archie was Joey, as if they were his parents. Obviously, this whole thing was a traumatic experience for them. Many people allow the organs of a loved one to be given to needy recipients, but to give the entire body of ones own child to another person, that would definitely cause anxiety. Still, the body now belonged to Archie, and he had no need of a mommy and daddy hovering over him through every breath. He couldn't understand why Colin tolerated this, why he coddled them so. He wouldn't allow Archie to address the issue with them, yet he wouldn't broach it himself.

It was nearly two weeks following the infusion when Archie was lifted into a wheelchair, and rolled into Colin's office where he could face his father alone for the first time since the procedure. Esther protested, demanding that she be present, but Colin was resolute. He needed to meet with the boy without them. If the Burke's would like a nurse present so that the two were not alone, that would be acceptable. At this, Esther scoffed and left the room, leaving Greg to trail behind with an apology tumbling from his lips, whether directed at Esther or Colin, no one was certain. Esther was very jealous of her time with Archie and he felt relief scamper over his form at her departure. The woman simply would not allow him a moment alone. And this, Archie had determined, was because Colin hadn't been entirely forthcoming with the young couple.

Colin sat behind his massive desk flipping through Archie's chart and popping peanuts into his mouth. "Well," he said. "You're showing remarkable stability. Vital signs—low end of normal. Coordination—acceptable."

"Acceptable?" challenged Archie. "I can't climb out of bed without a safety net. If I were to feed myself, I'd stick a spoon in my ear."

Colin chuckled and took a sip of lukewarm coffee. "Your brain is treating this body as if it were Archie's. Your mind still thinks the legs and arms are longer. It believes the limbs to be stronger and older." He took another sip of java and leaned back in his leather chair. "You'll adapt, I'm sure. But, you're overlooking the most encouraging element to this entire drama. You're coherent. You could have been comatose. You could have come out of this insane or imbecilic. But, Archie, here you sit, a rationale, fully functioning human being."

"Uh-huh," said Archie. "Tell me why the Burkes see me as their son."

Colin shuffled, spun his pen on the desktop. "They were his parents, you understand. Maternal and paternal bonds can be quite strong."

Archie wasn't quite sure what Colin knew about paternal bonds, but he let that one go.

"I understand that they were Joey's parents," he said. "What I need to know is why they think they're *my* parents."

Colin sipped his coffee and spun his pen. "That," he said, "is complicated."

Archie's stomach dropped, his worst fear realized. "You dropped me into this kid's body without telling the parents, didn't you?"

Colin said nothing, his gray eyes moist, but unreadable.

Archie dropped his head into his palms and said, "I need a smoke."

"No. Actually, you don't," said Colin, entirely avoiding the issue at hand. "Joey's body is not addicted to nicotine. Considering that your cancer began in the lungs and was likely the result tobacco usage, I'd suggest you allow it to maintain that status."

Archie sighed and shifted awkwardly in the wheelchair. "Yeah, yeah, yeah. I've heard it all before." He leaned forward, attempting to appear serious and in control, but knowing this to be impossible. "Listen, Colin, all I want is another shot at life. Simple. Easy. I go on my way—no baggage." He sighed, shook his head, attempted a weak grin. "What you did is incredible. You're a genius. You transferred my consciousness into another body. Amazing."

"Thank you, Archie. That's kind, but…"

Archie interrupted him. "I'm not trying to be kind, Colin. I'm simply telling the truth." He paused, attempting unsuccessfully to scratch an itch on his head. "Colin," he said after a curse and a stomp. "You need to tell these people that their son is gone."

Two peanuts, a swig of java, and a twirl of the pen. "Complicated. The parents, you see…"

"Forget the parents. What about me, Colin? Did you feel compelled to tell me—your own son—that I'd be forced not only into the body of a child, but into the life of one as well? I don't think I ever heard that one."

"Again, complicated."

Feebly, Archie rose from the wheelchair. His legs quivered and his arms began to spasm. He felt even more pathetic than he had rising from a different wheelchair, in a different body, in this same office only weeks before. "I'll show you complicated, *doctor*! You tell those people what you really did to their son, or I will."

"That wouldn't be wise, Archie."

"That's right," blurted the man in the boy's body. "You said it right there. I'm Archie. Not Joey, not a child. I'm Archie. A forty-five year-old man. And I expect to be treated like an adult."

Colin rose to meet Archie's gaze. "Yes. You are Archie. You will always be Archie. But, that is something no one can know—ever."

"And why exactly is that?"

"Because no one does know. Not Joey's parents, not the general hospital staff—certainly not the administration, not the A.M.A. It was the only way to save you. Authorization on this type of procedure is years away—if it ever comes at all. You must understand, this is a tremendous conundrum. Planting one person's mind in the body of another—the moral implications are tremendous."

"That's all well and good, Colin. But, none of that addresses the issue at hand. Greg and Esther Burke think I'm their son. That's unacceptable."

Colin snatched a handful of peanuts, slipping them into his mouth. "It's also unavoidable. Trust me, they would not have agreed to this procedure. Neither could I tell them that the boy had died. The Burkes would have wanted Joey's body. They would have planned a funeral." Colin paused for a moment. He stared at Archie, his gray eyes glinting from his desktop lamp. "Joey's parents believe their son came out of the coma unassisted. They know nothing of any procedure, legal or otherwise. They weren't made aware that Joey had been brain-dead. Brain damaged—yes. I told them that you have lost all memories. Complete, irreversible amnesia."

Archie's legs began to twitch, his balance to waver. Yet, he remained standing. He was tired of being an invalid.

What was that?

He'd just seen something in the corner of the room, beyond Colin and to the right. White. Perfect, clear, blinding white. Only a sliver. Just a narrow line slipping along the floor beside baseboard as might mercury on a subtle slope. Archie's stomach twisted. There was a vague hint of a memory, but it was elusive, a wisp of a thought, there and then gone. Where had he seen this before?

Colin stepped around his desk, seating himself on the front of the smartly polished surface and bringing Archie's attention back to the issue at hand. He smiled. "Sit down, Archie. You've made your point." Archie began to protest, but Colin waved his hand, stopping him before he'd really begun. "Archie, sit. It's clear you're not physically strong enough to remain standing. We can converse as father and son, not as adversaries."

His liquid gray eyes were soft, knowing, and Archie's legs were about to buckle. Archie lowered himself back into the wheelchair. "This conversation isn't over, Colin."

The doctor smiled. "No, I doubt that it is. And I'm sure there will be many others. But think this through. As far as the world's concerned, you're twelve years-old. You can't even get a job. You have no work history, no savings. Nothing. It seems to me you should take what the Burkes have to offer."

"You're insane."

Colin chuckled. "Yes, I'm Doctor Frankenstein." He paused, withdrawing his pen from his pocket. "Think of the advantages you'll have by growing into adulthood with over four decades of life experience behind you. Think of how advanced you'll be in school. Think of the wisdom you've already attained. You can bypass youthful folly and begin a productive life at a very young age. Personally, I say, embrace it." Colin leaned forward, a rare glint in his pale gray eyes. "And, Archie, longevity. You've already lived forty-five years. With good health and continuing advances in medicine, Joey's body might last another seventy-five or eighty years. You could live to be one hundred and twenty years-old. And by that time, infusion procedures such as this might be commonplace. You, quite possibly, could do this again, live another eighty years."

"Colin, have you lost your mind?" Archie paused, shook his head at the implications of what Colin was saying. "I'm no genius, but wouldn't this thing be limited to the number of available donors? I mean, Joey Burke was a fluke. How many healthy, brain dead bodies do you expect to find lying around? No matter what advances in medicine are made, this could never become a common procedure."

Colin nodded, grinned, and popped two more peanuts. "That's where my colleagues in the field of cloning could become quite useful. You see, the two arenas could be joined in order to grant near immortality to anyone desiring it. As a person's current body wore out, a new body could be cloned. The higher brain activity of the clone could be inhibited during pregnancy and infancy, and then an infusion could be performed, thus allowing an individual to live yet another lifetime in a duplicate of his own body."

Archie felt numb. His limbs twitched, and his stomach rocked from side to side like a rowboat in a hurricane. "I need a very stiff drink."

Colin smiled a subtle grin, rose, moved forward, and said. "No. That I won't supply. Not now at least. This is the best I have to offer." At that he bent at the waist, clasped Archie's head gently between his two palms, and kissed him on the forehead. Archie could not remember ever having been kissed by his father. "I couldn't let you die, Archie. I hope you'll forgive me for what I've done. But I couldn't let you die." Archie felt a single drop of moisture land atop his head.

Chapter Six

Archie made his escape six weeks later. During this period, most of his waking hours were spent in physical therapy, regaining his strength and attempting to establish coordination. The strength increased steadily through the weeks. The coordination was more of a challenge. Mealtimes were horrendous: food in the hair, the ears, the eyes. Archie just couldn't get his limbs to submit to his brain.

Still, he made progress. Archie soon found that, provided no buttons were involved, he could dress himself, and so took to wearing T-shirts, sweat pants, and Velcro shoes. Joey's head had been shaved for the procedure, and the hair hadn't yet grown out to beyond an uneven buzz cut, so Archie didn't yet have to worry about combing anything. But, brushing his teeth was a daily nightmare.

Archie had planned on waiting a few weeks longer before making his run. He'd hoped to somehow acquire money from either the Burkes or Colin, and he'd wanted to be physically more capable. But the day that Diana Mortonson stopped by his room, he knew he could wait no longer. Archie didn't know quite what position she filled, though he remembered having seen the woman in Colin's office prior to the infusion.

She entered Archie's room just after noon. He'd just returned from a therapy session, and, as the Burkes had finally gone back to work, neither Greg nor Esther had been present. Archie was seated in the loveseat situated in his room catching his breath after having walked the three hundred or so yards from physical therapy. He enjoyed these strolls, no matter how awkward and exhausting. These had given him a welcome sense of freedom and also served to further strengthen his previously atrophied muscles. Walking, though, still presented difficulties. Every step felt like he was stepping, unawares, off of a curb. It was as if his mind thought the floor was one place, but in actuality, it was another six inches below that. Archie cursed as he plodded disjointedly down the hallway, but he was up and about, and that meant he was closer to true freedom.

She introduced herself as Doctor Mortonson, saying she was a colleague of Doctor Lambert's, and that he'd asked her to check in on Joey. Suspicious, Archie simply nodded, silently waiting for her to proceed.

"I see you're up and around," she began.

"I walk like a retard," he said in an attempt to seem childlike in his conversation.

"Well," she said with a crook of a smile. "That was inappropriate." Her painted lips twitched only slightly, and she asked, "What happened to you? How did you come to be in this facility?"

"I was in a coma." Archie felt it best to remain vague, to allow her to do most of the talking.

"How did you come to be in a coma?" she pressed.

Archie shrugged. "I don't remember the coma. I was asleep through all of that."

She sighed, and straightened her form-fitting gray woolen sweater with tugs on either side. "What I meant to ask was how you came to be in a coma in the first place."

"I don't remember."

"You don't remember any of it?"

"The doctor says I have amnesia."

She nodded, her left eyebrow twitched ever so slightly. "So I've been told. Why do you suppose that is?" Her voice was as smooth and tart as buttermilk. There was something illogically seductive about this woman.

"You're the doctor, not me. Why are you here?"

This seemed to throw her off balance. Archie didn't think she'd expected confrontation from a child. "Well, to assess your progress," she replied, her voice stiff, her gaze dubious.

"Uh-huh. Why are you asking these questions instead of simply reading my chart?"

She cocked her head, her shoulder-length black hair spilling to her right. "Interesting question for a child to ask," she said. "I simply wanted to get some background on your case."

"And what is your connection to my case?" asked Archie with an intense stare inconsistent with his childish form.

"I'm Doctor Lambert's colleague. A very concerned colleague."

"Did he really ask you to come, or was this little fishing expedition your own idea?" Archie knew his questioning no longer resembled anything a child might ask. But he'd never been skilled at self restraint, and there was something suspicious about this woman.

Mortonson moved closer, so near, in fact, that Archie could smell butterscotch on her breath. Her lips narrowed, her gaze intensified. "Who are you?" she asked.

The question made Archie pause. All of his arrogance fled. She knew. Or at least suspected. Obviously, she was aware of the nature of Colin's research. And now, thanks to Archie's recklessness, she suspected that Colin had gone through with it.

"My name is Joey Burke," he replied. "But you already knew that."

"Yes," she said, her voice as soft as a serpent's hiss. "And what is your middle name, Joey?"

Archie paused, but only for a second. "No idea. I have amnesia, Diana." The use of her first name was purposeful. Archie knew she'd introduced herself only as Dr. Mortonson, but he remembered the name Colin had used in his office prior to the procedure. Archie hoped this move would unsettle her, giving him the upper hand.

Mortonson cocked her head, a hint of a smile at the corner of her rigid lips. "I never told you my first name."

"No," he replied. "You didn't. But someone in the hallway called you Diana just before you walked into my room."

Diana bristled. "I spoke with no one in the hall."

"Oh," said Archie, leaning forward and maintaining eye contact. "Then I wonder where I learned it."

Chapter Seven

That night, Esther Burke left Archie's room just after ten pm. Archie rose from his bed fifteen minutes later and opened the drawer to the nightstand, withdrawing a piece of banana bread wrapped in cellophane, a treat he'd saved from his evening meal, and slipped it into his pocket. Archie had no money, and had no idea where he would find any. This little piece of bread might be his only sustenance for days.

Over the past two weeks Archie had taken to roaming about the facility at odd hours of the night. In anticipation of his flight, he wanted the nursing staff accustomed to seeing him out of bed and on the move. As well, these midnight jaunts allowed him to learn the layout of the facility. Each night he ventured further from his room, exploring stairwells and fire exits, devising his escape route. Archie still became winded easily, and his progress was slow and awkward, but with each nightly excursion he became more and more capable of taking extended jaunts with only a minimum of breaks.

After fighting with his left shoe for nearly three minutes, Archie made his way to the door. He looked back into his room, not fondly, not for remembrance sake, but rather he peered at the phone. Colin would be gone for the night. He was an early riser, and would most likely be back on site by seven the following morning. That would give Archie about an eight and a half hour head start. He moved back into the room, picked up the phone, and after three attempts, managed to coerce his index finger into punching in Colin's extension. As planned, he reached voice mail. "Colin, Diana Mortonson knows, or at least suspects. Don't try to find me. Goodbye... Dad." He hung up the phone. Colin was warned. Archie had done his part. It surprised him to realize that he felt a pang of sorrow at the thought that he might not see his father again. Despite all that had happened between them, the human heart was a fickle and lonely thing.

He exited his room for the last time at 10:32 pm on June 22nd. There were three nurses at the nurse's station. One of them, a pretty black girl of about twenty-five, smiled and said, "Taking another midnight stroll, Joey?"

Archie nodded. "Yeah, I can't sleep, so I might as well work my legs."

She laughed. "You're coming along fine. Don't overdo it."

"I won't. But I feel restless. I might try to walk a little further tonight. You know, kind of test the waters." Archie noticed an apple lying beside her on the counter. "Is that your apple?" he asked.

"Yes, why, are you hungry again?" She had a cute smile and a giving heart.

Archie shrugged, which actually came off as an awkward twitch. "Well, yeah, but if it's yours, I don't want to take it."

Of course, she gave it to him. He also "borrowed" a dollar for a Coke, telling her that his mom would pay her back the following day. Archie had always had a way of getting what he wanted from women, a skill which often caused him more pain than gain.

The Edward G. Gowon Neurological Institute was a large and rambling building built sometime between the two world wars. Originally established as a sanitarium, it had been utilized in its current form for only sixteen years. The corridors were long, the floor tiles antiquated brown and tan nine-inch asphalt, and the walls were painted custard yellow on the upper and pea green on the lower portions. Aside from the bright neon lighting and state-of-the-art medical equipment, the place had an eerie, out-of-time feeling to it. Sometimes Archie felt he could still hear echoes of the old psych ward as he made his way through the halls, that long-dead patients were calling to him, chiding him, berating him. Sometimes they seemed entirely pleased at what he'd done in taking over Joey's body, other times it seemed they cursed his very existence.

Crazy thoughts. They didn't belong in his head.

Being primarily a research facility, most activity was relegated to daytime hours. There was no emergency room. Few surgeries or procedures were performed after dark, and the place took on the feeling of near evacuation after six pm, with only minimal staff and a handful of security personnel. Archie encountered only four people on his way to the elevator, and no more than a dozen as he reached the main floor.

The Gowon Institute was located on the outskirts of town and set some two hundred yards back from the tiny two-lane highway which was the only way to and from the facility. The founders of the institute had liked the remote setting, feeling their many research scientists and doctors would have fewer distractions than they had at the facility's former locale in Chicago.

The grounds were nicely manicured with multicolored flowers and shrubberies and surrounded by woods. It was common to see deer slink onto the property, nibble on the freshly mown grass and then dash away in a sable blur. Squirrels and chipmunks were plentiful, and half a dozen stray cats called the place home.

The exterior scene caused Archie to pause. Joey's young senses perceived the world sharper than had Archie's. Even in the dim moonlight, the flowers were vivid, with bright blues and reds. The gray/green stems jumped out at him in an enhanced brightness. Fragrance tickled his nose. Smells he'd forgotten even existed, danced about his olfactory system: cut grass, violets, diesel fuel. The world was once again a strange new place. Still in awe, he angled toward the adjacent woods. The night was clear and the moon three quarters full. On the off chance that one of the nurses decided he'd been gone too long and sounded an alarm, Archie didn't want to be visible to any passers by.

Even with the light of the moon, it was difficult to see. The massive oaks and scattered maples obscured most of the light and there were dark patches of brush all about. Small things scurried this way and that at his approach. Something, probably a rodent, brushed against Archie's right leg and then disappeared into the darkness. Branches and stems brushed against his sweat-moist skin and it seemed every mosquito in the county had been alerted to his presence. He found and followed a small trial that snaked through the trees, but often had to leave this and strike out through the brush in order to remain within sight of the nearby road—a necessity if he was to ever find his way to town.

The ground was uneven and he stumbled frequently, one time gouging his knee on a broken branch and ripping his sweatpants in the process. The injury hurt, but was minimal, only a jagged scrape really. The torn pants, though, bothered him. He had no other clothing, and no means of purchasing replacements. He needed to remain presentable or risk drawing attention to himself. Archie had no plan other than to get as far from the institute as possible. He knew he would need money, and he knew he had to stay out of sight, but that was pretty much as far as his thought process had taken him. Once again, Archie hadn't planned on making his escape so soon. As an adult he probably could have found some day labor, made a few bucks and moved to Florida or Las Vegas, someplace far away from Northwest Indiana. But as a child, Archie's options were limited. Sure, he could mow lawns, maybe walk a couple of dogs, but the few dollars he'd earn would hardly feed him, much less send him packing cross country.

The road was dimly lit and off to Archie's right. He stayed roughly two hundred feet within the brush, invisible to any of the few cars and trucks that passed by. He saw one bus go past; it was a city bus, not a Greyhound. He probably wouldn't find a Greyhound station this far out, and he wouldn't have the money to purchase a ticket anyway. But a city bus. The single dollar he'd borrowed from the nurse might just get him onto one of those and into town. Archie decided to keep an eye out for a bus stop. At this time of night, there would likely be few passengers, less people to remember him. Once in town, he'd have to find a place to hide till he concocted the next step in his plan. Swatting a mosquito, he gazed down the road in hopes of finding a bus. No headlights.

The following quarter hour offered two semi-trucks, a muddied SUV, and a 1970s era V.W. Beetle. No driver noticed Archie. He was pretty well hidden in the shadows, but with each passing vehicle, his heart quickened, and he inched just a little further into the shadows to avoid detection.

The comforting symphony of crickets and the rain-fresh air nearly lulled him into walking sleep, until headlights appeared in the distance. Archie couldn't yet see the form of the vehicle, but its shadowed outline was slightly jagged, as if something were on top of the car. A moment later it passed under one of the few streetlights illuminating the dark road: black fenders, white doors, red lights on top—a police car. Archie's heart fluttered and his limbs quivered as he scrambled further into the brush.

The car slowed as it passed. Had the cop seen movement beyond? He wasn't using a searchlight, so probably wasn't searching for Archie specifically. Still, if he caught sight of him, Archie's escape would be at an end. It was definitely past whatever curfew the county imposed, and, if found, Archie would be classified as a runaway minor. The car went past, its taillights vanishing around the bend. Archie released his breath—but only for a moment. The cruiser stopped, executed a three-point turn, and now a searchlight swept the landscape. Archie had either been spotted or his disappearance reported.

He bolted into the dense brush. The searchlight beam was almost upon him when he flattened himself to the ground behind a cluster of foliage. The beam nearly stopped as it moved over the spot he'd just occupied. Terror filled his being. Archie had no idea what Diana Mortonson might do if she discovered proof of the infusion. Could she force Colin to reverse the procedure? Was that even possible? If so, Archie would be dead. His adult body had died as soon as his soul fled into Joey's brain. There was nowhere for him to go back to.

But Archie's fears centered more on having some sort of normalcy in his life. He knew that if word got out about the infusion, he could count on being a sideshow freak. The world went gaga over a cloned sheep, he couldn't imagine what would happen if news of an actual soul transfusion were verified. The tabloids would be at his door inside of a week. And there might possibly be legal trouble as well. Who knew what charges could be levied for stealing a child's body for one's own use? Congress would probably pass new laws because of this. There might be protests, possibly even death threats. No, Archie wanted none of that. His one and only goal was to get through this second childhood with as few mishaps as possible. And that meant avoiding detection.

The police car stopped. The searchlight moved back and forth in front of Archie. It seemed at any moment it was going to zero in on him, but as much as he wanted to flee, he knew he must remain completely still. Any movement of the brush or fluttering of disturbed wildlife would draw attention. The mosquitoes took full advantage of Archie's inability to move, but he let them have their way. The beam moved back again, this time deeper into the woods, coming to rest directly behind Archie. A notch down and he'd be found.

He waited, breath held, not even willing to blink his eyes as the beam hovered for what had to be hours. Another mosquito. Archie ignored it. The rustle of some small creature behind and to his right. Archie prayed the thing would draw the cop's attention.

And then the light moved on.

After two more sweeps, the officer extinguished the light, performed a wide U-turn, and continued up the highway. Archie rolled onto his back, panting in the thick muggy air and swatting at bugs. That was much too close. His guess was that word of his escape had not yet reached the police. Otherwise, the searchlight would have continued sweeping up and down the road, instead of in one specific spot. Chances were the officer had caught a quick glimpse of him as he passed, probably wondered if he'd really seen anything at all, and then come back to investigate.

Archie needed to get out of the woods as quickly as possible, but now knew that utilizing a bus would be much too obvious. It was only a matter of time before he was reported missing. Greg and Esther would have the National Guard after him if they had any say in the matter. The cop, of course, would remember thinking he'd seen something near the road, and if a lone kid, dirty and winded, hopped onto a bus in the middle of the night, the bus driver would surely remember that as well. Archie considered hitchhiking, but came to the same conclusions. Wherever he went, Archie needed to get there alone.

Chapter Eight

Archie stumbled through the woods for nearly two hours, never leaving sight of the small two lane highway, but remaining several feet beyond the tree line as to avoid detection. The night air was cool, though the humidity remained. His damp skin added to the chill and goose bumps traversed his arms and back. The mosquitoes, though, seemed less interested in him than they had earlier. Maybe they'd already bled him dry.

Eventually trees gave way to cornstalks, then cornstalks to lights and scattered buildings. As Archie walked, he thought through his options and determined that his best option might be to make contact with someone he knew and trusted. Maybe he could stay with that someone for a few weeks, maybe try to come up with some money. He wasn't sure what he'd do, but there had to be something better than pretending to be a child for the next seven years.

The first building he encountered was a squat yellow brick square with no windows and a two hundred foot antenna situated behind the structure. There were two cars parked in the small gravel drive, an old Ford Taurus and a late-model Lumina. Light escaped from the double glass doors and Archie contemplated the wisdom of going inside. All he needed was a phone, and maybe to use a restroom for a quick cleanup. But whoever was here would certainly question why a child was wandering the streets alone at two AM.

But this might be his last opportunity to make a move before the greater world learned of his escape. Certainly a missing child would be all over the morning news; an Amber alert would be made. Risky as this might be, it was likely his best shot at contacting a friendly and vanishing before all hell broke loose.

He tugged on the handle. The door was unlocked. "Hello?" he said as he stepped into the small foyer and wiped the mud from his shoes onto a bright red welcome mat baring a flaming logo with the words *The Fire* arching across the top. "Is anyone here? Hello. I need to use a phone."

There was a radio station blaring through overhead speakers, a talk show about UFOs and Bigfoot. Archie had heard the show before—James T. Roswell, the local expert on anything paranormal. Perhaps a decade earlier, he'd been a big time syndicated radio hot shot out of Chicago, but his star had faded, some of his claims becoming so outrageous as to anger even his wide-eyed alien-loving followers. Eventually he'd lost his Chicago gig and landed at a small station in Norwest Indiana, broadcasting midnights to cows and insomniacs.

Archie heard a door open and then close to his right. A tall gangly kid, Asian, in his early twenties bobbed down the short hallway and into the foyer. "Hey," he said with a crooked grin and slouched shoulders. "I thought I heard something." He was munching from a Cheetos bag and wiping the orange residue off of his fingers and onto his black Ozzfest T-shirt. "You here to see J.T.?" he asked.

"J.T.?" asked Archie.

"James T. Roswell. You're a fan, right?"

It dawned on Archie that this was a radio station. Roswell was broadcasting from within this building. If Archie hadn't been so self-obsessed he would have picked up on this before setting foot in the place.

The guy took Archie's momentary silence for embarrassment, and said, "Hey, don't worry about it, kid. When I was little, I used to sneak out to see J.T. too. Now, look at me—I'm a producer for the show." He grinned a Cheetos grin, all orange and crunchy.

Dropping his head and flashing his best aw-shucks grin, Archie said, "You're not gonna tell my parents are ya?"

The kid laughed. "Nah. We're cool—Cheetos?" He extended the near empty bag.

"No thanks," said Archie, withdrawing the nurse's apple from his pocket and holding it up.

The guy bobbed his head. "Alright. Come on, I'll introduce you."

Archie followed the kid down the short pale hallway littered with black and white photographs of James T. Roswell and tabloid-like images of strange otherworldly creatures. There was one of a large, fury, mostly out-of-focus creature chasing an elderly woman who fled while still pushing her shopping cart. Another featured the same out-of-focus creature sporting a bra. Archie wasn't a James T. Roswell fan, but he'd heard about that one. The bobbing producer stepped through a door to the right and there was Roswell, on the other side of a Plexiglas barrier, headphones obscuring most of his dark mop of hair, and a microphone two inches before his narrow lips. "Now, Lana, what makes you think this was a legitimate sighting?" Roswell asked a caller.

"Well," came a disembodied female voice through the overhead monitor. "First, the government denied the whole thing. They said it was a satellite launch."

J.T. Roswell grinned, his pocked and craggy face stretching into deep crevasses. "And why do you think the government was lying to you?"

"Well," continued the woman with an air of importance. "It is the government, after all."

Roswell chuckled. "Well, I can't argue with you on that count."

"And," she said, her voice becoming more urgent as she continued. "I went online, and according to 'are-we-really-alone-dot-com' there were no scheduled satellite launches for that evening."

Roswell nodded, his dark face impassive, sincere. "Very good research, Lana," he said, his voice strong, authoritative. "And so typical of our government to conceal important information from those intelligent, well-informed citizens who pay for their private jets and million dollar lifestyles." He paused dramatically, and added, "Friends, like Lana, we need to remain vigilant in uncovering the truth. We need to bring into accountability a government run amok. No longer can we sit back and allow our elected officials to spoon feed us lies and deceptions, withholding from us information about dangers far greater than any terrorist threat or climate crisis. We must seek the truth at all costs. We, as Americans, need to band together, to become patriots of the truest calling, to reveal the dark and sinister plots hidden behind every headline. We must make a difference." Roswell punched a red button, causing his theme music to rise majestically from the speakers. "Coming up after our next break—Puppies! Do they carry the key to deciphering extraterrestrial hieroglyphics?"

Roswell punched another button and an advertisement for Screamin' Timmy's Lube and Wash filled the room. The man removed his headphones, massaged his heavily-lined temples with his fingertips, and then eased his husky form from his seat, crossed the small room, and into the adjacent space where Archie and the "producer" stood observing the show.

"Who's the kid, Ned?" asked Roswell. "I thought you went to get me a burrito."

Ned, the producer, bobbed his head. "Yeah, I haven't gone yet. This kid's a fan of yours. He came down here to meet you."

Roswell eyed Archie curiously. "You're a fan?" he asked, a sardonic grin on his lips. "Isn't my show on a little late for you?" There was a hint of a Mexican accent teasing his voice, an accent not present with his on-air persona.

Archie shrugged. "I'm not really allowed to stay up that late, but sometimes I turn the radio down real low so no one can hear it."

Roswell crossed to a coffee pot and filled his mug. "I'm guessing your parents don't know you're here."

Archie glanced down at the floor, an embarrassed child caught in a misadventure. "Any chance I can plead the fifth on that one?"

The man chuckled. "We'll leave that question open for the time being. What's your name?"

"Spock," he said.

Roswell shook his head and sipped his coffee. "Right. And my birth name's James T. Roswell. Come on, kid. A little more honesty than that."

"Alright, my name's Archie, but don't ask for a last name."

The radio personality grunted, setting his mug down and listening to the overhead speaker. An ad for Shoe Time was just wrapping up. "Listen, I've got to get back in there and do my show. Where do you live?"

Archie hesitated, but not for long. "Um, up the road, in Ephesus."

"Okay," said Roswell. "You can't stay, not without your parents knowing where you are. Next time bring me a note or something." He nodded in the direction of his producer. "Ned's doing a food run. He'll drop you at home."

Apparently, another word for "producer" was "gofer."

*****

The air conditioning in Ned's Taurus didn't work and his electronic windows didn't roll down. Though the air had seemed cool as Archie walked down the road an hour earlier, it felt stuffy and warm inside the enclosed vehicle. He couldn't imagine how Ned could stand the car in the steamy midday heat. Ned chugged a twenty-ounce Monster energy drink and cranked the local heavy metal station. Chuckling, Archie said, "Okay, if you're such a James T. Roswell fan, why aren't you listening to him right now?"

The kid shrugged. "I hear him all night. I need some jams sometimes."

Archie nodded. "So, do you believe the stuff on his show—UFOs, aliens, ghosts, goblins, all that?"

A smirk. "I believe there's life on other planets."

"But not necessarily in crop circles and Big Foot?"

"Nah, well, you know, some of his stuff, it actually seems to check out. Other stuff—you know."

"Checks out? The guy actually does research?"

"Yeah, sometimes—if it's something he can get a lot of mileage out of, he'll follow up."

"And what if he follows up and it ends up being a hoax?"

Ned laughed and bobbed. "That's the best stuff. See, if something checks out, then he just reports it as it is. Usually that stuff's pretty small, nothing big or exciting. But if he checks into something, and it comes up dead, well, then he gets on the air and says that he investigated this thing, and, well, it's classified or the details are too intense to reveal on the radio."

"So, when it's nothing, it sounds like he found something big."

"Yeah, yeah, but he never actually has to lie—too much."

"Brilliant," said Archie.

"Yeah, he is," agreed Ned as he downed another chug of Monster. "So, where do you live?"

"Yeah, about that, I can't exactly go home tonight."

Ned angled his head toward Archie, studying him for several moments before speaking. "You can hang at my place tonight if you want," he said at last.

Interesting. Did this kid have any idea of the trouble he could get into by harboring a runaway minor? Now it was Archie's turn to study his traveling companion. Did he trust this guy? Was he comfortable accepting the offer?

Did he have any other options?

No. He had none. And as to trust, Ned seemed more clueless than anything else. Archie didn't have the feeling the guy was a psychopath or a pervert—not that he had experience with either. Still, he wondered what the guy was thinking by making the offer.

They drove another five minutes before Ned spoke again. "Archie, right?"

"Uh, yeah. Archie."

"Right. Kid, I can tell you're not really a J.T. fan. That's cool. No problem. I don't know what your deal is but I get the feeling you need a little help. I can't keep you long term, got that?" He paused long enough for Archie to nod. "One night only. Time to get your head together. But then you gotta face whatever it is you gotta face. Deal?"

Archie nodded. "Deal." Apparently there was more to Ned than his stereotypical stoner persona might suggest.

*****

Ned's place was a sparsely-furnished one bedroom apartment, shared by three buddies. There were empty beer cans on the counter, video game boxes and controls attached to the television, and scattered posters of hot girls and super heroes on the walls. Ned's roommates, Lou and Waldo, were already sleeping when Archie and Ned arrived, Lou snoring peacefully on the couch and Waldo on a hammock stretched taut against the far wall. Apparently Ned, being gainfully employed, was the one who actually got to sleep on a bed.

Ned told Archie that he could crash wherever he wanted, then added, "Whatever it is, give it time, it'll work out. If it's big, I mean like legal big, abuse, that kinda thing, we'll deal with it while the vamps sleep. Got it?" He then retreated in search of James T. Roswell's midnight snack.

Too wired to sleep, Archie decided to check the fridge, where he found three pizza boxes, bologna, and beer. Assuming the food to be too old for human consumption, he took a hefty bite out of his apple and snatched a Sam Adams. Then, closing the fridge, he ambled back toward the living room. Archie tossed his head back, taking a swig of brew and nearly spit it across the room. He was amazed at how bitter it tasted, at how the alcohol burned at his throat. His head began to spin, and he suppressed the urge to retch. Apparently, Joey's body was unaccustomed to adult beverages.

Archie lifted the can to his lips, this time taking only a sip, and settled into a worn pea green chair situated between the sofa and the hammock. Taking yet another sip, he tried to relax. Archie wasn't tired, but couldn't turn on the television for fear of waking Ned's roommates, who, if they woke before Ned returned to explain that Archie was an invited guest, would undoubtedly wonder why some kid was crashing on the chair and drinking their beer. There was a continual drip coming from somewhere off to the left, probably the bathroom. The steady *plink, plink, plink*, lulled Archie into a calm sense of contemplation.

Taking another sip, he reached into the left pocket of his sweatpants and withdrew a small and crumpled picture. It was a photo of Archie and his daughter Jill, the one he'd asked Colin to save for him until after the infusion. Colin had been reluctant to return it to Archie, fearing the Burkes might find it and ask questions about who those people in the picture were. Archie had assured him that if the photo was discovered, he could simply explain that the girl was one of his classmates. They might mistakenly assume their boy had a crush on the girl in the picture, but that was a problem easily dealt with. Colin had given Archie the picture, and he'd studied it every night since. How Archie wished he could at least let Jill know that he was alive.

Chapter Nine

Archie quit his job, got sloppy drunk, and was arrested, all on the day his only child was born. Memories of that one precious day that should carry with them the warmest of emotions instead sank his heart into blackness and devoured his frail soul every time he dared to think of it. He'd been working for a rent-to-own outfit. They carried TVs, appliances, entertainment centers; pretty much anything a family might want or need around the house. Their clients were people who, though gainfully employed, didn't have much disposable income or solid credit, and therefore couldn't simply buy these items outright. Prior to accepting the job, Archie had been one of their clients.

Archie had a new store manager, Jerry, who, tall, dark-haired, and sickeningly confident, was sure he'd turn their little piece of the strip mall into the number one store in the region by the end of the fiscal year. Archie had applied for the store manager position himself, but was overlooked in favor of Jerry, a hotshot sales guy from the Hammond store.

Jerry knew nothing about management, though he did know how to wriggle customers into renting the highest priced items. He'd chat with them about the weather and how nice the wife had done her hair. He'd make a few sports references to the husband, then pull out an autographed Topps Mickey Mantle baseball card (1952, rookie year) from his breast pocket, and let them handle his prize. While the couple admired the fine condition of his collectable, pondering how much the thing was worth, he'd move them toward the higher-end items and help them to fall in love with something they just couldn't live without. On the management side he'd constantly forget to complete employee schedules, muck up the daily reports, over-order items the store could never move, and forget to order items promised to his customers. Archie's official title was assistant manager, which, in reality, meant scapegoat for Jerry's blunders.

Marcie had called the store around ten AM to tell Archie that she was in labor. This was before the cell phone revolution and so Jerry took the call on the store line. But since Archie was loading and delivering a Whirlpool washer and dryer set for one of Jerry's beloved customers, he conveniently forgot to tell Archie of the significant event. Two hours later Archie was back in the store, on the phone, receiving an ear-full from Samantha, his mother-in-law, who, since Archie was unavailable, had driven the frantic Marcie to the hospital. Archie confronted Jerry about keeping Marcie's call from him. Jerry shrugged, "You were busy. I was busy. It slipped my mind."

"Jerry," Archie protested. "My wife is in labor."

Jerry withdrew a pack of Camels from a drawer, slipped out a cigarette, lit it with his monogrammed gold lighter, and then leaned casually against the counter. "Labor takes hours," he smiled his best salesman's smile. "You'll get there in plenty of time." He paused. "Now, I need you to deliver a fifty-two inch Sony to Mrs. Cobb over in Saint John."

"Jerry," Archie repeated. "My wife is in labor."

"Yeah. Got that." He stood straight, took a drag, and winked as he led Archie through the store. "Trust me, buddy. I've got three ex-wives and four kids. Labor's no fun. All the lady's going to do is yell and scream at you. There's nothing you can do to make things go any easier for her."

"This is my wife, Jerry. Our first child."

"Trust me," he said. "There'll be other wives and other labors. Do this television delivery for me. I'll most likely let you leave after that."

"No." said Archie.

Jerry offered an amused grin. "No?"

"That's right—no. You have no right keeping me from my wife."

Jerry shook his head as if amazed at Archie's stupidity. "Archie, Archie. I thought I could count on you. But if you're going to defy a direct order, I could fire you. You are aware of that, I assume.

Archie's eyes narrowed, his stomach tightened. "No," he said. "You can't fire me," And then Archie withdrew his company keys from his right pants pocket, dropped them to the floor in front of Jerry, turned, and walked through the front entrance.

Jerry didn't protest. He didn't try to call Archie back or work things out. In fact, Archie had probably done exactly what Jerry had hoped he'd do. It was no secret that Jerry saw Archie as a rival. The guy knew he couldn't fire the man for having wanted the management position himself, but there was no company rule against being an ass.

Archie marched to his car in self-righteous anger. He had done the right thing. He had stood up for himself—for his wife, for his child.

He had quit his job and left his family with no source of income.

Archie sat behind the wheel, his little tin and duct-tape Chevrolet still motionless in the parking lot. Surely, Jerry was inside the store, looking out, smirking, wondering just how long Archie would sit there before crawling back through the front door and begging for another chance. Archie hated the guy, couldn't think of spending another hour in his presence, but he had a family to provide for, bills to pay, a new baby entering the world that very day.

Archie snatched his sketchbook from the seat beside him, withdrew a pencil from his breast pocket, and began flashing it across the blank white page. A moment later he sighed, ripped the page from the sketchbook, opened the car door, hesitated only briefly, rose, and strolled slowly back toward the building. Archie could see Jerry through the tinted glass of the storefront. He was pretending to straighten up around the store, but Archie could also see his frequent glances in his direction. Jerry was enjoying this.

Archie pulled open the door, approached him. Jerry adjusted the throw pillows on a sofa, then stood to meet Archie's gaze. He smiled, his yellowed smoker's teeth oddly out of place with his capped, nearly snow white, front tooth. Apparently, the teeth had continued to yellow at a different rate than the cap giving him an odd jack-o-lantern smile. "Archie," he said with faux enthusiasm. "You forget something?"

Archie lowered his gaze. "Yeah," he said. "Um, well," he took a deep breath. "I forgot this." Archie handed him the hastily scribbled drawing depicting an enraged Archie punching a surprised Jerry in the nose.

Jerry looked up from the page.

Archie decked him.

He heard the crunch of cartilage in Jerry's nose as he felt warm blood splay across his knuckles. Jerry's crisp white shirt was speckled with crimson as he gaped at Archie aghast, his face deformed in a hyena grimace, his eyes wide with shock. He sank onto the nearby sofa, blood running down his face and dribbling into his breast pocket where he kept his precious baseball card.

*****

By the time Archie had pulled onto Route 30 and turned in the direction of the hospital, he realized just what a horrible situation he'd created. He could be arrested. Jerry could bring charges against him, and Archie would be locked away, unemployed, and unable to provide for his family. Likely, he'd be released almost immediately, but surely he'd be convicted. The incident would dog him through life. Why couldn't he have just eaten crow and begged Jerry for his job, or maybe called the regional manager and pleaded his case? Anything but assaulting the S.O.B. But Archie was too prideful for that. He couldn't let anyone get the better of Archie Lambert.

They'd survive, he supposed. They always had. Yes, things were already tight, and they had no savings. But, he'd find another job. There was always another sales position available somewhere.

Archie needed to calm down, to take the edge off before waltzing into that delivery room and pretending he had it all under control. So he pulled into the first bar he saw, a dumpy little building with red concrete floors, green walls, and pictures of geese throughout. It wasn't one of his usual haunts. But it was there, and he had a need.

Archie only had two beers, maybe three—maybe four—and was only at the bar for about an hour. But by the time he finally made it to the hospital, Marcie had already given birth. Archie was confused. He'd been told that the first labor was always the longest. He'd heard tales of women pushing and screaming for twenty-four, forty-eight, even fifty-four hours. But Marcie had it easy. Six hours from first contraction till delivery. *Whamo!* Suddenly Archie was a father.

Marcie had no desire to see him. It was bad enough that he had beer breath, but the news that not only had Archie quit his job, but assaulted his loser boss as well had sent Marcie into a frenzy. "Get out!" she screamed through her tears. "I hate you. Do you hear that? I *hate* you!" She pounded her fists on the stainless steel bedrail, cursed him to hell, demanded a divorce, and threw her bedpan at him.

Despondent, Archie wandered into the bright sterile-looking hallway. The eggshell white walls were decorated with blue and pink painted balloons, cribs, and rattles. A couple of nurses stood talking, and a few men, probably new fathers such as he, strolled casually and somewhat aimlessly about the place. A nurse found him, asked if he was Mr. Lambert, and then led Archie to an observation area where he could view his daughter for the first time.

Jill was amazing. They had her in a room, behind a wall of glass, with a dozen or so other babies born that same day. She wore a pink knit cap, and fussed just enough to make Archie feel nervous. Her skin looked so soft, and her mouth curled just so. Archie knew that one day she'd break the hearts of every boy she'd ever know. He must have stood gazing at his child for nearly an hour before Marvin, Marcie's father, appeared by his side. "Archie," he said as he placed one of his large strong hands on Archie's shoulder. "You'd better go see Marcie. She needs you right now."

Marvin's deep blue eyes were soft, yet incredibly hard. It seemed he couldn't decide whether to reprimand Archie or congratulate him. Instead, he just remained silent as he guided Archie toward the room were his exhausted wife lay recovering from her ordeal.

"She doesn't want to see me," protested Archie as Marvin put his hand on the door handle to Marcie's room.

"That's true," he said, not yet opening the door. "And that's exactly why you must go in there." He paused, leveling his gaze at his son-in-law. "She's going to yell at you, Archie. She might even call you some names that you've only been called in bars and in locker rooms. Take your lumps. Roll with it. Duck, if you need to. But stay in that room. Because right now, most of all, she needs to know you're there for her—no matter what. When she looks back to this day, she needs to know that, even though you screwed this thing up, you still stayed by her side. That's what she needs to remember."

He then opened the door and fed Archie to the lioness.

*****

Archie left the hospital after Marcie finally drifted into sleep. It was somewhere around eight p.m. He carried no additional bumps or bruises, but had taken quite a verbal lashing. He called Colin from a pay phone and asked him to meet for a drink. Archie told him it was to celebrate, but really he needed to unwind after a truly horrendous day. Colin told him that he'd meet Archie at Jeremy's Warf, a nice little place off Route 41, centrally located, and not too noisy or crowded. He said he'd be there by nine. By ten-thirty, Archie pretty much figured his father was a no-show. He ordered another pitcher of Michelob, and continued to draw cartoons in his sketchpad.

At midnight, he tossed back the last of a beer, and contemplated heading toward home. But he was almost afraid to show up at his own place for fear that the police might be waiting. Archie didn't yet know that his coworker, Anna Marie, had intervened, and that Jerry would be pressing no charges. Still, the bar would be closing soon. Archie had nowhere else to go.

Stepping out into the cool night air, Archie thought of Marcie. Alone. Weary. He really should be with her.

Or maybe not.

She was furious at him. It was best to avoid her when she was furious. She was loud when she was angry. It hurt Archie's ears.

But, he was her husband. He should be with her at a time like this.

But, he feared he might be just a little drunk. Marcie hated it when Archie was drunk.

Squinting, Archie focused on a small shop just across the street from where he stood. Everything Coming Up Roses, was the name of the place.

A florist.

Florists sold flowers.

Women liked flowers.

Marcie was a woman.

With one unsteady step followed by another, Archie slowly made his way across the street.

Somewhere in Archie's blurred and anguished mind he knew this was a bad idea, that he would do much better to go home and sleep it off, but he was feeling quite abandoned—and quite drunk—and honestly, nothing seemed to matter very much just then.

The florist was, of course, closed.

Archie pounded on the glass.

No response.

He hollered, receiving the same silent reply.

Why couldn't a place stay open for a guy? Surely he wasn't the first to have a floral emergency.

This angered him. How dare these people—these flower people—stand in the way of him repairing his relationship with Marcie? What right did they have to deny him flowers, no matter what the hour?

Archie stumbled, caught his balance, and then nearly stumbled again. His head was swimmy and the sidewalk was behaving mischievously.

With a curse, Archie lowered himself to a sitting position, his back against the red brick storefront. Better to sit than to fall. This much, at least, he remembered from previous situations.

There was a chunk of concrete to his left.

A hefty chunk.

There was damage to the sidewalk, not an uncommon thing in the Midwest with its extreme temperatures both hot and cold.

The chunk gave Archie an idea.

Or almost.

He knew it was a solution of sorts, but couldn't remember the puzzle to which he sought a solution.

Archie sat staring at the jagged hunk of matter. He knew he could use it for something. What? What? What? Why couldn't he remember?

Finally, he gave up on the concrete and decided to rise. There it was, the florist shop. It was then that he remembered the flowers for Marcie.

The flowers which he'd been denied.

He needed those flowers. His marriage depended on him bringing flowers. What kind of man didn't give his wife flowers on the day she gave birth? Not Archie's kind of man, that was for sure.

He didn't remember picking up the chunk of sidewalk.

Nor did he remember hurling it through the shop window.

He did, though, remember the alarm.

And the police. He definitely remembered the police. They'd found him just as he stumbled out of the shattered window, a potted plant cradled to his chest.

Marcie never got her flowers that night.

Chapter Ten

Archie didn't remember falling asleep in the chair. Nor did he remember leaving Ned's apartment building, or wandering the streets of Ephesus for half a day. But apparently he'd done all of these things, for his first conscious perception after pulling the picture of Jill out of his pocket the night before was that he was standing in the intersection of Market and Main ogling a red traffic light. The faint odor of car exhaust and the warm summer breeze conspired to pull him out of the mystic haze he'd occupied. A UFC wannabe in a blue half-ton pick-up honked and hollered for Archie to get out of the road and Archie gave a weak nod, waved, and slowly made his way across the street as a clear white form scampered across the sky and beyond the horizon.

Archie's left forearm throbbed and stung. Once he was safely on the sidewalk he lifted it, finding five narrow cuts surrounded by purple-green skin. Four fingers and a thumb. As if someone had dug his nails into his arm—hard! By the angle of the wounds, it seemed as if they might be self-inflicted. With growing apprehension, he examined his right hand; there was dried blood under the fingernails. Archie's heart jumped and throbbed. Why did he remember none of this? Had he had a fitful dream and grabbed his own arm? Had an insect crawled onto him causing him to instinctively claw at it? If so, why hadn't the pain awakened him? And how had he come to be in the middle of town? Had he walked, hitched a ride? Archie closed his eyes, trying to reach back, to pull forward the memories of the past several hours. Nothing. Nothing but white. He remembered white—pure gleaming white. Whatever that meant. He needed to talk with Colin, but knew this wasn't an option. Any contact with his father would surely lead to discovery.

Confused and frightened, Archie jammed his hand into his right pants pocket. Yes, the picture of Jill was still there. As was the dollar he'd borrowed from the nurse the night before.

There was also an additional thirty-three dollars.

Archie stared at the mystery bills, attempting to pull forward the memory of how the cash had come into his possession. There had to be something, some whisper of a memory, some hidden trail leading back across the timeless void of the previous hours.

Nothing.

Only white.

It dawned on him that by this time—somewhere in the mid-afternoon—word would have gotten out of his escape and the police would be on the look-out. Fortunately, it was summer. The local kids were not in school. Archie wouldn't be overly conspicuous. Still, he felt it best to stay as well out of sight as possible.

Bewildered and disoriented, his stomach rumbling, Archie made his way up Market Street to the local diner he'd frequented as a child. He knew he'd be better served away from public scrutiny, but he was hungry and confused. This at least would get him off of the street while he sorted things out.

Archie's medium well burger was nearly rare, but still he chomped on it eagerly as he gazed through the front window of the diner and onto the street, keeping an eye out for patrol cars. The town was busy: traffic moving up and down Market Street, pedestrians scurrying this way and that, kids riding bicycles and scooters.

Archie felt a profound sense of longing for days gone by as he gazed through the subtly tinted pane.

Ephesus Indiana, population 30,000 plus and climbing, was a town in transition, and had been for quite some time. Located roughly an hour and a half southeast of Chicago, the town was birthed to be rural, aspired to be urban, and had settled into a fitful quasi-suburbia with an aw-shucks flavor and a boomtown attitude. There were still two small cornfields on the outskirts of town, but most of the true rural flavor had been nudged further south as populations increased. Where once everyone knew everyone, now most folks struggled to name the family living in the next house over. There was still only one high school, though another was under construction. Gangs and drugs had begun to creep in. The oldest part of the downtown area was mostly ignored and rife with the homeless and the desperate. Though Archie had grown up in Ephesus, and had worked there until the cancer flared up, he hadn't actually lived within the town limits for a number of years.

Still, this was home turf. He knew the town, knew the people, knew the ins and outs of the place. Despite the many changes, Archie felt a longing and a warmth as he mentally embraced the familiar structures about him. Hugh's Bakery where he used to buy donuts every morning on the way to school was immediately across the street. Market Street Pet Shoppe was adjacent that. He'd spent hours in that place as a child, talking with a parrot—Lolly—who he just had to have. A few doors further down was an old movie theater recently converted into a pizza parlor. He'd seen his first R-rated film there. He'd only been thirteen but he and Billy Jablonski had sneaked in through the back door. Next to the converted theater was a little thrift store. The sign read only "Thrift" and Archie never knew its real name—if indeed it had one. The kids called it Dotty's Place because that was what their mothers called it.

Archie was surprised to find a tear sneaking stealthily down his cheek. He would need to leave this place. Soon. Likely this very day. Never to return. Or, if he did, not for a decade or better. Not until he'd grown into his adult body and was unrecognizable to those who had known Joey.

Would that ever happen?

Even years later, wasn't it likely someone would recognize him? Joey's parents. Wouldn't they forever be on the lookout, scanning crowds for a sign of their missing son, wondering if ever he would come home to them, wondering if some pervert had secreted him away, wondering if he was alive or dead?

He wiped the moisture from his face with a paper napkin. He couldn't do this. Couldn't allow himself to follow that line of thinking. Right now, this day, everything was about avoiding capture, pure and simple. He could worry about the moral implications, about the fallout, about everything else once he'd found safety and had a chance to sort things through. For the moment, he had to keep moving.

Leaving the diner, he strolled gracelessly onto the street, deciding for no particular reason to turn left. His plan of the night before to contact someone from his adult past still tickled his brain, but he hadn't quite figured out who to call or what to say. Archie did know, though, that he'd need to change clothes if he wanted to avoid detection. The police would be on the lookout for an awkward kid in a yellow SpongeBob T-shirt. Stepping into Dotty's Place, he searched the racks for suitable replacements. There was a woman at the counter—not Dotty, though there was some resemblance—who followed him with her eyes. She was on the younger side, probably late twenties or early thirties, wore her blond hair in a pony tail, and stood with her broad arms crossed over her broader belly. Her gaze made Archie uncomfortable. Was the general public already aware of his disappearance, or was this girl simply the suspicious type? Archie selected a T-shirt, Navy, with no distinguishing writing or images, and a nearly matching set of sweat pants, paid for the items out of his remaining money, and left the store.

A shiver of dread danced about his limbs. Twice, as he moved down the sidewalk, he thought he caught a glimpse of something shimmering, something only a few feet behind him, hovering, watching. But there was nothing. Only the town. Only Ephesus. Still… Something wasn't right. He couldn't quite get his head around it, but there was something familiar and simultaneously alien—something deadly—and it was just beyond the scope of his memory.

There was a service station on the next corner. Archie struggled through the change of clothes in the men's room, and then tossed his old outfit into the dumpster. He then veered off of the main drag, thinking it better to walk the side streets where fewer people would see him.

The residential streets were flooded with kids: tossing balls, zipping about on skateboards, squabbling over game rules. Most ignored Archie, but some stared or pointed, whispering to their friends. Did these kids know Joey? Had they been his friends, his classmates? It had been a mistake to move into the residential area. He should have remained on the main streets, the domain of adults. Kids were almost invisible to most adults, being nothing more than unpredictable traffic obstacles. Here, he was likely among those who were most likely to recognize him.

White.

Everything white.

No variance, no shade, no texture.

Silent.

Utter void.

And then...

Archie was perhaps a block distant from where he'd been only moments—seconds, minutes? —before.

What in the hell had just happened?

*****

Archie made his way back to Market Street and moved further down the way until he reached an old two-story brown brick building. Curly Jake's Pub, one of his old haunts. Surely there would be someone he knew in there, someone he could talk with. He'd been a regular at the place right up until he'd landed in the hospital the first time.

Archie shuffled to the door and gazed at his reflection in the glass. The face of a child stared back, youthful and innocent, soft and frightened. What could he possibly expect to accomplish here? Would anyone really believe that he was Archie Lambert, that his soul had been transferred into another body? And even if some lunatic did believe, what could said lunatic do to help him? Did he really expect someone to take him in, to hide him for multiple years until he finally resembled an adult? No. None of it made sense. There was no reason to even try. Archie's best bet was to contact Colin and go with his recommendations. But that he couldn't do. There was too great a risk that someone would uncover Colin's secret and Archie would become a lab rat for the overly curious and the dangerously greedy. He gazed again at his reflection, sighed, reached out, clasped the door handle, pulled the door open, and entered the dark smoky room.

Archie scanned the familiar place, inhaling the mingled smells of tobacco, beer, and months-old frying grease. There was a row of TVs mounted above the dark wooden bar, each featuring a different sporting event: baseball, tennis, soccer, beach volleyball. The darkly paneled walls bore artistic black and white photographs of railroad tracks, ice-caked telephone lines, and turn-of-the-century buildings. There were only three patrons, all male, spaced along the bar. It was early. The place would fill up after five.

Curly Jake, the owner/bartender, a man of about fifty, balding, thin, and pale, leaned against the bar reading a National Geographic magazine. He was always reading stuff like that. National Geographic, The Economist, The New Yorker, anything that made him appear smart or sophisticated. Anything that made him look like someone other than the neighborhood bartender. He liked to dress as he imagined an ivy-league professor would dress. Today he wore a blue dress shirt, narrow tie, corduroy jacket—with obligatory elbow patches—and blue jeans.

Archie had to fight off tears at the sight of Jake.

They'd spent many hours laughing and joking together, shared personal problems; Archie had even helped him out with a couple of family crises. They went way back, not all the way to high school or college, but almost. Jake was one of the few people that Archie actually considered a friend. He hadn't seen him for months, not since he'd become sick. Now, Archie realized how much he'd missed the guy.

There was another familiar face as well: Doug Stobach, a real estate agent, heavyset, with bushy hair and eyebrows. Doug and Archie had been on friendly terms, not best buds, but they'd had their moments. Archie's stomach tightened. This was his old life. Right here, in this room. His feelings were mixed. Joy and sorrow. What had he missed? What was he missing now?

And suddenly, all eyes were on Archie. Jake lowered his magazine, eyeing Archie curiously. "What have we here?" he asked in a tone of curious annoyance.

Archie forgot himself, forgot that he was a kid, that Jake wouldn't know him. "Jake, you look great. How's it going?"

Jake chuckled. "Child, this is an adult establishment. Are you looking for someone specific?"

"Lou!" said Archie with sudden inspiration. "Lou, I should talk with Lou."

Jake set the magazine on the bar. "Lou's not here. Now, I need you to leave before I lose my license."

"Yeah, yeah," said Archie. "I'll leave. Just, I need to collect on an old bet with Lou. Um, for Archie Lambert." It had just dawned on him that he had placed a bet on the Patriots, just prior to getting sick. New England had romped, and Archie was owed nearly two hundred dollars.

Jake cocked his head. "Archie Lambert. I don't know the name."

Oh, come on, Jake. It hasn't been that long! "Archie Lambert. Six-foot-oh, hazel eyes, killer smile. You know, third stool from the right, always sat there with a sketchpad."

"He's talkin' 'bout Sketch," said Doug without looking up.

Jake laughed. "Ah, Sketch. You his boy?"

"No," said Archie after a pause. "I'm his, uh, nephew."

Jake nodded, staring at Archie, probably trying to search out some family resemblance. "I haven't seen your uncle in perhaps six or seven months. He still has an outstanding tab, maybe sixty dollars. Would you like to pay his debt?"

"I'll pass."

"Of course you will." Jake stepped away from the bar, reached down and opened the under-bar refrigerator, grabbed a bottled Budweiser, popped the top, and downed a swig. "Some advice for you, kid. Stay away from your Uncle Sketch. You'll be happier."

"He's dead," said Archie, his voice even and controlled, though he could feel the heat rising in his face, could sense the white slithering about his ankles, wanting to rise, to subdue. Archie exhaled, maintaining control. He didn't understand the sensations, but sensed danger.

"Figures," said Jake as he took another swig. "How did Sketch send you if he's deceased?"

The white scampered up Archie's leg, tickled his spine. "He told me about you before. He said you were his friend."

Jake shrugged. "He was my customer. I was his bartender. Whatever significance you wish to attach, that's fine by me."

With a shout, Archie raced around the bar in a stuttering gallop, tackling Jake at the waist. The bartender dropped his beer. It shattered with a loud *pop*, splaying suds and glass against their legs. But Jake remained standing. Archie just didn't have enough oomph to do any damage. Still, he pummeled the man with wild punches, forcing him to back away. Jake snatched his National Geographic, swiping at Archie as at an annoying insect.

"Just his bartender!" screamed Archie. "What about all those late night weeping sessions? What about when your sister needed a place to crash?"

Jake took another swing with his magazine. "Get off of me you little spaz!" He swiped again, this time slapping Archie across the face. "The only reason Sketch took my sister in was that he hoped to get laid." He swatted again, but Archie ducked, and somehow managed to land a solid punch to Jake's gut.

Archie flashed white. All about him, choking him, slipping in through his nostrils, his ears, his mouth. All was pure, gleaming white.

Archie blinked. He was still in the bar. Jake's ear was bloodied.

White again. Blinding. Frigid.

Jake was on the ground, gagging on the blood spilling from his mouth.

Doug was now behind Archie, wrapping his arms over him, pulling him back, trying to calm him. Arms no longer available to him, Archie kicked wildly, connecting with Jake's groin.

"Let me go," screamed Archie, still squirming and kicking. "Doug! I said, let me go."

But Doug wasn't listening. He simply lifted Archie from the floor and carried him gracelessly toward the front door. They knocked over a couple of bar stools in the process, and Archie bloodied Doug's lip with the back of his head, but none of this slowed him. "Nah, nah, nah," said Doug. "You just calm yourself down, kid. Calm her down."

With an icy tingle, the white slithered down Archie's leg and into oblivion. What had that been? What had just happened?

Doug backed through the door, still squeezing Archie in a tight bear hug. Archie could hear Jake screaming as the door swung shut.

Now in the daylight, Archie squinted, nearly blinded by the midday sun. Doug continued holding him tight, not yet ready to release him for fear the boy might race back into the bar. "Okay, kid," he said. "Calm down. Jake can get obnoxious. There's nothing you can do to change that."

"Let me go!" Archie screamed. And this time Doug released him. They were now out in the open. Cars were passing by and there was an elderly couple across the street glaring at them. Likely Doug feared someone would call the police and accuse him of child abuse.

Snorting, and clenching his fists, Archie turned to face Doug. The man's face was red from exertion and he was breathing heavily. "You don't understand," said Archie, still trying to catch his own breath and steady his quivering limbs.

Doug bent over, panting, and placing his palms upon his knees as he looked Archie eye-to-eye. "What's to understand?" he asked. "Jake disrespected your dead uncle. You took him to task. Fine. But you've got to understand, your uncle Archie, he was an okay guy. Nice, I mean. But…" Doug hesitated, maybe unwilling to continue his thought.

"Go on," prodded Archie. "But what? What is it about Archie you don't want me to know?"

Doug squinted, scrutinizing the boy. He was probably wondering if Archie would go off on him the same way he had on Jake. Archie wouldn't. Doug and he had been acquaintances. Jake and Archie were supposed to have been friends. The hurt was a lot deeper coming from Jake.

"Okay," he said finally. "Archie, well, like I say, he was nice and all, just, well, too into himself, you know. Big plans. Gonna be the next Charles Schultz and all that. Moping about after the divorce, all 'whoa is me,' as if he was the only guy to ever go through that. He was fine to have a drink with, but the whole thing got old, you know?"

They stared at each other for several silent moments, each trying to discern the other's thoughts. "No, Doug," Archie said finally. "I don't understand. Maybe you don't either. Archie thought you people were his friends; that you cared about what was happening in his life. That's why he shared his goals and hurts. I guess Archie really was a fool." And with that, Archie turned and marched away with his most dignified shuffling hobble.

Chapter Eleven

Archie made his way downtown, the thought being that Ned's apartment was on the southern outskirts of town; any search would center around his last known location. Downtown was much further north, and probably one of the last places anyone would expect a runaway kid to willingly go. There was a Greyhound bus station in town, but Archie assumed this would be under surveillance.

Archie's stomach growled, he felt lightheaded from hunger, but determined not to spend any more money till the following day. He'd gone through his limited resources far too quickly and needed to squirrel at least two more meals out of his remaining six dollars.

It was beginning to drizzle and distant thunder warned of a more intense rain to come. Archie needed to find shelter for the night, someplace dry and well hidden. Downtown Ephesus was not the jewel of the city. Mostly ignored and nearly forgotten, it was the kind of place respectable people didn't go, except when they took a break from being respectable. Most of the buildings were built somewhere in the first half of the twentieth century and many had fallen to disrepair. There were still businesses downtown, but the true economic growth had moved further south where strip malls, fitness centers, and Starbucks dotted the landscape. Most of the remaining storefronts in this older part of town were either ma and pa shops, barely scraping by, or bars, adult bookstores, and strip clubs, all of which seemed to feast on the decay. Downtown only encompassed an area of perhaps two square miles, but was distinctive in feel and tone, baring little resemblance to greater Ephesus. Probably, the whole place should have been leveled and rebuilt, but with the rest of the town so full of character and vitality, no one seemed to care about this tumor at its northernmost point.

A group of five young men stood on a corner, their expressions serious, threatening. Money exchanged hands. A drug deal, no doubt. Archie quickened his pace, turning right at the next opportunity. There was a middle-aged couple sitting on folding chairs under an awning. They were chuckling and pointing at the clouds, enjoying the rain-fresh air and debating whether or not this was tornado weather. They waved as Archie walked past. He nodded in return.

And everything went white.

Not a bright blinding white such as that caused by a floodlight shining in one's eyes, but more of a snowstorm white, as if someone had whitewashed the entire world in one quick stroke. Archie had no concept of what he did at that moment, if he stopped, moved forward, stumbled. He just knew white. And then it was gone. He was still on the street. The middle-aged couple sat staring at him, confusion, maybe even fear, in their eyes. They rose, moving quickly into their home and locking the door. Archie lowered his head and marched past without a word. He'd had a similar episode earlier, hadn't he? At Jakes. But... maybe not. Somehow he couldn't quite get his mind around it. Something had happened. He was certain of it. But what? Why were his thoughts muddled? Why was he missing pieces of the day? Little snatches, vignettes. Why did he feel as if time had become a jigsaw puzzle and that several key pieces were missing?

Physical pain brought him back to his immediate situation. Archie's legs ached and twitched. He'd been back and forth across town all day, and though Ephesus wasn't exactly a metropolis, he'd definitely covered ten or fifteen miles since morning. It was surprising he hadn't collapsed. Archie knew these limbs wouldn't carry him much further and feared they might go on strike the following day, leaving him helpless and vulnerable.

He came to a concrete embankment beneath a viaduct. The space at the top, just on the underside of the overpass, was well shadowed and dry. Clumsily, he climbed the slope, several times nearly losing his footing and tumbling down. The incline leveled off to a ledge at the top, perhaps four feet deep and with a four foot clearance below the iron and concrete bridge. A chill raced up Archie's spine as he settled into the dark uneven place and gazed down at the traffic passing beneath. It would be a cold night, probably dropping into the forties. While purchasing a T-shirt had made sense in the heat of the summer day, a wet and rainy night called for a sweatshirt, even better, a jacket or coat.

There was a blue and green towel rolled up in a ball off to Archie's right. Beside it lay a half-eaten Snickers bar and a dark green trash bag containing aluminum cans. Obviously, Archie wasn't the first to have sought shelter under this viaduct. He wasn't tempted by the candy bar, but the rolled up towel would make a decent pillow. He wondered if its owner had abandoned it or if he was simply out and about, soon to return to claim his space and his belongings. Archie decided it best to wait until he was ready to sleep before availing himself of the towel.

Sleep, he wondered if that was even an option. How does one sleep out in the open, in the middle of a drug-infested and nearly forgotten corner of town? Archie hoped that he would be mostly invisible up in his little sanctuary, but how many others would join him as night claimed its victory over day? What would these displaced people do to a lone child, weak, uncoordinated, and unaccustomed to life on the streets?

Archie stared out at the rain. It had now become steady and lightning and thunder punctuated the dusky eve. Rain smacked and pattered on either side of him as it ran off of the road overhead and collided with the concrete incline. The sounds of tires rolling across the rain-drenched asphalt sounded like bacon frying on a skillet. Dusk eventually rolled into night and the shadows darkened to a dirty charcoal. Occasionally, Archie heard voices as people strolled by beneath, sometimes pushing shopping carts containing all of their earthly possessions and other times lugging trash bags on their backs. Two men, both white, and both ill-tempered, seated themselves at the base of the slope, sharing a bottle and a quarrel. Archie didn't think they'd seen him. Maybe he would somehow make it through the night unmolested.

Another hour passed. The rain continued and several more people found their ways to the bottom of Archie's embankment. Some had sleeping bags; a couple even had small tents. Most stayed at ground level where the surface was flat, but a couple moved partially up the slope. Surely, some noticed the boy huddled toward the top, but none seemed overly concerned or threatening. They talked of sports, politics, religion, all the normal office chat, just, minus the office.

Archie finally decided to retrieve the balled up towel. Shaking it out and inspecting it, he found no obvious evidence of creepy-crawlies and so rolled it and positioned it behind his head, just above the neck. He lulled in and out of near-sleep, never fully drifting off, but not retaining full conscious thought either.

There was a sharp tug from just beneath his neck, the towel was whisked out, and Archie's skull *thunked* hard against naked concrete. "That's my towel!" screamed a man. His face just inches above Archie's own, his blue eyes wide and darting, his hair a tangled brown mop sticking out from beneath a fisherman's hat. His nose was red and bulbous, caked with dried matter at the nostrils. "That's my towel!" he repeated, as he whipped Archie with the thing. "This is my space—mine!"

"Leave the boy alone," came a voice from below, a woman's voice, high, but not shrill. "He's just trying to sleep."

"It's my spot!" cried the man, again, this time shoving Archie with both hands.

"Alright, alright," said Archie, still struggling with the remnants of sleep. "I'm moving."

"My place!" said the man.

"Leave him alone!" shouted the woman as she scrambled up the embankment, swatting at the man with her crocheted scarf.

Archie feared the man might to take a swipe at her, but instead, he cradled the towel under his left armpit, and shuffled away to the right. "My place," he muttered one last time, just to make sure everyone understood his claim.

"Well, that was fun," said Archie as he rose to a sitting position and rubbed the back of his head where it had connected with the concrete.

The woman smiled as she lowered herself to beside him. "You alright?" she asked.

"Yeah, fine," he said, still massaging his head. "Just a little startled."

She chuckled and nodded. "Yeah, I guess you would be." She was a short black woman, maybe five foot three, with large round eyes and a dark creamy complexion. Aside from the over-sized, stained and torn windbreaker she wore, and the mildly disheveled hair, she was quite attractive. Likely in her mid to upper twenties, she had an easy smile, dimpled cheeks, and an intelligent glint to her eyes. She didn't seem to Archie the kind of person he'd meet under a viaduct.

She looked Archie up and down, appraising him. "You're cold," she said.

Archie nodded and shrugged. "A little bit."

"It's going to get colder."

She was probably right. It had been twenty-five years or better since last he'd been camping. Archie had no idea how low temperatures might drop in the middle of the night.

"My place!" screamed the man once again, still cradling his towel, and huddling toward the edge of the embankment.

"Give it a rest, Freddie," said the woman as she began to unzip her windbreaker. Then, offering Archie a knowing smirk, she said, "Freddie can be a bit possessive. Here," she said, offering Archie her windbreaker. "You take this."

He shook his head. "No. You need that."

Ignoring Archie's protests, she tossed it onto his lap. "I'm still wearing a sweater and have been through worse nights than this. You put that on. Warm yourself." Archie made eye contact, and seeing that she was sincere, nodded.

"My name's Mercedes," she said.

"I'm, uh, Skip," he replied, feeding her the first random name that came to his mind as he slipped into the jacket. He'd foolishly told producer Ned his name was Archie, and the police would be looking for a kid named Joey. He felt it best to avoid any name associated with his real life.

"Glad to meet you, *uh*-Skip," she smiled, imitating Archie's hesitant response. "Are you going to be okay out here?"

Archie nodded. "I'll get by."

She stared at him, her large brown eyes seemingly x-raying his soul. "Why are you here, Skip? Did you run away from home?"

"You first," he countered. "I'm trying to figure how someone like you came to be here. You're not exactly like Freddy and his towel, or those guys down there arguing over a three-quarters empty bottle of J.B."

"Bad choices," she said after a moment's contemplation. "Bad choice in a husband, bad choice in... Well, let's just leave it at that. Bad choices."

"Well," Archie said. "I've certainly been down that road." He contemplated the rain for a moment, breathing in its freshness, shivering at its chill. "Have you been out here long?" he asked. "Do you have any prospects for getting an apartment, a job?"

"Any prospects?" she chuckled and ran a hand through her hair. "You're a strange kid, you know that?"

Archie shrugged.

"Any prospects," she repeated. "Yeah, I guess. I mean, I'm working on a couple of things. This is a short term problem. I've got options." She paused, cocked her head, and grinned. "Now, enough stalling. What about you—how did you come to be out here?"

"Bad breaks," he said after a beat. "A lifetime of bad breaks."

She shook her head and laughed out loud. "A lifetime of bad breaks. You're what—ten, twelve?"

"That," he said with a wry smile and piercing gaze, "depends on who you ask. But, you'd be surprised at how much I've seen, and how much I wish I could change."

"Well, I don't care how much you think you've seen. You still don't get it. I can tell that already."

"You have me figured out already?"

"Bad breaks. There's no such thing. People go through life whining, bad breaks, bad breaks. Every break you get is what you make of it. You make good choices, you get more good breaks. You make bad choices..." She shrugged.

"Says the homeless lady," snapped Archie in a bitter tone.

Mercedes leaned closer beside him, draping an arm across Archie's shoulders. "Why is it I get the feeling you're trouble just waiting for its moment to arrive?"

Archie smiled, shrugged, and then pulled away, reclining again on the bare concrete. The woman had no idea how perceptive she had been.

Chapter Twelve

Archie awoke to the subtle murmurings of voices below, of increased traffic from above, and the distant yapping of neighborhood dogs. Mercedes was curled next to him, her left arm draped about him, cradling, protecting. Archie could feel the warmth of her breath on the back of his neck, and the beating of her heart on his spine. It dawned on him that had he been in his adult body, he might be feeling different emotions toward this woman than the strictly platonic admiration for a caring soul.

She must have sensed Archie's stirrings because within moments of his awakening, Mercedes asked, "Are you alright, Skip?"

Archie offered an affirmative grunt, disengaged from her arm with a shiver, and lulled into a sitting position. His cheeks stung, his nose dribbled, and it seemed his ears might shatter at the slightest touch. "You were right—cold," he said, pulling her windbreaker tighter about his body and longing for a stiff drink to warm his belly.

She scooted to Archie's left and ruffled his fledgling hair. "You sure you want to stay out here? Maybe home doesn't seem like such a bad place after spending a night under a bridge."

"There is no home to go back to," he said, hoping she wouldn't ask for details.

She nodded, staring at the street below, at the occasional car or pickup truck, at the few people left at the bottom of the embankment. The sun was up, the rain gone; it was time to move on. "What about foster care?" she asked. "I can get you to protective services."

"No!" snapped Archie. "No foster homes, no government agencies. I'm on my own."

"No one's really on their own, Skip—ever."

Archie didn't need this, the moralizing of a homeless person. He had enough real issues to deal with. Who was she to give him advice? Obviously her life wasn't ideal. Without responding, he began scooting down the embankment. It was best that he moved on, that he got away from this woman.

Her intensions were good, but he couldn't escape the feeling that she'd lead to his discovery. Sooner or later he'd let too much information slip or she'd feel compelled to call the authorities. Archie needed to get out of Ephesus, maybe hitchhike up to Hammond or Gary, perhaps even Chicago or Milwaukee; someplace other than this town where the search was on.

"Skip," she called, when he'd reached the bottom.

Archie turned, gazing up at her. "I can get you some food," she said. "Maybe even a little bit of money."

Archie nodded and waited for her to scoot down the embankment. If she had food and money and was willing to share, that would save him some hassle. Depending on how much money she had, he might even be able to take a bus once outside of town.

They walked in silence observing the gray bleakness of downtown shift to vibrancy as they crossed into the living sector of Ephesus. There weren't any tracks to be on the wrong or right side of; rather, it was simply the crossing of Washington Street at Market. The north side of Washington was dark, disturbing, and dying, while everything south was alive and, at least apparently, well. The street was only four lanes, two in each direction, but there might as well have been a mile-wide chasm between the two neighborhoods. Several respectable south-side people eyed the pair as they crossed into reputable territory. No one wanted the boundaries expanding, and the Ephesus Police Department kept a close eye on the cracked and pitted asphalt border.

"So, where are we going to get this food and money?" asked Archie as they angled left across Market Street and down a single lane side street.

Her face became taut. "It's mine."

"If you have money, why are you on the street?"

"Maybe I shouldn't be," she said. "But life can be complicated, Skip. Things aren't always as they appear."

Archie couldn't argue with that, and slipped back into silence. It was probably best that he kept conversation to a minimum. The more they talked, the more likely she'd either catch him in a lie, or, worse yet, he'd let something slip that would give him away. She asked about his lack of coordination, if he had cerebral palsy. He told her that he'd been in an accident, and that he'd rather not talk about it. After that she stopped probing.

Eventually, they made their way down a quaint little street lined with red brick houses, green lawns, and Chevrolet automobiles. "Don't say anything," said Mercedes as she pulled a key ring from her pocket and climbed the front porch steps of a small one story home. "Stay here till I'm sure he's not home."

"He who?" asked Archie, beginning to wonder if this had been wise.

"My ex. Now be quiet."

She slipped a key into the brass-colored lock, twisted, and slowly pushed the door open. "Good," she whispered. "He hasn't changed the locks." Then she disappeared inside, gently closing the door behind her, and leaving Archie standing alone in the yard. He wondered about Mercedes then, why she would help a runaway child to flee the city. Was she really going to help him or was she calling the police? That would, after all, be the responsible thing to do. She seemed level-headed, not deranged or hopped up on drugs.

There were several children playing the game Running Bases in the next lawn over, and one vehicle making its way up the street. It was perhaps three blocks distant, and Archie couldn't yet tell if it was a squad car. He didn't like being exposed. Someone was bound to see him, maybe even recognize Joey. He needed to remain invisible.

After a three minute-long hour, Archie decided to move indoors. Pushing the door slightly open, he whispered, "Mercedes." She didn't respond. He stepped inside, closing the door behind him. "Mercedes," he said again, this time a little louder. Archie was in a small living room. The furniture was old, the colors and styles reflecting the tastes of the mid-nineties. But it was all in good shape, not stained or ripped. There was a low-sitting coffee table in front of a taupe-colored couch, scattered periodicals spread across it. A thirty-two inch high definition TV was mounted on the far wall. It was tuned to CNN Headline News. Someone other than Mercedes was here.

"You have no right!" came a male voice from the back of the house.

"I have no right?" hollered Mercedes. "Wait till you get served, then we'll see who has no right. You knew what you were doing. I'm the wronged party here."

There was a shuffle, running footsteps. "Give that to me." screamed the male in a near falsetto.

"No," said Mercedes. "These are mine. I worked for them."

"Give those to me!"

Then there was a loud crash, something—or someone—slamming against something else. Before Archie realized what he was doing, he'd somehow willed Joey's body to rush down the short hallway and to turn left into a small bedroom. Mercedes was against the far wall, on the floor, just beginning to rise. She had what looked to be stock certificates clutched in her right hand. Before her stood a plump Asian man with little hair, and hip-hop bling. "Those are ours, not yours."

"It was my money that paid for these," countered Mercedes as she turned toward the door.

The man moved to intercept.

"Stop," said Archie, not knowing what else to do.

"Who are you?" blurted the balding hip-hop Asian.

"Skip, stay out of this." warned Mercedes, her eyes narrow, the stock certificates clenched tightly in her fist.

"Hey, wait a minute," said the man. "I've seen you on the news. Johnny, Jimmy, something like that. You ran away from that hospital."

Archie's stomach tightened, his legs tensed to flee.

"Skip?" said Mercedes. "Is that tru…"

*****

Again there was white.

Only white.

Seemingly forever white.

But not forever.

Now there was something else. Pieces, different colors and sizes. Falling. From above, below, from the left, and from the right. They fell, silent and purposeful.

And as they fell, they collected, dozens of intersecting pieces: silver, black, brown, red. Piece by piece they tumbled, now interconnecting, assembling until Archie found that he was somewhere else: on an elevator, amidst a crowd of chattering, cheerful people. The pieces had assembled the reality.

He was Archie again. An adult. Not a child or the emaciated cancer victim he'd become, but the beefy, blustery Archie of perhaps ten years prior. A young woman, pretty and blond, with painted fingernails and a powdered nose, bumped against him as the crowd adjusted. Archie felt his heart thump at the accidental contact, at the smell of her perfume, at the hint of her smile. This wasn't a dream. He had physical sensation. He could feel, smell, hear. The colors were vivid, not shadowy and indistinct as they would be in a dream.

The stainless steel door slid open. The crowd surged forward carrying Archie with it. He found himself in a large windowed area. There were dozens of people present: families, businesspersons, tourists. Tentatively, he moved forward. His gate was steady, with none of the awkward missteps of the past weeks. He could hear people's conversations, the dad telling his toddler to hold his hand, two young women giggling about some actor named Edward. Archie could sense the movement of the air on his skin. He could feel the subtle pressure on his ears caused by altitude change.

Confused and apprehensive, Archie made his way to the edge of the room, squeezing between a young giggling couple and a lanky black man in a Michael Jordan jersey. He saw the John Hancock building looming before him. Scanning the horizon he also made out Soldier Field and Navy Pier. The traffic far below could have been ants darting about a picnic table. There were only a couple of clouds in the perfect sky, but they were at eye level. He was atop the Sears—now renamed Willis—Tower in Chicago.

Archie stepped back, his mind mired in a pit of impossibilities. He'd only been to the Sears Tower once in his life—years ago, before he'd met Marcie. It had been overcast that day, clouds embracing the huge structure, not bright and sunny like this day. He hadn't been able to see a thing. How had he come to be here now? Archie put a hand against the wall. It was cool, hard—real.

*****

Mercedes' ex loomed above Archie, his brow furrowed above bloodshot eyes. "Finney!" he heard Mercedes say. "What did you do to him? Is he okay?"

"I didn't do anything," replied the man as he extended a wary hand. "Kid, are you epileptic?"

"No," said Archie as he scooted out of the man's reach. "What's going on?"

"I was hoping you could help us with that," said Finney.

Archie glanced about the room. Mercedes was behind her ex, still clutching the stocks in her right hand. She seemed frightened. For Archie, for herself, he couldn't tell. Archie opened his mouth to speak but was not present to hear his own words.

*****

With a mighty surge, the white washed away the scene and Archie found that he was in a canoe. A whitewater river raged about him. The crashing of the waves thundered in his ears. The fresh smells of water and springtime filled his nostrils. Instinctively, he clutched the coarse wooden oar, jamming it into the cold, rushing spray. Once again, he was Archie, an adult, with an adult's strength and coordination.

A large rock jutted out of the water before him, gray and jagged. Remembering his few canoeing experiences from his scouting days, Archie attempted to use the oar as a rudder, to steer to the left of the looming obstacle. But the canoe failed to respond as quickly as needed. The current was too strong, the distance from the obstacle too narrow. Still disoriented, Archie plunged into the icy water as the small craft crashed into the cold gray stone, hung there for a moment as if deciding what to do next, and then pulled loose, racing away with the white and foaming water. Archie's body flipped about as he struggled to surface, to breathe. He struck something hard with his right knee. He twisted, the current pulling him under and…

*****

Archie was atop Finney. The man's face was bloodied, one eye swollen shut, his nose out of place. His face was crimson and glistening. Mercedes was behind Archie, weeping hysterically, pulling at him, trying to force Archie off of her ex. Archie's fingers were sticky with blood; Finney's or his own, he didn't know. Archie allowed Mercedes to toss him to the right, onto the slick hardwood floor. He tumbled, his elbow connecting with wood, a shot of pain racing up his arm. "You freak!" she screamed. "You animal! What are you?"

"I… I… don't… know," he stammered, gazing at the scene in disbelief. The blood on his hands. Blood. It was warm, tacky, repulsive.

There was a sharp knock at the door. "Police!" barked an authoritative voice. "Someone call nine-one-one?"

"Back here," called Mercedes as she moved toward Finney. "He's back here. Hurry!"

"The baby," moaned Finney as she cradled his head in her lap, his blood staining her clothing. "Did he hurt the baby?"

Mercedes touched her belly with her right palm. Only then did Archie notice that her face was scratched and swollen as well. "I don't know, sugar. It hurts."

Archie heard footsteps, sharp, deliberate.

"That's the kid," said a tall, red-haired officer. "The one from the institute."

Archie watched as the white scampered across the baseboard, fleeing the scene of the crime.

Chapter Thirteen

Archie sat in a cold vanilla conference room at the Gowon Institute. Dr. Diana Mortonson was seated across from him, a folder open on the long dull table and a yellow legal pad setting beside it. In her left hand was a number-two pencil, its eraser worn nearly to extinction, in her right, a pale green Granny apple, still uneaten. Her breath offered the feint hint of butterscotch. "What were you doing?" she asked as her brows converged above her petite angular nose.

Archie stared down at his hands balled together on the table and remained silent.

"I asked you a question," she said, her voice firm and authoritative.

Archie looked at her deep chocolate eyes, pale, almost gothic complexion, and bright red lips. She was a stern woman, someone unaccustomed to rebellion from those she considered to be inferior, an intelligent woman, someone who achieved and didn't have time for life's little detours. But she was also strangely frightened. Her face was taut, her grip on her pencil tight, rigid, not relaxed or controlled.

"Listen," he said. "I ran away. Kids do that."

"Why?" she pressed.

"Because I was frightened."

She nodded, jotted a note, took a bite out of the apple, chewed, then asked, "What happened with Finney and Mercedes Yamagata?"

"Apparently they're separated or divorced. Mercedes is living on the street, Finney still has the house."

Mortonson set the pencil down on the legal pad and then took a chomp from the apple. "The question I am asking is why did you attack them?"

Archie didn't have an answer for this. He wished he had. But Archie wasn't there, in that room, with those people at the time. He was somewhere else, in a raging river, being carried downstream. He had no idea of what had happened, if Finney had attacked first, if Archie had simply defended himself or if for some reason he'd gone after them. Apparently, Archie had attacked Mercedes as well as Finney. None of it made sense.

"Dr. Mortonson," he said, for once attempting to sound respectful. "I don't know what happened with those people. I have no memory of it. I wish I could tell you more."

Mortonson picked up her pencil and dashed a few quick notes. "Why can't you remember any of this?"

"You're the doctor. You tell me."

"Who are you?" she asked.

Archie had to stop himself from blurting the wrong answer. "My name is Joey Burke," he said in as even a tone as he could muster. "And I'd appreciate it if you'd remember that and quit asking me the same ridiculous question every time I see you."

"Do you know your middle name?" She took another bite of the apple, it was nearly three-quarters gone now.

Archie sighed. Another repeat question from their previous interview. "No I don't," he said, allowing his voice to become irritated. "I have amnesia. You may have heard of it. It's a condition where a person loses all memory. The only reason I know my first and last names is because they were told to me since I came out of the coma. Do you have any relevant questions, or are we done here?"

Mortonson jotted furiously on her pad as she continued chewing her treat. "Relevant questions. That's quite a vocabulary for a twelve year-old."

"Yeah those two and three syllable words—they're killers."

"Did you know that Dr. Lambert's son died in this same facility several days before you emerged from your coma?"

Archie scratched at the sweat on his palms. "I'll send a sympathy card."

Mortonson set the pencil down, making direct eye-contact, holding her gaze for several seconds before speaking. "Listen… Joey," she said, her voice softer, more feminine, nearly seductive. "You may not believe this, but I am not your enemy. In fact, I may be the only one who can help you. But I must know the truth. I must know exactly what was done to you and under what conditions. Otherwise, I fear we may have other incidents similar to what you experienced with the Yamagatas."

Archie stared at her, unsure of how to proceed. Her change in tactics had thrown him off guard. She sounded almost believable, as if her offer to help might actually be genuine. He ran a hand across the top of his head. "Dr. Mortonson. I don't know you. I have no faith in what you're saying."

She nodded, took a last bite of apple, and then casually tossed the core into a garbage can perhaps ten feet to her left. "I can appreciate your hesitancy. But understand this: those whom you trust may not be the ones whom you should be trusting."

At that moment a door opened behind Archie. He felt a cool rush of air from the hallway beyond, and then heard a familiar voice. "Dr. Mortonson. Thank you for tending to my patient while I was en route. I'll take it from here and debrief with you once I've had an opportunity to speak with Joey."

Mortonson continued to gaze at Archie, her dark eyes intent and piercing, but it was to Colin that she spoke. "Of course, Dr. Lambert. We were just killing time." With that she rose, collected her notepad and pencil, and moved around the table. Archie noticed a small white rectangle sitting where the yellow legal pad had been, a business card. For no reason, he slipped it under his palm before Colin could take the now vacant seat.

"That woman is not your friend," said Colin once Mortonson had exited the room.

"I know that," said Archie, still clutching the business card in his right hand. "I didn't tell her anything. But she knows, Colin. I'm sure she knows everything."

"Yes, well, what she knows—or thinks she knows—is entirely different from what she can prove." Colin seated himself across from Archie, pulled a thick navy blue pen from his breast pocket and twirled it between his fingers. "What you did, Archie, running away, that was quite stupid. The procedure you underwent was complex, experimental. You must remain under observation—under *my* care—for quite some time before you can be free to move about as you will."

Archie nodded. "Yeah, well, here I am. Observe all you want. Apparently, I'm not going anywhere."

Colin placed his pen on the table. "Ah, but you are, Archie, you are."

"Okay," Archie said. "I'm lost. What happened to remaining under your observation?"

"You see, there is the conundrum. Now that you've gone public, we are under scrutiny. The only way to facilitate your continued care is to move you off campus. Here, there will be excessive curiosity and prying. I've arranged for you to go home with the Burkes."

Archie leveled his gaze at Colin and said, "No."

"Archie, listen. I…"

"Colin, I said no. I'm sure the Burkes are nice people. They were probably good parents for Joey, but…"

"But," interrupted Colin, leaning forward, his liquid eyes intense and relentless. "They're your only hope for a normal life. Listen to me, Archie. If I could keep you with me, I would, and most of your difficulties would subside. And in truth…" Here he paused as if searching desperately for an elusive and foreign thought. "I think I would have liked that very much. Very much. But, that is not an option we've been granted. The Burkes were terrified when you ran off. Furious. They may still sue the facility. But I've been in contact with them throughout. I assured them that you would be found. The only way that I could convince them to keep you under my care was to agree to let them take you home."

"Tell them I'm not ready to leave, that you still have more tests to run."

"Well, you ruined that approach, didn't you? Any claims I had that you weren't physically capable of living beyond these walls evaporated when you hiked clear across town."

"I'm not going," said Archie in as firm a voice as he could muster through Joey's prepubescent vocal cords.

"No," said Colin as he clicked his pen open and then closed. "In fact, you are going, and within the day." Colin shifted just slightly, leaning on his right elbow. "Archie, do you know what happened out there? You attacked two people—savagely. From my understanding, you have no recollection of the encounter."

Archie nodded in agreement.

"Does that seem normal to you?"

Archie shrugged. "Well, there have been some pretty heavy nights of drinking in my past."

"Archie, I'm serious. I need access to you. I need to monitor your progress, analyze any abnormalities. We're at the beginning of this thing, not the end."

"And there's no way for me to stay here?"

Colin gripped Archie's hand in his, squeezing as he locked eyes with his son. "Would you like a chance encounter with Diana Mortonson every day for the next several months? Would you like her to visit you during physical therapy, or while you're in your room at night? Would you like her to gain your trust, to slowly confirm her suspicions? No. This is not ideal, but it is what we have." Colin released his grip, glanced down at the table, fiddled with his pen, and once again met Archie's gaze. "It's all we have, Archie. Our position is precarious. I'm... sorry, son."

Archie nodded. Something strange stirred in the pit of his belly. For a moment he foolishly thought it might be a long lost love for his father, but dismissed the thought even before it was fully formed. Pity, perhaps. Nothing more. Colin had put his career on the line for Archie. He supposed he should be thankful for that, but he could allow his emotion to progress no further. That would be unacceptable. Too much had happened over the years, too much damning history to ever hope to mend the frayed and fragile tie between these two men. "There's one other thing," said Archie. "When I blacked out, it wasn't exactly a blackout. I went somewhere else, somewhere far away."

Perhaps sensing that something elusive had just passed between them and then fled, Colin offered a tight grin. "Tell me about it."

"It happened twice," said Archie. "The first time, I found myself at the top of the Sears Tower."

"You were dreaming," said Colin with a nod.

"Not at all. It was… I was myself again, an adult. The sights, the sounds, smells, everything was real. I touched a wall and it felt cold and hard. A woman brushed against me, I could smell her perfume."

"A memory?" he asked.

Archie hesitated for just a moment, gathering his thoughts. "No. I don't know what it was, but it wasn't a memory. I've only been to the Sears Tower once. What happened here, it was nothing like that day."

Colin placed his pen on the table and then smoothed his hair with his palm. "You said this happened twice."

"Yeah. The second time I found myself in a canoe, in white water."

"And this is when the Yamagatas were attacked."

"Yes."

"Did you experience anything similar when you stole the money from that young man's apartment?"

Archie hesitated. Stolen money. The mystery thirty-three dollars. Apparently he'd lifted it from producer Ned's apartment before fleeing. "No," he said. "I have no recollection of that. Until an hour ago, I didn't even know where the money had come from.

Colin fiddled with his pen. "Were there any other incidents?"

Archie considered telling Colin of the creeping white, but feared his father might become fearful and further limit his freedom. Better to stick with the major events and feed Colin additional information as Archie deemed it necessary. No need to complicate matters further. "No. Nothing," he said.

Colin contemplated him for a moment and then said, "This isn't entirely surprising, is it?"

"Meaning?"

"For someone in your condition, that things could be jumbled, cluttered perceptions, breaks with reality."

Archie stared at him, still clutching Diana Mortonson's business card in his palm. "Colin, how would you know what is and isn't normal in this situation? I'm the guinea pig, right? I'm the first. How can we know what is and is not unusual?"

Colin smiled, his thin lips curling back to expose a straight line of off-white teeth. "Of course. Exactly. You are the first, the procedure experimental; therefore, the unusual quite literally may become the usual."

"Sounds like double-talk to me."

Colin nodded and twirled his pen on the table. Whatever emotion had gripped the man moments before, Colin had slipped back into safe mode. He was again the scientist, nothing more. The fragile father persona had crept quietly away to hide and cower in its hovel until another day. "I'm sure it does," he said, snatching his pen in mid spin and slipping it into his breast pocket. "Listen," he continued. "Though we had no way of knowing what was going on in their minds, we did observe similar behavior in some of the primates to receive infusions: sudden aggression, fits of rage in some. Others, the opposite, sudden bouts of apparent apathy or disinterest. Obviously, in your situation, aggression seems to be the issue at hand."

"And?" prodded Archie.

"And we were able to medicate them with much success."

"I won't let you turn me into a zombie, Colin."

He shook his head. "Of course you won't, but neither will I allow you to become a psychopathic killer."

Archie clutched Diana Mortonson's business card, nearly crushing it in his right hand. What wasn't Colin telling him?

Chapter Fourteen

Archie sat on a brown vinyl reclining chair in a dreary unoccupied room. The nurse had given him a cup of butterscotch pudding and he was struggling with the plastic spoon, attempting with little success to get more pudding into his mouth than on his face. Colin strolled into the small room followed by the Burkes. "Hello, Joey," he said, attempting to sound perky and unconcerned with the events of the previous days. "Are you ready for your big day?"

Archie pointed at his pudding covered face. "Is there anything about this that looks ready?"

Colin smiled. "Coordination will come. There's already improvement. Your stride, for instance."

Colin was correct in that Archie's excursion into Ephesus had helped his leg coordination considerably. Probably, just the fact that he'd done so much walking had forced him to smooth out his gate. Archie wasn't ready for ballet, and his strut would make Quasimodo look graceful, but he was no longer in danger of losing his balance with every step.

Esther Burke moved forward, a napkin magically appearing in her slender hand. Silently, she wiped the caramel-colored goo from Archie's face. Archie glared at Colin.

Finishing with her task, Esther said, "I taught you how to feed yourself once. I suppose I can do it again."

"Well," said Colin with a grin and a click of his pen. "I've signed Joey's release papers. I'll look forward to seeing him this Thursday. And, Joey, be sure to take your medication."

Colin had prescribed a drug called AF367D-2, saying, "This is a non-commercial cousin to a promising Alzheimer's drug. It is known to enhance the activity of certain receptors for the neurotransmitter acetylcholine. The compound binds—or grips—to these M1 receptors. In doing so, it boosts the levels of the enzyme, alpha secretase, while simultaneously reducing the activity of the enzyme GSKbeta."

When presented with this information Archie had said, "English, Colin."

Colin rephrased, stating, "It won't turn you into a zombie."

That was all Archie needed to know.

Archie was to take two pills daily, three if he had any additional episodes. And, any such episodes should be reported directly to Colin, and not to the Burkes or any other physicians—i.e., Diana Mortonson.

*****

The Burke's home was a woodworker's paradise, offering the warm aromas of sawdust and various shellacs and stains. Guitars, both acoustic and electric, littered the modest middleclass residence. Each was unique in design, each of high quality, with fine inlay and delicate filigree. Three or four were on guitar stands, but the majority hung from the paneled walls of the living room.

Archie paused, staring at a framed calligraphy on the wall near the fireplace mantel.

"God, grant me the serenity to accept the things I cannot change,
Courage to change the things I can,
And wisdom to know the difference."

The Serenity Prayer.

Every twelve-step program's mantra.

Interesting.

Archie sat at the dining room table with Esther to his left and Greg to his right. To Archie's dismay, they were eating smoked sea bass. He wasn't fond of seafood and only nibbled at the meal. To make it worse, he was forced to use his left hand to steady his right in order to bring the fork to his mouth.

Clapton, the family mutt, sat on the floor to Archie's left. He seemed to be mostly a Labrador, with his short golden hair and expressive puppy-dog eyes, but something else was mixed in as well, maybe shepherd or collie. The dog's breath was hot, moist, and unpleasant, but Archie was able to slip him pieces of fish with hopes of creating the illusion that he'd eaten more than he had. Upon first encountering the animal, Archie had feared the dog would sense that he wasn't really Joey, but after an initial hesitation, Clapton had warmed to him. Archie wasn't normally a dog person, but he was glad to count the animal an ally and not a foe.

"I hope you like the bass," said Greg between bites. "I wanted to fix you your favorite meal on your first day home."

"Oh, uh… yeah, Greg. Thanks," he said as he pretended to chew a piece. He would have loved a Sam Adams just then.

Esther's eyes locked with Archie's. Her demeanor was not that of a mother toward a child. No hugs, no kisses, her voice did not become sing-song in his presence. Did she know something? Had she figured it out? Or been told? Had Mortonson gotten to her? Archie lowered his eyes, studying his plate. He was being paranoid. If she knew, she'd have never brought him home. Still, there was a peculiar tension radiating from the woman. It caused Archie to avoid eye contact, to retreat even further into his shell. He just couldn't help but feel she suspected something.

"It's good to have you back," said Greg.

Archie remained silent. Esther continued to stare. He'd yet to observe any outward physical affection between her and Greg, no pet names for each other, no hand-holding. They seemed an odd pair; Greg laid back and casual, likely never sporting a necktie unless required by God himself, and Esther dynamic and driven, a quintessential type-A personality. Archie knew that the loss of a child often resulted in the parent's divorce or separation. He wondered if the near-loss of a child could have a similar effect, possibly creating a near-fatal fissure in an already-mismatched relationship. Perhaps each blamed the other, maybe one had not responded to the crisis as the other had hoped.

"It's been quiet," said Greg, obviously attempting to break the tension in the room.

Silence.

Awkward glances.

Greg noticed the dog begging from Archie. "Clapton's happy to see you."

Archie nodded.

"I'm a luthier," said Greg. "I make guitars. You used to help me with my work, but then you…" He paused, glancing at Esther before continuing. "I guess you had other things to do. I was hoping you could help me again soon. Do you remember any of this?"

"Sorry," said Archie. "I don't."

"Nothing?" asked Esther. "Not one thing?"

Archie shook his head.

Esther offered a tight grin and a terse nod, before selecting a bite of fish.

Archie felt bad for the Burkes. This was supposed to be a happy occasion, the homecoming of their only son. But he had nothing to say to these people. Even if he'd wanted to engage them in conversation, he'd have been afraid to do so. What topic could Archie possibly broach without unwittingly exposing himself? Colin had put him in an untenable situation.

Several silent moments passed. Finally Greg smiled, setting his fork on his plate and leaning forward on his elbows. "This is hard for you, isn't it?"

Archie nodded. "Yeah. I'm still not hitting on all cylinders."

Greg spotted Archie slipping a piece of bass to the dog. The man grinned and chewed. "Lost your taste for fish?"

"Uh, no, er… Yeah. I mean… my favorite."

"What's your favorite color?" challenged Esther.

"Um, I don't… know."

"What school do you attend?"

"Um…"

"Esther, what are you doing?" It was Greg asking, his voice hinting at annoyance.

"I want to see just how complete his amnesia is."

"Don't push him, Ess. It's his first day back."

"Shut up, Greg."

The man offered a minor grunt and then picked at his food, apparently sidelined by the command. Archie had witnessed this dynamic while still at the clinic, though it was more pronounced in the home setting. Archie felt for Greg. He seemed an okay guy. It was a shame to see him cowed like this.

Esther's eyes locked on Archie. Her questioning confirmed that she suspected. Maybe it was his mannerisms, perhaps some of the things he'd said over his several weeks of recovery—maybe things that a twelve year-old would not say or have knowledge of. But for whatever reason, Esther was suspicious. She might not understand just what had happened, but her maternal instinct alarm was obviously blaring.

"Esther, I really don't remember any of this," offered Archie in hopes of settling the issue at least for the time being.

"Really? None of it? You don't even remember your own mother—not a thing about me?"

"I'm sorry. No."

The eyes narrowed just that little bit more. There was the slightest twitch to the lips. "I see," she said.

*****

Joey's room featured posters of heavy metal rock bands, a computer on a desk in the corner, an X-Box gaming system, a guitar leaning against a dresser, a boom box on a shelf. Archie found a picture of Joey holding a large fish with another boy. The boys were at a lakeside, and the amber leaves told him it must have been in the fall. Joey looked younger than his body did now, and Archie guessed the picture to be two or three years old. Joey had piercing green eyes, tasseled hair, and a sly grin that hinted at precocious secrets.

Archie moved to the closet, a row of black T-shirts, each featuring a heavy metal band logo or some variation of a skull stared back at him. Two sheathed hunting knives sat on the shelf atop a small stack of comic books, and a fishing pole was lodged in a corner next to a tackle box. There were a few board games, some guitar magazines—along with two skin mags hidden beneath these. Stepping to his right, Archie turned on the boom box. Rap/thrash music blared from the speakers. Startled, he immediately turned it off. Archie turned and stared down at a half-finished jigsaw puzzle situated on a folding card table. Had Joey been working on this the day of the accident? Had it been a big deal to him? Had he been into puzzles or was this one just a fluke. It was a dark, gothic-looking seascape with towering waves beating against the shore, a foreboding castle of coarse stone and weathered metal stood sentinel against nature's onslaught. Archie would need to remove the thing. It was almost as if the puzzle was accusing him, taunting him with Joey's unfinished life.

But what had happened to Joey wasn't Archie's fault. He'd come along well after the fact. Joey was gone and Archie should feel no remorse for using his body. He'd heard rumors of heart transplant patients that felt the desires and needs of the person from whom they'd acquired the heart. Some of them even began to like the same foods as the donor had liked, or maybe to smell phantom fragrances associated with the other person's life. Archie had always assumed these instances to be imaginary; that the recipient felt guilt, and somehow projected these things into their own lives. He closed his eyes. He could not allow this line of thinking. He could not give in to the urge to learn more about Joey. Certainly, a thorough inspection of his room would tell a tale. Simply going through the history on the boy's computer would paint a picture of Joey's interests. And while this knowledge might help Archie to better settle into the role of Joey, it would also bring him face-to-face with the kid. Despite his conviction that he'd done nothing wrong in taking Joey's body as his own, this was something he could not do. Guilt, he knew, could cripple. What had been done had been done. Move on. Don't look back.

Archie dropped onto the bed. Clapton hopped beside him and laid his big slobbery head on his lap. Archie fished in his pants and removed his prized possession: the photograph of him and Jill. Gazing at the picture for several moments, he then flipped it over, reading the words he'd written before handing the photograph to his father on the day of the procedure. Tears trickled down his face. Move on, he told himself. Don't look back. That life was gone. He'd never see his little girl again. Never.

Chapter Fifteen

Archie hadn't meant to miss Jill's performance at her school's Holiday Celebration. It was just that the hours of the day moved faster than he could keep up with. It was snowing fairly heavily, vision was minimal, and the roads were more slippery than not. Archie was on his way home from work, but had promised Curley Jake that he'd stop by his bar for a complimentary beer to help the guy celebrate. After several years as a bartender, Jake had finally accumulated the funds to purchase the place from the owner, who had retired to Florida.

Archie hung around the bar for maybe an hour listening to Jake make grand pronouncements such as, "Entrepreneurship is the great American dream, obligation, and right. It is the force that drives our land." And, "This establishment has been established in the fond hopes of establishing a greater establishment." Archie had drawn a caricature of him in a business suit with a briefcase labeled "Boss." Jake hung it above the bar, but some weeks later it had disappeared to be replaced by a poster of Jake's favorite "Bud girl." He said he'd taken it home to display above his fireplace, but Archie later saw it on the storeroom floor adjacent the restrooms.

After three rounds, plenty of backslapping, and several friendly jabs at the new proprietor, Archie glanced at his watch and dutifully made his way to the door. The snow storm had gotten worse. What had begun as a steady flurry had now escalated into an all-out blizzard. Archie flipped his collar up, pulled out his hat and gloves, and trudged to the car. It took nearly fifteen minutes to clear the snow and ice from the windows. By then, new snow had taken residence on previously-cleared areas.

By the time Archie made it onto the road, he could tell that the drive from Ephesus to St. John was going to take well over an hour. Not yet having a cell phone, Archie had no way of reaching Marcie and of telling her of his predicament without first pulling over to use a pay phone. This, he decided against, fearing that if he let the car sit still, even for a few minutes, he might become snowed in. It was best to keep moving and to suffer the consequences when he finally made it home. Besides, chances were that the holiday celebration would be cancelled due to weather. Marcie would certainly understand.

*****

Jill's holiday celebration had not been cancelled. The house was empty. It was after seven-thirty. The program had been scheduled to start at seven. Under most circumstances Archie would have headed to the school, but he'd just spent an hour and twenty minutes on Route 41, and was not about to climb back behind the wheel of the car again until morning.

Slipping out of his snow-covered coat and shoes, Archie trudged through the small, chilly living room and into the kitchen, opened the fridge and withdrew a six-pack of Sam Adams. He made his way back into the living room and plopped down in front of the TV.

Marcie and Jill arrived home six beers and two shots of J.B. later. Archie was warm and cozy on the couch, semi-conscious, and now more or less unaware that he'd missed the big event. "Hey," he said. "Where have you two been up to?"

Jill's seven year-old eyes averted Archie's stare, finding instead the carpet at her feet. For some reason, she was wearing green tights and had bells on her shoes. Marcie, though, had no reservations about making eye contact. "Where have we been up to?" she blurted as she pulled snow-covered knit gloves from her hands. "Do you have any idea what day it is?"

Archie stared at her dumbly.

"How about what planet we're on, Archie? Can you get that one right, or is your brain too clouded for that too?"

"The Christmas program," he said, as his mind synthesized the details of the day. "I got home late. The snow was bad. I thought it'd be cancelled."

"Cancelled. And where did you think we were all this time? Or did you even think of that? You probably just figured we'd fend for ourselves out in the blizzard, and so you decided to get comfortably loopy, just you and Jim Beam."

Archie stared at Marcie for a moment, but even through the clouded haze of his mind, he could tell that he would get nowhere with her this evening. He turned his attention to Jill. "Hey, Sweetie," he said. "Daddy's sorry he missed your play. How was it? Tell me all about it."

Jill stared at him. Her hazel eyes moist and evasive. "Not many people were there. Too much snow."

"See!" he said to Marcie. "See? Not many people. Too much snow." Archie looked at Jill again. "Did you have fun? What did you do?"

She looked down and away. Her lips scrunched. She blinked, maybe trying to clear something from her eyes. "I'm cold, Daddy. My clothes are wet. I'm going to go change."

She walked past Archie without a hug or a kiss, without even a "Good night." Marcie stared down at him. "You can't keep letting her down, Archie. She loves you. She wants you to be a part of her life, but you never seem to figure out how to be a dad."

"The snow, Marcie. Do you know how long it took me to get home from work?"

Marcie sat down beside him on the couch. "This isn't about the snow, Archie. If we had come home to find you here—sober—waiting for us to get back, worried that we'd gotten stuck somewhere, that would have been okay. I could understand you not going back out unless you had to. But you weren't worried about me driving in that mess, you weren't standing by the phone, ready to race out and dig us clear if you got a call. You decided to make an evening of it and didn't stop to think that we might need you."

It took several moments to process what she'd said and then to formulate a response. Eventually, he said, "Sorry."

Perhaps he should have spent more time in contemplation, because "Sorry," though it seemed to him like the perfect solution, did nothing to calm Marcie. Archie thought of following it up by stating that he was really sorry, but wisely decided against this proclamation.

"Archie," said Marcie. "I know you think you're sorry. But that's not enough. You need to be a father for Jill, a fulltime dad. She wants to look up to you. She wants you to teach her things, and to be there for her successes and failures." Marcie put her hand on Archie's lap, it was quivering. "Archie, you either need to be a real father for Jill, a real husband for me, or you need to leave."

There was still snow in her disheveled hair. Her hands were chapped and red. Archie stared into her beautiful blue eyes. He could see the tears straining for release, but she was holding them back with all of her will, trying to be strong, in control. "Sorry," he said. And then she left the room without another word.

*****

It was two a.m. and Archie contemplated the living room walls. They were uneven, with minor dips and bulges, nothing anyone would notice. But to Archie they seemed monumental. Massive flaws that might bring the roof cascading down. He figured this might be a bad thing, but really wasn't inclined to do anything to prevent it. Archie wanted to leave, to get out of that place, even for an hour. He wanted to go back to Curley Jakes, or maybe even to just run up the road for a sack of White Castle hamburgers. Archie needed escape. Those walls, so uneven, so vanilla, just kept getting closer.

He thought of Marcie's admonition, that he either be a better father for Jill or leave. A part of him wanted to say, "Fine. I'll leave." But that was only his craven side wanting to avoid conflict. Deep down, Archie knew he wasn't a good father. In truth, he was a pretty poor one. But that didn't mean he didn't care. Archie loved Jill. He longed to be around her. It was thoughts of her that got him through the work day. She was the reason he came home when he'd rather have stayed at the bar. He didn't know what this said about his relationship with Marcie. But, so be it. Marcie and he had lost the magic years before. She hadn't tried any more than he had to recover it. Admittedly, Archie missed their relationship, the laughter, the kisses, the mummers of love. But he'd settle for peaceful cohabitation and a chance to redeem himself in the eyes of his daughter. But the only way he'd manage this would be to start acting like a father.

Slowly, Archie rose from the couch, scolded the floor for shifting beneath his feet, and shuffled toward his daughter's bedroom using the hallway wall as a support. He stumbled on a stuffed rabbit and then broke a happy meal toy with his full weight as he made his way to her bed. A real dad would discipline her for having such a messy room, but Archie figured he could give her grace. He had more parental matters on his mind. He would show Jill and Marcie just how much of a dad he truly was.

Archie flicked on her lamp and then seated himself on the corner of her bed. "Jill," he whispered, nudging her just a little. "Jillie-bean, its Daddy." She moaned slightly, just a little sound from a little girl. "Jillie, wake up. Daddy needs to tell you something." She rolled over, pulling her green fuzzy blanket over her face. "Jill, Daddy wants to talk with you. Wake up."

"Daddy, I'm tired."

Archie pulled the covers away from her little oval face. "That a girl. I knew you could hear me. Open those beautiful eyes. Let me see my girl."

"Daddy, where's Mommy?"

"Mommy's sleeping. But Daddy's here for you."

"I wanna sleep."

"Daddy wants to tell you where babies come from."

"Huh?"

"Babies, they come from mommies and daddies. I'm going to tell you all about it because I'm a good dad and good dads tell their little girls the things they need to know."

There was a soft shuffle behind Archie, then a sigh. "You have got to be kidding."

It was Marcie, standing in the doorway, wearing a decade-old Indiana University sweatshirt and sweat pants, her sleeping getup. Her expression was one of weary disgust.

"Marcie," said Archie. "What are you doing here?"

"Apparently, rescuing our daughter from your monumental misjudgment. Do you have any idea how loud you are when you're drunk?"

"I was just about to tell Jill about the birds and the bees."

"I know what you were about to do," she said as she moved toward the bed, somehow managing to avoid stepping on any toys. "What I'm wondering is what you were thinking."

"Isn't it obvious?" he asked, sure that his logic was crystal clear. "You said I should try to be a better dad for Jill. So, I'm trying to be a better dad for Jill. I'm taking your advice. You should be pleased."

Marcie shook her head and rolled her eyes. "Archie, she's seven. She's expressed no curiosity concerning that topic—and its two o'clock in the morning and you're drunk."

Archie stared at her, cocking his head, trying to stay focused. "And your point?"

Her sigh became a growling moan as she shook her head, gazing at Archie with a curious mixture of love, pity, and loathing. Extending her hand, she said, "Come here you big, loveable, pathetic loser. We'll talk about this in the morning."

Archie started to weep, right there on his daughter's bedside. Quaking sobs shook his entire frame. Marcie had called him pathetic and a loser, but she'd also called him loveable. There was hope.

Chapter Sixteen

The first two weeks in the Burke's house crawled by like a drunken tortoise. Archie did some minor rearranging of Joey's room, taking the jigsaw puzzle apart and putting the guitar in the closet, shifting underwear to the top drawer where he'd more likely find it. But he left all of Joey's posters and pictures in place and the boom box was still dialed to Joey's thrasher station— though, admittedly, it was never again approached. Fearing discovery, Archie wanted the room to appear as if Joey lived there. If he made major changes too soon, he'd arouse suspicion. If nothing but classic rock emerged from the room, Greg and, in particular, Esther would wonder where Joey had acquired his appreciation of fine music. If pictures of Joey and his friends were boxed and stored, the couple would worry about the boy's rejection of his earlier life. Better to ease into this existence, make subtle changes over a period of time, make the process seem natural.

Greg worked away in his garage workshop, not yet expecting Archie to resume Joey's role as helper/apprentice. At least twice a week, he drove to Chicago where he did guitar repairs and custom work for one of the city's major music stores. Esther worked furiously in her little cubby of an office adjacent the kitchen, making calls, printing contracts, typing away. But frequently she would stop and simply stare through the window toward the pool where Joey had nearly drowned. Archie felt bad for her, that she was being deceived, that her true son was gone and, more than likely—hopefully! —she would never know the truth. Frequently, he caught her staring at him as well, often pestering him about his memory, asking pointed questions, observing the differences in Archie's personality from that of Joey's. He still wasn't sure if the woman suspected something or if she was simply attempting to challenge him, to possibly stir some dormant passions or pent up aggression that would open the floodgates and send the memories cascading in. The lady was sharp. Archie doubted she did much without purpose. Certainly her maternal programming was going haywire. This was her boy, but not at all her boy. In her eyes, Joey had returned from the grave a stranger and it made full sense that she would be suspicious.

What had this experience done to her internally? Did she lay awake at night worrying about her peculiar son? Did she blame herself for not being there when he needed her most? Was she trying to make sense of his altered personality? Her near constant questioning and lingering gazes would indicate so. But, deeper yet, how had Esther, the woman, changed? Photographs of her about the home showed a much different Esther: a broad smile, intense, yet vibrant, long luxurious hair, form-fitting outfits that enhanced her natural beauty and probably gained her the attention of many men. Now, she appeared the antithesis of that woman. Hair cut in a short, utilitarian bob, loose-fitting outfits that deemphasized her figure. And as to the smile, Archie wasn't certain that he'd yet seen this. How horrible that such a seemingly joyous event, the resurrection of her near-dead son, had brought with it a gray and threatening cloud of uncertainty. But, despite this, despite his concerns for the pair, Archie had to be on guard where Esther was concerned. She was the one that would push and prod. She was the one that would do research and ask pointed questions. She was the one that might just figure this thing out. As much as Archie felt for her situation, he resolved to remain wary where Esther was concerned.

*****

It was Archie's third Tuesday with the Burkes. His dreams were of a dark shadowy form. Turning. It was forever turning. Both clockwise and counter-clockwise simultaneously. He knew this form. Knew it to be malevolent, but couldn't remember where previously he'd encountered it. The thing was watching him, observing, waiting for opportunity.

But, opportunity to do what?

It was an object—round, rotating, surreal. This was no person. It could have no purpose, no motivation.

Yet, still it drew closer, closer. Archie could sense dozens of eyes upon him; he could feel the malignant spirit of the thing. Closer still, nearly upon him, surrounding him, enveloping him, squeezing the very breath from his lungs.

Archie awoke.

He was in the hallway bathroom. How had he come to be there? He'd gone to sleep in his bed the night before and had no recollection of moving.

He was drenched with sweat, his palms clammy, his breathing quick and shallow. What had just happened?

Attempting to regain his composure, he turned, catching his reflection in the mirror. Pale. Nearly pasty. The dream had obviously been frightful, yet even now it scurried away on the lingering mist of memory forgotten.

Archie blinked the sleep from his eyes, ran cool water into the sink and splashed it onto his face with his palms.

Gone. Already the dream was gone.

He'd had other dreams as well. He was certain of it. But, like this one, they fled the light of day, fearful of conscious scrutiny.

Strange, he attributed thought and purpose to a dream, and yet it somehow seemed right to do so.

Exiting the bathroom, he heard voices coming from downstairs. One was Esther's; the other was female as well. It was the first time a guest had entered the home since Archie's return and his stomach took a twist. The voices were serious with no hint of banter or familiarity. This was not a friend dropping by for tea or coffee.

All thoughts of dreams scattered. As a result of his current situation, Archie had become quite cautious and couldn't help but assume that he was the topic of conversation. This wasn't egotistical, it was simply logic. Surely Joey's miraculous recovery and strange new behavior would be the number one topic of conversation. Archie decided this might be a prime opportunity to learn just what Esther might be thinking where he was concerned.

Creeping slowly down the stairs, trying to maintain both balance and si-lence, Archie drew closer to the voices. The stairs did have a tendency to creak, but he found that if he stepped far to one side, avoiding the center of the steps, he could minimize the sound and, with luck, descend undetected. The two women were in the family room. That was a good thing as the stairway emptied into the living room. Neither woman would see him from their current positions.

Esther's voice, flat and thin, was distinct. The other voice was business-like yet hinted at an underlying sensuality. It was also quite familiar to Archie. "Tell me, Mrs. Burke, what other changes have you noticed?" asked Dr. Diana Mortonson.

Archie's heart quickened, his legs shook. That woman again! Diana Mortonson wasn't going to let this thing go. She wasn't going to wait for another violent episode or some obvious inconsistency, she was going to play Sherlock Homes and follow her hunch through to the end.

God, he needed a drink.

Archie wondered if he should have called her. He still had her business card. Perhaps making contact could have lessened her suspicion. But that was only his fight/flight instinct rattling for attention. Meeting with Mortonson would have caused more suspicions than it would have allayed.

"Changes," said Esther, obviously contemplating a question. "Joey has complete and total amnesia. Everything has changed."

"Allow me to rephrase. Does he have different likes and dislikes? Have his speech patterns altered? Does he seem to have knowledge of things that he didn't know prior to the accident?"

There was a short pause, and then Esther said, "He doesn't like to eat fish. He doesn't play music—at least not loud enough for me to hear." Her tone offered an underlying suspicion with which Archie was quite familiar.

"Anything else?"

"He stays in his room most of the time. He doesn't socialize."

There was a short pause. Archie could picture Mortonson scribbling notes with pencil and pad, her eyebrows converging in a furrow above her slight, yet pointed nose as she concentrated. "How about his speech patterns? Has his vocabulary changed since his return? For instance, does he use larger words than before, more syllables?"

A pause, and then, "Perhaps. But, he says very little."

"Has Joey renewed any past friendships?"

"No. He really only had one close neighborhood friend, a delinquent. I've not yet allowed the boy access to Joey. There may have been other companions at school, but Joey is a bit of a loner."

Archie could hear the flutter of paper as Mortonson flipped a page in her notebook. His stomach took a dive as she asked, "Does Joey display knowledge of things that he didn't know prior to the accident?"

"That's a strange question, Doctor. What are you suggesting?" Esther's voice was curious. What was she thinking just then? She had to be suspicious of this peculiar line of questioning.

"I suggest nothing, Mrs. Burke. We still know so little of how the cerebrum functions in instances such as these. We must explore every facet."

"I understand that. But, how could Joey possibly know things now that he didn't know before?"

Mortonson sighed. Archie could picture her bright red lips thinning, her dark desolate eyes narrowing. "Perhaps I should rephrase the question," she said. "Sometimes, in cases such as this, the obvious memories, the common memories, are erased. But occasionally there are hidden memories of actual events, or of things seen in a movie or read in a book, or possibly of inconsequential life events that were buried beneath the more immediate and central memories. These sometimes survive, and when everything else is erased, they come to the forefront. A person may even act like a person from a book or a movie. He might remember places that he'd only passed through but never visited, or recall the lyrics to songs that he'd heard only once."

What a load of crap. Mortonson was inventing a cover story as she went along, tossing out fabricated half truths to derail Esther's line of questioning.

"That's an interesting theory," said Esther. "But, no. Nothing like that has happened here."

Once again, Archie heard Mortonson flip a page. "One last question. Has Dr. Lambert mentioned any other patients, perhaps someone else with the same condition as Joey?"

Archie's breath stilled and his hands quivered. Why was Mortonson asking about other patients? Archie had been the first. There were no others.

Or so Colin said.

Esther responded to Mortonson's question. Something about Colin being a researcher, that when he'd heard about Joey, he'd requested that the boy be transferred from Saint Margaret's Hospital in St. John to the institute, that he might be able to help him. He had not mentioned any other patients to Esther. Archie stood up, peeked around the corner to make sure no one was coming, moved to the front door, opened it, and stepped outside.

*****

"Nice car," said Archie as Mortonson slid into the driver's seat of her yellow 2015 Mini Cooper. "Though, I pictured you as more of the Lexus type."

She gasped at the sight of him and fumbled with her notebook and purse. "Joey! Um, what are you doing here?"

"I live here. What's your excuse?"

She reached over the seat to place her purse and notebook in the back. "I gave you my card. I was hoping you'd call."

"No need. I'm doing well."

"I'm told your coordination is improving."

Archie shrugged. "It has its moments, both good and bad."

She stared at him, nearly grinning, but with an expression of contemplation, not of amusement. Diana Mortonson could best be described as irrationally attractive. Though she was slender and well-proportioned, with smooth skin and high cheekbones, she didn't have the air of beauty that normally accompanied these features. Her skin was white to the point of appearing unhealthy. Her brown eyes were so dark as to seem black, giving them a strangely reptilian vibe. He'd never seen her without lipstick, bright and red. Her black hair was styled in a pageboy cut, with short even bangs above expressive brows, and she favored gray business attire, skirts and blazers, mostly. She shouldn't be attractive, yet she was, and yet she wasn't.

"Why were you questioning Esther?" asked Archie.

"I'm a doctor, she's the mother of a patient."

"Not the mother of one of *your* patients."

She smiled. Her teeth were as white as liquid paper, straight and shinning. "The Gowon Institute is a research facility," she said. "Many different doctors may have interest in the same patient, though, quite possibly, for very different reasons."

"What's your area of research?" he asked.

"Gowon is a neurological institute. All patients are studied within the various confines of that discipline. Like your father, I'm a neurologist."

Somehow Archie managed to smile. "You must be mistaken. My father's a luthier. He builds guitars."

She nodded noncommittally. "Of course he is, *Joey*." She paused long enough to slip a butterscotch candy from atop the dash, unwrap it, and slide it slowly between her lips with just a hint of a saucy smile. "My area of research is very similar to Doctor Lambert's," she said. "We work closely."

Archie nodded and decided to throw her off guard by saying something only a child would say. "My dog's name is Clapton. Do you have a dog?"

Mortonson cocked her head. "No, Joey. I don't have a dog."

This was no surprise. Archie pictured her more as the boa constrictor type.

"Why did you ask my mom about Doctor Lambert's other patients? What would she know about that?"

Mortonson sat rigid, her face taut, revealing nothing. "Surely you must know you're not the only one," she said, her voice warm, smooth, almost playful.

"Excuse me," said Archie, trying not to sound too jittery. "I'm not the only one?"

"Of course not, Joey," she said with a saucy cock of the head and just a hint of a smile. "You're not the only patient ever to come out of a deep coma." She paused. "That is what we're talking about, isn't it?"

Her near-black eyes bored into him, her near grin goaded him. For one of the few times in his life, Archie Lambert could think of nothing to say.

Chapter Seventeen

Archie stayed in his bedroom for the rest of the day, mostly staring out of the window into the back yard, doodling in a half-filled notebook he'd found in Joey's desk drawer, and cursing Colin to the very depths of fiery brimstone. He'd tried calling his father three separate times, leaving increasingly agitated messages. Colin didn't return the calls. Archie's next appointment with him wasn't for nearly a week. He didn't think he could wait that long. Diana Mortonson had hinted at something, goaded really, probably looking for Archie's reaction. Surely Archie's bloodless face and sudden loss for words had verified her direct hit. All the more reason to talk with Colin.

Mortonson had implied that Archie had not been the first infusion. If that was the case, Colin had lied to him. The deception bothered Archie, but not as much as the motive behind the lie. This was what kept him up all night and into the next morning. If there had been other procedures, and they had been successful, there would be no reason to hide this information. It would be an encouragement. "Nothing to worry about, Archie. I've done this a dozen times, every one a success." No, the only reason for Colin to keep this from Archie was that the other infusion—or infusions—had not been successful. And if that was the case, Archie needed to learn what had become of the others, what the failure had been, what it was he could expect. Archie needed to wring his father's smarmy little neck.

Eventually morning came. The night had been silent and lonely. It was a very isolating feeling to realize that there was no one to confide in, that the one person who knew a secret may be the one person who could be trusted least. Archie considered Mortonson. He could give her all of the juicy details she'd been begging to hear. It was obvious she already knew the truth, that she was simply looking for that last little confirmation to put the whole thing together. But then the question became: what would she do with that information once her theory was confirmed? Would she work in Archie's best interest, would she be forthright with him, giving him even better care than had his own father, or would she turn Archie's merely miserable existence into an outright horror?

And could any other doctor treat him? This was Colin's procedure, his so-called gift to humanity. Was there another person on the planet that could tend to Archie's needs? He hadn't had any more episodes, hadn't slipped back into a raging river or climbed the Sears Tower. He hadn't attacked anyone since Mercedes and Finney Yamagata.

He hadn't battled the white.

But, hadn't there been that dream? Or dreams?

No.

Maybe.

The memory was a wisp at best. And a dream was just that—a dream. A phantom of the unconscious mind. Under the circumstances it was amazing he didn't wake up screaming with night terrors every time he dared close his eyes.

But what if he developed a tolerance to his medication? What if there was another incident? To whom should Archie then turn? He knew too little about Diana Mortonson. The risk was too high. Maybe being confronted with the fact that Archie knew there had been other subjects would force Colin to be forthright. Knowing Colin, this was unlikely, but it was all Archie had.

It was midmorning. Esther was at her desk in her cubby office adjacent the kitchen. Her eyes were red from lack of sleep. She and Greg had argued late into the night—not an uncommon occurrence. The topic of the disagreement: Greg's lack of ambition. This, as well, was not unusual. Though, Archie wasn't sure he'd call Greg unmotivated. His skills as a guitar builder were amazing, his craftsmanship inspired. Maybe that didn't make him ambitious but the man was far from lazy.

Greg's counter charge was that Esther had changed, that somewhere along the way she'd lost her playful spirit—even before "the incident." She was too intense, said Greg. Intense and secretive. He wondered how ever they'd found each other in the first place. Esther would then jab at him, dredging up his drinking, a crutch he'd apparently overcome a couple of years before, but not soon enough to have avoided Esther's scorn.

As she sat, making a sales call while tapping at computer keys, Archie wondered what motivated the woman. Who was she really? His nemesis, cer-tainly, the one person who was most likely to uncover his deception. But that was only Archie's situational take on her. How did she see herself? As a mother, a salesperson, a wife? Certainly all of those at some level. But those were just roles. Who was Esther Burke, the woman? What motivated her? What was she thinking when her cobalt eyes narrowed and her lips drew thin? What occupied her thoughts as she gazed for minutes at a time through the kitchen window, her face a porcelain mask, hard and cold? Did she think back to when Joey was younger, perhaps a toddler racing about the back yard, stumbling and giggling, or back to when she and Greg had first met, when their love was fresh and young and true? Or was she really so rigid and cold? Was there a frightened woman—or even a little girl—slinking just behind the irises or a lioness crouched and prepared to pounce? There was no way of knowing for certain. But Archie sensed that she was complex and perhaps conflicted. This caused him wonder.

Apparently, she heard Archie as he entered the room for she glanced in his direction and said, "Yes, Bill. I'll see you then," and disconnected the call.

As usual, Archie could hear the band saw whirring in Greg's woodshop. The smell of sawdust tickled Archie's nostrils. He'd never been the handy type, never built anything from wood or metal, but now found the smell of sawdust rather nice. It had a warm, comfortable air about it. It just felt right.

Archie nodded toward Esther and padded across the tile to the cupboard, opening it and examining its contents. "Got anything with more roughage?" he asked. "You know, a guy could get cancer without enough roughage."

Not that Archie had ever been health conscious before. Prior to his new life as a child, Archie existed primarily on burgers, tacos, and pizza. He'd learned that one could subsist virtually on pizza alone if the food was ordered from various pizza establishments, alternating between New York thin crust, Chicago-style deep-dish, meat-lover's, vegetarian, and Hawaiian. But now, having been down a deadly trail once before, he figured it wouldn't hurt to eat in at least a moderately healthy fashion.

This went for alcohol and tobacco as well. The boy's body was not addicted to the stuff and tobacco had been the instrument of his death. Logically he shouldn't desire it. But he did—sometimes passionately. And the alcohol?

Archie knew he'd had a problem. Alcohol had led to his divorce, to his separation from Jill, the only person he truly loved in this hellish world. And though Joey Burke's body had likely never tasted either, Archie desired them both more fervently than he could have believed possible. It was a mental game, he knew. But he was thankful that, for the time being at least, these two crutches were not readily available. With luck, he'd have them both licked by the time he reached an age where these could be easily secured.

Still tapping at her keyboard, Esther said, "All we have is what's in the cupboard. Let your father know if you want something special." Her tone, as usual, was flat, emotionless. It was as if Joey's near-death experience had drained her of life, as if it had been her that died that day and not Joey.

"How about an allowance?" asked Archie. "Can we negotiate a raise? You know, after all I've been through." Archie needed bus fare and had no other avenue to acquire capital.

Esther swiveled to face Archie, arms now crossed at the chest. "Well, you do know how to play an angle, don't you?"

Archie shrugged.

"You don't get an allowance. We do pay you for work around the house, though."

"Thanks, no," he said, closing the cupboard and turning toward the family room.

"Joey."

Archie turned to face Esther.

She stared at him intently—expectantly. "What do you plan to do?"

"Plan to do?" It seemed she might have something in particular she was thinking, that perhaps the question had another, deeper, more unsettling significance.

"Yes. What are your plans?"

Archie shrugged. "I think I'll go outside for a while."

"And do what?"

"Play, I guess."

"Play?"

"Yeah. That's what kids do, right?"

Again, Esther simply stared. Was that fear he saw in those fathoms-deep cobalt eyes? Surely, the near loss of a child could make anyone skittish.

"Don't worry," he said. "I'll be careful—and I'll stay away from the pool."

Esther offered a slow nod and a forced near-grin.

Archie turned, walking through the kitchen and into the family room. His stomach rumbled but he ignored it. Opening the sliding glass door, he stepped onto the patio overlooking the swimming pool. Joey had nearly drowned here. Apparently the boy had been a good swimmer. At least according to Greg. But still, he'd lain at the bottom of this pool for several minutes, his brain deprived of oxygen. No one talked of the details and Archie didn't push for information. What was done was done.

The yard was alive with birds: sparrows, robins, even cardinals, all chirping and chattering, darting in and out of the many birdhouses mounted on poles about the perimeter. The midsummer breeze danced about Archie, nipping and caressing. It was fresh and moist, but not oppressive, seeming nearly to call his name in a lover's whisper, inviting him into its embrace.

Archie turned right and made his way to the side of the house where he found Joey's dirt bike, yellow and black, tires caked with dried mud, leaning against the red brick wall. He thought of Diana Mortonson, her insinuations, of Colin and his deceptions. Colin wasn't returning his calls, but Archie needed to talk with him. Could Archie possibly ride this bike all the way to the Gowon Institute? How many miles was that? Five? Seven? More? He really wasn't sure.

Grabbing the handlebars, he rolled the bike to the fence, opened the gate, and stepped into the driveway. Now at the street, Archie put his left foot on the corresponding peddle, gave a press on the ground with his right foot, swung his right leg over the bike, seating himself on the hard black saddle. He wobbled left, right, left again, and fell off of the bike with a hearty curse. Fortunately, he was near the curb and was able to angle onto the nearby grass. If he'd pulled that same maneuver in his adult body, he'd have been feeling strains and pulls for a week.

Rising, he wiped the dirt and grass from his palms, and then mounted the bike again with the same result.

This time he fell onto the hot summer asphalt.

A third try.

A fourth.

On the fifth attempt he ran off of the road and into a neighbor's oak. The front wheel bent slightly, and Archie tossed the bike onto the curb in disgust.

Archie turned toward the house, defeated. How was he to see Colin?

Steal Greg's car?

No. That would cause more trouble than it was worth.

"Hey!"

There was a voice behind him.

"Hey, Burke!"

Archie turned. There stood a kid, about Joey's age, a bit taller, a bit chunkier, but not heavyset. He looked to be of Middle Eastern stock. There was a long scratch on his left cheek, his right eye was blackened, and his spiked hair purple. There was a white ear piece inserted in each ear, and a cord trailing into his front pocket. Loud thrasher music pulsated in the air about him. The kid wore a jet black T-shirt, black baggy shorts, and tall squared-off boots, black with numerous buckles. Chains hung from his belt and neck. There were no visible tattoos or body piercings, but the kid was only eleven or twelve years-old. They would come. He seemed rather young to sport this semi-goth look, but what did Archie know? He was forty-five years-old and, by definition, out of touch with youth culture.

"Hey," said the kid in a tone of cautious familiarity, the music still throbbing about him.

Archie felt a sudden surge of indefinable—what? —emotion, apprehension, wrath?

The white.

It was flitting about the periphery, testing, examining, attempting to find a way through, to encroach on this reality. Tickling at his spine, it scurried over his head, across his face and settled on his chest. His heart beat triplets and it seemed he might lose consciousness.

Breathe. Breathe. Relax. It is nothing. Nothing real at least.

Archie squinted, concentrating as best he could, attempting to push it back, wanting to scream, to run into the blinding and purifying sun. But how does one flee that which is within?

"You okay?" asked the kid, a tone of caution in his young voice.

Archie blinked, swore, stomped his foot.

And the white fled. Not far. Definitely not far. It sat, waiting, watching. Archie almost believed it to be sentient.

Blinking again, Archie addressed the boy. "You're the kid in the picture, in my room—with the fish," he said.

The kid shrugged. "Guess so. We used to fish."

"Your hair, in the picture, wasn't so… purple."

The kid grinned revealing a missing tooth just to the left of center. "Cool, huh?" Archie didn't respond and so the kid asked, "So, what's your deal? You got outta the hospital like, I dunno, a month ago. But every time I call, your mom says you're busy."

Great, thought Archie. As if it wasn't bad enough to have Diana Morton-son investigating him, now he had some kid prying into his life.

"Listen," said Archie. "I don't have time to be social. I have things to do." He felt bad being harsh to the kid. Obviously, this was one of Joey's friends, but Archie had no desire to complicate his life further.

The kid cocked his head and smiled an unsettling smile. "Damn, Burke. You've got things to do? Like what? Sitting in your room doodling?"

"How do you know what I've been doing?" shot Archie, a surge of anger rising from within his belly.

The kid shrugged. He had a hard and cocky look about him. "I've been watchin'."

"You have no right," Archie began to step forward, his fist clenched, though he had no real idea of what he might do. Something about this kid unnerved Archie.

"Get a grip, idiot," said the kid, obviously not the least bit frightened by Archie's aggression. "You survived—chill."

Archie had nothing to say, but the kid seemed to consider the issue was settled.

"So, I'm supposed to know you?" asked Archie after a moment.

"Man. Your brain did fry."

Archie nodded. "Something like that."

The kid's face darkened, but only for a moment. Something was on his mind, but Archie wasn't in the mood to care what that something might be. "So," said the kid. "You don't remember anything—nothing at all from before you drowned?"

Archie shrugged. "Nothing."

The kid contemplated Archie for several moments. Eventually he nodded and said, "I'm Bug."

"Bug?"

"My real name's Justin," he said. "But anyone cool calls me Bug."

Justin. Not a Middle-Eastern name, but then, why would it need to be? Archie was old enough to know not to make judgements based on appearances alone. If he let his mind go in that direction, he'd be thinking this kid was a suicide bomber by noon. Small minded, yes, but still the thoughts crept in. Another reason for self-loathing he supposed.

Archie gazed at Bug. "So, uh, what happened to your face—that scratch?" Archie asked, not really interested, but trying to at least appear moderately social.

Bug shrugged. "Melvin."

"Melvin? Who's he?"

"Duh! My cat. Man, I've got some work to do on you."

No he didn't.

"Listen," Archie said as he took a step away, and leaned down to pick up Joey's bike. "I need to get going." The front tire of the bike was bent, but not too terribly so. Archie wasn't sure if he was yet ready to give bicycle riding another try, but it seemed as good an excuse as any to ditch the kid.

Bug laughed. "Dude, I saw you try to ride already. I *know* you're not goin' anywhere on that thing."

He was right. Archie knew it. Bug knew it. Archie nodded and let the bike drop. Apparently, he was going nowhere.

"What's-a-matter?" asked Bug. "You got somewhere you really gotta go?"

There was no real reason to answer the question. But there was no real reason not to either. "I wanted to go out to the institute, to see my doctor."

"What? Are you afraid to go in the car with your mom?"

Peculiar question. "No," said Archie. "It's a secret." Archie knew Bug would understand this. There's an unwritten law with kids, a kind of code. Parents are useful. They're well-meaning, and you can love them all you want. But at some level, they were always the enemy. No kid would ever tell another kid's secret to his parents.

Bug smiled, but not a joyful smile. More of a curious one. "Why can't ya tell your parents you're goin' to the doctor?"

"They wouldn't understand," Archie said, leaving his response to hover in ambiguity.

Bug nodded and gazed at Joey's bike. "I can get you there," he said with an air of cocky self-assurance.

"How? Your parents?" asked Archie. The last thing he wanted was other adults drawn in.

"Nah," said Bug. "My older sister has a Vespa."

"A what?" he asked.

"A Vespa, a motor scooter. You don't need a license to ride them. I'll drive, you hang on the back."

This seemed a truly horrendous idea, dragging this kid into his mess. Joey had known him. Esther had frequently alluded to Justin—a.k.a. Bug—as being a delinquent. But he was a stranger to Archie. Obviously, he couldn't allow Bug to sit in on his meeting with Colin, but still, Bug would know that he'd gone to the institute, that he'd met with Colin. Was it worth the risk?

Archie gazed at Bug, with his purple hair and black shirt and shorts, at his missing tooth, his smudged and dirty face. It didn't seem he had any other options.

"Okay," he said. "Get the scooter."

Chapter Eighteen

Colin was in a meeting when Archie and Bug arrived. Archie told the receptionist that he'd check back in a bit, but not having time to be patient, immediately made his way to Colin's office, keeping an eye out for Diana Mortonson as he slinked up the corridor. Bug was full of questions, and Archie wished he could have ditched the kid.

The door to Colin's office was unlocked. A surprise. Archie assumed that his filing cabinets and anything containing sensitive documents would be secured. Still, he marched across the room and tugged on a handle. His pulse quickened. The drawer slid open. Archie didn't care what type of meeting Colin was in, he knew his father wouldn't leave his office and files unlocked unless he expected to return within minutes. Glancing over his shoulder, Archie flipped through the folders, hoping to find his own file, or any others indicating an infusion. Of course, aside from looking for his own name, and Joey's, he had no idea of how to locate the desired files. It was highly unlikely he'd find anything titled, "Illegal Mind Infusions in Here!" Glancing at Colin's laptop computer, he wished he had hacking skills. Certainly, there was useful information on the computer, but Archie knew Colin well enough to know that it would be password protected. Better to start with paper files. At least those he could access.

"So, you gonna tell me what this is all about?" asked Bug as he grabbed a handful of peanuts from Colin's carnival glass bowl. Archie had almost forgotten the kid was there. Not too bright, going through the files in front of him.

"Can't. Sorry," said Archie as he studied the names on each file, vainly hoping he'd discover something of significance. Joey Burke's name was not in this cabinet—at least not under the letter "B." Archie glanced over his shoulder. No sign of Colin.

"What ya looking for?" Bug was eyeing him wearily.

"A file," said Archie, scanning through "L." Nope. No Lambert.

"Duh!" said Bug. "What file?"

Archie opened the next drawer down. "Mine," he said. Archie was becoming increasingly uncomfortable. Even if he found something, he couldn't view it with Bug present and it was unlikely he could get rid of the kid.

"Who's this?" said Colin from the doorway. Eying Bug with a dubious stare, he entered as Archie slammed the filing drawer shut and stood upright.

"This is Bug," said Archie.

"Bug, hmmm. Have some peanuts." Colin glanced at the half-empty bowl. "Or, yes, it seems you already have." Colin stared at Archie for a moment and then back to Bug. "Would you mind leaving Joey alone with me for a few moments? His medical information is confidential, you understand. As is everyone's," he added with a nod. "Not that I would allow anything classified to be left unlocked and accessible."

Colin ushered the boy out, directing him to a lobby where he could thumb through year-old issues of Better Homes and Gardens and Newsweek. Bug glanced back at his onetime friend with something akin to disdain. Archie wasn't overly concerned about offending the kid.

"You've been avoiding my calls," said Archie once the door had been closed.

Colin strolled across the deep plush rug, seating himself behind his vast mahogany desk. "I'm frequently in the company of colleagues and patients. It's sometimes difficult to return confidential calls. You should have been patient. I would have called." He snatched some peanuts. "Now, who's the boy? Have you told him anything?"

Archie plopped into the seat before him, gazing directly into Colin's cool gray eyes. "He's one of Joey's friends. He drove me here on his motor scooter. Why didn't you tell me there were other infusions?"

Archie's father stared at him through his thick plastic glasses, his gray eyes glinting subtly from the light of his simple, yet elegant desk lamp. "What makes you think there were others?"

"Diana Mortonson paid a visit. I'm still waiting for your answer."

"Hmmm, of course she did. A bull dog, that one."

"Colin, the other infusions," Archie had no patience for his father's evasiveness.

"There were none." Colin set his pen on his desktop.

"You're lying."

Colin looked down, fiddled with his pen. "I have never before performed an infusion on a human being. Primates, yes. But we've already discussed that."

"That's your final word?"

"Yes, my final word," Still, he failed to make eye contact.

*****

White.

Everything white.

Archie felt no sensation, heard no sound. It wasn't that he was floating; it was more that he wasn't there at all. That he had no substance, no being.

*****

"It happened, Colin. Just now."

"Hmmm? What was that, Archie?" Colin popped two peanuts into his mouth.

*****

White again. Everything: utterly white. No color. No shadows. No walls or dimensions. In the distance, Archie sensed, but did not see, an emerald ring. A wheel within a wheel. A wheel with eyes, with purpose. Pulsing. Growing. It was strong. And it was becoming stronger.

*****

Archie blinked.

There had been a tall standing lamp in the rear right corner of the office. It was now on the floor, the pole bent into a V. The bulb and stained glass lampshade were broken, pieces of glass scattered about the room. Archie's right hand was sticky. He glanced down to find that he was cut. It wasn't a deep slice, nothing requiring stitches, but it was enough to bleed.

Colin was just rising to his feet after apparently tumbling to the floor. "Archie?" he asked, a hint of fear to his formerly controlled tone.

"Yeah. I'm back." Archie stepped forward, intending to grab tissue from Colin's desk.

Colin took an involuntary step back.

"It's happening, Colin."

"Please explain. What exactly is happening?" He was regaining his composure now, slipping back into his detached air of professionalism.

Archie snatched three tissues from the square Puffs box atop the desk and moved several feet distant. He didn't want to be too close to Colin should he have another episode. "I went away. Just now. Somewhere else."

Colin bent, righting his toppled chair. "Where did you go?"

Archie began to pace. His legs were trembling and his arms tingled with pent up energy. "White," he said, pressing the tissue firmly against his palm, staving the blood flow. "Everything was white. There was something else. In the distance."

"Yes, what was it?" Colin slid into his seat, his throne, his power position behind his austere desk. Not once did he inquire about Archie's injury.

Archie crossed the room, shaking his arms, trying to calm himself. "A wheel, I think. It was… I'm not sure. I couldn't see it."

"Then, how do you know it was there? Could you hear it, smell it?"

"No!" he blurted. "It was just… I could sense it. I could feel it watching me."

Colin leaned back, opened a desk drawer, and produced a pocket-sized audio recorder. Placing it on the desk before him, he depressed the record button. "Please repeat everything you've just shared. I need an accurate record."

Archie rolled his eyes. "Everything white. I was somewhere else. A wheel was watching me."

There was a subtle twittering at the far edge of his perception, a clatter, a shuffle, tiles cascading into position.

"Colin, am I losing my mind?"

The doctor drummed his fingers on the desk. "This white place, have you been there before?"

"A couple of times. The day before I attacked Finney and Mercedes Yamagata, another time. I think it was the same day. It's hard to remember these episodes. They fade."

"To clarify, you're referring to the day before you found yourself—as an adult—in the Sears Tower and in the whitewater?"

"Yes. The white was there then too. The experience began white and then pieces of the Sears Tower reality fell into the white."

"Pieces?"

Archie nodded. "It's tough to explain. Fragments of the reality. They assembled."

Colin scribbled a note on a yellow pad. "Describe for me the first experience. Was there a wheel?"

Archie paced, thinking back, trying to remember. He'd been in downtown Ephesus, walking, trying to find a place to spend the night. There was a couple on their porch, and then—white. But only for a moment. Just one very brief moment. "No," he said. "No wheel. At least I didn't sense it, but I only went white for a few seconds. I can't say that it wasn't there." Archie paused, squeezing the tissue hard against his cut. It seemed the bleeding had subsided.

"Any other instances?"

"The first night, after I escaped the institute. I think I went white in an apartment. Just as I went to sleep. I didn't come back to reality until the next day. Colin, what's happening to me?"

Colin steepled his index fingers beneath his chin. "Archie, honestly, I don't know. Stress could be a factor. It seems this occurs when your stress level is elevated: you fending for yourself out on the street, Finney Yamagata recognizing you from a news broadcast, you confronting me about your suspicions."

"But, what do we do about it? I can't live like this, knowing that at any moment I could go off somewhere else, knowing that I could hurt someone while I'm wherever it is I go."

Colin nodded, snatching some peanuts. The face of normality. Everything was fine. There was no reason to fear. If Archie hadn't been sired by the man he might have even found comfort in his demeanor. "Ultimately, I'm unsure as to how we'll proceed. Initially, though, we'll increase your medication. With luck, that will suppress further episodes."

Archie walked around the chair and stared down at his father. Colin couldn't help but to scoot several inches back. "That's not the answer, Colin. You know it's not. That medication worked fine—for a few weeks. But not now, not today. I may be developing a tolerance. If so, increasing the dosage will only delay the inevitable. We can't keep upping my meds until I land in the crayon club at the psych ward. I won't live that way."

Colin shrugged. "Be that as it may, for the time being, it's what we're stuck with."

"What about the other patients?"

"Pardon?"

"The other infusions. The ones you claim don't exist. What happened to them? Did they go to a white place? Did they go somewhere and never come back?"

Colin cleared his throat and gazed at his empty peanut bowl. "I've told you, Archie, there were no others."

"Right," said Archie. "You've told me." He left his father's office, unsure if he'd ever return.

Chapter Nineteen

As expected, Bug was full of questions. "What was that all about?" "Are ya cured?" "Why do ya look so mad?" Archie remained mostly silent, offering only cursory responses. They motored north on the winding two lane highway, passing the wooded area and crossing Plummer's Creek as they made their way toward town. Archie's mood was sullen. Colin was not going to be forthcoming, and that left him with only one option—Diana Mortonson.

But could he trust her?

Archie's mind slipped back to the wheel. That emerald wheel within a wheel, pulsing and venomous, eyes all about an uneven and corrosive rim: scrutinizing him, studying him, assessing his strengths and weaknesses.

A wheel that was not a wheel. There were no spokes, no hubcaps, no center or axel. The outer wheel was disconnected from its inner companion, yet both were part of the same whole. It breathed, expanding and then contracting. The eyes were of different sizes and shapes—round, oval, box-like, narrow. The substance of the thing was malleable, never consistent, never at rest. A growing ooze, roughly round in form, but creeping, spinning, infecting.

Madness!

Archie came back to rational thought. He needed to make decisions, decide who to trust, what to do about his condition. Colin infuriated him. Colin: smug, brilliant, deluded, callous.

Father.

Colin had never been a real father to Archie and his sister, nor a husband to his wife. It was amazing he'd ever sacrificed enough research time to find a woman willing to marry him and to then produce two children. Maybe he'd been different as a young adult. By the time Archie was old enough to comprehend his situation Colin was off in his lab early every morning and late into every evening. He'd show up at eight or nine PM, give Archie's mother an obligatory kiss, offer the kids some peanuts, and then sit at his desk with his reheated meal, pouring over notes and mumbling six-syllable words into the condenser microphone of a large black Montgomery Ward cassette tape re-corder. He'd nod when Archie showed him his drawings, um-hmm when he saw his grades, and ask Archie's mother to "cover" for him when Archie asked him to play ball. He did, it seems, remember Archie's name, for he bellowed it when attempting to quiet the boy.

Archie glanced past Bug's purple head and saw a squat, pale yellow, brick building coming up on the left. There were five cars in the small gravel parking lot, one of which was a deep blue late-model Lumina. Archie recognized the car. A crazy thought tickled the corners of his brain.

It was risky. Riskier even than going to Diana Mortonson.

"Bug, pull over."

"What?"

"Pull over. Let me off here."

"How you gonna get home?"

"I'll figure something out. Maybe I'll call my parents for a ride. What can they do—ground me? I don't go anywhere anyway."

Bug shook his head. "I dunno, Burke. I think you're missing somethin' in your head."

"No argument there, Bug."

*****

It had been in the middle of the night the first time Archie visited the radio station. There had been no receptionist, only James T. Roswell, the radio UFO guru, and his trusty producer Ned. This time, he was greeted by an enthusiastic young woman with a perky grin and perfect hair. "Hello," she said. "Welcome to *The Flame*, northwest Indiana's number one source for news and oddities."

"Well, I'm sure I qualify as at least one of those," he said.

"Excuse me?"

"I need to see Roswell."

If possible, her already expansive smile grew broader. "His show's not on till ten."

"Yeah, but his car's here. I have a story for his show."

*****

Roswell was a big man. Not fat, not overbearing, but middle-aged chunky. He wasn't exceptionally tall, maybe five-eleven or six foot. It was more that he gave the impression of being large. He had that big guy feel to him. His hands were over-sized with thick, chapped fingers. His frame was wide, broad-shouldered. He had a dark mop that hung above heavily-lined temples. His eyes were chocolate brown. The kind of eyes that look right through a person. They weren't mean eyes, nor particularly compassionate, but they managed to appear mildly gentle while still revealing nothing of Roswell's intent. His thin lips occasionally slipped into a wry grin, and his golden brown complexion disallowed the opportunity to foresee embarrassment or anger.

He leaned back in his squeaky navy blue office chair, clutching a steaming cup of black coffee in a purple and orange *The Flame* mug, and tossed a stapled stack of papers onto his already cluttered desk. They landed atop this week's *The Globe* supermarket tabloid. "You're the kid who was here that night, the one who stole the money from Ned's roomie." His tone was casual, almost bored, not accusatory.

"Yeah, that's me," said Archie.

"You're not planning on stealing anything from me, I hope." He sipped his coffee with a subtle slurp.

"No stealing. I promise."

"Your name's not really Archie either."

The guy had a good memory. "Nope. Call me Spock."

Roswell chuckled and leaned forward. "Do you really have something for me—*Joey Burke*—or are you just here to chat with a radio guy?"

Apparently, he'd heard the local news report on Archie's escape from the institute. Maybe he'd reported on it himself. "Ned told me that you actually research some of your stories, that they're not all entirely fabricated."

"What makes you think any of it is fabricated?" His face was deadpan, no hint of sarcasm in his voice. Surely, he'd perfected this skill after numerous years of on-air nonsense.

"Silly me," said Archie. "What could I have been thinking?"

Roswell didn't grin or chuckle, but simply nodded for Archie to continue.

"Do you believe any of the things you report?" asked Archie. "Or is it simply for entertainment value?" He wanted to know if Roswell had a reporter's instinct, if he believed in anything enough to track down the truth.

Another sip of coffee. "What's not to believe?"

"Puppies," said Archie, quoting Roswell from the night they'd met. "Do they hold the key to deciphering alien hieroglyphics?"

An accidental smile slithered across Roswell's lips disappearing before it was fully formed. "What do you need, Joey?"

Archie sighed, still not sure that he wanted to confide in this man, knowing that if he did—and if Roswell believed him—he could be opening the institute, his father, himself, up for a media storm of controversy such as sleepy little Ephesus had never before seen. Except that James T. Roswell was considered a kook and a fraud by most rational human beings. True, he had listeners, most of which believed virtually nothing he said. And yes, there were those few who did believe, but Archie's guess was that they lacked personal credibility as well. J.T. Roswell might actually be able to do the digging Archie needed, find out about the other infusion recipients, broadcast his findings to the six or seven communities that received his show, and never have a word of it taken seriously.

But Diana Mortonson would know. She would believe.

"Okay," Archie said. "If I tell you this, my name—any reference to me at all—needs to be kept out of it. You can tell the story. Use the others as your examples, but I don't exist—got it?"

Roswell smiled and raised his cup to his lips, his eyes glinting as he said, "Right now there is no story. Tell me what you've got and then we'll talk deals."

"No," said Archie. "What I'm offering is of mutual benefit. You get a spectacular story—a real one for a change. And I get some much-needed information. But I need some guarantees before we begin."

Roswell shrugged, sipped his coffee, glanced at the wall to his left. There was a poster from the movie Jaws, one of Darth Vader, another of Spider-Man.

127

There was a photo of Roswell with the mayor of Chicago, and one of Roswell with William Shatner, Captain Kirk from the original Star Trek series. Beside that was a 2006 award for "Broadcast Excellence" and a picture of what appeared to be a three-headed alien in drag. Roswell remained silent.

"Okay," Archie said after a moment. "I'm sorry for wasting your time. I'm sure you need to get back to scanning the tabloids for tonight's broadcast content." He rose to leave.

"Who are you, Joey Burke?"

"Excuse me?"

"Why did you run away from the Gowon Institute? Why did you attack those two people? Why did you steal the guy's money?"

Archie paused. Roswell was obviously quite familiar with the story of his escape and subsequent adventures. "Do we have a deal?" asked Archie. "Will you keep my name out of it?"

Roswell sipped his coffee, scrutinizing a tribal mask hanging on the opposite wall. "You're a minor. By law I must keep your name out of it. Besides, you're just a kid. How big could this be?"

Archie reseated himself, meeting Roswell's gaze. "Well, to begin with," he said. "I'm forty-five years old."

*****

Not only had Roswell not believed Archie, but he threatened to call Joey's parents and warn them that he was attempting to cause trouble for them and everyone who had helped him come back to consciousness after his near-fatal accident. Roswell invoked the legal ramifications of broadcasting the tale, that he could be sued for slander by the institute, by Colin. Archie had told him of his suspicions, that he wasn't the only infusion, that he needed to locate the other patients, find out what had happened to them, if they'd survived, if they'd kept sound minds, if they'd experienced the same inner-mind experiences as he.

Roswell led Archie to the door.

Bug had not left as Archie had instructed him to, but rather stood in the hallway, his brows arched in curiosity, his lips curved downward in mistrust. "What was all that about?" he asked when they'd exited the building, stepping out into the early evening mugginess of an Indiana summer.

"Oh," said Archie. "Nothing. I just wanted the guy's autograph."

"Liar," said Bug as he stomped toward his sister's scooter. "I heard you in there. Not all of it. But you said your name's Archie—that Joey's dead."

Damn!

Archie stared at him for a moment, maybe for several moments, his pulse quickened and then slowed to near nonexistence. His fingers tingled, his head felt light. Archie concentrated on Bug, on his features, his purple hair, his round face and pouty lips. He feared going white, going to where the wheel waited. He feared that he'd attack this boy; hurt him, maybe even kill him. Yes, he knew that capacity was within him and so he concentrated on the reality about him, holding onto it with every nuance of his being. Bug, this snotty little twelve year-old goth wannabe knew his secret. He was a danger.

The white knew the danger.

Or was it the wheel that understood the risk? Were they one and the same? It didn't matter, he supposed. What mattered was that he had no control over this entity, whatever it might be.

White trickled from his fingertips, pooling on the pitted asphalt. It rippled and hopped, inching this way and that before slithering up Archie's legs, contracting, squeezing, controlling.

Archie took a deep breath, calmed himself, focused on damage control. The two boys stood, eyes locked. "I made it up, Bug," said Archie finally. "My doctor, he made me mad. The medication he has me on is too strong. He wouldn't do anything for me, so I made up that story to tell Roswell, you know, to get back at my doctor."

The white quivered and darted, threatening to seize control, to run amok, inflict damage. It tickled at his brain. Burrowed deep within. Images flashed in Archie's head. Terrible Images. Grotesque. Gory. Images of Archie popping Bug's eyes out with his thumbs. Images of a decapitated Bug. Images of…

Archie breathed deep, averting Bug's gaze, trying to think of anything but the problem at hand. Bringing up the most innocent images he could think: Mickey Mouse, Spider-Man, Jill. When finally he met Bug's gaze again, the boy was speaking, oblivious to the deadly danger only four feet before him.

"No," Bug said. "I don't believe that crazy crap you told the radio guy. But I don't believe what you're tellin' me neither."

Bug climbed onto the scooter, turned the ignition, and sped off with a wobble and a lurch, leaving Archie standing in the parking lot of, "*The Fire*, northwest Indiana's number one source for news and oddities."

And the white squeezed. Oh, did it squeeze.

Chapter Twenty

Joey's father picked Archie up about a mile north of the radio station at Mama Sophie's Hoosier Grille, a little green brick building that oozed the tantalizing odors of flavorful grease and high-octane coffee. Archie had made his way there after having been abandoned by the angry and sulking Bug. He hadn't wanted Greg to know he'd been at the radio station. The last thing Archie wanted was for Greg or Esther to sit down with Roswell and learn what he'd told the man. The white had subsided soon after Bug's departure, but not fled. Archie could sense its presence, lurking just beyond the veil of reality, waiting and watching.

Greg was concerned that Archie had slipped away without telling him where he was going, but hadn't seemed angry. He had more of a boys-will-be-boys attitude and let it go without asking for much in the way of explanation. It seemed to Archie that Greg was likely glad to see his son get into just a bit of normal childhood mischief. Esther Hadn't been so forgiving, berating him for his act of defiance and demanding a detailed account of his day.

Over dinner, Esther revealed that Colin had called while Archie was gone. Naturally, this caused Archie's stomach to twist and curl, he hadn't told Greg and Esther that he'd seen Colin. "What did he want?" Archie asked in a voice that was surely weak.

"He wants to run some follow-up tests on you: an MRI a CT scan. He wants to see what's happening inside that precocious head of yours." Archie nodded, attempted to seem unconcerned, and asked Esther to pass the green beans.

Archie returned to Joey's room after dinner, dejected and guilty. Colin had cared after all. He'd ordered more tests. He wanted to explore Archie's condition, to find out what had gone wrong. He was seeking the solutions Archie sought, but Archie hadn't given Colin the time to plan a course of action. He'd expected Colin to tell him exactly what needed to be done, right there, right then as if this was nothing more than a scraped knee.

And Archie had betrayed him.

In the racing tide of fear and anger, Archie had exposed his greatest secret to a stranger. And not just any stranger, but a radio personality. Someone who had the capacity to broadcast this information to thousands of area citizens. Colin could be ruined. He could lose his medical license, wind up in jail. Was there any way Archie could undo what he'd done? Roswell hadn't believed him. He'd berated him even. Probably, the encounter had already fallen off of his mental radar. But what if he'd rethought his opinion? What if he'd decided it was worth a look, that it might be a good story after all? The story was homegrown. This wasn't happening seventeen hundred miles southwest in Area 51 or back east in Washington D.C. This was a down home, corn-fed, local scandal.

Archie had to make this right.

He slipped his cell phone from his pocket. Why a twelve year-old needed one, he couldn't say, but here it was. He dialed information, received the number for *The Flame*, and called Roswell. "Yeah," said Roswell after nearly a five minute wait. "This is J.T."

"Mr. Roswell, Joey Burke here."

A sigh. "Again? Kid, no offence, but you're becoming a pest."

"I won't bother you any more—I promise."

"Uh-huh. What now, an alien chimpanzee with Hitler's mustache?"

"No, no. Listen, all of what I told you this afternoon, about the institute, the mind transfusion, it was a lie. I was just trying to see if you'd put it on the air."

"A lie?" Roswell's voice was quiet, contemplative. "You sure sounded like you believed it then."

"Yeah," he said. "Kids, huh?"

"Yeah... Kids."

After disconnecting, Archie had focused his worries on Bug. The boy had heard part of what he'd told Roswell. And on top of that, he was angry with Archie. Who knew what the boy could do, what he'd tell. Archie needed to talk with Bug, act like Joey, be his friend—just a little.

Archie stared at his phone, intending to call Bug, to fabricate a story. Maybe he could tell the boy that his brain was still jumbled, that sometimes he couldn't tell fantasy from reality, that everything he'd told Roswell had been a dream.

But the phone hadn't been in Archie's palm. In truth, he had no palm, but only white. Pure, colorless, lifeless white. He'd attempted to squint, but didn't have control. He'd tried to remember Joey's room, to picture it in his mind, to focus on the reality that he knew to be around him. The white shifted, rocking from side to side. Archie felt nauseous, like he was about to lose his dinner. Something appeared in the distance—or was it just in front of him? He really couldn't tell. At first he thought it might be Joey's room, that he'd actually concentrated himself out of the spell.

But it wasn't the room. It was a shopping mall.

The white was gone, though Archie had not perceived its retreat. He never really noticed as the mall enveloped him, wrapping itself about him, closing in, permeating his reality. But he knew that it had done this. He knew that it folded over the white, obscuring it, that it slipped unnoticed beneath his feet, that it enclosed the emptiness above with florescent lights and ceiling panels.

Colin had speculated that anger or fear might bring about these episodes, but Archie was coming to believe that it was more than this, that perhaps it was any strong emotion, good or bad. Perhaps it was at these times that his mind was less focused that the barrier was breached. He speculated that should he, when Joey's form was more mature, ever fall in love, that the white would encroach upon his love making, that perhaps if he was to ever become a father again, that the white would intrude upon that precious moment of birth, or at the child's first step, first word, first day of school.

But there was deeper fear as well. In his heart he knew the white was becoming stronger, that the slender veil that separated his two realities was wearing thin, that if nothing was done he would soon cross over never to return.

Archie brought himself back to his current situation—the mall. Perhaps there was something to be learned while in this strange purgatory. Maybe there were answers here, perhaps even solutions.

He observed an older couple sitting on a bench eating pretzels. So normal, so common. Moving closer, he asked them something inconsequential, what time it was, where they were, something not entirely abnormal. They didn't respond. Archie said something again, louder. "Where'd you get the pretzels?" he asked. Archie didn't care about the pretzels, he just wanted a response.

They continued as if he wasn't there.

Archie touched the man on the shoulder. He was solid. Archie could feel the wiry fibers of his tweed jacket. He could smell the garlic on his pretzel and hear the subtle wheezing of his breathing. Still, the man didn't acknowledge his presence. Archie turned, stepping in front of a threesome of teenaged girls, giggly and animated, carrying packages from the Gap and Sam Goodies. They separated, walking around him, but not acknowledging him. "Hey," he said. "Hey! Excuse me!" Archie grabbed one of the girls by the arm, just above the elbow, turning her to face him. She continued talking with her friends as if she hadn't been obstructed. Archie could smell bubblegum on her breath, hairspray in her hair. "Can you see me?" he yelled, holding her at arm's length by both shoulders. "Can you hear me? Do you know that I'm here?" She kept babbling about some guy named Ron and giggling at the responses of her friends though they were now several feet away and out of earshot. When Archie released her, she turned and quick-stepped back to her friends, still chattering as if she'd been beside them all along.

Frustrated, Archie attacked an over-sized potted plant. The pot itself was probably three feet high and equally as wide, the plant, a small tree really, extended an additional five feet toward the ceiling, with green, leafy branches extending out in all directions. It wasn't that Archie was taking his anger out on the plant; it was more that he wanted to see if he could draw anyone's attention.

Archie had to rock it four or five times before it toppled, but when it did, dirt and leaves spilled onto the shiny vinyl floor, dozens of leaves detached, spreading about in the dirt. The passers-by, though, paid it no mind. Yes, they stepped around it as if they saw it, but they didn't stare at Archie, they didn't ask what he thought he was doing. They simply moved about it as if it was a normal part of the scenery.

Cursing, Archie kicked the planter. It hurt.

He made his way through the mall, rushing forward, pausing, turning, gazing at the people: the mothers with kids, the bored employees, the unconcerned security guards. He had no real purpose in mind. There wasn't anything he could do but wait to return to the real world and learn of what awful things he'd done while he'd been away.

But this world seemed so real: the sights, the smells, the feel of everything he touched. Even his own body felt the way it had felt just a few years before. There was the slight stiffness in his neck, the constant reminder of a traffic accident some years before. His left knee twitched, just a bit. He had never known why. It had started somewhere during his college days. It wasn't painful, nor did it inhibit his movement, it just twitched every so often; just a little reminder that it was there. Archie could smell his own cologne, Aspen, a kind of sweet musky fragrance that mixed with the stale smell of cigarette smoke that permeated his wardrobe. He was himself. He was Archie Lambert. And he was in some Twilight Zone world with no escape.

Bug was there too.

Standing in a pool of blood. It wasn't Bug's blood. At least Archie didn't believe so. It was more that Bug had stepped into it.

Archie saw him, across the way, maybe thirty yards distant, headphones in his ears, bobbing to his jams. He'd just exited Spencer's, a novelty store, though he carried no bags. His hair was black, not purple, his clothes were bright and colorful. "Bug!" he cried, as his stroll became a jog. "Bug! Over here!" Archie crashed into a middle-aged woman in a green flowery dress. She fell to the floor, her many bags scattering across the tile, spilling blouses, shoes, lingerie. She acted as if nothing had happened, continuing her conversation with a man of about thirty as she rose, leaving her spilled purchases behind to be trampled by others who were equally oblivious to Archie and his deeds.

Archie weaved through the crowd, trying to catch the boy, bumping into and knocking over any zombie-like forms obstructing his way. Why did no one notice him? What was this place? Archie caught Bug as he stepped into a dimly-lit clothing store featuring loud, throbbing music and flashing, multi-colored lights.

As with the other residents of this bizarre reality, Bug was oblivious to Archie and so he shook the boy, yelled, cursed, even slapped him once. Nothing. Bug simply bobbed to his music and, when released, made his way about the crowd tracking sticky red goo with every step.

Why was he here? Why was Bug in Archie's brain? Because that was where Archie was, somewhere in his deep subconscious, locked away with Alice and her rabbit while Joey's body did who-knows-what in his absence.

And then he sensed it. Somewhere near. A presence.

Archie's stomach took a dive as he glanced left and then right. He could feel it, almost like an electric tingle through his being. It was the ring, the wheel within a wheel, its numerous eyes watching him, studying his every move. It was to his right. Archie didn't know how he knew this, but he was sure of it. He moved in that direction, weaving about the oblivious patrons, jogging, gazing in every storefront as he moved past.

Blood. Splotches of blood on the tile floor. Thick, spreading as with purpose, leading the way, beckoning Archie onward. Archie's body tingled. He was getting closer. He must follow the blood. The crimson flow knew the way, just around a corner, or behind a clothing rack. Archie slowed his pace, panting, trying to catch his breath. His body was not accustomed to heavy physical activity. Too much smoke in the lungs, too much hops in the gut. Archie slowed to a halt, turned steadily, a full three hundred and sixty degrees. Where was the phantom wheel? He could feel it, practically taste its emotion, its anger, its fear and wrath.

There. Not twenty feet distant. The wheel within a wheel. Floating, hovering. One oozing rim spun clockwise, the other, counterclockwise. The eyes, all about the rims, blinked and gazed, some stared to the ceiling or off to the left, some focused on Archie, and some focused on nothing at all. Archie stepped forward and then thought better of it. The thing enlarged and then contracted. Its brightness intensified and then diminished, its hue lightened and darkened. The rims seemed like tentacles more than metal casts: living, squirming, hating. And still the eyes blinked and gazed.

"What are you?" he asked, but received no response. Archie ventured another step. The blood was pooling about the thing and Archie nearly slipped in the wriggling substance. The wheel did not advance or retreat, but enlarged, perhaps as a warning to stay away.

Why are you here?

It wasn't a voice. It wasn't a transmission. It was more that the question encased Archie, surround him, causing him to shudder, to vibrate in a most unsettling way.

"I'm Archie," he stammered, not knowing what else to say.

Why are you here?

Some of the eyes narrowed, the rims rotated, the outer one pulsing at a frantic rate.

"I don't know why I'm here," he said. "I don't know where here is."

The thing flared bright green, nearly blinding.

Why are you here?

"I don't know where 'here' is!" he screamed.

The thing pulsed, growing larger, six feet, eight, ten. The mall became dark, the colors shattering and breaking away in jagged mirror-like pieces to reveal an intense white. The floor oozed, becoming pliable. Archie wanted to run, but to where? The mall no longer existed. Only the wheel remained. The wheel and the white and the blood.

*****

Archie awoke with a shiver. He was in Joey's body. On an unfamiliar lawn—naked, wet, cold. An in-ground sprinkler system splayed waves of water, drenching him. Blades of freshly-mown grass stuck to his damp bare skin. Archie sat up, cradling himself in his arms, trembling from the cold. Clear water dribbled across his face. There was a chain-link fence, a garage in desperate need of a paint job, a patio area. Where was he? Where were his clothes? Archie noticed blood on his hands. They were sticky, red, sickening to the sight. An awful taste pervaded his mouth. Something like hair stuck to his tongue. He spat several times in an attempt to clear it. Deep scratches, like claw marks, snaked across his chest. Archie rose, surveying his surroundings.

He was in someone's back yard. It was fully dark and few houses were illumi-
nated. Archie guessed for no particular reason that it was sometime after midnight.

There was something on the ground, perhaps ten feet distant. A lump,
maybe a pile of something. Still cradling himself against the midnight chill,
Archie shuffled over to the thing, curious as to what it might be. The light was
dim, only a small porch light from maybe fifty feet behind, but Archie could
see the diminutive form of the cat as he stepped closer. Brown and white and
splattered with blood. Hazy green eyes stared unseeing into eternity, head
cocked at a grotesque angle. A portion of the neck had been torn away. At once
Archie knew that he had done this.

Archie didn't cry out or shriek, though tears did mingle with sprinkler water on his cheeks. He wanted to collapse into a babbling heap on the water-
soaked lawn, to cry out, to give himself over to hysteria, maybe even slip over
into blissful insanity. But instead, he simply sprinted from the yard, out into
the empty street. He was in a residential area, vaguely familiar. He wasn't far
from the Burke's home, though he wasn't sure of the specific street. Archie
chose a direction and ran. Running still wasn't easy for him, but his coordination had improved dramatically. He moved onto the lawns, out of the center of
the street, away from the street lamps. He was naked, lost, covered with blood.
He couldn't allow himself to be seen.

A block distant, a van rounded a corner. Its headlight beams landed on
Archie. He froze for a moment, unsure of which direction to turn. The van
moved steadily forward, closer, closer. Recovering from his momentary paral-
ysis, Archie moved to his right and crouched behind a low hedge of shrubbery.
The van rolled past without slowing, the driver facing forward, talking on a
cell phone, not scanning the area. Apparently, the woman hadn't seen him.

It took Archie only a few more minutes to find his way home. He'd been
only a couple of blocks distant. He crept along the side of the house and could
see the glowing light in Greg's garage woodshop. Greg often worked late into
the night, long after Esther slipped into their shared bedroom. He said it was
more peaceful then, less distractions. And, apparently, he had enough clients
as to need extra hours in order to complete projects by customer deadlines.

Archie also recognized that this was an escape from his wife. The relationship was strained and brittle. Greg accepted this with a quiet stoicism and an aversion to confrontation. Whatever vigor the man may have once possessed, it had been sucked from him by the cruel tricks of life.

There was a spare house key in a magnetized container under the mailbox. Archie slid this out, and then quietly unlocked the front door. The air conditioning caused goose bumps to rise on his damp naked flesh. The entrance to the garage was off of the laundry room. Archie was nowhere near Greg, but Clapton, the dog, had heard him come in and offered a low growl from atop the stairs.

Archie shushed Clapton, and comforted him with a pat to the head as the animal approached. Archie heard the latch of a door from beyond the kitchen and family room. Greg was coming in from the garage. He would need to walk past Archie if he intended to get to the master bedroom. Quickly, Archie moved to the stairs, crept up, turned left into the hall bathroom and closed the door behind him. The master bedroom had its own facilities. Greg never used the hallway bath. Still, Archie held his breath as he heard Greg making his way up the stairs. Would he wonder why the bathroom door was closed? Archie should have gone straight to his room, but he was wet, filthy, bleeding. He needed a towel and bandages.

Archie listened closely as Greg padded up the stairs, continuing past, opening the master bedroom door, stepping inside, and closing it behind him. Archie had made it.

A moment later, he found his prescription bottle and took three pills, no longer concerned whether they would turn him into a zombie or not. In fact, the prospect seemed rather welcoming.

Chapter Twenty-One

With the exception of a rather nasty scratch on the back of his right hand, all of the claw marks were on Archie's chest, easily concealed with a T-shirt. He told Greg and Esther that he'd scratched his hand on one of the rosebushes on the side of the house. They had no reason to disbelieve him and readily accepted the explanation. Bug, though, was more suspicious.

The boy sat cross-legged in the front yard fiddling with dew damp dandelions and staring coldly at the house. Archie had no desire to speak with the kid, but after two hours of this figured he'd better see what Bug wanted. Esther was cautious where Bug was concerned. He was a delinquent, she said. Not the kind of boy he should befriend. But, in the same breath, she asked about Bug's parents, in particular his father, how much contact the boy had with the man, if he'd heard anything concerning the custody battle. She wondered if she, herself, had come up in conversation, if Bug had talked much about the weeks leading up to Joey's accident. It all seemed a little weird to Archie, but there were so many bizarre things happening in his life that "a little weird" didn't even register on the radar. Likely, Joey had fallen in with a rough kid and Esther was hoping to extinguish the renewed relationship before her son was influenced toward antisocial behavior.

Archie strolled onto the front lawn, chomping on a Pop-Tart, and stared down at the black-clad boy. Even at several feet away he could hear the music blaring from Bug's earphones. The boy's eyes were half shut as if he was in some transcendental trance, and his mouth, though expressionless, seemed to have just the slightest quiver at the corner of his lips. "Hello, Bug," said Archie.

Bug dialed down his music and said, "Hey."

"What are you doing out here?" asked Archie, not really in the mood to be bothered with small talk.

"Keepin' an eye on you."

"Why?" he asked.

"Because I don't trust you." Bug's voice was even, his stare cold.

Archie took a bite of his Pop-Tart and squatted down on his haunches so he could speak eye-to-eye with the boy. "Why, Bug? Why don't you trust me? We used to be friends before the accident, right?"

"What happened to your hand?" Bug asked in reply. He'd noticed the bandage.

"I cut myself on a rosebush," said Archie.

Bug responded by saying, "Melvin's dead."

"Who?"

"My cat. Melvin. The one that stayed at my dad's house. Somebody killed him last night."

Archie's legs went weak. He was sure they shook. Until that moment, he hadn't known whose cat he had killed. He'd assumed it had been some random feline. But this changed things. This was no chance incident; this wasn't an accidental encounter. This was a deliberate attack against Bug. Why? What could his subconscious mind possibly have against the kid? And was it even Archie's subconscious mind that guided him during his absence? What if it was the emerald wheel? What if it was something else that had somehow gotten into his head during the infusion, some malignant force or consciousness?

He shuffled into a sitting position, fearful that if he didn't he might tumble. "Killed?" he said, not knowing how to reply.

"Yeah," Bug said. "Killed." His eyes were watery, on the brink of tears, his voice even, controlled, but with just a hint of underlying waver. Archie didn't really like Bug. He didn't seem like the kind of kid Archie would have hung out with even if he had really been twelve; not with the purple hair, black clothes, and tough guy attitude. And since Archie wasn't really that age, well, Bug seemed to be nothing more than an additional annoyance in an already insane existence. But the kid's pet had died; Archie had been responsible. Who knew what other pain he might eventually cause the boy.

"Bug... I'm so sorry." Archie's voice was weak. Emotionally, he was still reeling from the implications of the night before. Bug had seemed depressed, even suspicious before, but Archie hadn't paid it much mind. But now, the guilt he felt, the pain he saw in those young eyes. "I'm so sorry," he said again.

"What are you sorry for?" Bug's tone was one of suspicion, accusation.

"Bug, I... I didn't kill your cat." This was true, in a sense. Archie's conscious mind hadn't been present when the atrocity had occurred. He'd been in a shopping mall, talking with a floating wheel that had dozens of eyes. How could he truly be put to blame?

Bug pursed his lips, melancholy and wrath, eyes locking with Archie's own. "How did ya say ya got that scratch?"

"Rosebush," Archie replied as evenly as his voice would allow.

"You used to like Melvin. You knew him. He wasn't like the others." A tear made a break for it, racing down Bug's cheek before being whisked away by a shirtsleeve.

The others? What was this kid talking about? "I have no memory of meeting your cat, Bug—either now or before." Archie rose. He had to get away from this kid before his emotions betrayed him, before tears escaped his eyes or confession his lips. "I'm sorry for what happened. I truly am." Archie turned and slowly made his way across the lawn to the front door.

"I'll be watching," called Bug.

Chapter Twenty-Two

Archie met with Colin several times over the next two weeks. Colin ran tests: a Magnetic Resonance Imaging (MRI), a Single Photon Emission Computed Tomography (SPECT), a Computed Tomography (CT), a Positron Emission Tomography (PET), and several others that Archie could neither spell nor pronounce. Colin was serious throughout, muttering thoughts into his hand-held recorder. He'd said that it was rare to run such an array of scans on one patient, but that each brought with it its own nuances, and since they were dealing with essentially uncharted territory, he needed to be as thorough as possible. Everything came back within Colin's acceptable expectations; no anomalies were apparent, no evil apparitions floating on the borders of Archie's consciousness.

"Colin, this thing," said Archie, not really wanting to broach the subject, but knowing he must. "This thing that happened. The things I'm feeling. The things I saw. They can't have anything to do with Joey, can they? I mean, he's not alive in here somewhere?" This thought still plagued Archie, that somehow the boy was alive and he'd stolen the body of a child. As selfish as Archie could sometimes be, he couldn't live with himself should he learn that the boy had perished in order that he might live.

Colin shook his head with an audible scoff. "Don't trouble yourself with moral dilemmas when there's no need. The boy was dead—is dead. There was no brain activity." Colin offered the hint of a grin. "Remember, the parents were prepared to discontinue life support until I intervened. These problems you're facing, they have nothing to do with that child."

"You're sure of that?"

"I'm certain." Colin had nothing else to offer and so, jotting notes on Archie's chart, turned away, effectively concluding the conversation.

And so Archie resumed his new life, continuing with his elevated daily dosage of AF367D-2, had no episodes, but knew deep within his being that the issue was far from settled.

Greg and Esther wondered why Colin was suddenly running so many additional tests. Hadn't everything been going well? Joey was behaving normally. Colin covered these questions by telling them that Joey had experienced some migraine-type headaches, but that the boy hadn't wanted to worry them before first confiding in his doctor. Archie had received a mild scolding from Esther for keeping this from her, and a chuckle and a slap on the back from Greg who congratulated him on taking it like a man.

Archie tried to shove thoughts of other infusion recipients, of Diana Mortonson, and of gleaming emerald wheels from his mind. He knew that at some point, maybe hours distant, maybe months, he'd be forced to deal with these all again, but at the moment there were no other avenues to explore, no other tests to run. Besides, he had more pressing—more frightening—issues to deal with.

It was the first day of school.

Middle School. Sixth grade.

Kids vying for social stature. Girls and boys suddenly attracted to one another. Hormones grossly out of balance. Mood swings of Jekyll and Hyde proportions. Archie had been through it once; he had no desire to experience it again.

He had protested to Greg and Esther, claiming that he wasn't ready yet, that the amount of social contact required would be too much for his muddled brain. Greg told him that he was doing fine and that he needed to relearn how to associate with others, though, for once, Esther seemed she might take Archie's position, stating that maybe this was a little quick, but in the end no medical reason could be found to exempt him from continuing his education. Archie had pleaded his case before Colin, but the man allowed him no quarter. "Archie," he'd said. "Education is a wonderful thing."

"But, Colin—sixth grade?"

Colin stared at him for several moments, some underlying emotion creating a ruckus in his brilliant mind. "This is an opportunity, Archie. Perhaps the greatest gift you've been given. Think about what you're being offered. I so wish I'd taken the time to impress this upon you thirty-plus years ago. Perhaps you would have led a more fulfilling life."

Typical Colin. Even when he tried to be helpful he managed to insinuate his displeasure with his son. "Colin, this is not a gift. You're not getting me into Harvard. It's sixth grade. Spit wads, bullies, bored teachers and bad cafeteria food."

"No, no, no. Archie you're missing the point. Think of this as a chance to distinguish yourself. A four-point-oh GPA should be within an easy grasp. Embrace this. Going through school a second time with all of your life experience behind you, well, if you apply yourself, you might even be allowed to skip a grade level or two. Then, Archie—higher education. Perhaps even a distinguished university. Opportunities you neither had nor could have appreciated on your first go-around. A chance to make something more of your life. To make a contribution."

The implication, of course, was that Archie hadn't made a contribution during his first go-around. One more reason to resent Colin. Maybe if he'd been more of a father, Archie would have had a better example to follow.

*****

Archie strolled into his first sixth grade class wearing new clothes and lugging a blue backpack loaded with spiral notebooks, pens, pencils, and a calculator. Back in his school days, they hadn't had backpacks. Those were for hiking not for schoolbooks.

Archie gazed about the classroom. The teacher was not yet present. Someone had written, "Suzy loves Matt" on the chalkboard. Several kids wore headsets and Archie could hear an assortment of musical styles as kids scurried about selecting seats, shoving, laughing. Bug sat at the back of the room, the far left corner, blowing bubbles of saliva, and then puffing them into the air. Talented kid. They made eye contacted, but neither nodded nor waved. Archie sat on the opposite side of the room.

No one approached Archie. Instead, they watched and whispered among themselves. Eyes darted toward him and then away—and then back again. There were guilty giggles from the girls and narrowed gazes and smirks from the boys.

145

Archie supposed Joey's story had become school folklore. The kid who nearly drown, who was rumored to be brain dead, but somehow had recovered to full health. It was a great story. Surely adults in an office setting would have responded similarly to a returning coworker.

Archie stared about the room. Eyes dropped. They all wanted to hear the story, but no one had the guts to open their mouths. "What?" he asked finally. "I used deodorant today."

None of them got the joke. All was now silent. The undead kid had spoken.

Archie reached down, unzipped his backpack, and withdrew a notebook and pen. Everyone stared at him. He looked up. All eyes dropped.

"Excuse me. Did I do something to entertain you?" This was going to get really old. Archie needed to address it somehow. But they all acted as if he hadn't said a word. "Alright," Archie said. "Come on. Does anybody have anything to say to me, or are you all just going to stare?"

Silence. Stares.

"Anybody? I don't bite—honest."

More silence, more stares.

Finally, an athletic looking boy with sandy brown hair and cool green eyes responded. "Okay, freak," he said with a clear air of caring and diplomacy. "Is it true you died?"

"Excuse me," Archie said. "My name's not freak." Archie supposed he'd asked for it. It would have been better to let them come around on their own timing. Now, he'd have to deal with the "cool" kid. The one who felt he had something to prove.

"Okay, *FREAK!*" the kid said, with an emphasis on what was sure to become Archie's new nickname. "Everybody says you died and came back to life. Did you die?" He crossed his arms, cocked his head, wanting everyone to know that he was in control, that he was the brave one, the cool one.

Archie shrugged, trying to make it seem like no big deal. Though he supposed this was pretty much impossible. These were twelve year-olds. At that age, farting practically made the front page, how much more so rising from the dead? "Yeah," he said. "In a way, I suppose I did die."

"You're full of it, Dweeb," said the cool kid.

Archie fixed his eyes on him. The room hushed once more. "If you weren't going to believe me," he said. "Then why did you ask the question?"

The kid flushed. He wasn't used to being challenged. "You were a freak before, Burke. Anybody ever tell you that? Everybody was glad when they thought you'd died. Too bad it was a lie."

Archie didn't know why he did it. Maybe it was because, as a child, as Archie, he had let aggressive kids bully him around. It wasn't that he was small or scrawny, it was more that he simply wasn't aggressive. Archie avoided physical confrontation, attempting to joke his way out of situations. So, when this kid called him a freak, he decided to embarrass him. This type was mostly bluster. Archie could see the kid's eyes shift as Archie rose from his seat. He could sense the tension as he stepped forward. "Oh, but I did die," said Archie, his voice low and breathy, almost a hiss. "It was amazing too. I went through this long tunnel of light. And at the end I saw…"

"Jesus?" asked a girl from the front of the room.

"No," said Archie. "Oh, but how I wish it had been Jesus." He paused for dramatic effect. All eyes were on him. All breath held. "It was Satan."

Several children gasped, a couple chuckled.

"No way," said the cool kid, though the boy shrank back just a little as Archie stalked dramatically about the room.

"Oh, yes," he continued. "It was Satan. And there was fire all around. And my skin was melting, and there were thousands of people screaming   maybe even millions!"

"Naw," said a sniffling boy.

Archie marched menacingly toward his antagonist's desk. "Do you know what he said to me?" Archie asked as he loomed over the boy.

"This is bogus," said the kid, though, there was a hint of a quiver in his tone.

"He told me to collect all of my classmates and bring them back to hell with me." Archie snatched the kid's arm. General commotion filled the room. Some kids screaming, others cheering. Archie caught sight of Bug at the back wall, staring calmly, observing, no expression on his dark round face.

"Let go of me, you freak!" screamed the kid. But Archie didn't let go. He'd had his fun, taken it too far, and now realized that he didn't know what to do next. The kid was bigger than he, stronger. Archie couldn't beat him in a fight. What had he been thinking? All he'd wanted to do was to sit by himself and get through the travesty of middle school. He wasn't looking to make friends—or enemies. He just wanted to do his time and get out. But the kid had irked him, pushed his buttons. Archie had always hated kids like him, but as a child, had never been able to do anything about them. Well now, as an adult, he'd made matters worse. Now there was no doubt that he was a freak, that he was a sideshow waiting to happen.

The kid wrested his arm free. He stood, his fist raised. Archie took a step backward, stumbled against a desk. He felt a tingle slither across his skin, a flash of white in his eyes. Was it happening?

No.

Not here.

Not in a classroom filled with innocent children.

Archie's vision remained clear, but it was hard to concentrate. His flesh felt electrified—alive. Had it been this way the last time? Had he had these sensations before escaping the real world? He couldn't remember.

Archie took another step back. The kid advanced.

"Gavin!" yelled a girl. "Leave him alone. He was just having fun with you."

The kid, Gavin, continued forward. Archie glanced to his left. Bug had a curious, almost amused, look on his face. He'd probably like to see Archie get trashed.

The tingling persisted. Archie had to get out of there before something horrible happened. He felt like Lon Cheney Jr. watching the full moon rise while surrounded by unsuspecting villagers. He took another step back, bumped into a ponytailed girl. White slithered and oozed across the blackboard. Gavin lunged at him, but Archie sidestepped, slipping around another desk. The white leaped and bubbled. Gavin took a wild swing, across the desk, connecting with Archie's chin but causing no pain or damage because of his awkward angle.

Archie focused on the nearest desk, something concrete, something tangible and real as the white traversed the room, floating on an invisible cloud of horror.

Archie caught a glimpse of movement to his left. It was Bug. He'd stood up and was spitting onto his fingertips. He raised his hand and then flicked the saliva halfway across the room where it smacked against Gavin's right cheek. This kid was like the spit Spider-Man.

Gavin cursed. The room erupted in laughter. Archie took the opportunity to flee into the adjacent corridor and out through an emergency exit, a brilliant stream of white trailing closely behind.

Bursting onto the pitted asphalt of the staff parking lot Archie glanced over his right shoulder. There it was, a pulsating white blob, roughly the shape of a kidney, floating twenty feet off of the ground, growing, oozing, changing. Despite his fear, Archie was mesmerized, he wanted desperately to flee, but his strength deserted him, his legs felt weak and ineffectual. He stopped, turning to face the thing, barely maintaining his position as he resisted the call of the white. Bright tentacles of nothingness shot randomly into the cool morning air simply to dissipate into wisps of vapor. Drops of white oozed from the rim, dripping in every direction with no regard for gravity, logic, or even sanity. The white now occupied over fifty percent of the visible sky.

It grew. It breathed. It called to Archie, beckoning him, tantalizing, purring, seducing.

And there was something within. At the heart of the phenomenon. Something tangible. Vital. Menacing.

The wheel.

It hovered at the threshold between realities gazing down at Archie with numerous eyes. And though the wheel had no face, no means of expression, it seemed it nodded and grinned before retreating into eternity. Whatever it had hoped to accomplish through this encounter, it had been successful.

Chapter Twenty-Three

The sound of the crash brought Archie out of the white. It was the first time, to his knowledge, that external stimuli had done so. Still, the experience sent a shiver of terror racing along his spine. Unlike his previous experiences, he had been unaware of going to the white. He'd been asleep, in Joey's bed, like every other evening.

And now here he stood.

Gazing down on Esther's inert form.

Naked.

A hunting knife in his hand.

There was blood on the blade, and a thin line of red on Archie's chest, almost indiscernible, but there nonetheless. From time to time he had noted other such lines on his body. Nothing big, no real damage, just simple lines of no more than an inch in length. Often they disappeared within a day's time, disregarded and forgotten.

Archie glared at the knife, trembling at the implications.

How often had this occurred without his ever realizing? Did he go to the white every night, or had the stress of the day brought about the episode?

And the knife, his state of undress, the cuts?

Had he completely lost his mind? Was he truly a threat—to others and to himself?

Archie tried to move, to step away from the bed, but stark terror bound him to the spot. What was he to do? Could he dare tell Colin of this—or maybe Mortonson? If ever he'd felt directionless and alone, it was in that moment.

And then the color spilled from his face. The blood. On the knife. Was it his alone or had he attacked Esther?

She was alone in the bed. Greg had left several hours earlier after a heated debate concerning Joey's behavior at school. Greg, according to Esther, had taken the boy's week-long suspension too lightly. To Greg, it was simply middle school nonsense. He felt Joey had handled a difficult situation with a clever sense of humor. Esther had argued that Joey was displaying signs of aggression and should be monitored carefully, that his use of Satan as a threat was disturbing and not something a well-balanced boy would do.

Greg argued that this was exactly what any middle school boy would do. Esther retorted that this had always been the problem, that Greg was never willing to acknowledge any true problems with Joey—or with anything else for that matter—that he never took severe issues seriously. The fight had become heated, Esther scoring numerous verbal knockdowns. Greg had stormed from the house. And now here was Esther, alone in bed, Archie standing over her blade in hand.

Archie leaned closer to the unmoving form. So still. So lifeless. Had he attacked her? He couldn't have, and yet here he stood, clutching a knife. Closer, he looked, closer. She rolled, offered a subtle whimper. Startled, Archie stepped back. The knife handle was moist with sweat and yet it felt so very right in his hand. She was sleeping. He could do almost anything.

My God! What was he thinking?

Why was he even here?

Why hadn't he fled the room?

It was then that Archie remembered the sound of the crash. The sound which had drawn him forth from the white.

Cautiously, he moved to the window, pushing back the curtains. The family van, engine running, headlights bathing the house with a dull white glow, was pressed against the lawn's only tree.

He moved quickly now, to Joey's room, slipping into sweat pants and a T-shirt and depositing the hunting knife in its appropriate spot atop the comic book stack. He then descended the stairs and, opening the front door, strolled onto the lawn. The driver-side window was open. Greg sat behind the wheel, rocking from side to side. Head lulling in Archie's direction, he smiled. "Joey… Champ. I… had a few drinks."

"No kidding," said Archie wishing he could have joined the man.

"Never become a drunk, champ. Not worth it."

"Preachin' to the choir, Greg." Archie stepped forward, clasping the door handle. "Let's get you out of the van." He opened the driver-side door, reached in, and turned off the ignition. Archie grasped Greg's left hand and guided him out of the vehicle. The man's stance was wobbly, unsure. Fortunately, the van was only mildly dented. Greg would certainly endure a healthy tongue lashing from Esther, but the vehicle was still operable.

"I went six and ah haff yers, ya know. Six and ah haff yers! Then stuff started ta happin'."

Archie narrowed his eyes. He really didn't need this just now. There was too much happening for him to worry about Greg and his issues. But the man had been kind to him, he was in a caustic relationship, and Archie had had need of someone to come to his aid in similar circumstances. The least he could do was help the guy into the house. "There'll always be stuff that happens, Greg."

Greg shook his head violently. "Not this stuff! This stuff is big stuff. Stuff you don' know 'bout. Stuff you forgot after you… After your accident. Stuff I wish I could forget."

Archie's stomach took a rollercoaster dive. "What stuff? What did I forget?"

"See," said Greg triumphantly. "You don' remember."

"Remember what, Greg? What is it I should remember?" Archie had never considered that anything concerning Joey's life pertained to him, but something about Greg's tone—even through the haze of alcohol—caused him pause. He thought of only minutes before, standing naked before Esther, a knife in hand. What was that about? Certainly there was no connection, but knowing a bit more about significant incidents involving Joey couldn't hurt. He wasn't sure why, but this was an opportunity, while Greg's guard was AWOL.

"Things," said Greg. "Bad things. What you used ta do. What you wanted ta do. Oh! I shouldn' say tha'. Esther'll be really pissed."

There it was. Bad things Joey used to do. Could any of this be connected to him? "What things, Greg? Don't worry about Esther. Tell me what I need to know."

"Esther!" He said the name with such violence that Archie nearly stepped back. "You don' know anythin' 'bout Esther."

"Then tell me. What about Esther?"

Greg's expression went cold, his eyes focused on Archie. After several moments he moved his head first right and then left. "No, Joey. There are some things a boy should never know about his own mom." And then he pulled away to stagger toward the house.

"What about Joey?" called Archie. "What bad things did Joey do?"

Greg shook his head violently, nearly stumbled, and said without turning, "If you don' remember... Thas' best for all uh us." And he proceeded in a disjointed march toward the front door.

Chapter Twenty-Four

September 13

Seven year-old Niki Sullivan discovered Penelope's body just after break-fast. Penelope, the faithful beagle, only eight months old, and Niki's dearest friend in the world, was strangely absent when she woke. Niki didn't think much of it at the time. Sometimes Penelope needed to go out before she got up. Daddy would tend to the pup and Penelope would greet Niki when she came downstairs for breakfast.

But Penelope wasn't there.

Mommy didn't seem worried. Penelope had gotten out a couple of times before. She was a sneaky little pup and sometimes slid unseen through the doorway when someone was coming or going. On both previous occasions, she'd appeared in less than a quarter hour, prancing about and howling to be allowed inside.

After breakfast, Niki and her mother began searching. Daddy had already left for work and Niki's older brother had left with his friends for school.

Penelope was two lots north, swinging from a maple tree by a noose made of clothesline. There was an incision beginning at the base of the neck and extending down to between the rear legs. Most of Penelope's entrails lay on the dew-covered grass beneath.

Niki didn't go to school that day.

*****

September 26

Scott Doyle heard the sounds shortly after one a.m. At first, he was tempted to ignore them. Likely it had been nothing. He was half asleep and had to rise for work in just over four hours in order to arrive in the city on time for a seven a.m. sales meeting. The meetings were useless. The same thing every month. Rah, rah, rah. Sell, sell, sell. Have a doughnut and hit the floor with a smile and a goal. What a load of crap.

The sound had probably been the wind, he thought. It was whipping around pretty good out there. As well, it was raining and he was warm beneath the covers.

Scott closed his eyes, pulling the thick blankets closer about his form. He wasn't too jazzed. He'd be able to fall asleep.

There it was again.

That wasn't wind or rain. It sounded more like, what, an animal of some sort?

He was alert now, eyes wide, though it was on sound that he focused.

Two minutes passed.

Three.

Nothing. Perhaps he'd been hearing things after all.

Another minute, lethargy returned, creeping across his form, tantalizing his eyelids, demanding that they close.

There was a yelp. Loud. Distinct. No question this time. It sounded like an animal in pain.

With a grumble, he rose, snatching his red I.U. sweatshirt from the floor beside his bed, he slipped it over his head and plodded through the doorway and down the narrow staircase.

The sounds had ceased by the time he reached the bottom landing. Still, he snatched a baseball bat from a corner closet, and proceeded slowly through the house, turning on each light as he went.

The dog was on the driveway, just to the left of his black Kia Forte. It was a mangy thing, a stray mutt he supposed. Scott thought he might have seen it around the neighborhood a couple of times. Its throat was opened in a jagged tear, its blood still seeping onto the rain-drenched concrete. Its vacant eyes stared unblinking into the gentle rain.

*****

October 3

Brian Rizzo discovered three dead kittens on his back patio. Assaulted.

*****

October 9

Shirley Collins walked the three blocks home from The Village Pizzeria. She had worked the late shift for another waitress, Tara, and was tired and frustrated. It was a weeknight; the place was nearly empty save for John and Maria Gaines, a middle aged couple who wouldn't leave until the final credits rolled on their four decade old movie. Shirley regretted ever offering to change the channel away from ESPEN. They ate only an order of breadsticks, tipped a dollar thirty-seven, and asked for constant refills of sweet tea.

Shirley sensed more than heard the sound behind her. Perhaps she'd noticed the shadow in the streetlight; maybe she'd heard the shuffle of footfall but hadn't registered it as such.

She quickened her step.

Now she was certain. Someone was behind her. Close. Moving quickly. She turned, half expecting to see some hulking thug preparing to lunge.

No. Not a thug. Not some creature from the ridiculous horror films her younger brother watched. A boy. He was perhaps fifty feet back, partially obscured in shadow. Was he naked? There was something in his hand. It glinted in the artificial light.

And then he was gone, a shadow racing between buildings. By the time Shirley arrived home, she'd half convinced herself that it had all been an illusion.

By morning, she'd forgotten the incident altogether.

Chapter Twenty-Five

Archie sat in the school cafeteria. It had been six weeks since he'd awakened to find himself standing naked over Esther. He'd learned nothing more of Joey or of Esther. Greg's drunken rants had probably been just that, the ramblings of an inebriated mind. There had been no discernable white episodes, though he suspected several midnight forays into this unknown realm. From time to time there were still unexplained marks on his body, twice he'd found grass stuck to the bottoms of his feet, but nothing more dramatic. Maybe he sleepwalked a bit. If that was the worst of it, he could live with that.

He'd learned to plod through his classes with silent consistency, mostly ignoring the other students, taking notes, and answering as few of the teacher's questions as possible. There were still stares and whispers.

Archie and Bug had made an uneasy truce after Archie inquired as to why the boy had flung spit at the bully that first day of school. "He was ready to kick the snot outta you," said Bug. "And you're my friend." He hadn't said anything further about the cat. While Archie wouldn't seek Bug out, neither did he chase him away. Bug, an apparent outcast himself, was the only kid that really talked with Archie. That was fine by him.

The schoolwork was mostly easy. Archie was able to slip by with only minimal study time and ace all of his tests and quizzes. Though, he was surprised to find that they were teaching algebra to sixth graders. The algebra, remedial though it was, did require some study. It was basic, but math had never been Archie's thing and he remembered very little from his schooldays three decades gone.

Archie was beginning to embrace the idea of school. Colin had a point. If Archie was stuck in the body of a child and forced to attend school, why not treat it as an opportunity? With his four and a half decades of life experience, he had a focus that he could never have attained as a true youngster. It had never been that Archie was unintelligent; it was more that everything other than schoolwork was a priority. Archie simply couldn't be bothered with homework, though he'd read books on battleships, and sports, and dinosaurs all evening long. But here he had an opportunity to excel, to perhaps get a scholarship to the Art Institute or another prestigious university. He could forgo youthful folly and start setting the pieces in place for a successful career as a cartoonist even while in school.

Archie sat alone at a table toward the back southwest corner of the cafeteria, reading the Ephesus Gazette and sipping on a now-cold Starbucks coffee he'd purchased during his walk to school. Bug frequently teased Archie about his newspapers, stating that he could read the same boring crap online and not look like such a dork doing it. Archie simply smiled, claiming to be an old fashioned kind of guy.

Archie's coffee was cold, terrible really, but still he sipped it. Somehow, it gave him just a little sense of normality in his otherwise insane existence. He flipped a page, sipped again. This actually wasn't turning out to be a bad day.

Archie sensed, more than heard, the girl approach his table. He was engrossed in the comics section and didn't bother acknowledging her presence. Soon he heard the rustle of a lunch bag and a soft, cautious voice. "Is anyone sitting here?"

"Nope," he said, roughly flipping a page, attempting to send a non-verbal signal that he didn't want to be bothered.

"I'm new at the school," said the girl after she'd seated herself. "Um, what grade are you in?"

"Sixth."

"Oh," she said. "I kind of thought you were older."

Archie snorted an ironic chuckle. "Yeah, tell me about it."

"I'm in eighth," she said as she opened her lunch bag and began emptying the contents onto the table before her. Archie turned another page, still not lowering the paper or making eye contact. "Am I bothering you?" she asked, her voice perhaps a bit disappointed. "I can move. I mean, if you want."

Archie sighed. New kid in school. No friends yet. Why did she have to pick him? "No," he said. "You're not bothering me. I'm a fan of the Sunday funnies."

"Really? My dad used to love the Sunday funnies."

"Sounds like my kind of guy."

"Yeah. He'd just been picked up to draw his own strip like a couple years before he died."

Archie lowered the paper and looked into the eyes of his daughter.

Archie wasn't quite sure what he did first, drop the paper, scream her name, quiver uncontrollably. Truly, they were probably simultaneous. "Jill!" he said. "Jillie!"

Archie began to rise, as if to hug her, but sat back down almost before he'd begun. Tears tumbled across his cheeks. He didn't know what to do, what to say. He'd thought he'd lost her forever. She and her mother had been living further north, in Munster. Why was she here? Why was she in Ephesus?

The white sought to intrude.

"She's beautiful!" he cried. "My baby's beautiful."

Flitting about the periphery, darting up and then down. White.

Archie noticed something quite different about Jill. Not her hair, though it was longer and maybe a shade darker brown than before. Not the lengthening of her face, or the extra six inches in height. Not her hazel eyes—she'd gotten those from him, along with her narrow lips and slightly lopsided smile. "You're wearing a bra!" he screamed. "My baby's wearing a bra!"

Archie rose, nervous energy racing through his veins as laughter erupted from the next table over.

The white scampered across his vision, a multi-legged hole in his reality. Archie squinted, shaking his head.

"Are you alright?" asked Jill, her voice tentative. She'd set her apple down and looked as if she might flee.

Surely, Archie was frightening her, but he couldn't control himself. He began to hick and jerk; his body trembled, his vision faded about the edges as the white encroached, seeking to overcome his will.

"Somebody help!" screamed Jill. "Ohmygosh! He's having a seizure or something! Help!"

"No! Jill! No! I'm okay!"

Archie blinked, attempting to recover his vision, to stay with reality, to not slip away. He couldn't let it happen. Not with Jill so close. His right arm jerked, flopping out to the side. He worked his fingers, closing, opening, trying to maintain control. He had to maintain control.

"No, Jill, please!" he screamed as he reached out, across the table, grabbing her arm. Later, Archie thought he'd been trying to pull her into a hug, but he couldn't be sure of what had really happened. Images were cascading, flashes of Jill as she'd been when he'd seen her last, of Joey's bedroom, of the night he'd lost both Jill and Marcie. Of white. Pure colorless void—evil.

"Jill!" he screamed, wanting nothing more than to tell her who he was, how he'd missed her, how sorry he was for all he'd done.

"Help! Somebody help!" she hollered.

Archie pulled her closer, the table still a barrier between them. He stared into her face. She tried to pull away, but in his energized state Archie was much stronger than her, much stronger than he normally would have been.

"Help!" she screamed again. Surely a teacher would intervene, pulling Archie away, forever separating him from his Jill.

"No!" he said, placing a hand over her mouth, stifling her pleas. He couldn't allow her to alert anyone else. He needed to see her, to hug her, to love her the way a father should love his one precious daughter.

It was growing now, creeping from every angle, the nothingness that claimed him as its own. Archie sought to say something, but his voice would not comply. He had no control of his own actions.

Girls were screaming, boys yelling. He heard an adult's voice somewhere in the distance.

And that was when his entire world went white.

Chapter Twenty-Six

Car sales hours were long and relentless. If a guy was going to make money at it, he needed to be there when the customers were available. That meant working evenings and weekends. Archie frequently worked nine till nine and thus didn't see Marcie and Jill much. Marcie had been growing steadily distant. She didn't like that Archie habitually tossed a couple back at Jake's on the way home. She didn't like that he worked nearly every Saturday, missing most of Jill's soccer games. She didn't like that he sometimes came home frustrated and angry because of a lost deal, or that his paychecks ranged from almost wonderful to nearly nonexistent. She seemed only to remember the nearly nonexistent variety.

At some point, Archie supposed, he'd stopped caring about what Marcie thought. He was sure that at some level he still loved her, but he didn't think she really loved him, or even respected him. That made it hard for him to care for her in the way he should.

All he sought was a peaceful coexistence until Jill was grown. Then, he figured, Marcie and he would drift away from one another only meeting at weddings and funerals. He'd tried reconnecting, but Marcie's resentment was too deep. She had no interest in flowers or romantic getaway weekends. She had no interest in Archie or in his feeble attempts at making things right.

All she saw was a drunk who spent more time away than he did at home.

Well, maybe he wouldn't need to drink so much if Marcie was more responsive. Not that she'd ever accept that point of view.

He'd gotten off of work reasonably early on this particular Tuesday, six o'clock; and had only stayed at Jakes for one beer and a quick sketch. With luck, he'd be home almost in time for dinner. He'd see Jill while she was still awake, and he'd catch an hour or two of television before dozing off on the couch, heading to bed, and starting it all over again the following morning. It sounded like a nice Midwestern American evening. But when Archie pulled into the driveway and saw Marvin's car, he knew his plans of mid-week bliss would go unfulfilled.

It wasn't that Archie disliked his in-laws. Marvin Briggs and his wife Samantha were fine caring people. He got along with them as well, he supposed, as any guy gets along with his wife's parents after she's informed them that he's a good for nothing scoundrel. It was mostly that Archie just didn't want company that night. He had so little time with Jill and felt justified in being possessive. Marvin and Sam had been spending more and more time visiting with Marcie. Maybe she just wanted some adult conversation, and since Archie was rarely around, she sought this from her parents. But when Archie was home, and they were present, he somehow felt it was he, not them, that was the visitor.

Archie's relationship with Marvin had deteriorated over the years. At first Marvin had thought Archie clever and ambitious. But eventually this was downgraded to mildly offensive and lazy. Archie didn't think he'd ever been lazy. He'd always found a job, was always willing to pull whatever hours were required, work whatever overtime was offered, he just never stuck with one position long enough to climb the corporate ladder. After all, these jobs weren't his career, but simply a means by which to make money until he sold his strips.

Marvin was sitting on Archie's recliner when Archie arrived. He glanced at his watch and said, "Hello, Archie. I thought you were supposed to get off at six."

Archie opened the closet door, hung his jacket, and set his sketchpad on the shelf. "Yeah, I stopped for a beer on the way home."

Marvin nodded his slow contemplative nod. "I suppose a man's got to have his beer."

"Yeah," agreed Archie. "I suppose."

Archie excused himself, making his way to the kitchen where he found Marcie and Samantha. Nothing was on the stove, there was no aroma seeping from the oven. Even the microwave sat still and dormant. "Hey, Sam," he said to his mother-in-law. Then, turning to Marcie, he asked, "Where's Jill?"

"Upstairs," she said.

Archie nodded. "No dinner?"

Marcie didn't bother looking at him. She was folding a towel, keeping her hands busy. "We ate at five."

"Guess I'll have leftovers." He started toward the refrigerator. It was only seven-fifteen. They could have waited for him.

"There are none," she said. "I guess we were all pretty hungry." She re-folded the same towel.

"Yeah," he sighed. "I guess you were."

Archie heard Marvin's voice from behind. "Why don't you and I run out and grab a bite. Marcie hadn't expected company and hadn't fixed that much. I could use a little more myself."

"Yeah, okay," Archie said after a pause. "Just let me run upstairs and say hi to Jill before we go." He turned, offered Marcie a meaningful glare, and marched from the room. She folded the towel a third time.

Archie was angry. Marcie had known this was one of his few early nights home, knew that at the very least he'd want some leftovers, and ideally that they could hold off an extra hour or so and let him eat dinner with them. Five o'clock. Marcie never had dinner done by five o'clock.

He marched up the stairs, attempting to calm himself before knocking on Jill's door. She was twelve now, and liked her privacy. "Hey, Jillie-bean, it's me."

"Come in," she said in a too-grown-up voice.

Archie strolled in. She was sitting on her bed, staring out of the window at her own reflection. Her hair was in a ponytail and she had a gaggle of little dolls sitting next to her on the bed. Beside that, her room looked remarkably clean and neat. "What are you doing?" he asked.

"Nothing."

"You cleaned your room."

"Yeah. Mom made me."

"You did a good job of it."

"Thanks."

Archie stepped forward and sat beside her on the bed. "How was school?" he asked.

She shrugged. "Boring."

This was the standard answer to the standard question. "Huh. I never would have thought. Any homework?"

"Nope. Already done." Her voice was soft, almost a whisper. She sat fiddling with a doll in her hands, not looking at Archie.

He patted her head playfully. "Good girl." He paused for a moment, just looking at her, at how she'd grown, at her glistening eyes and freckled nose, at the new grown-up tooth forcing its way up through her bottom gum. "Hey," he said. "Your grandpa and I are going to grab a bite. You want to come with?"

She hesitated, dropped her head. "No," she said.

"Why not?" he asked. "It's early. Maybe you could get some ice cream." Archie knew ice cream would seal the deal. Jill never refused ice cream.

"I can't," she said.

This was a surprise. "Why not?"

"Homework."

Archie cocked his head. "You said you were done with your homework."

She paused. "I forgot to study my spelling words."

"Okay," he said, conceding defeat. There was probably some critical television show that came on at seven-thirty or eight. "Well, I'll try not to be gone too long," he said. "We'll still have some time together this evening." Archie ruffled her hair again, and rose to leave.

"Daddy?" she said.

"Yes, Jillie-bean."

She stood up and gave him a tight bear hug. He didn't get many of these from her these days. It was sweet.

*****

Archie and Marvin went to Schoop's Hamburgers, a mostly regional chain that likely served the best burgers on the planet. Filled with taste and grease, the burgers were huge, the meat extending beyond the ample bun, and the patty being about an inch and a half thick at the center. Archie joked that they should serve them with a side of defibrillator. Jukebox tunes lilted about the room over the sounds of sizzling burgers and clattering plates. Two waitresses leaned against the counter complaining about some guy named Hugh and a two year-old raced up and down the aisle, easily avoiding his father's frantic grasp, and giggling at every attempt. Archie and Marvin talked about nothing: the Bears, the Bulls, the weather. Jill was a safe subject, her grades and her soccer. Marcie, though, was off limits.

"So, what are your goals, Archie?" asked Marvin at one point.

Archie took a sip of his shake—a real shake with real ice cream, not the synthetic fast-food variety—and shrugged. "What do you mean?"

Marvin gazed at Archie, his deep blue eyes focused on him from below thick, arched brows. "Goals, Archie. Surely, you know what goals are." Sometimes Marvin could be condescending.

"Yeah, I know what they are. I just wondered what you meant by the question. My career goals, family goals, personal goals?" Archie took a hefty bite of his burger, relish and onion spilled from the backside.

Marvin chuckled a humorless chuckle. "It wasn't meant to be a deep question, son. Do you really have that many different goals, or are you just biding time?"

"Biding time," Archie said with a chuckle and a pause. "Same goal as always. I'm still trying to sell a comic strip to a syndicate. I have a new one called Gilly Baskerville. I think I could actually hit big with this one."

Marvin's eyes were large, empathetic. The blue orbs, deep and moist, studied Archie for a moment. At first Archie thought he read judgment in them, but later thought it may have been sorrow. "Do you really believe that, Archie? Do you really think you have what it takes to break into that line of work?"

Now it was Archie's turn to study him. Marvin's face was lined, his mouth expressionless. His large hands were folded before him, his barely-touched burger and fries having been pushed off to the side five minutes earlier. "I need to believe it, Marvin. If I never make a go of it with my toons, then who am I? I've been pursuing this for over twenty years now."

"And that's how you see yourself? As a failed cartoonist?" His tone was quiet, warm, almost intimidating. It seemed he really wanted to know how Archie saw himself.

Archie didn't respond to his question. There was no need.

Marvin sighed and dabbed the corners of his mouth with a crumpled napkin. In the background, John Mellencamp sang about little pink houses. "Archie, you've had the role of a husband, of a father. You've got a beautiful little girl, and all that matters to you is selling jokes with pictures?" He set the napkin aside and waved off Archie's stammered attempt at a response. "Don't get me wrong. I understand your desire to succeed in this one particular arena. We're men. We define ourselves by professional success and failure. That said: if you're going to pursue this thing, then pursue it with vigor. You need to fight for your chance."

"And my family?" asked Archie after taking one last bite of his too-large burger. "I thought you were going to tell me to stop wasting my time on cartooning and spend all the time I can with Jill and Marcie."

Marvin picked up his napkin again, dabbed his lips. "Spend what time you can with Jill. Try to be some kind of father. But aside from that, make something out of the rest of your life."

*****

Marvin was generally quiet on the way home. Traffic was sparse. They caught mostly green lights. He sat behind the wheel, contemplative and solemn, neither offering new conversation, nor encouraging any from Archie. He had the radio tuned to a talk station. It droned on and on in the background, neither enlightening nor entertaining. It seemed Marvin was nearly worn out. Up until that night, Archie had admired the man greatly. Marvin had always seemed wise and fair. Despite Archie's struggles, Marvin had still treated him as a man, as an equal, someone whose opinion he sought, whose company he welcomed. But that was prior to this night. Afterward, Archie would despise him with all of his being.

They pulled into Archie's driveway. The house was dark, not even the porch light shining. The family car was gone, in its place, only a couple of half-dried oil spots. Marvin threw his Caddy into park, but left the engine running.

"Huh?" said Archie. "I wonder where Marcie went."

Marvin opened the driver-side door as if to get out of the car. Archie followed suit, stepping out onto the driveway, staring at the strangely dark house.

"Maybe she had to run to the store," offered Marvin from his seat.

"Yeah, maybe," Archie said as he moved around Marvin's car and up the drive toward the front door. "But I don't know why all of the lights would be out. Even if Marcie ran out for something, Sam and Jill should still be here."

Archie heard the car door slam, the engine rev. Marvin nearly peeled rubber in his Coup Deville as he slammed the car into reverse, and bolted into the street, leaving his son-in-law gaping and alone.

Archie's stomach almost rejected his dinner as he watched Marvin's tail lights diminish in the distance. He knew. He knew right then, standing alone in his driveway what had just happened. Still, like a car crash on the highway, he had to see for himself. It took him a few moments to work up the courage to approach the porch, to pull his keys from his pocket, to unlock the door. Archie flicked on the lights. Everything seemed so normal. The television still sat on its stand beside the pressboard shelving unit. The TV Guide was open on the coffee table beside issues of Sports Illustrated and Newsweek. His brown vinyl recliner sat upright, waiting for Archie to plop into it, beer in hand. The smell of Glade air freshener still tickled at his nostrils. The carpeting was still stained with grape juice just behind the couch where Jill had had an accident. This was home. This was where Archie belonged, where Marcie belonged, where Jill belonged.

Archie turned left, strolled over to the dining room table. This was where he and Marcie left notes for one another when they were out. It was there, of course—the note. As was one from Creators Syndicate. It was a letter of acceptance. Archie had sold his Gilly Baskerville strip. But, Archie wouldn't read that until the next morning. It was Marcie's note that mattered now. Archie didn't know what he'd expected. Maybe some sort of explanation. But he supposed there really was no need of one. They both knew the issues. There was no point in rehashing them yet again. Still, she could have said something more than this. She could have apologized for the way she'd done it. She could have given him a phone number, assured him that he'd still have access to Jill.

Archie stared at the plain white piece of paper on the Formica tabletop. It wasn't even hand written. It'd been done on the computer.

Archie,

We've left.

Marcie

That was it. So simple. So direct. Like a ninja's blade to the aorta.

The tears came slowly at first, as did the anger. Archie snatched the offending paper; holding it in his hand. He read it, reread it. Though there really wasn't much to read.

He let it drop, not crumpling it, not tearing it to shreds. He simply let go, allowing it to float lazily to the floor as Archie raced across the room and bound up the stairs. He knew what he would find, but had to check, had to see for himself.

Archie didn't knock this time. He knew there was no one to bid him entrance. He simply flung the door open. "Jill!" he screamed. "Jillie-bean!"

The room was empty. The furniture was still there, yes. But the heart of the room was gone. Jill was gone. Archie scanned the shelves. They were still lined with plush, fluffy faces, but her favorite stuffed animals were missing, the ones that mattered, the ones she'd named and cherished. Her favorite outfits were not in the closet, the remaining clothes were ones she'd outgrown or hated from the get go.

Her bed was made.

Jillie's bed was never made. It was almost a final insult, dirt on the top of a lowered coffin. The room screamed, *"Jill does not live here any more!"*

"You took my daughter!" screamed Archie to the uncaring walls. "Marcie, baby, you took my daughter!" He collapsed onto the bed, weeping, cradling his aching belly in his own trembling forearms; rocking himself, twitching, shuddering. "You took my daughter!" It was nearly four hours before he finally staggered, weak, and entirely spent, from the room.

Chapter Twenty-Seven

Archie wasn't transported to a mall this time. He didn't find himself at the Sears Tower or in a raging river. He was on Market Street in Ephesus, outside of the old movie theater-turned-pizza parlor. The breeze was cool, the air fresh with the smell of rain. The sun glinted down from between parting clouds causing him to shade his eyes with his hand. A dog yapped from somewhere down the street and birds chirped and chattered as they stabbed at worms on the puddled grass. The wheel within the wheel was there. Not hiding this time. Just watching, observing. It hovered just two doors distant, in front of the Market Street Pet Shoppe. It pulsed and throbbed, enlarged and then deflated. It seemed a living thing, monstrous, yet somehow intimidated. Archie screamed at it, told it that he needed to get back, to see his daughter, that it couldn't hold him, that it couldn't keep jerking him away from his life. But the wheel within the wheel remained silent, hovering, pulsing, never heeding his voice.

Still reeling from the shock of seeing Jill, Archie forgot to be afraid. He stepped forward, toward the gently rotating wheel, the outer rim spinning clockwise, the inner, counterclockwise. "What are you?" he screamed. "What do you want from me?"

The emerald ring flared bright, but retreated perhaps seven feet, its many eyes blinking independently of one another, darting in every direction with no sense of coordinated movement. *Joey!* It said. As before, the voice was not a voice, but rather, more of an all-encompassing vibration or sensation. Archie felt it course down his spine, race through his arms and legs to his furthermost digits. His face tingled with a static surge. Salvia evaporated from his mouth like a spilled drink under an August sun.

"I'm not Joey," said Archie, taking another tentative step forward. An elderly man was riding an orange Huffy bicycle down the sidewalk; he veered left around the pulsing wheel, and then slid in front of Archie, passing on his right, without notice of the strange occurrences on this normally docile Midwestern street.

The wheel flared bright. Archie felt a radiant heat. *JOEY!*

"I'm not Joey," he said again, his dry throat raspy and weak. "Joey's gone. He's dead. Joey's dead."

JOEY! It screamed. The heat intensified, causing Archie to shield his face. He felt something akin to sunburn on his brow as the thing pulsed and radiated. *JOEY!* it screamed one last time.

And then it was gone.

And Archie was gone.

*****

Archie felt the jolt against his back; saw the hard lunchroom floor rushing before his eyes with just enough time to stick out his right arm and attempt to break the fall. He landed with a jar, the impact knocking the wind from his youthful lungs. There were shouts, commotion, girls screaming, boys hooting. Archie thought he may have heard Jill crying in the background. He'd been tackled. His assailant was on top of him, holding him down. Archie scrambled, trying to role over, to see who had attacked him. It took him a moment, but the guy's grip seemed to lessen slightly, just enough for Archie to spin onto his back and stare into the face of his assailant, but not enough for him to break free or to fight back.

It was Bug. He sat on Archie's belly, straddling him, peering into his eyes, his expression dark and humorless. "Bug? What are you…"

"Shut up, Burke," he hissed as his brown eyes darted from side to side. "How many times am I gonna have to save your ass from doing somethin' really stupid?"

Archie blinked, still clearing his vision. In a matter of moments he'd gone from seeing Jill in the school cafeteria, to confronting the mysterious floating wheel on the streets of Ephesus, to being attacked by Joey's only friend. "What are you talking about?" he asked, still trying to catch his breath.

Bug's eyes narrowed. "Never mind," he said, his voice nearly harsh. "It's nothing you need to remember."

"But…"

"Shut up!" he screamed, giving Archie no option but to comply.

The clamoring kids hushed. All grew still, save for a few muffled giggles and gasps. Archie glanced up and to his right, seeing a pair of black wing-tipped shoes marching steadily in his direction. Mr. George Lang, the principal, had arrived.

*****

Archie sat in Joey's bed. It was late evening. The curtains were drawn, the wind *wooing* between the Burke's home and the next house over. He was in his bedclothes, an old Brookfield Zoo T-shirt and baggy gym shorts. Archie would have given anything for a beer right then. Or a vodka, gin, anything to dull the internal torment.

There was a soft knock at the door. "Hey, Champ. Can I come in?"

It was Greg. "Sure," said Archie. "Why not?"

Greg entered, closing the door behind him. He had sawdust in his hair and on his clothes and a Band-Aid bandage on his left thumb. "Your mother's downstairs," he said. "You've got her worried. I convinced her to let me talk with you. You know, man-to-man. But we both know she'll be up here any minute."

Archie nodded. He wasn't looking forward to the encounter with Esther.

Greg strolled across the room and seated himself beside Archie on the bed. "I talked with Dr. Lambert after you left his office today. He assured me you hadn't had a seizure, but he wants to see you again tomorrow."

"Sure, I'll see him," said Archie. "Why not?"

Colin had run some basic tests, no MRI or SPECT scans though. Archie got the impression he was baffled, concerned, but didn't want his son to know this. In their few minutes alone, Archie described the wheel, what it looked like, how it behaved, the sensations he'd felt as it spoke. Colin had passed it off as hallucinatory, but his disjointed verbiage and averted glances told Archie that Colin wasn't quite so sure. Maybe this was because they were confronted by something completely outside the realm of conventional science. Floating, multi-eyed, talking wheels aren't the stuff of respectable neurology. Therefore, in Colin's eyes, they simply must not exist.

171

Greg readjusted himself on the bed and contemplated his dusty Adidas tennis shoes. "So, what really happened at school today? I mean, there's got to be a better way to get a girl's attention." Greg offered a feeble smile. He was trying.

"Didn't Colin tell you what happened?" asked Archie. He wanted to make sure he didn't contradict anything Colin had said by way of explanation.

Greg nodded, meeting Archie's gaze with sad green eyes. "Yeah, he did. But I want to hear my son's version."

Archie shuffled uncomfortably. He couldn't stop himself from seeing Jill's beautiful face in his mind, how she'd grown, how radiant she looked—how horrified she'd been as he'd assaulted her. "I remembered her from before the accident," he said. "I lost my head, overreacted. End of story."

Greg offered a weak grin and gazed down at his folded hands. "Yeah, about that: the principal said this girl didn't remember you. She's just moved into town from Munster. Even if you'd met before, you couldn't have known her well. Why would she be the only person you recognize from before the accident?"

Archie shook his head, attempting to seem as bewildered as he should have been. "I don't know," he said. "She's just a kid. She started asking me questions, and all of a sudden, I don't know, she seemed familiar, like I might know her. I guess I just lost control." It sounded weak, he knew. But it was all he could come up with. Truly, he needed to stay as vague as possible. The whole incident was prompting questions, drawing attention to him, to Jill. The last thing he needed was to light a blow torch and illuminate the whole body of inconsistencies before them.

*****

Archie's world went white, but only for a moment.

He was in the same room. But not the same room. It was different. It belonged to a younger boy, to someone much further away from the threshold of puberty. A poster of Big Bird hung on the baby blue wall. A birdhouse shaped like a balding clown hung above the closet door. There was no C.D. player, no computer. Spider-Man and Batman action figures littered the floor. A baseball bat leaned in a corner.

Greg was sitting on the bed, just as he'd been. But it was a different Greg. Younger. His hair was longer, redder. There were no hints of gray forcing their way into his now full beard. His eyes glistened with a vibrancy Archie had yet to witness in the man. He said, "It'll be alright. I'll build you a new one." But Archie couldn't make out who he was talking to; only that there was a faint green glow on Greg's round red cheeks.

*****

Archie was back again. To his version of Joey's room. He blinked, clearing his vision. Greg still sat beside him on the bed, looking down on him, the beginnings of crow's feet in the corners of his eyes, scattered gray hairs intermingled with the reddish brown stubble on his chin. Archie wondered how much of the man's aging had been a result of the passage of time and how much had come about due to the stress of the past several months. He thought of Greg's cryptic comments that night he'd come home drunk, of mysteries concerning both Esther and Joey. And for the first time he wondered what struggles this gentle man faced and how the weight of life's horrors must crush down upon him. He was so quiet. And secretive. Archie had never really thought of this before, but the man held things close to his chest. Something was there. Some event, some mystery or misfortune. There was more to Greg than Archie had previously grasped. In that moment Archie wished they could sit together over a couple of cold ones and bare their souls. It could never happen, of course, but Archie felt a new wave of guilt where Greg was concerned. This man did not deserve the lot he'd been given.

*****

White again.

Young Joey's room.

Greg paces. He apologizes for something. His speech is slurred.

*****

And then it was over. Archie shook his head, disoriented, confused. His muscles ached. He didn't know if it was from the body slam Bug had given him earlier, or if it was the result of the tension of slipping from one reality to another. Greg caught his eye. There was concern on his face. "Joey, are you alright?" he asked. "What just happened?"

Archie shuddered and blinked, gazing about the room, at the Slipknot poster, at the electric guitar sitting where a baseball bat had once leaned. Big Bird was no where to be seen, Spider-Man and Batman had fled the scene of the crime. Archie clutched the sides of his twin mattress, attempting to hold on to this present reality.

"Joey. Are you alright?" Greg asked again, his tone more urgent yet.

Archie thought he might have nodded, but continued to clutch the mattress.

"Listen, Joey," said Greg, his voice tight, nervous even. "You're my son—my boy. Nothing in this world will ever change that. No matter what happened between us in the past, no matter what you've been into, we're bound together. You got that? No matter what you may have done in the past—or have been planning to do—you are not bad. None of this is your fault. You must remember that. We've had this kind of conversation before, but you never wanted to listen. I'm hoping that's different now."

Archie didn't respond, but simply stared at him, thinking of his own relationship with Jill, and of how Joey's relationship must have been with Greg before the accident.

"Don't shut me out again, Champ," continued Greg. "The past is the past. You have a new start. I'm trying to help you. But you're... different now. I'm trying to understand exactly how and why. I need to know how I can help you better."

"Why don't you go on another binge?" said Archie in sudden fierceness. "That's what I'd do. Life always seems a little clearer with a few brewskis in the belly." Archie didn't know why he'd lashed out at Greg. Hadn't he just lamented that he couldn't share his troubles with this man, hadn't he—at least for a moment—seen him as a kindred spirit? And, Lord knows, Archie didn't have any room to talk where alcohol was concerned. Maybe he was really chiding himself through this attack on Greg. Or, perhaps it was just his way of avoiding the real issues at hand, of derailing the conversation. Whatever his reasoning, Archie had been cruel, uncaring. He could tell the words struck Greg like harpoons in a whale's hide.

Greg dropped his head, bit his lower lip. "Not fair, Champ. My drinking days are long past. This last thing; that was just one unfortunate slip."

"Yeah, Greg," said Archie, continuing with the attack almost against his will. "But how do you know when it's just one unfortunate slip too many? You never know just how far you can take it before your wife decides that enough is enough."

Greg stared at the man he believed to be his boy, his light green eyes searching something beyond the realm of the seen. "My wife? Your mother? You bring her into this? After what happened? I hope you never have to…" He paused, fought back tears, fidgeted with his bandaged finger. "Forget it. We're not going there. Just be better and know that I'm doing what I can to protect you." With that, Greg ruffled Archie's hair and strode silently toward the doorway. Pausing, he turned. "Is your amnesia really complete, or are there memories you're hiding from us? You can trust me, Champ. I'll keep your secret from your mother."

"I remember nothing."

Greg studied Archie for a long moment before nodding and exiting the room.

Chapter Twenty-Eight

Archie sat on Joey's bed, holding the phone in one hand and Diana Mortonson's business card in the other, his fingers trembling. It was nearing midnight, but she'd written her cell phone number on the card, and could be reached at any time. Archie didn't want to call her, surely didn't feel that he could trust her, but he needed to talk with someone other than Colin. It wasn't so much a matter of trust. He believed Colin had Archie's best interest in mind. But Colin was part of the problem. He was baffled by the more inexplicable aspects of Archie's experience such as the wheel and the incredible tangible aspects of his inner mind experiences. Archie needed unbiased ears, a medical mind free of preconceptions.

In his life as Archie, he'd been a loner, but a very social loner. This may seem contradictory, but it was the case nonetheless. Archie had surrounded himself with people: his wife and daughter, his buddies at the bar, his coworkers. They shared jokes and drinks, stories of their pasts. But that was as deep as it went. No one, not even Marcie, was allowed into the inner-sanctum of Archie Lambert's heart. He walked alone through a life filled with friends and family, never revealing his deeper struggles and failures for fear of the rejection that would certainly follow should anyone glimpse the blackness at the center of his being. He'd longed to share his struggles, his failures, his lapses, with Marcie, but he didn't trust her to understand, and feared he might have lost Jill years sooner. Archie often thought of bringing his failures to Curly Jake, of asking him to cut him off at two beers. Obviously, Archie was well beyond bringing himself under control without the aid of another. But Jake, as he'd recently proven, was not a true friend. Perhaps Archie had sensed this all along and thus avoided Jake's inclusion in his misery. Archie had even considered confessing to Marvin, his father in-law. Archie had felt a near kinship with the man, at least, until Marvin had betrayed him. But, again, Archie had remained silent. Likely because, at his core, he really didn't want anyone hindering his excess. It was his life, his problem, his decline. Why should loved ones be granted a voice in his personal destruction? In the end, Archie hadn't even shared the fact of his cancer with friends or family. He still wasn't sure how Colin had learned of it. Most likely, Archie's oncologist had realized that Archie was the son of a colleague and notified Colin. Ephesus wasn't that big after all.

This burden, though, Archie needed to share. He'd revealed much of it to J.T. Roswell, but the man had rejected it outright. But, Diana Mortonson. She would believe. She wanted to believe. She'd practically begged Archie to tell her his secret. But Mortonson wasn't impartial. She was a researcher at the clinic, maybe a rival of Colin's. She was someone who could just as easily cause more complications as she could less.

Still, who else to call?

Archie stared at the phone. He thought of the wheel, of Bug's cat, of the mornings he'd awakened dirty and naked, of how close he may have come to actually hurting Jill. He looked at Mortonson's cell number printed neatly on the back of the card in sharply angled black letters, and began punching out the seven digits, focusing on each tone as the buttons were depressed. Her phone rang, once, twice, on the third ring she answered. Her voice was soft, groggy, but not that of someone just wakened from a deep sleep.

"Hello?" she said. "Joey, is that you?"

Caller I.D., thought Archie. But, for some reason he couldn't bring himself to speak.

"Joey, are you there?" Her tone, as usual, was professional, yet she sounded slightly anxious.

Archie pulled the phone away from his ear, prepared to hang up, and then pulled it closer once again. He couldn't decide what to do. This reminded him of the first time he'd called a girl for a date. Maggie Hershey. Archie had called when he'd thought she'd be away, hoping for a kind of trial run, to leave a message with her parents, thinking that this way she'd know he'd called and maybe call him back, relieving Archie of some of the burden. She'd answered after only one ring. Archie had stuttered a couple of unintelligible words, and then hung up. He never went out with Maggie Hershey.

"Joey, say something. I know you're listening. I can help you, Joey. Please let me help you."

Suddenly, there was a sharp rap from behind.

Startled, Archie dropped the phone. He could still hear Mortonson's voice, raising in pitch and volume, but no longer cared that she was speaking.

There was a shape, a form, at the window. How could that be? He was on the second floor. Had the wheel somehow followed him into this reality? Was it just beyond the pane, hovering, waiting, seeking a way in? He went cold. Its pulsating vibrations could shatter the thin membrane of glass. It would chase him down, engulf him. If it had followed him this far, there was nowhere else to run.

Another rap.

Soft, yet urgent. A face pressed against the glass.

"Bug?"

Archie snatched the phone from the floor and disconnected without uttering a word to Mortonson. Surely, his mysterious midnight call would prompt yet another of her visits, but he'd worry about that later. Right then, he had to worry about getting a sixth-grader in through his bedroom window before Greg and Esther woke up to the commotion. Archie crossed the room in four easy strides, unlatched the latch, and lifted the window.

"'Bout time," Bug said with an annoyed pout. "Whatcha doin' on the phone this late?"

"What are you doing at my window this late?" countered Archie. And then, "How did you get up here?"

Bug shrugged and grinned, revealing his missing tooth just to the left of center. "Easy. Your bedroom's right above the patio. I just climbed up the trellis and onto the patio roof."

"And why?" prodded Archie.

"Duh!" said Bug. "We need to talk 'bout what happened today." His tone made it clear that there would be no arguments.

*****

Archie and Bug walked along a rust and iron train trestle that stretched over Plummer's Creek, the little gurgling stream located several blocks south of Joey's home. Fallen leaves crunched beneath their feet and the not-so-fresh smell of the Creek tickled their nostrils. The autumn air was cool and bit through Archie's red, hooded, Indiana University sweatshirt. Bug, in his army jacket and with a pet rat hitching a ride on his shoulder, seemed oblivious to the chill. He was more concerned with getting his questions answered.

He wanted to know who that girl had been, why Archie had gone ballistic on her. He pressed Archie again on what he remembered from before the accident. Bug wanted to know what he'd told the doctor, what he'd told Joey's parents about his memories. He couldn't understand why Archie was so different now.

And then, without thinking it through, for no good reason other than the fact that Bug was there and Archie needed to relieve his burden, Archie told him.

Everything.

Colin, the infusion, the strange floating wheel. Everything.

It was a stupid thing to do, but Archie was desperate. And the more he thought about it, the more it made sense. If Bug chose to break confidence, no adult would believe a twelve year-old with a preposterous story. Archie could tell Bug anything he wanted to tell him, there was no risk of him taking it to the media, or notifying medical boards and getting Colin's license revoked. There was very little Bug could do to harm him. Just as J.T. Roswell had scoffed at Archie's claims, likewise would any adult Bug should approach.

But the relief.

The relief was real. The sharing of a burden, the passing of a load from one person to another—incredible.

Of course Bug was skeptical. He was twelve—and he now had green hair and a rat on his shoulder—but that didn't make him stupid. Still, childhood is that miraculous time of life when the unbelievable is not quite so unbelievable, when the fantastic seems just a grasp away, where spaceships do fly from distant planets, where ghosts do haunt abandoned houses, where super heroes might just soar the noontime sky if only someone would care to look. Childhood is a time when a person may know what is real and what is imagined, but is not yet so jaded as to stop wishing that something just a little extraordinary could actually smack down in the middle of every day existence.

"Okay," Bug said with a knowing smirk. "So, this doctor takes some guy who's dying, and zaps his brain into your body?"

"Not the brain," Archie corrected. "The essence, the memories—the soul."

Bug rolled his eyes. "Come on, Burke. I'm not a kid, you know."

Archie grinned, seating himself on the edge of the trestle, his feet dangling over the Creek below. "Bug, am I the Joey you knew before?"

"In your dreams."

"Exactly. I'm the guy—Archie."

Bug squinted. "Yeah? So, where's Joey?"

Archie gazed at the peculiar boy. The kid deserved the truth. "Dead," he said.

Archie could tell the word stung him. Bug started—almost as if he'd been smacked in the face—and then remained silent for several moments, staring out into the darkened woods. A crow cawed, and the sound of a distant eighteen wheeler sliced through the tranquility. "No," said Bug in a voice so tiny as to be nonexistent.

"What?" asked Archie.

"No," he repeated. "Joey can't be dead. He lived. They brought him back."

Archie shook his head slowly, hating this, the bearing of horrible truth. He already carried a guilt that weighed on him, he loathed to pick at the scab and expose it anew. "He was brain dead, Bug. Machines kept his body alive, but nothing of who he was remained."

"No," he said a third time. "Joey's alive—you're alive."

Archie placed his palm on Bug's back. "I'm alive. But I'm not Joey."

A tear raced down the boy's cheek. He quickly whisked it away. Bug was a tough. He'd not allow this sign of weakness. "How do you know he's dead?" he asked. "I mean, like, where did he go? Did he evaporate, go to paradise? Is he still inside of you? Why did you have those, I dunno, flashbacks, inner-mind trips, whatever they were?"

"No idea. I'm just some poor creep that got a lucky break."

Bug picked up a rock and lobbed it into the Creek below. It entered with a garbled *plunk!* "He was my best friend, ya know. I mean all the way back to kindergarten."

Archie nodded, remaining silent. It was Bug's turn to unload.

"We had some bad fights. Especially the last few months. You know, before he drowned. He was, I dunno, changing. But we were still, you know…"

"Yeah. I know."

"Man!" Bug exploded, slamming his palm down on a wooden train tie. "Is there anything else I need to know?" His voice was harsh, accusatory.

Archie met his gaze. "Well, yeah. But I don't think you're going to want to hear it."

Bug eyed him. His dark eyes intense beneath his new lime green hair. "I can handle it."

"Well, that girl, the one in the lunch room."

"Yeah?"

"My daughter."

Bug shook his head. "Leave me alone, Burke. Just leave me alone."

Chapter Twenty-Nine

October 30

Eight year-old Carrie Turner had never been out so late before. Her bed-time was eight PM, eight-thirty at the latest on a weeknight. Some weekends she'd stayed up as late as ten, but this was really late. It was past midnight, a time she'd heard of but had never before experienced. This was the time, she knew, when ghosts walked the graveyards and witches stirred mystical potions in big black caldrons. This was the time that adults didn't want kids to know about. Because they thought kids didn't understand such things. But, kids knew. They knew all about the things of the night.

Carrie's family lived in a two story Tudor only a block from Plummer's Creek. She walked along the muddy riverbed calling after her dog, Hermione. The two year-old border collie had escaped before, each time running directly to the creek where she'd dive in and return home smelling rank and dripping river water onto her parent's precious carpet. Carrie's father had announced that if Hermione did this again, he'd take her to the pound and let someone else deal with her mess.

Carrie had awakened to the sound of Hermione nudging the patio door open and slipping out into the night. Somehow the clever creature had figured out how to get past the lock on the flimsy door.

Carrie had to find her pet before she jumped into the river. And if she was too late, well, she'd bathe Hermione herself. She'd seen it done. It couldn't be that hard. Her dad would never need to know.

"Hermione!" called Carrie, though not too loudly. She couldn't risk wak-ing someone in a nearby house. The area was wooded, but not densely so. And besides, she didn't want to alert any ghosts or witches. It was the day before Halloween. Surely they were out looking for victims.

"Hermione!" she called again.

She moved further, frequently glancing through the trees toward the three-quarter full moon half expecting to see the silhouette of a witch passing before the giant orb. Wasn't the moon always supposed to be full on Halloween? It was in the movies. But it wasn't quite Halloween. She was certain it would be full tomorrow.

There was a snap from behind. The sound of a twig breaking underfoot. "Hermione?" she asked. Certainly it was the dog. Ghosts and witches didn't make sounds when they approached.

There was no reply.

Suddenly frightened, she quickened her pace. "Hermione! Hermione, come here, girl." Her summons was nearly a plea.

There was another sound, a subtle slosh in the river. Carrie glanced over her shoulder. Nothing. It was too dark. Even in the moonlight, there were too many shadows. Suddenly, she wished that her dad was with her. A daddy was a good thing to have when frightened.

"Hermione! Please!" she called.

No response.

She moved further up the riverbed, still calling for her dog. After a couple of minutes, she began to calm down. Her palms weren't quite so sweaty, her breathing not so quick. There were no witches in these woods. That was silly. These were barely woods at all. A witch would find a big woods and a big river. They wouldn't bother with this puny place.

Rounding a subtle bend, Carrie noticed a shape just ahead, at the edge of the water. It was kind of a lumpy thing. At first she thought someone had left a big trash bag beside the creek. Her third grade teacher, Miss Barton, would have a fit if she heard about this. She was always talking about recycling and littering.

Coming closer now, Carrie realized that it was no trash bag.

Her stomach took a hollow dive into her bowels. Her hands quivered, even before she'd identified the still form before her.

"No." the word was no more than a choked whisper. "Hermione, no."

Tears spread across her tiny cheeks.

Hermione's vacant eyes gazed sightlessly toward Carrie, the dog's head hung at a strange angle, there was a large slash at the neck from which blood dripped into the murky green water.

"No."

Carrie didn't know what to do. Move toward her pet, run away, scream? She wanted her mommy. She wanted her daddy. There were witches here. Mean witches. Evil witches. Probably from Slytherin.

Now there were footsteps from behind. Close. Nearly upon her. Why hadn't she noticed them before? Turning, she said, "Daddy?" for surely her daddy would know that she was frightened.

It was not Daddy.

It was a boy. Older than Carrie, but still a boy.

He wore no clothes.

Carrie almost giggled at this, but she was frightened and angry and sad.

The boy did not smile. He did not try to hide his nakedness. He stepped forward, a strange look in his narrow eyes.

It wasn't until he was nearly upon her that Carrie noticed the knife. There was blood on the blade. She knew that she should run, that she should scream, but her legs would not obey and her voice was suddenly quiet. Carrie's last thought was that a spell had been cast. Witches did that, cast spells on their victims so they couldn't run away or call for help.

Carrie and Hermione's bodies would not be found for nearly two months. The grave, though shallow, was well hidden beneath brush. Dead fish from the river were placed over the bodies to mask the smell from search dogs. A nearby fallen Maple, not fully mature, but still over twelve feet in length, was shifted over the spot. The grave was not obvious.

Chapter Thirty

Black and orange crape paper steamers arced across the gymnasium walls. Similarly-colored helium-filled balloons, anchored to chairs and tables by colorful ribbons, drifted subtly from side to side as chattering youngsters moved about, munching on iced cookies and red punch. But today they weren't kids. Today they were vampires, ballerinas, princesses, hobos, and super heroes. It was the annual Halloween dance at Rutherford B. Hayes Middle School. Though, why they called it a dance was entirely suspect. For the most part, the boys congregated on the west side of the room, the girls on the east. Only a need for sugar and drink would cause a boy to venture into neutral territory, and then only for a quick snatch of food and a drink.

A D.J. was spinning tunes, encouraging the students to dance with snappy patter and promises of first, second, and third place awards. A handful of girls braved the dance floor, but few males dared the potential embarrassment and certain ridicule. The function was obligatory, and held during the school day. Archie assumed this was meant to force boys to attend. At twelve or thirteen years of age, no boy would voluntarily attend a dance, no matter how much he secretly hoped for a moment with one of his cute, giggly classmates. Boys learn early how to keep real desires close to the chest and far from the glaring eyes of potentially cruel peers.

Bug stood beside Archie, dressed in his standard attire. On this particular day, it seemed appropriate. Archie had forgone a costume as well.

Archie hadn't been suspended for the incident with Jill, though he had stayed home "sick" for three days. The episode had been chalked up to mistaken identity and mental anxiety caused by the trauma he'd so recently endured. Though, Archie had been warned that no other such offences would be tolerated, and that should he cause another disturbance, the administration would consider sending him to a "special facility."

As traumatic as that incident had been, something deeper plagued Archie to his core. He'd gone white the night before. He was sure of it. There had been dirt beneath his fingernails this morning and he'd found bits of leaf on his mattress. The towel was still damp in the hallway bathroom. As Esther and Greg had their own facilities, Archie was the only one to shower in this room.

And there had been a news report of a missing girl.

Archie couldn't imagine that he was connected.

He couldn't!

Yes, there had been the incident with Bug's cat, but that was months ago. As well, there had been the episode while Esther slept, but the only damage had been to himself, the tiny self-inflicted cut. True, he was fairly certain that he took occasional midnight jaunts—including this past night—but he'd never seen any further evidence of deviant behavior. Certainly not kidnapping or murder!

But, this thing nettled at his mind. His gut was hollow. A missing child. He couldn't be connected. To think so would be such an assumption, such a leap in logic as to not even bare any real consideration.

"There she is," said Bug, breaking Archie's concentration. He was nodding in the direction of a group of three chattering girls.

It was Jill. Dressed as an angel—of course. Her long wavy hair had glittery sprinkles, her smile radiated warmth and joy. Archie could almost believe that her velvety white wings were real. A quiver ran through his body. No, he wasn't about to lose control, to go into the white, or attack anyone, he was simply nervous about seeing her again. This was the first time since the incident. Archie still couldn't believe how tall she'd become, how her face had matured, how her figure now resembled that of an hourglass.

Bug glanced at Archie and flashed an amused smile. "Now or never, Burke."

Archie nodded. His stomach went tight, his palms clammy. He had decided to talk with Jill, to get to know her again on different terms. No, he wasn't going to reveal his identity. That would be insane. But maybe, as a friend, he just might have a positive influence on her life; he might even be able to make up for some of his past mistakes. But right then, with her standing just a few yards distant, laughing and giggling, so carefree and young, his plan seemed preposterous. What could Archie possibly offer that she didn't already have? "No," he said. "It's not right. I can't do this." Archie turned to walk away, intending to leave the building.

Bug grabbed him by the arm. "Not so fast, daddy boy."

Archie gazed at the kid. "Bug, what are you doing?"

"I know chicken when I see chicken. You're sprouting feathers. Just get over there and talk with your… Whatever she is."

Archie shook his head as he pulled his arm free of Bug's grasp. "This is a mistake. I can't do this." Archie shook his head, paced a few steps away, and then returned to Bug. "What am I doing here? I have absolutely nothing to offer Jill."

Bug stared at Archie, then over at Jill, then back to Archie. "Love," he said. "I guess you could offer her love."

Archie gazed into Bug's dark eyes. His green hair stuck out in subtle anarchy. "That's ridiculous," said Archie. "What can I possibly say that's going to make anything better? 'Hey, it's me—Dad. I've lost a few pounds, and a couple of decades, but, hey, roll with it.'" Archie waved his hands. "No, I should just let her be and move on with my life."

"Yeah, well, maybe that's what your brain's thinkin'. But I bet you heart's sayin' something a little different."

This was a very strange aspect of Bug's personality. Archie hadn't seen him as someone who would care about something like love or relationship. To Archie, Bug had seemed nothing more than a mildly obnoxious punk who used to hang around with Joey, a walking contradiction, someone who fit no well-ordered stereotype. "I can't tell her who I am," Archie said. "You know that."

"I never said you should. Just talk to her." He paused to take a sip of punch. "You're a dad," he said. "Dad's are supposed to be there for their kids. They're supposed to be good people." He hesitated, some hidden emotion gripping him. When he spoke again, his voice was weak, nearly cracking, though he never allowed his gaze to falter. "Some dads aren't too good. Don't be one of those."

Archie knew little of Bug's family life other than the fact that his parents were divorced and that Bug lived with his mother, spending only the occasional weekend with his father. Archie was beginning to see that there were issues here, things that Bug had never revealed, hurts he hid fiercely behind his green hair and Goth look.

"Okay, Bug" he said as he patted the boy on the back. "Okay."

Archie steadied himself and began walking slowly, nervously, toward his unsuspecting daughter. She was so beautiful, so precious, standing there, animated and chatty, smiling and laughing with her new friends. Amazing. Everything in his being screamed to hold her, to squeeze her. Archie had no idea what he was about to say, so he simply stopped perhaps five feet distant, staring at her as his stomach performed intricate gymnastics.

One of Jill's companions, a tall African American girl named Mary, noticed him, giggled, and pointed. Jill turned. Her eyes widened just a bit. Archie thought he might have seen fear in her sparkling hazel orbs.

"Uh, hi," he said. Not exactly suave, but it broke the ice.

Jill hesitated before saying, "Oh, um, hi. I heard you were back."

Archie smiled. "I'm guessing that's not all you heard."

Jill shrugged. The shorter friend, Shelly, whispered a not-so-subtle warning in Jill's ear.

Archie took a tentative step forward. It was amazing how horrified he was to speak with his own daughter. "Can we talk?"

Jill glanced at her friends, who'd gone silent. The incident had already become a school legend. "I guess," she said. Her voice was small and tentative.

"Listen, I'm… sorry about… you know."

She dropped her head. "You really freaked me out."

Archie nodded. "I don't doubt."

There was an awkward silence. Archie glanced at Jill's friends, both of which avoided his gaze. "Can we talk alone? No crazy stuff. I promise."

She glanced at her silent companions. Both shook their heads gently, as if to say, "Don't go, he'll kill you."

Jill shrugged and nodded. "Okay," she said. "But only for a minute." Good girl, he thought. She's not afraid to go against the advice of her peers—even when theirs was the better judgment.

They strolled across the gym floor and sat down at a table near the north-ernmost wall. "So, what happened the other day?" she asked. "I mean, you really lost it."

Archie set his newspaper and drink down before him. "It's complicated."

"Some kids say you came back from the dead and you were trying to cast a spell on me."

Archie chuckled. "Yeah, I'm sure they did."

"Oh!" she said as if he might think her an idiot. "I don't believe them. I mean, that sounds pretty stupid. The principal, Mr. Lang, he said you died, that your brain was damaged, and that now you sometimes have fits."

Archie shrugged. "Technically, I guess I did die—for a couple of minutes."

"I heard you're really brainy now, but you weren't before."

"Nah, I just know more than I did before. It makes me look smarter. Mostly, I'm just different. I'm not like most kids."

She smiled her precious smile. "That's okay," she said. "A lot of the kids I know are jerks, anyway."

Archie laughed. This was going much better than he'd anticipated. "So, you just moved here?" he asked. Archie wanted to learn what had caused Marcie to relocate to Ephesus. He wondered if she'd found a new job or perhaps a great deal on real estate; she'd seemed pretty well settled in Munster.

"Yeah," said Jill. "Just a couple of weeks ago."

"Why did you move?" he prodded.

Jill cocked her head, speaking matter-of-factly. "My mom just married a guy who lives here."

Archie felt as if she'd punched him in the gut. He no longer thought of Marcie as his wife, hadn't for quite some time. Truly, most of his feelings for her had fled before the divorce. And his outright loathing had begun the evening she'd slipped away, taking Jill with her. But for some reason Archie just hadn't thought of her marrying again. This was silly, he knew. She was attractive, bright, self-assured. Archie guessed that with everything else going on, he just hadn't let his mind go there.

But now she'd brought another man into her life, she'd moved into his home. This man, this stranger, would be raising Archie's daughter, his precious Jillie-bean. He'd be filling her head with his ideas, his world view, his opinions on right and wrong. It would be this man that boyfriends feared, this man who walked her down the aisle. Archie felt short of breath. Surely he had gone pale.

"Are you alright?" asked Jill. She looked frightened, perhaps fearing that Archie would repeat the incident of their first encounter. She began to rise, as if to flee, then reseated herself.

"I'm alright," he said, though his voice was weak and his hands trembling. "I'm just… Your real father… It must hurt him to know that your mom remarried."

Jill's eyes dropped, she fiddled with her hands in her lap. "My dad died."

Idiot! What was he thinking?

"I'm sorry," he said. "I didn't think about that."

She looked up at Archie and smiled a thin but supportive smile. "That's okay," she said. "My parents were divorced. I didn't see my dad much, at least not for the last couple of years. I'm kinda glad I didn't. He was a real jerk."

Archie gazed at her, trying to think of some appropriate response, but knew that any verbal expression would be accompanied by a tight strangled voice and a rush of cascading tears.

Marcie! She had done this. She had poisoned Jill's perception of him. She'd been a vengeful ex-wife, fighting him at every turn, seeking to deny him access to the one person he truly loved. And Archie had let her do it. He hadn't wanted Jill to be caught up in the midst of a brutal custody battle; he hadn't wanted to put her through that. And he'd been weak. And he'd been frequently drunk. And all through it Marcie had fed Jill lies and half truths about him, corrupting her memories, telling only the bad and none of the good, forcing her to choose sides. Marcie. It all came down to that self-righteous, oh so perfect Marcie.

What had Archie expected to happen after such indoctrination? What had he expected Jill to say, that Archie was the best dad ever, that she'd loved him so much and couldn't bear life without him, that she thought of him every moment the way that he did her? Ridiculous! There was no good that could come of this—none! He'd been an idiot to even think of reinserting himself in her life.

Willing his voice to remain steady, avoiding eye contact, Archie stood. "Listen, I've, uh, got to go," he said before walking silently from the gym, his gaze on the shiny wooden floor, his fists balled in anger, a tiny wisp of white trailing in his wake.

Chapter Thirty-One

Nov 8

Stephanie Munson, a guidance consoler at William C. Bowdon Elementary School in Ephesus Indiana did not report for work this overcast Monday morning. Two days later she was officially reported missing and was never seen again. Though there was wide speculation that she'd run away with a former lover with whom she'd recently resumed contact. No one was ever arrested in connection with her disappearance, though the remains of an unidentified female would be discovered nearly seven years later buried in the basement of a long-abandoned building situated only two blocks from Stephanie's apartment.

Chapter Thirty-Two

It was now three weeks since Halloween. The car had been following them for five blocks. Archie and Bug were on their way home from school. The smell of burning leaves wafted through the air and random drops of moisture escaped the cloud-covered sky. A Picture of Carrie Turner, the missing eight year-old, fluttered on a pole.

Archie, being in a state of deep contemplation, missed the car entirely. He was thinking of Jill who he now saw on a semi regular basis. Their conversations had been short, and yet… fulfilling. There was something there. Some connection, though one not easily defined. Bug, though, had been paying attention to his surroundings. He glanced over his shoulder and said, "Go this way." His voice was urgent and hushed as he veered through a nearby alley-way.

"Why?" asked Archie, only half caring. He assumed Bug was simply showing him a new shortcut home.

"Just wait," said Bug in a sharp, urgent tone. They marched through the gravel drive, avoiding two overturned garbage cans and a rather testy-looking feline, and then paused at Bug's command before exiting onto the next street only two doors down.

Thunder rumbled somewhere off in the distance as Bug glanced behind, then left and right, before urging Archie on. "What's going on?" asked Archie, now understanding that this wasn't just a shortcut.

"Someone's following us," said Bug in a conspiratorial whisper.

"Who?"

"A car," whispered Bug. "It's been following us for, I dunno, five blocks."

Archie smirked, writing this off as a young boy's over active imagination. Everything was a mystery, everything was an adventure when one was twelve. "Who'd want to follow us? We're just a couple of kids."

"*I'm* just a kid," he said. "You're a freak. Maybe the FBI wants you, or the CIA. Maybe they want to probe your mind an' learn how to turn kids into cyborgs."

Archie doubted cyborgs had anything to do with it.

A shiny navy blue car turned the corner a half a block up. The windows were tinted nearly to a deep charcoal, obscuring the driver from view. "There it is," said Bug. "This way."

He bolted across the street and vaulted a couple of shrubberies. Still not believing they'd been followed, but not feeling inclined to be left behind, Archie raced after his companion. For a moment he actually felt like a twelve year-old, racing about for no reason, making adventures out of nothing at all.

The car accelerated.

Bug veered right into another alleyway. The car followed, its tires noisy on the gravely surface. Archie's heart rate clicked up a notch. Maybe Bug wasn't so far off base after all.

They shot between two houses, over a short chain-link fence. A small shaggy dog, a shiatsu, yapped and chased, snapping at their heels. Archie and Bug raced across the yard, skirting several doggy land mines, and scrambled over the opposite fence, narrowly escaping the frenzied pup. Turning left toward the street, Archie nearly collided with the dark blue Lumina.

Bug was right. It had been following them.

Once again, they turned to run as the dark tinted passenger-side window slid down revealing a single occupant. The horn tooted twice. "Gilly Baskerville!" barked the strong baritone voice. "Not a bad strip."

Archie stopped, turned. Whoever this was, he knew Archie's true identity. There wasn't any use in running. If this man knew who Archie was, he also knew, or could find out, where he lived. Better to have whatever conversation the man wanted to have here, as opposed to in the Burke's living room where closely-held secrets could be spilled before potentially horrified ears.

Archie stared through the now-open window at the stocky middle-aged man, at his dark mop of hair, pocked complexion, and piercing brown eyes. "Roswell," he said.

The man nodded as he sipped from a white Styrofoam cup. "Yeah. Get in."

Archie supposed he should have recognized the car, but it had been months since he'd visited the radio station. He'd had no reason to believe he'd ever see the man again. Winded, Archie stepped forward asking, "What do you want?" Bug stood in the background, eyes narrowed, and breathing heavily from the exertion.

"Isn't it obvious?" Roswell asked. "I want to talk."

"Wait, wait, wait," said Bug as he moved forward, limping just slightly, probably working out a cramp. The kid wasn't overly athletic. "Who is this guy?"

"James T. Roswell," Archie said as he approached the Lumina. "The UFO guy on the radio. Though, I doubt that's his given name."

Bug's eyes brightened with recognition. "The guy who didn't believe you?"

"Yeah. That guy."

"Why were you following us?" asked Archie, now leaning on the open window. Roswell's car smelled of White Castle hamburgers and stale coffee.

The man shrugged and took another sip of his drink. "Like I said, I wanted to talk."

"Why didn't you approach me directly?"

Roswell inclined his head toward Bug, who now stood directly beside Archie. "I was hoping you'd lose the kid before you got all the way home. Less complications." There was just a hint of a Mexican accent to his otherwise Middle American speech.

Archie nodded. Roswell had no way of knowing that Bug knew his secret. "Okay," said Archie as he grasped the handle and pulled the door open. "We can talk."

"I'm goin' too," said Bug.

Roswell eyed Bug. "No," he said. "I don't think so."

Bug turned to Archie, likely hoping Archie would refuse to go without him. "Sorry, Bug. Roswell's right. We've got to talk man-to-man."

Bug glared a hurtful glare. Archie felt bad for the kid. The situation could have handled that better.

*****

Roswell drove aimlessly through the streets of Ephesus, rain pattering lightly on the windshield, no destination in mind. He sipped coffee as Archie gazed absently at the children parading down the sidewalks on their ways home from school. "So," Archie asked finally, "What made you decide to believe me?"

"Who said I believed you?"

Archie shrugged. "I'm here right now, and you don't strike me as the pedophile type."

Roswell nodded and chuckled. He reached down and grabbed a crumpled fast food bag from beside Archie's feet and tossed it into the rear. A dog-eared paperback copy of Steinbeck's East of Eden sat between them on the seat. "It was your follow-up call that got me thinking," he said. "When you called to tell me it was all a gag. You sounded almost panicked, like you thought you'd made a mistake by bringing me into it."

Archie nodded, knowing he should have left well-enough alone. "Okay," he said. "That got you thinking—months ago—but what convinced you?"

"At first I wasn't convinced. I still thought it was hokey."

"Hokier than Bigfoot in a bra?" asked Archie in reference to Roswell's most infamous radio broadcast.

Roswell chuckled. "Yeah, hokier than that. But the thing kept nettling at me. I kept wondering about it. I remembered that first night when you came to the studio. You were dirty and messed up. Your clothes were ripped. Then you stole money from Ned's roomie and attacked that couple the next day."

"A normal kid could have done any of that," offered Archie.

Roswell nodded and sipped his java. Making a right onto Eisenhower Lane, he slowed to allow two schoolgirls to stroll across the street. "Exactly," he said. "That's what I thought. You had been at the institute, something happened that you didn't like. You fled and were eventually caught just like any other twelve year-old runaway."

"But?" prodded Archie.

"But, why come to me with that crazy story? That is, unless something serious did happen, something you didn't feel you could tell your parents, but something you wanted uncovered." He took another sip from his Styrofoam cup and smacked his lips. "I let it sit for a long while, but the whole thing kept nettling me. What if something had happened to you in there and by doing nothing I was allowing that same thing to happen to other children? So, finally I checked into this Dr. Colin Lambert you'd mentioned. I wondered if there'd been instances of abuse reported, if he had any kind of history with young boys." He glanced in Archie's direction and offered a wry smile. "You'll be happy to know your father came out clean." Roswell took a moment to observe Archie's expression before continuing. "But, now I had the bug for this thing. I knew something caused you to run. Besides, a place like the Gowon Institute, there's got to be a story there somewhere. Surely I'd uncover something worth airing. I'm surprised I'd never thought of checking into the place before. You did me a favor, Arch."

Archie wasn't quite sure that doing James T. Roswell a favor was exactly a good thing, but he nodded. "Obviously, you found something."

Roswell nodded, and then reached into the back seat with his right hand, maintaining a hold on the wheel with his left. Archie could hear rustling bags as he drove. "I think I've got a couple of White Castles left. They're probably cold. You want one?"

Archie declined.

Roswell grunted and shrugged, pulling a tiny, half-eaten burger from a bag, finishing it in two bites, and chasing it with coffee. "I began talking to institute staff about your father, Colin Lambert," he continued. "It took some digging. I scanned the internet and local newspaper sites for articles about the institute." Roswell turned the wheel again; this time rolling south onto Poplar Street. "I was beginning to think I'd been suckered into a wild goose chase till I found an article on a former patient at the institute stalking a woman he claimed to have known in another life."

Archie remained silent.

"An isolated incident," said Roswell. "Or so I thought." He glanced at Archie, a wary look in his eye. "Then I read of another instance, and another, and another, each connected with the institute."

"Other infusions recipients seeking out people from their previous lives." Archie stared through the window, avoiding Roswell's gaze. The rain was heavier now.

"I checked police reports," added Roswell, his tone quiet, informative, not booming or dramatic like his radio voice. "Over the past several months there have been animal mutilations here in Ephesus. And on the same nights, sightings of a boy running naked in the street. Some reports indicate the boy had an awkward gate. Yours has gotten better since our last encounter, I see. But the obvious similarity and the boy's basic description, it got me thinking."

Archie didn't respond as he was besieged by his own personal horror. Not only had there been animal mutilations—ones of which he had no knowledge—but there had been other infusions. Colin had lied. And not only had he lied, but he'd known what could happen to Archie, and yet still he performed the procedure—without informing his own son of the risks. "What happened to these people?" asked Archie. "What was the ultimate outcome?"

Roswell sighed and took another sip of his coffee as he turned east onto Nixon Boulevard. "I can't give you a full rundown on all of them. I haven't learned everything." He slowed to allow a mother and her young daughter to cross. "I tracked down a former employee of Gowon Institute," he said. "A nurse. She'd worked under a Dr. Diana Mortonson."

Archie's face must have registered shock because Roswell said, "You know her?"

"We've met."

Roswell nodded and stopped for a red light at Market Street. "Former employees are sometimes the best sources of information. They're no longer in fear of losing their jobs or of being passed over for promotion. They tend to be freer with the tongue than current employees—especially the ones who left on less than friendly terms." The light turned green. Roswell accelerated, passing Hughes Bakery on his left and proceeding back into residential neighborhoods. They were now only a few blocks from the Burke's home.

"I learned of six infusions," he said. "There may have been more, but I've confirmed six. All were patients of Dr. Mortonson."

This was a surprise. "Not Lambert?"

Roswell shook his head. "If it was him, he's done a great job of shifting the blame to Mortonson."

"What happened to them?" Archie's voice was tiny, retreating into his throat, resisting the command to voice these crucial questions.

"My information is sketchy. Some of it is not verified. All six had some level of mental instability. Many had instances where they were not in control of their own actions, not even consciously present. One," he said, "killed a man for marrying a woman he claimed as his wife."

Archie allowed this to register, wondering what Colin could have been thinking, why, knowing the risks, he would perform such a procedure on his own son. And was it true? Had Mortonson performed the other infusions? If so, what had been Colin's role? Had she stolen his procedure from beneath him, performing it on humans before it had been properly tested? Or had Colin been involved at every level, allowing Mortonson to continue regardless the risks? "Where are they now? Have any returned to the institute?"

Roswell contemplated this before speaking. Archie wondered if he was pondering whether or not to tell the truth. "One's at the institute," he said through an exhaled breath. "Another's up in East Chicago, at a psychiatric facility."

"And the others?"

Roswell turned right onto Old Oak Drive and slowed to a stop. The Burke's home was a half block down. Bug sat waiting on the front lawn. The kid was probably soaked.

"The others," said Roswell as he slipped the car into park. "The others, Archie, are dead—suicides."

Chapter Thirty-Three

"Peanuts?" asked Colin as he extended the carnival glass bowl toward Roswell and then to Archie. Both declined, and Colin set the bowl down, snatching a couple of treats for himself as Archie and Roswell each settled into the cushioned leather seats situated before Colin's expansive mahogany desk.

Archie hadn't allowed Roswell to drop him off at the Burke's home. He needed to talk with Colin, and Roswell had a car. They'd paused only for a moment, a few doors down, and then moved past the house. Bug, still sitting on the rain-soaked lawn, stared as they drove past, his expression a mix of anger and concern. Despite it all, he still didn't get that Archie was no longer his best bud Joey.

Archie wasn't entirely comfortable having Roswell present for this particular confrontation with his father, but there was little he could do about it. Roswell was his ride and he'd provided valuable information. In truth, the man might prove useful. The details Archie now knew were ones Roswell had uncovered. Maybe he could give Archie leverage with Colin, or maybe ask probing questions that Archie hadn't yet conceived.

"So, Joey," began Colin. "Again, who exactly is your friend?"

"I'm James T. Roswell," offered Roswell before Archie could respond. "I'm a radio personality on The Flame." This was his radio voice, no accent.

"Yes. Bigfoot in a bra, if I remember correctly."

"Guilty as charged," chuckled Roswell. "I must not have slept well that night. How was I to know it was actually a tutu he'd been wearing?"

Colin nodded, but did not smile. He wasn't a man of much humor.

"Colin," said Archie. "Roswell knows."

Colin shifted his gaze to Roswell, staring at him directly. "He knows? What knowledge, exactly, does he purport to possess?"

"I could outline that for you, Dr. Lambert." Roswell pulled a small spiral notebook from his breast pocket. It was bent, the pages dog-eared, the deep blue cover only holding on by two wire spirals. "I've uncovered evidence of at least six mind infusions—seven, if you include Archie here—performed in the past seven years. The first was a woman named Susanna Fontaine. She was a French immigrant to this country, apparently had a very strong accent, that is, until after the procedure, then, no foreign accent, but she did have a bit of a southern twang—*y'all*." Roswell smiled. Colin did not. "Miss Fontaine was never released from this facility, though she did escape on three occasions. Would you like me to detail the results of her excursions?"

Colin's face was ashen; he spun his pen before him on the desk. For the first time, Archie's father actually looked his nearly seventy years. "There will be no need of that," he said with an accusatory glance in Archie's direction.

"Of course there won't," said Roswell. The man seemed self-assured, almost cocky, but Archie didn't get the feeling he was enjoying this. More, that he was simply doing what he felt must be done. "The next infusion was performed on a young man named Shepherd. He was only twenty-three at the time. The third was another male, this one named Guidarelli."

"Enough," said Colin slapping his palm on polished wood. The two men stared at each other, silence between them until finally Colin spoke. "What is it you want, Mr. Roswell?"

Archie answered the question for Roswell. "What Roswell wants isn't the concern, Colin. We're here because I need to know the truth."

Colin remained still, his jaw working slowly on a peanut, his hands clasped before him on the desk.

"Why didn't you tell me about the other infusions? Why didn't you give me some warning as to what might happen? The other patients all went insane." Archie didn't know what he felt most: anger, pain, disappointment. This was his father who had done this to him. His father!

"Why didn't I tell you about the other infusions?" asked Colin. "Why not tell you that you just might endure a catastrophic neurological episode? Why not tell you that there were others, nearly all of whom took their own lives?" Colin leaned forward, his pale gray eyes locking on Archie. "I didn't tell you because if I had you wouldn't have gone through with the procedure."

Archie stood, paced the room, glared at his father with all of the contempt a son could muster. "How could you do this to me?" he screamed. "How could you do this to your own son?"

Colin met Archie's gaze. "How could I not do it *for* my son?"

"Damn it, Colin! Be honest for once. This wasn't for me. Nothing you've ever done has been for me. I was just one more lab rat for you to study."

Colin was up, out of his seat, rounding the desk, waving his upturned index finger in Archie's face. "Do you think that? Do you really believe that?"

"What else is there for me to believe?"

"Believe that I'm your father. Believe that I would do anything—anything! —to keep you alive." Colin bit his lower lip, clenched his fists. His face reddened and his brow crinkled. Archie didn't believe he'd ever seen true passion in the man before. "Do you know where you would be right now, right at this moment, if I hadn't infused your neurological energies onto the boy's hippocampus?"

Archie didn't answer. There was no need.

"You'd be dead. Right now. This day. You would no longer exist as anything but decaying flesh. How could a father let that happen? Not when there's an option, not ever when there's even the slightest chance. Not even when the potential outcome is near as frightful as the certain death you faced without it. At least this way there was hope, a chance—something!"

Avoiding Colin's gaze, Archie glanced at Roswell. The guy looked at him and shrugged. He wasn't taking notes, at least not on paper. Archie moved away, putting distance between he and his father. "Colin," he said. "That's a nice speech. I'm sure anyone who heard it would be moved. But that would only be because other people don't know what it means to be Colin Lambert's son."

Colin threw up his arms as if in exasperation. "I have no heart, is that it? I'm a soulless husk? Is that truly what you believe? 'Dad wasn't around much when I was a boy. Therefore he must not love me.' I've heard it before, you know. From your sister. She wasn't afraid to tell me of her failings. She relocated halfway across the country simply to make her point." He paused, attempting to calm himself. When he spoke again, his voice was soft, controlled. "I never saw her again after our last fight. I don't believe you ever knew that." Colin turned away, moving first toward his desk and then veering to the bookshelf, before circling back in Archie's direction. "I may have been distant. I, well, I'm not entirely a social animal. But my dedication to my work, my lack of physical affection… These do not denote a lack of emotion."

Archie stared at his father, at his steel gray eyes, at his dark hair now laced with silver, at the lines, so uncharacteristic on his once-taut face. Archie's sister had been dead for several years now; the victim of a drunk driver on a Manhattan New Year's Eve. Archie had attended the funeral. Colin had made a brief appearance, approaching the coffin for only a moment before turning to march quickly from the room. Archie had always assumed Colin had been in a hurry to return to his precious research. Perhaps he'd been mistaken.

Roswell cleared his throat. "Listen," he said. "I don't want to intrude on family business, but I do believe there are other issues at hand." Neither Archie nor Colin spoke, so Roswell continued. "Archie's already exhibited some rather dramatic symptoms. What are you doing for him, doc?"

Colin pulled his pen from his breast pocket and clicked it several times. "That is a complicated question. The boy, Joey, was somewhat unique in that there was no physical damage to the brain, no brunt-force trauma. He'd become brain dead due to lack of oxygen, not as a result of a fall or a blow." Colin gestured for Archie to return to his seat and then strolled around his desk and lowered himself into his chair. "In the other cases, healing of the brain matter was required prior to the infusion. I had hoped that in Joey's case, the lack of prior physical damage would work in our favor, perhaps diminish some of the less desirable effects of the procedure."

Roswell stopped him. "Wait a second. You say you repaired brain matter? I was under the impression that the brain can't regenerate or repair tissue."

Colin nodded, leaning forward on his elbows. "Very good, Mr. Roswell—and correct. That is, except in the arena of experimental medicine." He paused, glanced at Archie, and then continued. "We have developed a nanofiber capable of reknitting severed neurons—quite extraordinary, really. The compound is composed primarily of a special ionic peptide. Once injected into the damaged area, tiny amino acids erect a net or scaffold, which bridges gaps created by injury. Regrowth is rapid. Complete healing—at least, from an observable standpoint—can occur in as little as thirty days."

"Okay," said Roswell. "Interesting. But, how does any of this help Archie?"

Colin nodded. "We had previously assumed that these breaks with reality in infusion recipients were somehow linked to former damage to the brain, that as extraordinary as the nanofibers might be, some damage had remained."

"In other words," pressed Roswell. "Joey's brain had not suffered the same kind of injuries as the others; he hadn't been treated with nanofibers, and therefore, you didn't expect the same problems." Archie was impressed with Roswell's line of questioning. The man was obviously much more intelligent than one might be led to believe by listening to his radio show.

"Oh, Joey's brain did receive nanofibers," replied Colin. "Nano technology was used to create a duplicate of Archie's neuro-net on the boy's brain, thus allowing the infused energies to seek the familiar terrain and adhere properly. But on the other patients, we'd used similar fibers for repair as well."

"And about these breaks with reality?"

"The brain is a complex organ, Mr. Roswell. Even the most brilliant among us must concede to its many mysteries."

"In other words you're stabbing in the dark, trying to figure out what to do next before Archie comes completely unglued?"

Colin's jaw tightened. "One would hope it wouldn't come to that."

"One would hope you would have thought of that before performing the procedure," shot Roswell.

Colin made eye contact with his son. "I am doing everything within my power to correct whatever complications you're experiencing. Archie, you must trust me." His voice was simultaneously firm yet pleading.

Archie stared at his father, a strange rush of emotion surging within. "I want to trust you, Colin. But how? You've kept so much from me." Archie paused, glanced over at Roswell, and then continued. "The only reason you're opening up now is because Roswell uncovered your secret. Otherwise, I still wouldn't know of the others, or of what happened to them."

"What else is it that you want to know?" asked Colin.

"Diana Mortonson," said Archie. "What's her connection?"

Colin offered a weary chuckle. "Her connection," he repeated. "It's her baby. Well, it is now. Diana and I began research together, years ago—as equals. There were disagreements, of course, differences in focus. Unfortunately, it was she that found funding for the initial experimentation. As such, she was able to assert her control upon the project."

"Funding?" asked Roswell. "I'm guessing, military funding."

Archie chuckled slightly. Roswell, the conspiracy theorist.

Colin, though, simply twirled his pen, making no comment. Perhaps Roswell was correct.

"Could Mortonson be of assistance in Archie's situation?" asked Roswell.

Colin lifted his gaze to meet Roswell's. "Diana Mortonson is brilliant," he said in a cool even tone. "And by all means, avoid her at all costs."

Chapter Thirty-Four

It was nearly a week before Archie's next face-to-face encounter with Roswell. The radio personality intercepted Archie and Bug two blocks from Rutherford B. Hayes Middle School. Lowering the driver-side window, he sipped his coffee, and gazed out at the two young faces. Classical music lilted from within. Bach, thought Archie, but he wasn't sure. "Got your tag-along, I see," said Roswell, nodding toward Bug. The boy scowled.

"Bug's okay," said Archie in an attempt to defuse the tension. "You can talk in front of him."

Roswell gazed at Archie askance as if to say, *"If you say so. But it seems pretty stupid to me."*

Archie asked, "So, can we get in to see the others?"

Roswell reached toward his dash, turning the radio down, and then taking another sip of coffee. "I think I'm going to have quite a ratings boost when I air this," smiled Roswell. "But that's not what you asked, is it?"

"You're gonna let this jerk-off put this stuff on the radio?" shot Bug. Archie felt the boy might just slug them both.

"Not just yet. And when he does, my name and any reference to Joey's family will be kept out of it—right Roswell?"

Roswell shrugged. "Whatever you say, Arch." He took another swig of coffee and said, "Listen, one of the infusion recipients, a man named Neil Frisk, is a patient up in East Chicago. I know your dad refused to allow you to meet with the recipients, but I can get you in to see this man. Can you make that happen?"

East Chicago Indiana was a good half hour to forty-five minutes north of Ephesus. Between travel and meeting with the man, Archie would be gone nearly three hours. This would be difficult to explain to Greg and Esther. "Sure," said Archie. "I'll make that happen."

"Good," smiled Roswell. "I'll pick you up on the corner of Kennedy and Old Oak, say six o'clock?"

"I'll be there," said Archie.

"Good, I'll see you at six." And then, just before retracting his window, he looked at Bug and said. "Kid, you really should do something with that hair. Green just isn't your color."

Bug gave him the finger. Roswell nodded, saluted with his Styrofoam coffee cup, and rolled off. "I'm going," said Bug as he kicked a small stone onto the grassy parkway to his right.

Archie glared at Bug. "No. Allowing you to tag along would just complicate things."

"So?" he said with a child's innocence.

"It would make it harder for this to happen."

Bug stepped toward another stone. Archie could see the tension in his brow. "Listen. I don't wanna make things hard for you, but I'm going."

"Bug, no. I can't…"

"Listen to me!" he said, giving the stone a hefty punt and sending it skipping down the street, narrowly missing a black Toyota. "I'm goin' with you." He gazed at Archie from below his brooding brows. "I know ya don't understand, but I've gotta figure out what's goin' on just as much as you do. I've gotta know if Joey's really gone. If…" He trailed off. His lip seemed to quiver. Abruptly, he turned his back on Archie, marched to where the stone lay, and gave it another solid boot. "If you don't let me go, I'm gonna tell Joey's parents everything. They may not believe me right away, but I bet it gets 'em wonderin'."

"Bug, don't do this to me."

"I'm not doin' nothin' to you. I'm just doin' what's gotta be done." Bug stopped pacing, stared at Archie for a moment. "I know ya just think I'm a kid. Ya probably think I'll screw everything up. But I won't. Besides, I don't trust that Roswell jerk. Someone's gotta look out for you."

"I can look out for myself."

Bug frowned. "Me and Joey, we were friends, kinda forever, ya know. But, some stuff happened. Between us. Between our parents. Joey didn't… He kinda…" He paused, not knowing how to continue. "I think I could a done more ta help Joey. Maybe I still gotta."

Before Archie could respond, he heard a familiar voice from behind. His stomach jumped. Despite it all, an irrepressible grin rolled across his face. Jill was calling Archie's name. "Hi, guys," she said as she stepped to beside them.

Archie gave Bug one last serious stare and then greeted his daughter with a grin that wiped his concerns away. "Hi, Jill," he said. Why was it that his palms were suddenly sweaty?

"Hey," said Bug.

"Hey, Bug," said Jill. "You have your rat with you?"

Bug smiled briefly. He frequently carried his pet rat in the sleeve of his oversized jacket. "Always," he said.

"You look pale," said Archie after a moment. "Are you alright?" It seemed ridiculous, even to him, but Archie couldn't help himself. Paternal instinct, it seemed, could even transcend mind infusions.

Jill pulled her backpack around to where she could reach it, unzipped it, and retrieved a clear plastic bag, tossing it to Bug. "I'm fine," she said. "Swiss cheese. Left over from my lunch." Her smile was broad, her hazel eyes bright and alive. She still had a few of the freckles Archie remembered from two years prior, but they were fading as she flirted with adolescence. He was amazed that she'd continued to seek him out; that she was befriending him.

Bug grinned, unwrapped the cellophane-encased treat and slipped it inside his jacket, giving it to the eager rat in his sleeve. How the thing could breath in there, Archie would never know. And there were other possible problems with keeping a rat in a sleeve that he wouldn't even broach.

"Are you sure you're okay?" asked Archie. "You look pale."

Jill rolled her eyes. "I'm fine. Okay? You're not my mother. Jeez, Joey, it's a girl thing, okay?"

Bug chuckled as he patted his rat's gray and white head. "Well, that'll shut him up," he said.

They walked up the sidewalk, cut over to Spruce Drive, before crossing Main Street, and angling toward Old Oak. They talked mostly about nothing. Jill had an English exam, and hadn't yet read the material. Bug claimed that he never read anything. Archie, though, encouraged Jill to do her reading before turning on the Disney Channel. It was what a dad would say.

Bug split from the two, giving Archie the opportunity to spend some time alone with Jill. He glanced at Archie saying, "I'll see you later. Don't forget." His stare was forceful, conveying all that needed to be said.

They walked a little further as white flecks flitted from above. Jill grinned and giggled, sticking out her tongue to catch a snowflake. "First snow," she giggled. "It's so… I don't know—cool."

Archie chuckled, pulling his jacket closer about his form and zipping it to his chin. "Yeah, me, it makes my back scream just thinking about lugging a shovel full of that stuff."

"You're no fun."

Archie smiled. "That's me, Mister Grinch."

They walked silently for a few moments, Jill darting about, catching more flakes with her tongue, Archie simply admiring her youthful exuberance. Her hazel eyes truly did sparkle, and her smile, so broad that her face might just crack. He wondered why he'd allowed himself to stay away for so long, to allow himself to slip so completely from her life. True, Marcie had been a bulldog, battling Archie at every juncture, but Jill was his daughter—his life— why had he rolled over and played dead so easily? Why had he allowed himself to miss so much of her childhood, both before and after the divorce?

"So, uh, how's your mom?" he asked after a time.

Jill caught another snowflake and then twirled with a laugh. Her wavy brown hair was covered with little white flecks. "Okay, I guess. Why do you always ask about her?"

Archie shrugged. "Call me weird."

"Too late!" she laughed.

The snow had created a glistening white film on the narrow sidewalk. Jill began to run and slide on the now slick surface, often nearly losing her balance, bobbing forward then back, angling just slightly to one side as she struggle to stay upright. Infectious bursts of laughter erupted from the girl. "Come on!" she yelled. "Have some fun."

Archie smiled and shrugged. "Nah. Not today." He'd suddenly become melancholy, thinking about what might have been, at how he'd let his life— his real life with Marcie and Jill—slip away without a fight. He wished he could go back and change his past, to make things right, to just take a big old whiteout brush and erase all of his stumbles and blunders.

"Listen," he said. "I know your dad, well, it seems maybe he wasn't all that great at the job."

"No duh!" said Jill as she bent down and slid her gloved hand across the sidewalk, trying to scoop up enough snow to make a snowball.

"What I mean is… Well, don't let that tear you up."

Jill gave up on the snowball, shaking the bits of white from her gloves and moving toward Archie. "Why should I? I mean, I'm over it, I guess."

"Are you sure? That type of thing, you know—traumatic."

"Jeez, Joey. What's with you?"

Archie attempted a nonchalant shrug, but he was too tense. It seemed forced, unnatural. He should never have brought this up. "Well," he said. "I don't want you to be messed up because of your dad. You're a special person no matter what your old man did or didn't do."

Jill smiled walking alongside Archie. "You like me don't you?"

"Uhhh—no! I mean, yes, but…"

Jill giggled. "I thought so."

Archie's heart leaped and thumped. This was wrong. All wrong. "No. Uh, not like that. I mean—not like *that!*"

"Like what?" she smiled, a playful tone to her voice, a coy glint in her eye that was never intended to be seen by her father.

Archie had no idea of what to say, of how to handle this gross miscommunication. "You know," he said. "Like *that*. I mean, you're a great friend. I mean a *great* friend. But, we can't… We need to… just be friends."

Jill cocked her head, pretending to be serious. "Wow, the 'friends talk' before we ever even go out."

"No. Not the friends talk. Just…"

Jill leaned over, giving Archie a quick peck on the cheek and then ran away giggling. "I get it," she said. "But, don't worry. You won't be twelve forever."

Chapter Thirty-Five

Archie hadn't known what to expect of the mental facility. He supposed it would be something like what the Gowon Institute must have been as a psychiatric institution: old and foreboding, dimly lit, with screams and cackles echoing off of yellow tobacco-stained walls.

This was nothing like that.

Archie guessed that maybe no place beyond Hollywood really was.

The place was modern, not new, but contemporary still. It was brightly lighted, with shiny vinyl tiled floors, an upbeat staff, and an antiseptic hospital smell. There were pastel-colored paintings on the walls, couches and tables on the floor, and a busy buzz of chatter wafting through the air. Patients milled about the common area, none in straight jackets, mostly watching TV and staring into other universes. A short line had formed at a nurse's station where patients were given medications in two Dixie cups, one for the meds, the other for water with which to wash them down. Occasionally, there were spats in the common area, mild things, squabbles over a game of cards or whose slipper was whose. But Archie didn't feel threatened or endangered. It was all more of a curiosity than anything.

Bug, though, walked slowly, with eyes wide, jaw half open, staying close to Archie and even to Roswell (who had objected strongly to the boy's presence). In truth, Bug's tag-along had helped Archie's case. Both boys had told their parents that they were going to see a movie together. That would easily cover them for at least two and a half hours, maybe more if they claimed to have stopped for a snack. Greg had been happy to see his boy becoming social once again; Esther had been leery but agreeable, restating her dislike of Bug.

Roswell had used his pull as a local celebrity to get them into the psychiatric unit. One of his rabid listeners, a man nicknamed Sasquach Sammy, who called into the show at least twice weekly, worked in maintenance there, and Roswell had told him that Neil Frisk, the infusion recipient, was a cousin, that he wanted to do a favor for his aunt and check in on her son. Roswell had no verification that he was a family member, but the fan had managed to get the threesome though the thick double doors of the ward.

They walked through a long straight hall, away from other visitors, meandering residents, and the commotion of the common room. This was where the residents stayed, each room having two beds, and usually two occupants. Mental wards were rarely anything but at full capacity, a fact Archie found disconcerting. The rooms were small, but mostly neat. Some had knickknacks or furnishings supplied by loved ones. Some of the rooms had TVs. One young twenty-something year-old man sat on the edge of his bed. A hand-painted poster taped to the wall above his head read, "Shingles the Cat, Gone but not Rottin'." Archie nodded a nervous greeting to the man as they strolled past, then avoided glancing into any of the other rooms along the way. Roswell, though, seemed to scan every inch, studying each room as he walked slowly past, making a mental recording for future reference.

There was a soft shuffle behind, and then Archie felt a tug at his elbow. He whirled, prepared to fend off some crazed assailant.

"Smoke?" said a short balding man, slightly chunky, wearing pajama tops and blue jeans. "Smoke."

Archie pulled his arm free with a swift jerk, causing the man to flinch. "No. I don't have any smokes," he said, a little more harshly than he'd intended.

"Smoke?" the man's voice quivered as he looked from Archie to Bug to Roswell. Archie didn't know what to say to the man, so remained silent. Best, he figured, not to encourage the poor guy. "Smoke, please," the man persisted, his hazy blue eyes pleading, his hand outstretched with a slight tremor.

"Sorry fella," said Roswell. "I quit years ago, and these two boys—too young and too smart to think about it."

The man nodded and turned. Hand still outstretched, he shuffled toward his next prospect.

*****

Neil Frisk was quite thin. So much so that it seemed his elbows might pop through his onionskin flesh, that his huge deep brown eyes might tumble out of their sunken sockets. His face was that of a shrunken head, skin pulled tight against bone, cheekbones protruding, lips pulled back revealing gum and tooth. His chin was sharp and narrow; his nose small, receding, but with nostrils large and flared. Shoulder-length brown hair, clumped and greasy, spilled across his pin-striped shirt collar. Short uneven bangs hung above his nearly non-existent brows. He sat cross-legged on his bed, elbows on knees, hands balled under his chin. He was facing a blank vanilla wall, neither acknowledging nor ignoring his approaching guests.

"Why's he so skinny?" whispered Bug as he drew closer to his companions.

"I'm guessing the staff is having a hard time getting him to eat," answered Roswell with a slight twitch of a grin on his lips. Roswell was likely thinking this the scoop of his career.

"Mr. Frisk," began Roswell as he stood just inside the doorway. "May we come in?" Archie hated letting Roswell take the lead, but was hampered by the boy's body. They had agreed that Roswell was the "adult." He would be the one respected, whose questions would be taken seriously.

Frisk remained silent, staring at the blank wall, possibly contemplating its irregularities or peering off into some unknown world. Archie gazed at the man. This was another infusion recipient. This man had endured the same tortures as he. This man, Neil Frisk, might grant a glimpse into Archie's own future, into his own pending horror. But this man was not really Neil Frisk. He was someone else, a man, woman, maybe a child. Someone the world thought dead. But where was that man now? Assuming it was a man. Was he chasing an emerald green wheel? Had he finally just slipped away into another reality, never to return? Roswell was the adult, but Archie was the one with the real need. He stepped around Roswell, coming to just before the man, obscuring the patient's view of the wall. The deep brown eyes, two golf balls set in shallow indentations, stared blankly ahead. Frisk had not been staring at the wall. He hadn't been staring at anything. Not, at least, in Archie's world.

"Who are you?" asked Archie. "I know you're not really Neil Frisk."

Frisk said nothing.

Archie took a step forward, to within an arm's length of the man. Frisk's breath was hot, stale, like a dog's, but Archie remained close.

"Joey, don't," said Bug. The boy's voice was tight, frightened. Archie was sure that Bug now regretted his decision to accompany him on this adventure.

"Shhh!" said Archie. Then softly, he said to Frisk, "I'm Archie. But I live in Joey's body. I'm not really a kid. I had a mind infusion."

Archie gazed into the large eyes, so absent a soul, so devoid of knowledge or intelligence. They seemed the eyes of a dead man, or of a coma victim, hazy, hollow. "Dr. Colin Lambert performed my infusion," he said. "I believe Dr. Diana Mortonson performed yours." Archie hoped the familiar names would spark something in the man, draw him back to this reality. But Frisk continued staring, hands knit in a ball, legs crossed, jaw slack.

"Roswell," said Archie, while still gazing at Frisk. "What information do you have? How long has he been like this? Did he slip gradually, or was he irresponsive from the beginning? When was his infusion?"

"From what I've found," said Roswell. "His infusion was eighteen months ago. He was never quite stable afterward, but managed to function at least well enough for Mortonson to release him after four months. After that, it looks like he fell pretty quickly. He's been here for almost a year."

Archie nodded. None of this was good. He, himself had only been released several months ago and he was far from what he'd consider stable. Archie looked intently at the man, at his tight pale skin and jutting bones, at the broad mouth and empty eyes. And then his attention was drawn to the man's left arm, just below the elbow. There was bruising, bite marks, apparently self-inflicted. He let a slow stream of air escape in a subtle hiss. He remembered a similar wound on his own arm soon after he'd fled the institute.

"Neil," said Archie. "Can you hear me? Do you know that I'm here?"

The golf ball eyes remained lifeless, the hands pressed tightly together. There was no movement. But something had changed, though the expression seemed the same, as did the posture. What was it he saw?

"Neil," he said again. "Neil, can you hear me?"

There. At the corner of the mouth, ever so slight, a tremor.

"Neil," said Archie. "Neil, I know you can hear me. Say something."

Silence.

Roswell took a step forward. "Arch, maybe he's not…"

"He can hear me," shot Archie. "Let me do this."

Roswell raised his hands as if in mock surrender, but didn't retreat. The man made Archie uncomfortable. He'd been a great help thus far, even sympathetic to a point, but Archie still wasn't sure how far he could trust him.

"Neil Frisk," said Archie. "That's not your real name. Who are you really? Who were you before the infusion?"

Frisk blinked once, slowly, purposefully. "Barry," he said, his voice husky, dry, like he hadn't spoken in days, maybe weeks.

"Barry," said Archie as Roswell and Bug pulled closer. "Barry what? What was your last name?"

"Barry," said the man with the same raspy voice. "Barry." He pressed his lips together, his expression stoic.

"Barry, where are you from? Where did you live before the infusion?" It was Roswell this time, leaning over Archie's shoulder, his eyes intense, studying Frisk, apparently memorizing the details.

Frisk's eyes lulled in the direction of Roswell. They appeared as two cue balls rolling to a lazy stop. "Barry Lind," said Frisk in a husky moan. "Rock Island, Illinois." Frisk smiled. His teeth were yellow, but intact. His gums, though, were nearly transparent, causing the teeth to appear large and malformed.

Archie leaned closer yet. "What do you remember, Barry? What do you remember from before and after the infusion? What goes on inside your head?"

"Slow down," urged Roswell. "Let him answer."

Frisk allowed his hands to drop into his lap. His fingers twitched. He sighed, blinked. Even these small actions seemed to require a huge amount of effort. Perspiration glistened on his forehead. His breathing became labored as if he was fighting for the breath to speak. "Barry Lind," he said. "Dead, not dead, dead." He blinked again, nodded at something internally, and then stared at Archie. "Here comes the Chattanooga Choo-Choo, boy. Sure do wish I could ride it."

"Barry," said Archie. "What happened to you after the infusion? Were you stable or did you slip into other realities?"

"Is that the Chattanooga Choo-Choo?"

"Barry," said Archie, now with a hint of urgency in his voice. "How did you get like this? Did you slip into the white? Was there a wheel?"

"Choo-Choo!" he said in a raspy falsetto. "Choo-Choo!"

"Barry, listen to me. I need to know what was done. What medications you took. What worked, what failed?"

"Choo-Choo!"

"Barry, I need your help."

Archie felt Roswell's hand on his shoulder. "He can't answer you, Arch. Ease up on him."

"Yeah," agreed Bug. "Maybe we should, I dunno, get outta here. He seems kinda freaky."

Archie shook Roswell's hand free with a harsh jerk. He had no time for interference. This might be his one opportunity to speak with another infusion recipient. He felt a connection to this man, and even more, a rolling dread brought about by the sight of him. He had to learn all that he could, find out what worked and what didn't, try to learn how to avoid Barry Lind's fate. How was it that Colin and Mortonson had let this man free of their care? How could they allow him to sit in a psych ward when they were the only ones with a chance at helping him? "Barry, what did Dr. Mortonson tell you about your condition? Did she help you?"

Barry's head swung violently to his right, his eyes landing on Bug, who took a quick step back. "Not alone," he hissed. "Not alone."

Bug gasped, Roswell scribbled on his notepad, Archie leaned forward placing his hand gently on the man's shoulder. "What do you mean, 'Not alone?'"

"Choo-Choo!"

"What do you mean, Barry?"

The man lulled his head toward Archie. Ball-like eyes were wide and hazy, his lips pulled taut in an uneasy grimace. His breathing became louder, more labored, and sweat rolled freely over his sharp, angular cheeks. "Frisk is here," he said. "Choo-Choo! Frisk is here!"

"What do you mean, Barry? Frisk is here. Are you saying that you're in Frisk's body?"

"No," said Bug, excitement replacing fear in his voice. "That's not what he means." Bug stepped closer, too quickly, startling Frisk, who pulled his arms tight about his body, cradling himself. "He means Frisk is still alive. Frisk is still in him."

Archie's stomach took a dive and a twirl. This was the one thing, the one horrifying thing, he refused to believe. If Frisk still lived, that meant there was a possibility that Joey still lived, and that simply couldn't be true. "Bug, you don't know what he means. Let me talk with him."

The man squinted, his eyelids seeming to stretch over his large ball-like orbs. His bony arms flexed, then relaxed. His breathing steadied, his frame shuddered. And when at last his eyes opened, they darted back and forth, seemingly taking in the scene. When he spoke, his voice had a different timbre, higher, more nasal. He had a bit of an accent, something from the east coast. Boston, perhaps. "How did you find me?" he asked. "What do you want?"

"Barry," said Archie. "We're not going to hurt you."

Frisk eyed Archie curiously. "I don't think I should be talking with you."

"We'd better get someone in here," said Roswell. "I think this has gone further than we can handle."

"You're Frisk," said Bug, excitement in his voice. "You're really Frisk. How do we get you back?"

"He's not Frisk," said Archie. "He's…"

Frisk lunged forward, grabbing Bug by the biceps and putting his face within an inch of the boy's. "I am always here. I am never here. Do you understand? Always! Never! Always! Never!"

Frisk then scampered away to huddle in the far corner of the room, shivering and fearful. "Choo-choo," he said in a tiny voice. "Choo-choo."

Chapter Thirty-Six

Archie lay awake, thoughts of Neil Frisk floating through his mind. He couldn't lose the image of this tortured soul, so fragile, yet so fierce—so lost. The man was what Archie would become, maybe in a few months, maybe even a few years, but Archie could sense the inevitable. At some level he'd nearly resigned to his fate. Colin was stymied, with nothing more to offer, and Archie knew he could slip away into another reality at any moment. And maybe that other reality wasn't so bad—if he could stay there, not bopping back and forth between worlds, not facing the consequences of whatever horrors his body performed while his mind was gone. Yes, his physical body would likely be institutionalized and sedated, much like Frisk, but if Archie was off somewhere else, well… Maybe he'd learn to accept it.

But, what of Jill?

Precious, wonderful Jill.

He'd never be her father again. He knew that. But she'd befriended him. There was hope of some type of relationship. He'd have to be careful never to allow her to again get the impression that he was romantically interested. But aside from that, his goal would be to become her best friend. He could counsel her, guide her, give her fatherly advice and wisdom through the mouth of a caring friend. He had a second chance. A chance to actually make a difference in her life. But only if he could maintain his sanity. Archie couldn't bear the thought of losing Jill a second time. And therefore, he needed to be stable, to be in his own mind, his right mind, twenty-four hours a day, without fear of slipping away and becoming some frightful, animalistic being.

But he also had to consider Joey Burke.

Was Bug correct? Did Joey yet live within him? It seemed Barry Lind and Neil Frisk shared a skull. What were the implications? Was Archie guilty of murdering this innocent kid? And even if so, wasn't it too late? To his knowledge there was nothing that could be done to reverse the process. Archie suppressed these thoughts. Joey was dead. Despite whatever supposed evidence, he was dead. That was the only outcome Archie could accept, anything else made him a monster. And though he could be selfish and boorish, he was still something less than monstrous.

His phone chimed. Withdrawing it from his pocket, he glanced at the caller I.D. and answered. "Bug, what do you need?" asked Archie, irritation in his voice. "It's after twelve-thirty."

"Turn on your radio. Your jerk-off friend's blabbing the whole thing to the world."

Archie disconnected the call and flicked Joey's radio to on, changing the setting to the AM band, and twirling the tuner to the left. He found Roswell's broadcast within thirty seconds.

"...more insidious than space aliens," said Roswell in his booming on-air voice. *"For this threat did not originate in the cold blackness of space. No, my fellow Americans, this plot was concocted and implemented not three miles down the road from where I broadcast. Mind infusions!"* he continued. *"The transferring of one man's mind into the brain of another. I've met two of these infusion recipients, and the experience is most frightening. Why, just this evening, in an area psychiatric ward, I and two companions encountered one of these freaks of science. The man is far from stable and, if released, would be a certain menace to society."*

Archie's legs went weak. His breathing quickened as he dropped to a sitting position at the edge of his bed. He had done this. He had opened this door, allowed this man, this stranger, Roswell, into his life, revealing to him his darkest, most disturbing secret. Archie had known that Roswell would one day broadcast his findings. But he hadn't cared. Not then, anyway. Archie had been thinking only of the immediate. Roswell was a means by which to get the information he sought. So what if the man wanted something in return? So what if he planned on revealing this terrible secret to the world, bringing untold attention to Colin and his colleagues? Archie just hadn't cared enough. Not then, he hadn't. But now. Now, it had happened. The door had been opened. And there was no way of knowing where this road might lead.

*****

Diana Mortonson was waiting for Archie that next morning. She'd parked in front of the next house over, and stood at the foot of the driveway, cradling herself against the cool November wind as Archie marched through the doorway, backpack hanging from his shoulders, the weight of the world pressing down from within his mind. "Hello, Archie," she said as he drew close. Her voice was sweet, like candy. "It sounds as though you had an adventure last night."

"My name's not Archie," he said as he crossed in front of her, barely glancing in her direction. "And I have no idea what you're talking about."

How could she already know? Did this woman—this brilliant scientist—actually listen to James T. Roswell's ridiculous on-air antics? And Roswell had not mentioned names, not of the infusion recipients, at least. Mortonson's name had been mentioned as well as Colin's, but the names Archie Lambert, Joey Burke, Neil Frisk, Barry Lind, none had been voiced.

"The institute phone has been ringing all morning," she continued, rising her voice above a frigid gust of wind. "There was a broadcast last night. Certain things were revealed."

"And that has what to do with me?" asked Archie, finally stopping and turning to face his adversary. She wore a knee-length, woolen coat, gray, and pulled tightly about her slight form.

"Neil Frisk is beyond help," said Mortonson as she stepped closer, her eyebrows seeming darker than midnight against her pale, white skin. "But you are not," she added. "Let me help you, Archie. Let me give you a sound and stable mind."

"I need to get to school," replied Archie.

"You're a grown man. What good is sixth grade to you?" Her eyes narrowed, causing those sinister brows to converge above her tiny triangular nose. "How many episodes have you had? How many breaks with reality, visits to someplace else?" she asked, her tone now softening, but her eyes remained intense. "Five? Ten? I hope no more than ten. If you've reached that state, it might already be too late."

Archie hesitated. How many had there been? He'd never thought to count. There'd been two at the Yamagata's house. But they were close together.

Would that be counted as one? He didn't remember the episode, per se, but he'd somehow lifted money from one of producer Ned's roommates. That would be another. There was the time with Bug's cat, the time when he'd met Jill, a couple when Gary had sat talking with him in Joey's room. The time he'd stood naked over Esther's sleeping form. How many times had he woken with grass or dirt on his feet—two, three, more? Roswell had alluded to animal mutilations. As much as Archie hated to admit it, he knew in his gut those had to be him. How many were there?

"I don't know how many, exactly," he said finally. His voice was weak, resigned.

"Then we'd best not waste time," said Mortonson as she stepped toward her Mini Cooper and opened the passenger-side door for Archie.

Chapter Thirty-Seven

The Positron Emission Tomography scanner was a tall, square machine, silver-white, with a tapered donut hole in the center where a patient could be slid in and then scanned. Numerous rings were within this. These were detectors that would record the emission of a radioactive substance which had been injected into Archie through an intravenous drip. He knew from previous experience that the substance would "tag" certain tissues such as glucose or ammonia and allow the doctor to identify anomalies in his brain. Archie had had these "PET" scans before, and was accustomed to the procedure; still, this time was different. In addition to the radioactive material, Diana Mortonson had injected Archie with a drug designed to induce one of his episodes. She wanted to scan his brain while he was separated from this tangible reality.

Archie understood the logic of this, but it frightened him still. Mortonson had inferred that if Archie had too many episodes before they devised a treatment, that he could lose his mind, that he'd forever exist somewhere between these two worlds. What if purposely initiating an episode caused him to slip over into that final oblivion? Was agreeing to this test essentially suicide?

Archie was strapped to the narrow examination table, cushioned, but stiff, his head held immobile. Normally, patients weren't restrained for this procedure, only asked to remain still. But as Archie would not be in control of himself once he slipped away, precautions needed to be taken.

"How do you feel?" asked Mortonson from just beyond Archie's peripheral view.

Archie tried to angle his head in her direction, but the restraint held firm. "Perfect," he said. "How could I feel any better than this?"

Mortonson chuckled. It was low, throaty. "I understand, Archie. The restraints make it uncomfortable. But you won't be aware of them most of the time."

"Yeah. Now I feel better."

She moved closer, leaned over him, smiled, her dark eyes glinting in the neon light. "Is this better?" she asked.

Archie grunted. "I'll be better when all of this is over."

Mortonson nodded. "Well, it shouldn't be long now. The episode should be at hand."

"Great," said Archie. "I can't wait."

They remained this way for several moments, Mortonson now leaning close enough to kiss, each studying the other, her warm butterscotch breath tickling his nostrils. Mortonson's lips curled seductively, her eyes glistened in anticipation; her expression intense, scrutinizing, aroused. What motivated this woman? What did Mortonson truly hope to gain? She was brilliant, her work amazing, but Archie sensed something deeper in her. There was no professional detachment where Diana Mortonson was concerned. Rather, there was a passion, a fire, nearly sexual in its intensity. Every syllable spoken dripped with zeal. Every movement shuddered with anticipation. Every fiber in her being thrived on the thrill of this accomplishment.

Archie felt an electric tingle race through his form, beginning in his torso and then moving into his limbs, all the way down to his extremities, and then reversing, rushing back to the point of origin. He began to sweat. There was now white at the corners of his vision.

No!

He did not want this.

He'd changed his mind. There was too much risk. He needed to make it stop.

"No," he said, though his voice seemed far distant. "Don't…"

Mortonson moved closer yet, the tip of her nose meeting his. There was no longer any restraint in the woman. She was smiling, broad, enthusiastic. "Relax, Archie," she said, her voice a husky breath, tinged with excitement, maybe even lust. "This needs to be done. Relax. Give in. Give in."

Their eyes locked, Mortonson's and Archie's. He watched as her pupils contracted, as her lips curled, as she caught her breath short in expectation.

*****

Archie was in the wooded area at the southern border of Ephesus. Plummer's Creek gurgled, and a gentle spring breeze caused the tree leaves to flutter. Bug was talking with someone nearby. His tone was terse, his comments pointed. Archie scanned to the right.

It was the wheel. Bug was arguing with the emerald wheel within a wheel. Archie could see the subtle green glow reflecting off of Bug's cheeks, the pulsating throb of eerie color that bathed the area. Archie tensed, unsure of what to do. Should he warn Bug, try to intervene, distract the wheel? What did the wheel want with Bug?

There was a sound, a rustling. Archie looked down to see a small dog, a shaggy mutt of no particular breed, lying on its side. Its breathing was labored. There was blood about the neck, a jagged slice. Emitting a final gurgle, the cute little animal breathed its last, the brown eyes becoming clouded as it stared into eternity. Disgusted, Archie turned back toward the gurgling water. Bug was gone. As was the wheel. In their stead was a young doe lowering its mouth to the short brush and nibbling.

Archie took a step forward through the tall grass. Something moved from beside his feet, a rodent maybe, or a snake. He quickened his step. The doe, like everything else in this reality, ignored him. He knew that he could approach it, touch it, feel its soft, subtle coat, but the creature would never respond to him. He scanned the riverbed, nearly slipping on the muddy ground as he approached the narrow creek.

There was a sound from behind. A voice. A child's voice, but not Bug's. Archie knew Bug's tone, and this was different, yet, somehow, familiar. "Hey, old man. Come here." hollered the child's voice, a voice that nearly surrounded him.

Archie twirled toward the sound, nearly slipping again on the muddy surface. He scanned the clearing and gazed into the trees beyond, but saw nothing.

"Over here," yelled the voice. "You ain't a pussy are ya?"

Archie took a tentative step forward. He was sweating now. The muggy air was thick and heavy. His limbs trembled with nervous exhilaration. This was it. He could sense it. The impending moment he dreaded like no other.

"It's just a memory," said the voice. "Nothing can hurt you—pussy!"

"I can't just walk into your memories," said Archie as he took one cautious step forward. He loosened his tie. The heat was getting to him.

"Sure you can. I'm just using the memory as kinda, I dunno, a meeting place or somethin'. Come on."

Archie moved tentatively forward wanting with all his being to flee into the surrounding white never to return. He could see a faint green glow just beyond the line of trees. He removed his suit jacket, dropping it in the grass. There was no need of the thing here. Scanning the area he said, "Where are you? I can't see anything here."

Why didn't he turn? Why didn't he flee? He did not need to do this. Wasn't it better not to know? Wouldn't it be better if he could continue to plead ignorance?

But he did know.

If he was to be honest with himself, he'd known—or at least suspected—for some time now. But still he'd held out hope that this could not be, that there was some other explanation.

"Just follow the path," came the distant voice, childlike, yet filled with venom.

"Follow what path?"

Archie scanned to his left and to his right. There was no visible path. He moved forward two steps, pushing a drooping tree limb aside, and not releasing it until he'd passed it completely. When, finally he let go, it snapped back with enough force to put a good size knot in someone's forehead. He glanced about, still trying to locate the path, angry that he was being forced to play this ridiculous game of hide and seek. He contemplated turning around, returning to the clearing, and waiting there, either for whatever was going to happen here, in this reality, or for his return to the real world. And though he so desperately wanted to turn his back on that which waited, he needed answers. And for the first time, he felt he might just be on the brink of putting this whole thing together. Horrified, yes. Terrified of what he already sensed to be true, absolutely. But still, he was compelled forward as if by a will beyond his own. Or maybe by his conscience or his soul. Something within him that for once sought to do the right thing despite Archie's own best interests.

"A little help here," he called. "I don't see any path."

"Look harder."

Archie pressed through the dense woods, smacking at mosquitoes, maneuvering around trees and brush. Several birds fluttered away, and he could smell the musty/fresh fragrance of water and foliage. He tripped once, over a tree root, stumbling to the ground with a curse. Then, rising slowly, he brushed the dirt from his pants and moved onward. The voice laughed, urging him to find the path.

"I'm working on it," shouted Archie in frustration. "Why couldn't you just meet me in the backyard? You've got to turn me into Grizzly Adams."

"Who?" asked the voice.

"Never mind," grumbled Archie as he ducked beneath a branch, then sidestepped a rather large stone. A tiny, gray squirrel scurried before him and then shot up an oak, settling itself on one of the lower limbs and nibbling on some unknown goody. The green glow was brighter now. Archie was getting closer. He continued forward, sweat dripping into his eye, stinging. He had to angle slightly right, as the glow was now in that direction. The brush was lesser now; he was able to move with relative ease.

Stepping into a clearing, he heard the rush of water to his left. A young doe dipped its head, dining on a low bush. He was back where he'd begun.

"It would have been easier to follow the path," said the voice.

Archie stepped forward, brushing twigs from his hair and dirt from his clothing. It was there—the wheel. One pulsating rim spinning slowly clockwise, the other, counter clockwise. The dozens of eyes scrutinized him, none blinking, none wandering. The thing shimmered and slithered, appearing almost as two circular tentacles, spinning lazily in each direction, eyes intermingled with tumors and sores. It was grotesque, loathsome even, having become viler with each encounter.

"What are you?" asked Archie, still panting from the exertion.

The thing expanded and then contracted. "You already know that," it said. And it was right.

Archie knew, but hadn't known. Or refused to know. At least until he'd heard the voice call across the clearing, until he'd seen Bug arguing with the wheel, until the mysterious, other-worldly object had taunted him in a child's voice, so strange, yet so familiar. It hadn't been until this experience that Archie had truly known. Oh, he'd suspected, but had not allowed these suspicions to progress. For if this speculation proved true, then Archie was the villain, the intruder, the thief that had stolen a living child's body, and in doing so, ended his life. It was much simpler to bury these thoughts, these fears and assume the wheel to be some outside force, some demon or ghoul that had slipped into his brain during the infusion.

Archie watched as the wheel contracted, folding in upon itself, shifting, changing. An arm emerged, first green and rubbery, but quickly gaining form and flesh tones. The fingers wriggled, grasping at nothing, but working out whatever insane kinks it had from the transformation. A leg followed, but not exactly where it belonged. There was more shifting, reshaping as the form of Joey Burke slowly replaced the maddening wheel. The boy looked smaller than the current version. Apparently the body had grown some while Archie inhabited it. Joey had Greg's light green eyes and broad mouth, and Esther's hair, light brown, cut short and spiked. He wore black, head to toe, no hint of color, no adornments. The boy flipped a hunting knife from hand to hand as he seated himself on a large rock, a boulder really, and glared at Archie.

"You really are an old guy aren't ya?" asked Joey. His voice was now that of a normal child, nothing otherworldly about it whatsoever.

Archie stepped forward, but not too close, not yet. "Yeah," he said. "I guess to you I probably seem ancient." Archie scrutinized Joey for a moment, staring at the face that he saw in the mirror each morning. "What am I doing here?" he asked. "What are you doing here?"

Joey cocked his head. "I could ask you the same thing."

The boy slid off of the rock and walked across the clearing toward the little river, still flipping the knife. There was no evidence of the wheel, nothing to indicate that he'd ever been anything but a boy.

Archie followed, unsure of what to do or say. "You're supposed to be dead," he said finally.

Joey continued walking. Once at the river's edge, he bent down. Selecting a few small stones, he began skipping them across the water. "You're supposed to be dead too," he said. "Bet there's a grave out there somewhere with your name on it."

Archie stepped to beside him, looking down on the boy, wanting to touch him, but fearful to do so. Everything in this world seemed so tangible, so real. But none of it was real. It was all in Archie's mind. "You're not real," he said in a final futile effort to deny the obvious. "This is some sort of hallucination."

Joey positioned the knife tip on his left index finger and pressed, drawing blood. "Is that what your dad told you?" he grinned, displaying the bloodied digit.

"Colin doesn't believe that anything I see when I come here is real, if that's what you mean."

Joey examined the bloodied blade. "I wonder if Daddy could be wrong."

The boy moved toward the tree line. Archie stood motionless, unsure whether or not to follow. How could Joey be here? How could he still exist? He had been brain dead. Gone. There was not supposed to be any of the boy left. It should have been a clean slate, a sterile environment for Archie's consciousness.

Archie turned toward the tree line where Joey had disappeared. There were colorful lights beyond, and loud distorted music. Archie had noticed none of this before. He moved in that direction, passing quickly through the trees. As he came through to the other side, he realized that it was suddenly nighttime. The sky was inky black, dotted with sporadic stars and only a wisp of clouds. Carnival music swelled about him. There were crowds of people, laughing, joking, playing games. Barkers called out, drawing the unsuspecting to their tricks and schemes. A group of teenagers screamed and whooped as the Tilt-O-Whirl spun them this way and that, a toddler with cotton candy raced giggling past Archie, his weary father in close pursuit. There was a Farris wheel to the right and a fun house directly ahead.

Joey stood at the entrance to the fun house. Bug stood beside him.

The boys stepped in.

Archie rolled his eyes, cursed, and made his way to the fun house. The five stairs up into the thing—a refurbished double wide—were rickety, swaying and creaking with Archie's weight. Archie marched past the scraggly looking ticket attendant unnoticed, and stepped into the dark, narrow space. He squinted as his eyes adjusted to the darkness. The place smelled of sawdust, enamel paint, and stale popcorn. The walls, floors, and ceiling were all of black painted plywood. Colored strobe lights flickered from around a corner and painted clowns and jesters eyed Archie from the walls. Archie saw movement further up the way, Joey and Bug. The boys split, each moving down a different corridor. Archie followed Joey.

There were mirrors, the wavy kind that distort the reflection. Archie could still hear muffled carnival music from beyond the thin walls, and he barely had enough room to maneuver in the tight corridor. "Joey!" he yelled after turning a corner to the right. "Where are you?"

"Look in the mirror," said Joey's voice from behind.

Archie looked in the mirror. His distorted image made him look short, like a child, while Joey, standing just behind his left shoulder, appeared tall, lanky, towering over Archie.

Archie turned to face the boy. "Why am I here?" he asked.

Joey shrugged. "Nobody else to talk to."

"What about Bug? He's here, isn't he?"

"Only memories of him. He can't do anything except what I remember him doing. We can't talk."

Archie stared at the boy. It seemed somehow bizarre seeing him here like this, talking with him face to face. In some ways it was like having a conversation with one's self. In others, it was like meeting a stranger, someone he'd heard about, someone he knew by reputation, but not anyone he'd ever encountered. "You're driving me crazy," said Archie. "These flashbacks, or whiteouts, whatever they are. I can't sleep, can't think. I'm constantly wondering when your next mind theft is going to pull me away from reality."

The boy remained silent, carving a curse word into the wall with his knife. Bug ambled by, oblivious to anything but his predetermined path. There were other people in the funhouse as well: a father with a young son. The boy was frightened, probably too young to understand his surroundings. He clung to his father's leg, whimpering, pleading to see mommy. A young couple turned the corner beside Archie, nearly plowing into him as they hugged and kissed, giggling at their ridiculous reflections.

Finally, seeing that Joey wasn't going to respond to his previous statement, Archie said, "I was told that you were dead."

Joey stared into Archie, seemingly examining his soul. Archie felt invaded, violated. "My body's still alive. So am I."

"Just because you're here," said Archie. "Doesn't mean you're alive."

Joey slid the knife an inch into his mouth, licking the blade as one might a popsicle. "I'm not a ghost, if that's what you mean."

Archie shook his head. "Nah. Not a ghost. I'm thinking more like a really deranged memory."

Joey stared at him, his green eyes bright, intelligent. "Memories can't think. I think."

"Like I said—deranged."

Joey shrugged. "I don't know that word."

Archie stared at the boy. It was impossible that he was real. Yet, he was carrying on a conversation, reacting to Archie. This was too real to be a dream or a hallucination. But then, what was it? What was this boy? "Listen, Joey," said Archie. "I saw your charts—before the infusion. Your brain was flat-lined. It had been for quite a while. Now you're back. It's not all coming together for me."

Joey smiled an ironic smile. "Ever think there might be stuff that doesn't show up on a chart?"

Before Archie could answer, the boy turned, following the dark, musty maze of a corridor through the funhouse. Not knowing what else to do, Archie followed.

"You know my dad, Greg?" asked Joey. "He'd beat the drinking thing. But then Esther did her thing, he let it get to him."

"Yeah. What did Esther do?"

Joey leered and made a thrusting motion with his pelvis.

A clown mannequin popped up from the floor, laughing a loud, bizarre laugh, startling Archie. He stepped back, nearly tripping over his own feet.

Joey continued on, unsurprised. He'd seen it all before. Archie composed himself with several deep breaths. "Thanks for the warning, kid."

"Oops. Did I forget to tell you about that?"

Archie stared at the kid. "Tell me about Esther."

Joey shook his head, and turned, stepping away.

Okay, thought Archie. None of his business. Better to stick with what really mattered. "Kid, I feel bad for what happened to you. I really do. But you've got to stop dragging me around like this. You saw Neil Frisk—right?"

Joey nodded.

"Barry Lind was the guy who was infused into Neil Frisk's body. But Frisk, I think, keeps trying to come back. I don't know how. But I think that's why he's insane. I think it's why they're both insane. If you keep pulling me back and forth like this, I think we'll both lose our minds."

Joey's face was that of a mannequin, cold, hard, emotionless. "Have ya ever thought that maybe I'm not the one who's supposed to be dead?"

Archie's heart leaped. "Joey," he said. "You were already gone. You were kept alive by machines. I was the one who still had a shot."

Joey stepped forward, lifting his blade and placing it against Archie's jugular in calm defiance. For some insane reason, Archie did nothing to prevent this. "You sure about that, old man? Lambert's your dad. You think maybe he was so set on saving you that he missed something he could have done for me?"

"Not a chance. Colin's my dad, yeah, but, no. We hadn't talked in years. He just doesn't care that way. He wouldn't sacrifice a kid for me." Joey applied just a little pressure, the blade bit into Archie's flesh producing a trickle of blood. "Joey, you were brain dead. Do you get that? Brain dead."

Joey shook his head, smiling a jack-o-lantern grin. "Do I look brain dead to you?"

The blade slid effortlessly through Archie's exposed flesh.

Chapter Thirty-Eight

Colin was there when Archie returned to reality. Somewhere between the time Archie had come back, and when he'd regained full clarity of being, his restraints had thankfully been removed, thus allowing him to angle his head and see his father moving about the room as Mortonson sat stoically at a computer station, legs crossed, head inclined toward Colin. Colin's face was taut as he worked his jaw, probably wishing he was in his own office where he could snatch a handful of peanuts. His pen was in his left hand, twirling between his fingers as he paced the floor. "This project was ours," he said. "Ours. Not yours." Colin paused, eyed Mortonson, moved toward the far wall, pivoted, and spoke. "That is my son on the table. My only remaining child. You had no right, Diana. No right."

"Nor did you, Colin. Regardless of what you may have felt." Mortonson's voice was calm, businesslike. There was no hint of her earlier exuberance, no allusion to her twisted glee. "You should have consulted me. This was not your choice to make alone."

"He is my son, Diana."

"Yes. And your son has brought a storm of attention onto this very secretive project because of your carelessness. If you'd included me from the beginning, perhaps we would have kept the boy here instead of sending him home with strangers and leaving him to his own misguided devices."

"And if you'd refused to allow me to perform the procedure?" said Colin. "You are, as we both know, the lead researcher on the project—despite the rather lascivious manner in which you established that credential."

Mortonson smiled, just ever so slightly. This woman wasn't ruffled easily. "If I'd have refused, it would have been for sound medical reasons. Not influenced by mundane paternal emotion."

"And if you'd refused, Archie would be dead by now."

Mortonson nodded. "Yes, Colin, that is likely." She turned toward the computer, tapping the keys. "You've been giving the boy AF367D-2 to suppress his episodes."

"That's correct," said Colin.

"Of course you understand the ramifications of such suppression."

"Following the extended loss of brain oxygenation, the boy suffered total necrosis of the cerebral neurons. The condition had remained as such for weeks leading up to the infusion. There was no reason to believe there would be residual activity."

"Then why the need to suppress the episodes? In theory, there should have been no episodes."

Colin smiled, paced, twirled his pen. "Theory is a wonderful thing, Diana. But, there are things we have yet to learn."

Mortonson unfolded her legs, re-crossed them, now the left over the right, and laced her hands over a knee. "But we do know that suppressing these episodes can have a counter effect, that eventually the psychosis pushes through, becomes worse than perhaps it would have otherwise."

"And that is precisely the reason I've continued research on the matter. An increased dosage appears to offset the side effects."

"You don't know that."

"Archie has functioned quite normally for nearly six months," said Colin. "He's shown more promise than any previous recipient."

"More promise? He has frequent breaks with reality; his consciousness mingles with latent memories. And while his mind is otherwise occupied, his body reverts to aggravated behavior. He's admitted to me that he slew a boy's cat. There have been reports of other animal mutilations as well. There's a missing girl, Colin. And now, a missing woman, a counselor at the elementary school Joey Burke attended. Tell me there's no connection."

"There is no evidence tying any of that to Archie."

"Are you telling me you don't even consider it a possibility? Colin, your judgment is impeded by your feelings for your patient."

Until this point, Archie had been content to lay still and listen quietly. But he had questions. Both Colin and Mortonson were present, each with their own assumptions concerning his condition. With a grunt, Archie rose to a sitting position on the narrow examination table. He was wet with perspiration and shivered sporadically. "Okay, you two," he said. "What's the real prognosis?"

Mortonson stared at him, a crisp smile on her painted lips. Colin paused, rolled his pen between his fingers, and said, "Archie, you're with us. Are you alright? Do feel any lingering effects?"

"I'm stable, Colin. For now." His voice was no more than a whisper. The episode had left him weak and shaking. "And I'm wondering why none of this was brought to my attention. My medication could make me worse? Don't think I ever heard that one, Colin."

"You're father's trying to protect you," offered Mortonson. "He doesn't want to frighten you."

"Too late," said Archie. He leaned forward, sliding off of the table and onto his floor. The tile felt cold on his bare feet, and he shivered again. "We're all three here now," he said. "I assume there's no other significant party that needs to be present." He looked from Colin to Mortonson and back again. Neither responded. "Good. Now, I believe I asked for a prognosis."

"You're functioning rather nicely," offered Colin. "Few episodes. Your mind is sound, your thinking clear."

Archie turned to Mortonson. "You disagree."

Mortonson nodded, allowing a devilish smile to crease her lips. When she spoke, there was a tone of excitement. Archie was again reminded that she lived for this project, for this research, regardless of the consequences to the infusion recipients. She wasn't evil or uncaring, but she was narrowly focused and committed to a point of fanaticism. "I believe you to be in grave danger," she said. "The PET scan showed some disturbing anomalies. You've been overmedicated, which, in the short term, has allowed you to continue functioning, but ultimately could cause the nano-web to deteriorate. You should expect more severe breaks with reality."

"Nonsense," shot Colin. "That's nothing more than an assumption."

Mortonson did not look at Colin, but continued with her gaze settled on Archie. "Everything is an assumption, Colin. But some assumptions are based on science rather than emotion."

"What are these episodes?" asked Archie. "How can the things I see during them be so tangible? I can touch things; feel heat or cold, sweat, cut myself. If none of it is real, how can that happen?"

"They are memories," offered Mortonson. "Very vivid, tangible memories. The brain is a powerful tool. An amputee often 'feels' the severed limb, though it is no longer connected to the body. It tickles, hurts, burns. Very tangible sensations. These latent memories are similar."

"But they're not my memories. They belong to Joey."

"Yes," injected Colin. "Quite possible. You see, we affixed a nano representation of your neuro net onto the boy's brain. When we infused your neuro energies onto this brain, they sought the familiar landscape and adhered. You, your consciousness, continued to exist. You have your own memories, your own personality. But, Joey Burke's neuro net was not destroyed, but rather suppressed. The physical remains of his memories still reside within the contours of the cortex."

"You told me Joey was dead."

Colin nodded. "Joey Burke is dead. He had no brain function whatsoever. All that was left was the physical remainders of his life, not his consciousness."

"I've met him," said Archie. "We've talked."

"Impossible," snapped Colin.

Mortonson was on her feet. "What do you mean, you've talked? When was this? Under what circumstances?"

"It happened today," he said. "During the PET scan. I've seen him before, just in a different form. I hadn't yet realized it was Joey that I was seeing." Archie paused, glanced from Mortonson to Colin and back again. Both were intent on his words. "But today," he continued, "he spoke with me."

"No," said Colin. "You simply encountered a latent memory."

Archie smiled an ironic smile. He was recalling something the boy had said. "Memories don't think," he said. "Joey thinks."

"And you know this how?" asked Colin.

"We talked, had give and take. He responded to my questions."

"That still doesn't mean he was alive."

"He was real. I was there. He was there. Now, what am I supposed to do about this?"

Mortonson moved uncomfortably close to Archie, a peculiar twist to her brightly colored lips. "What did the boy say? What did he desire?"

Archie met her gaze. "I think that's pretty obvious. He wants his body back."

"No," said Colin. "These are residual memories lingering in the cortex. Perhaps the hippocampus still recognizes input related to him and sends new data to the repressed portions of the psyche."

Mortonson's grin broadened. Archie felt her presence, her command of the situation, even her strange sensuality. "Well," she said. "I suppose we need to determine a course of action. If by chance you are right, Archie, we have two distinct personalities vying for control of the same form."

"How is that possible?" asked Archie. "If the boy was brain dead?"

Mortonson slipped a butterscotch candy from her right lab coat pocket, unwrapped it, and slid it slowly between her lips. "I'm not convinced, yet, that the boy truly exists," she said. "Your father may be correct—a latent memory. Perhaps the nanofibers we used to create your neuro net have deteriorated sufficiently to allow these to surface. This does not mean he exists, but only that his memories now litter the landscape of your subconscious."

Archie cocked his head and gazed intently into her deep brown eyes. She did not avert, or even blink, but simply sucked on her butterscotch. "Is that true? Or are you fishing for an explanation?"

She chuckled. The butterscotch was on the right side of her mouth, pinned between upper and lower incisors. "A bit of fishing," she admitted. "But, it is the most likely scenario."

"And this leaves me where?"

Colin moved forward, clicking his pen. "I suppose we could strengthen your hold by adding additional nanofiber, essentially reinforcing your brain map, making it more difficult for the underlying memories to surface."

"The other option is to reverse the process," said Mortonson. "In preparation for the procedure, the child's brain was mapped as well. We could create a nano-web of the boy's neuro web, allow the natural contours of the brain to reconstitute. There would no longer be the vying for dominance. The child's persona would reemerge."

Archie's stomach turned. His throat went instantly dry. "And this means what to me?" he asked. "I mean, you just said the boy was most likely dead."

"What she's suggesting," said Colin. "Is this. Assuming the boy is dead, that his neuro energies had dissipated entirely prior to the infusion, you would remain you. That is, your personality would guide the body; your consciousness, your being would be the one to exist. But, you would now carry young Joey's memories rather than your own. You would be Archie, but with Joey's history."

"And if Joey somehow does still exist?" asked Archie, fearing, yet knowing the answer.

"If Joey still exists," offered Mortonson. "Then your personality would be repressed and Joey's pulled forward. You would likely slip into nothingness."

Chapter Thirty-Nine

Cancer.

The diagnosis had been cancer.

Archie had breathed deeply of the cold December air and then shuddered with hacking spasms, spitting blood onto his already-stained handkerchief. He shouldn't have been surprised really. He'd been smoking since he was twelve. The tobacco Nazis always claimed the stuff would kill him one day. Who'd have thought the tight-assed pricks would be right? He'd always shrugged these doomsayers off claiming that he could lead a perfectly healthy life and then get struck by a car, thus dying years before a guy with a two pack a day habit.

Could that happen? Yeah. Of course. But it didn't. Not often. In the general sense of things, people that led healthier lifestyles lived longer. No guarantees, no promises, but a heck of a good shot at it. That was, after all, why their lifestyles were considered healthy. It was like betting on sports. Was it possible for the thirteenth ranked team (Mr. Two-pack) to beat the number one ranked team (Mr. Health conscious)? Of course it was possible. But the vast majority of the time, the number one walloped the number thirteen. It was just the nature of things.

And so logically Archie should have seen this coming, should have re-sponded to the emerging symptoms months sooner. He should have been men-tally prepared. But he didn't. He hadn't. He wasn't. The news had been a prizefighter's blow to the gut. He'd wept like a two year-old who'd just broken his favorite toy. The doctor had given little hope. The cancer was too well entrenched. It had spread to too many organs. Maybe if they'd caught it sooner… There was always the possibility of remission… But Archie knew the score. Sure, they'd toss the standard battery of near-death remedies at the beast: chemo, radiation, the minuscule hope that some miracle procedure would light up the horizon in the nick of time. But this was game over. A done deal. Archie was at the end of this thing. There was little doubt that this would be his final Christmas. He wouldn't live to see another birthday.

His first impulse had been to call Colin. He'd dismissed this lunacy nearly as quickly as it had flitted through his brain. Colin was his father, yes, but only in biological terms. The two rarely spoke. And when they did, they had so little in common, so few shared experiences, that the conversations inevitably tumbled into awkward silence until one of them claimed a feigned urgency and ended the torturous call. Perhaps Archie should have tried harder as an adult, tried to bridge that gap, tried to build the relationship that wasn't. But he'd never had the energy or the inclination for such things. Easier to just let it ride.

The person he wanted most to tell was Jill. But they'd seen so little of each other since the divorce. She'd be nearly thirteen now. Old enough to handle the news, but too young to deal with Archie's cascading emotions. He wanted nothing more than to hold her in his arms, to hug her, to tell her that she meant everything to him.

But that would be unfair to her.

They'd drifted apart in these past two years. It wouldn't be right to come back into her life, renew their relationship, and then die, leaving a father-sized hole in her heart. Her grief would be much more manageable if they were to stay distant. If they were to remain as strangers.

Like he and Colin.

He would never see her again. Of that he was nearly certain. And this knowledge was far more devastating than the knowledge that he was entering the final weeks of his life.

Archie had spent very little time in churches. There, of course, had been his wedding, and the weddings of family and friends, the funerals of both his mother and sister. He had attended Sunday school with friends a few times when he was growing up, but the Lambert household was not a religious one. Colin was an avowed agnostic, and Archie's mother just didn't seem to have the energy to care one way or another.

Archie felt at odds with God. He supposed he believed in the deity's existence, but had never taken it any further than that. His lifestyle didn't leave much room for a God that wanted a say in things. Eternity, with all of its unanswered questions and mystic truths, could wait for another day. He'd assumed that if God did exist, that he'd still be around when—and if—Archie ever felt the need. Even now, when the need was greatest, he felt like a coward and a hypocrite walking through the unfamiliar doors of a random church. Who was he to ask God's help? He was even less connected to his supposed heavenly father than he was to his biological equivalent.

The church secretary instructed Archie to walk down the long hallway to her left and to go to the third door on his right. The door was open and loud rap music pulsated from within. Archie peeked into the office. The walls were covered with posters of Christian rock bands. A half-eaten pizza sat on a chair near the desk and a lanky young man—Superman T-shirt, spiked bleached blond hair, pierced nose and eyebrow—sat at the desk flipping through a Bible.

Archie knocked rather loudly, attempting to be heard over the blaring music. The man looked up, smiled a broad and toothy grin, and reached back, turning off the music. "Come on in," he said. "Have a seat. I was just setting Psalms to a rap beat. Wanna hear?"

Archie remained at the doorway, still surveying the scene before him. "Psalms to rap music? Shouldn't that be blasphemous or something?"

The man laughed a hearty laugh, his pale blue eyes glinting with humor. "Lightening hasn't hit yet. Pizza?" he asked, indicating the lukewarm food to his right.

"Um, no. Uh, sorry, but you're—a pastor?"

"Yep. Igor's the name."

"Igor, okay, sure. No offense, but you're what, twenty?"

"Twenty-six. I'm the youth pastor. Come on in. I don't bite."

Youth pastor, it figured. The secretary had said most of the staff had already left for the day. Apparently Archie had been relegated to the B team. With a weary and wheezing sigh, he entered the room, taking a seat on the metal folding chair before Igor's cluttered desk.

"And you are…?" asked Igor, as he leaned forward, extending his hand to shake.

Archie took his hand. "Archie Lambert." Why was he here? Was there any purpose in this? Archie shuffled, resisting the urge to flee this obvious mistake.

Igor smiled. It was a broad smile, sincere and endearing. "Okay. What can I do for you, Archie Lambert?"

Archie adjusted yet again, meeting the young man's gaze. "I… um… need to know the meaning of life."

Igor broke into good-hearted laughter. "Oh! Is that all!"

Archie shook his head. This was wrong. He had no idea what to say, what to ask, or even what he truly sought. "No," he said. "Not really. I guess what I'm really trying to figure out is what happens after someone dies? Do we live on or fade away? And how do we know for sure?" Archie lowered his gaze, still contemplating his rationale in being here. He hadn't even consciously decided to seek spiritual help, he'd just… driven here as if on autopilot, he guessed. Apparently, at some deeper level, he sought comfort. Likely, he simply needed someone to talk with, a listening ear. He didn't think this man— this kid—could help him on any deeper level. He doubted he'd believe the young pastor's spiritual claims no matter how well intended or sincere.

Igor studied Archie, his right hand massaging his jutting cleft chin. "I don't know you," he said. "But I'm guessing you have reason for asking that particular question. Something in your life that's caused you to think of things eternal."

Archie shook his head. For some reason he couldn't spit out the word cancer, or dying, or beyond hope. He couldn't say what this was really about. Couldn't say that he was terrified to the point of madness, that it wasn't fair, that he was too young to die and what right did some invisible god have to take him so soon! Ultimately, he just shrugged, doing battle with the tears brimming in the corners of his eyes.

Igor nodded. "Hey, I'm sorry. I wasn't trying to be insensitive. You don't need to tell me any more than you feel comfortable with, okay?"

Archie nodded, still unable to speak without fear of his voice cracking.

Igor offered an encouraging grin. "Let's see if I can lay this out for you." The young pastor leaned forward, elbows resting on his cluttered desktop. "The soul is basically the nonmaterial aspect of a person in its relationship with the physical being. There's the body, soul, and spirit. The spirit is entirely nonphysical, but the soul is normally considered to be tied to the body. Some theologians hold that the spirit and soul are separate aspects of the same entity."

"Soul, body, spirit?" asked Archie. "Could those correspond with id, ego, and super ego?"

Igor pondered this for a moment. Archie could tell the question surprised him. "Nah…" he said. "Well, maybe, but not in any real sense. I think, well… who came up with that? Freud? Skinner? Whoever. I think maybe they were trying to conceive a scientific explanation for a spiritual reality. Even if no one cops to it, science often seeks to explain the things of God."

"That's how you see it? Science seeks to explain God. I know some scientists that would disagree."

Igor chuckled. "Yeah. No doubt. And I know some theologians that think all science is atheistic crap. But, the two don't need to be mutually exclusive. Each can learn from the other."

"Okay," said Archie, not convinced, but seeing no reason to argue the merits of issues about which he knew nothing. "Fair enough. Now, when a person dies, what happens to him?" This was the key element. This was the information Archie's subconscious apparently sought. What some part of him contemplated though his conscious mind had given it little or no attention. Amazing what learning of impending death can uncover.

Igor nodded. "Well, the eternal destination depends on a person's relationship with God. Is the person a believer or not? If yes, then the spirit/soul goes to heaven, if not…" Igor shrugged. "Buy stock in sunscreen."

*****

Archie left the church grounds nearly a half hour later more confused than when he'd entered. He supposed he'd hoped some spiritual light would ignite, that he'd find peace and solace in his situation. That, apparently, was a much too simplistic expectation. The young pastor had been sincere, his answers forthright, his concern real, but despite everything, Archie wasn't quite ready to leap off of some spiritual springboard just yet. Maybe as this thing progressed he'd think differently. Maybe.

He slowed the car as he neared Curly Jake's Tavern, pulling into the gravel lot and parking adjacent the cinderblock building. It was late into happy hour and Archie was anything but happy. A blue haze hung in the stale air. There was the buzz of chatter punctuated by the occasional laugh. The Chicago Bulls were on the screens above the bar. Archie spotted four or five familiar faces, no one he was particularly close with, no one he wanted to see. Jake was leaning on the bar with one elbow, chatting up some twenty-something year-old blond, undoubtedly using every six syllable word he could remember in a futile effort to impress the pretty young thing. He glanced up as Archie entered, but didn't offer so much as a nod. He was trying to get lucky. He wouldn't succeed. Archie knew this and likely so did Jake, but it didn't mean he'd reclaim any dignity and walk away.

This was probably for the better, Jake being distracted. Now that Archie was here, he realized that he just didn't feel comfortable unloading this burden on the bartender. He could think of no particular reason for this. Maybe just jitters and cowardice. They were, after all, friends. Certainly Jake would do anything he could to comfort his buddy, "Sketch." But, then... Archie figured it better to wait. He'd see Jake tomorrow, or the day after, or...

Archie offered a weak grin and a nod, and turned to leave. He would wait for Jake to call. Certainly Jake would be concerned when he realized that Archie had been AWOL for so many days—weeks, months. But the call would never come, and as Archie's illness progressed, he just didn't have the energy to think about it. By this point it would be all he could do to move from one room to another, much less hang out at the bar.

After leaving Jake's, Archie drove randomly about with no particular purpose in mind, flipping from radio station to radio station, popping CDs into the CD player only to eject them midway through the first song. He went through a drive-thru burger joint and then tossed the bag, burger and all, into the trash receptacle as he exited the lot. He drove past his apartment, but didn't bother to stop.

Eventually he wound up at a strip club situated at the northernmost border of Ephesus. A little whole-in-the-wall dive with a bright pink neon sign and two street punks—probably drug dealers—hanging out front. Archie landed at the bar, ordered a Jack Daniels, and stared up at the middle-aged stripper, all celluloid and rouge, twirling about the pole in an unenthusiastic attempt to arouse the handful of glassy-eyed men sitting about the dark and smoke-filled room.

After his second whisky, Archie perceived a woman lowering herself onto the stool to his left. Placing her palm on his thigh, she said. "Buy a girl a drink?"

"Um… Oh, uh, yeah. Why not?" Archie didn't even look at the woman.

The stripper nodded at the bartender who poured a small tumbler of golden liquid and passed it across the bar.

"So, you looking for some fun tonight?" asked the girl.

Archie glanced at her. She was thirtyish going on forty, dishwater blond, relatively slender, but only just, with sad eyes and an eager smile. "I'm not sure what I want," he said finally.

She leaned closer, removing her hand from his thigh and slipping it around to his back. Her perfume was nearly as overpowering as her tobacco breath. "Hey, that's alright. We can just do drinks if you want. I'm cool with that."

Archie remained silent, avoiding eye contact, attempting to focus on the girl on the stage.

The woman slid her fingernails across his back, giving him a gentle rub. "What's your name, honey?"

Archie said nothing.

"I'm Daisy. Have we met before?"

Archie managed a shrug and a grunt.

"Would you rather I go? I can leave you alone if you'd like. Maybe I could send another girl over."

Archie turned, burying his face in the startled woman's chest. "I'm dying," he cried into the stranger's suddenly tear-damp bosom. "I'm dying."

Chapter Forty

The fireplace crackled and popped, initiating the winter season. The smell of burning oak floated gently through the room, permeating fabrics, the sofa, the curtains. Greg opened the screen, picked up another log, large and knotty, and dropped it into the flames. A splay of dancing sparks shot and twirled, before evaporating like fireworks on the fourth of July. Esther sat in her cubby office berating some faceless technician about an incompetent installation while simultaneously abusing her computer keyboard with a series of furious strokes. Archie sat cross-legged on the couch, surfing the internet on Greg's laptop computer. Clapton nestled against him, occasionally allowing a soft moan to escape his mouth. Archie took no more notice of the dog than he did the family about him. His world was coming to an end. And there was nothing he could do to stop it.

Greg glanced at Archie, a mischievous grin on his broad lips. "Game of chess, Joey? Bet I can take you in under twenty moves." More likely ten. Greg had a good mind for the game. Archie was only vaguely aware that there was such a game.

"Not now, Greg. I'm busy."

"Facebook doesn't constitute busy, Champ."

"Research for school. Not Facebook," said Archie, without bothering to meet Greg's gaze. It was research, but not homework. In truth, he was scanning theological websites. When Archie had agreed to the infusion, he'd thought of eternal matters, of God and Satan, of heaven and hell, of Pastor Igor and his earnest thoughts on eternity, and had concluded that his number one priority was to remain breathing. Eternity, with all of its unanswered questions and mystic truths, could wait for another day. He assumed that if God did exist, he'd just cheated the big guy, and had most likely damned himself for eternity.

But eternity was exactly what he'd been trying to avoid.

Science had failed Archie as well. Both Colin and Mortonson were stymied. They wouldn't admit this, but things were happening beyond the scope of their knowledge. The problem with science, he'd concluded, was that despite its amazing accomplishments, it was still fluid. A fact was only a fact as long as no one discovered another fact that contradicted the original fact. Archie still wasn't ready to join the hallelujah chorus, but he at least felt the need to get an opposing perspective on things.

He wanted a different perspective on what happened to the soul after someone died? Does a person live on or fade away? How could anyone know for sure? For that matter, was there even such a thing as a soul and could it be separated from the body?

Did Joey live?

That was the burning question.

Was it possible that Archie had stolen a body from a living person? And if so, what was he to do?

But Archie was looking for something that didn't exist, an explanation to his specific and highly unique situation. He sighed. Nothing on these sites pertained to his condition. Scripture didn't address the concept of mind infusions. He clicked back to Google, deciding to hop onto the Mayo Clinic site. He wondered if even that prestigious institution was aware of this area of research.

The doorbell rang.

Esther rose, closing her browser and moving toward the doorway.

It was Bug.

Snowflakes dotted his hair and tears wetted his cheeks.

"Justin," said Esther. "You're crying." A crease slipped across her brow as the two locked eyes. Archie didn't know the history, but obviously there was a history. The two didn't care for one another in the least. He'd picked up on this from the very first mention of Bug's name.

Bug stepped through the doorway, not waiting to be invited. "My dad's dead. It's your fault."

Esther lost three shades of skin tone in a single instant. "Justin, what are you talking about?"

"Somebody killed him."

"Justin... I didn't... I wouldn't," stammered Esther, tears creeping from her eyes, hands quivering. Her reaction was extreme, as if the news had been of a family member. This was more dramatic yet in light of the woman's traditionally stoic and near frigid disposition.

"I didn't say you did it," said Bug. "I said it was your fault." He turned toward Archie, a little boy, fragile, damaged, and furious. "Burke, we need to talk." His voice, commanding though it was, could have belonged to a six year-old. It was tiny and filled with fear.

Archie set the laptop aside, rising to face the boy. He knew. There was no evidence, no indication that he'd gone to the white the previous night, but in his gut he knew there was no other possibility. It was all he could do to meet Bug's gaze, to subdue the tremor slinking through his limbs, and to dissuade the slithering white tickling at his ankles.

"Justin, is there anything we can do for you?" It was Greg; he'd risen and was moving toward Bug. His expression was one of shock and disbelief. "You said someone killed him?"

Bug nodded. "My mom and me found him when she dropped me off for the weekend." The boy turned to face Archie. "We're going for a walk."

"Already on it." Archie was slipping into his shoes. What could he say to this boy? Or should he say anything. Maybe he should just run—and keep running. Forever. Or at least until the white took him once and for all.

"Joey, I didn't say you could leave."

Archie rose. "Esther, I never asked."

The mid December night welcomed Archie and Bug with a stirring breeze that danced across their spines like tiny icicle fingers. It was cold but not horrible for a Midwest winter, likely somewhere in the mid-twenties. The boys walked south on Old Oak Avenue, away from both of their homes and toward the wooded area at the southern border of town. "Tell me what happened," said Archie. It seemed the cascading breeze followed three steps behind, dancing, tickling, desiring to be in on the scoop.

"No," said Bug. "You tell me." His visage was dark and uncompromising. Secret fears and realizations cowered just beyond his eyelids.

"Bug, I have no idea what happened." This was true in so much as Archie had no memories of the event. In that regard, his thoughts were as speculative as Bug's.

"But you know it was you."

"I don't know that and neither do you."

"Liar."

"I don't even know your dad. Why would I attack him?" Archie was getting angry now, self justified. He had the sense of being wrongly accused, though his rational mind knew better than to investigate too closely.

"You don't know my dad, but Joey does. He knows what my dad did."

"Bug, what are you talking about?" The kid was being cryptic, alluding to something outside of Archie's limited knowledge.

Bug rocked his head from one side to the other as if in contemplation. "You don't know Joey. You don't know what he was like. What he got to be like after... things."

Well, what the hell was that supposed to mean? "Then tell me, Bug. Clue me in on the mystery."

Bug paused and turned to face Archie. It seemed the tears were freezing to his cheeks. "Joey likes to kill things."

Archie went hollow. Of course Joey liked to kill things. How could Archie have not realized this? Every incident pointed to it. "Not people," he said, thinking of the missing girl, the missing guidance counselor. "Please tell me no people."

"Animals. Cats, rabbits. Anything he could catch. He liked to torture them. I think maybe people someday, but... not before what happened."

"Why? Why did he kill things?"

"How the hell do I know? He's in your head. You tell me." Bug was pacing now, his fists clenched, eyes narrow. "It's your fault. You let him do it."

Archie was about to protest when Bug's fist found his jaw. Archie lost his balance, slipping on the icy sidewalk and falling to the snowy ground. Bug was on top of him before he could respond. The best he could hope to do was to cover his face with his arms as Bug pummeled him. He tried to throw the boy off to his side, but Bug's blind fury gave him a strength well beyond his normal capacity.

"You should have left Joey dead!"

Archie tasted blood.

"Even his mom was glad he died!"

He felt two teeth shift.

Bug's knee found his gut and Archie nearly vomited his dinner. The kid was venting tortured emotions that had obviously built over a very long time. Another blow to the face, one to the groin. Still, Archie did not fight back, but only attempted to defend himself. Bug was not to blame. But neither was Archie. Not entirely. Not consciously so.

"Tell me!" screamed Bug. "Tell me what happened!"

Another smack to the face. Another knee to the gut.

"I don't know! I wasn't there! I wasn't there!"

*****

"I can tell you. I can even show you."

It was Joey.

Archie had tumbled into the white. But the white remained white for only seconds as thousands of tiny fragments of reality tumbled onto the landscape, assembling into an interior seen. Archie found that he was standing in a living room area of moderate size. No lamps were lit, though a thin beam from the porch light slipped in through the thin vertical window adjacent the front entranceway. Archie surveyed the room impressed by the fifty-two inch Sony flat screen television mounted on the far wall and the neat row of golf trophies lining the mantle. There was a salt water fish tank as well. Colorful clown fish, a purple firefish, an eel slithering between rocks; it was beautiful and well kept.

Joey was on the stairs, naked. He looked as Archie did in Joey's body, not as the smaller child he'd encountered before. This was a more recent memory. This was last night while Archie slept, oblivious to all that had happened. Already, Archie knew guilt. Diana Mortonson had wanted Archie readmitted to the institute. She said that in his current state he was a danger to himself and to others.

But Archie knew that if he was readmitted, he would never again be released. Roswell had brought attention to the place, surely they would be under investigation, and Archie's own condition was dubious. He'd wanted to step away, to think things through, to consider his options before committing. In truth, he felt that if there was a real likelihood that Joey was still alive, he would allow Mortonson to draw the boy forward, causing Archie to cease to exist. He simply didn't think he could live with himself knowing that he'd chosen his own life over that of a young boy. All he'd really wanted was to get away from the place, from Colin, from Mortonson, so that he could get his head around it.

Now, watching the child climb the steps, naked, a five inch knife clutched in his hand, and the visage of hate and loathing on his features, Archie wondered if it truly was the boy who should be allowed to live.

"Don't do it," called Archie.

The boy turned, his pale skin porcelain in the dim light. "Already did it, old man. I'm just reliving the good times so you can share in the fun."

Archie stepped forward, hesitated, and then followed him up the stairs. "But why did you kill him?"

"That's easy. He screwed her."

"Who?"

Joey leered and, placing his hand on the doorknob to the first room on the right, pushed open the door ever so quietly.

"No!" screamed Archie, realizing what was about to take place. "Wake up!"

Though he knew the deed was already done, he raced up the steps hoping to somehow, some miraculous way, intercede.

Bug's father was a tall man, dark of complexion, lanky, yet muscular. Despite the winter cold, he lay in only a T-shirt and boxers atop his bed covers. The heat was turned up high, and he was comfortably slumbering as death loomed above him.

Archie grabbed Joey from behind, pulling the boy backward as he raised the long hunting blade for the kill. They slammed against the wall, twisted, Joey's elbow connecting with Archie's gut. Undeterred, Archie slammed doubled fists against the back of Joey's head. The knife fell to carpet with a subtle *thunk*. Joey laughed, twirling and smacking Archie across the face with the back of his hand. He'd felt none of Archie's blows.

There was a scream from behind.

Blood appeared as if by magic on the fallen blade as a gaping gash opened on the slumbering man's back.

And then another and another.

The man writhed, pitching and screaming, crying for mercy from an invisible assailant.

For even though Archie had pulled Joey clear of the man, still the event continued.

An artery was sliced. Blood splayed against the nearest wall.

The man gurgled, grasping at some unseen savior, before tumbling lifeless to the floor.

Joey laughed and danced, thoroughly amused by it all. Had he always been this sadistic or had near death and imprisonment within his own mind sent him over that delicate edge? Bug had said that Joey killed things—animals, not people. What had pushed him to this ultimate depravity? Had it been inevitable? Was this the Joey that would be had he not drowned all those months ago, or was he more troubled yet for being locked away in Archie's subconscious all this time?

I.e., was Archie responsible for this killing?

Another slash, this one across the man's left cheek, opening a jagged gap from mouth to ear. The man mumbled incoherently, tumbling about the carpeted floor in pain and confusion as his life fluid spilled from his veins.

Joey smiled down on him, bent, picked up the fallen blade, and proceeded to castrate the man. This was obviously the part he enjoyed the most. Rising with an enthusiastic grin, Joey turned right and then left in excited confusion and then marched toward the adjacent bathroom.

Bug's father bled out while Joey showered his blood away.

*****

Archie tumbled out of the white to find Bug bloodied and still beneath him.

Chapter Forty-One

Archie kneeled on the snowy grass and pressed two fingers against Bug's neck. The wind wrapped about him like an icicle blanket. His fingers were numb from the cold. It was difficult to feel anything—in particular, a pulse.

Archie pressed harder.

Bug had to be alive, had to be breathing.

Archie couldn't have killed him. He couldn't have. If it was Joey's mind controlling the form while Archie was traipsing white, it would make no sense for Bug to die. Joey and Bug were friends. Bug was perhaps Joey's only friend.

Archie readjusted his fingers, buried his ear in Bug's chest.

The boy coughed.

He coughed!

He was alive!

Archie exhaled in a long grateful stream, tumbling almost gleefully onto the snow-covered lawn, lying face-up beside Bug.

The boy was alive. That was all that mattered.

But Archie couldn't relax. He couldn't allow himself to think this was over. He was losing control. With every day that went by, Joey asserted his dominance all the more. Archie couldn't allow that to happen. The boy was too volatile, too insane, troubled. A sociopath. Wasn't that what they called someone like him? What caused that? The Burkes weren't horrible people. There was tension in the home, true. But there was love as well, at least where Greg was concerned.

Archie sat upright. The snow was heavier now, coming down in a continuous stream. "Bug. You with me? Bug!" He patted the boy on his belly only getting a moan in response. There were no obvious broken bones, no puncture wounds, though the boy's face was puffed and swollen. Bug had been unconscious. He'd need medical attention. There could be internal bleeding, perhaps a concussion. Archie had no way of knowing what Joey had done to the poor kid while he was AWOL. Reaching into Bug's pocket, Archie withdrew his cell phone and punched in 911. Rising, he stepped toward the nearest house and read the address to the emergency operator now on the line. He stated simply that there had been an accident and that an ambulance was needed at this address. He then disconnected.

Archie turned to leave and then paused. Kneeling beside Bug, he withdrew something from his own pocket and slipped it into Bug's front pant pocket. Placing the boy's phone on his chest, Archie then rose and ran between houses. Hesitating, he glanced back at Bug's inert form and wondered if he should remain until help arrived. Bug was alive, but not conscious. What if he stopped breathing? What if he went into convulsions or had a seizure? Chances were that the injuries were minor but there was no way of knowing for sure. Could Archie live with himself if the boy died? Bug's death truly would be his fault. There'd be no skirting the blame. Joey had been the one to attack him, yes, but it would have been Archie that left him to die.

But there was another more pressing issue.

The white.

It slithered about his legs, climbing, squeezing, taunting. It tickled and pinched. It sucked at his life force like hell's own leech, and Archie swore he could hear it giggling in demented glee as his heart raced and his limbs grew weak. Archie focused on Bug's still form, attempting to ground himself in this true reality, but already the white encroached on his vision. How much longer could he stem the flow? A minute? Two? Certainly not long enough to do Bug any good.

Glancing one last time at Bug, moving quickly through the narrow gaps between brick houses.

He made it less than a block before succumbing to the white.

*****

Joey was staring at him, his green eyes iridescent in the low light. He was clothed this time, several months younger. Wearing a black T-shirt emblazoned with the image of an inverted cross, tight black jeans, black leather boots with miscellaneous chains scattered throughout the ensemble. Twelve was far too young for a kid to dress that way. "Hey, old man. Wanna see something kinky?" he asked, and then turned aside before Archie could respond. The setting was familiar. Archie had been here only minutes before. It was Bug's father's home. Everything was pretty much the same, with the exception of a few different fish and one less golf trophy. Joey motioned for Archie to follow him up the narrow staircase and Archie couldn't help but follow. Maybe Joey had some sort of hold on him in this landscape. Or perhaps the kid had simply worn away at his will. Regardless the reason, he followed.

"Sometimes she slips away during the day," said Joey, apparently feeling he had to set the scene for Archie. "It happened enough that I decided to follow her. Then I kept coming back when she was here. Bug's dad never locks the patio door and it's a pretty freaky show."

"She who?" asked Archie though he was pretty certain he knew the answer to the question.

Joey grinned and stopped before the master bedroom door. Sounds were coming from within, a man and a woman, lovemaking. Joey cracked the door ever so slightly, peeking inside. Archie had a clear view as well. Esther was in the bed. Her hair longer than Archie had seen it. She was naked except for tall black stiletto boots and was straddling Bug's father, oblivious to the fact that she'd been seen. The man was blindfolded and cuffed to the bedpost. The sex was aggressive, with shouts and moans and slaps. A whip lay on the carpeted floor. The kind of thing no kid should witness.

"That's my mom," said Joey with a lusty leer. But there was something else in his gaze as well. Perhaps hurt, maybe a sense of betrayal. The kid was pretending this didn't bother him, that it didn't dig into his gut and twist it into origami.

Archie wondered how much of this Greg knew, and how many times Joey had witnessed such acts. How could the kid keep coming back to this? What twisted motive made the boy watch his mother performing such lewd acts? What did this do to his young psyche? What did this do to his soul?

And how was it that he was never caught spying? Were these people that oblivious, that caught up in their own pleasure to have no sense of their surroundings? Or were they so twisted as not to care? Did they know? Had they seen Joey but just not let onto it? Maybe they were afraid to confront him.

Perhaps they felt it better to pretend not to notice rather than be forced to deal with the ramifications of their adultery once it became public. Even so, couldn't they at least lock the door?

*****

The scene vanished so quickly as to shock Archie. Again he was outside, in Joey's body.

"Oh my God," he said. Jill was in his arms, holding tight. She kissed him on the cheek and giggled an embarrassed giggle.

"What?" she asked as he pulled away, nearly stumbling.

"I'm sorry. Are you alright? Did I hurt you? I didn't hurt you, did I?"

"What are you talking about?" She seemed truly perplexed.

"Did I hurt you?" he nearly bellowed.

"No."

How had he come to be here? He didn't even know Jill's address. How had Joey known? What had Joey Burke been doing with his daughter?

"Sometimes you slip away and never know you've been gone," said Joey from somewhere deep within. His tone was taunting and superior. *"Just for a few seconds or a minute. Just long enough for things to happen."*

"Joey, what's the matter?"

Archie had to regain his composure. He had to reassert his dominance. He could not allow this to continue.

"Joey, are you okay? You said you wanted to kiss. You said you wouldn't leave until I kissed you."

She blushed. Innocent. Confused. The first awkward foray into middle school romance.

"Answer her—Joey!"

"Um, sorry. I... Sometimes things still get jumbled in my brain. You know, from when I had the accident."

They stood in silence for several moments, neither knowing what to say. Archie focused on her, using all of his mental energies to stay within reality. How often had he slipped away for a few seconds and said or done something horrible? Was Joey telling the truth or was this a skill he'd only just now acquired. There was so much that he longed to say, but every moment endangered Jill further.

Archie had always wondered why Jill had sought him out as a friend. Joey was a year an a half younger than Jill, and a boy. Maybe, he thought, it was because she somehow saw some of her dad in him. That maybe his mannerisms, his speech patterns, maybe when she saw Joey, she also saw Archie, and was somehow drawn to him. They had had an okay relationship when he'd still been married to Marcie. Things had been strained and their relationship distant after the divorce, but maybe deep down she still longed for a relationship with her father.

But there was no more time for such contemplation, no time to build a relationship anew. Archie knew now that this needed to be the final time he would see her. The risk was too great to pursue this further. "Jill," he said. "I saw your grandfather last week. He's my doctor."

"My grandpa's not a doctor."

Even now, Archie could feel the white tugging at him, slithering about his limbs, coiling, squeezing, seeking entrance into his conscious existence. Was there no rest from this? No break, no opportunity to recoup, to gather his thoughts? Had he finally slipped over that precipice of no return?

"She's hot, old man. Your daughter's hot," leered Joey from within.

"Colin Lambert. Your dad's father," said Archie, almost abruptly. It was so hard to follow the thread of conversation with oblivion knocking at the door. "Colin Lambert's the grandfather I was talking about."

Jill smiled and nodded. "Oh. That grandpa. I don't think I ever met him."

Tighter, tighter, the white squeezed, nearly tangible. Archie struggled to force the air through his lungs to speak. "Jill, my prognosis. It isn't good. I'm not going to be at school anymore. But, your grandfather gave me a message from your dad. He was your dad's doctor when he died."

Jill stared at him, silent and confused.

A single tear escaped Archie's eye and raced the length of his cheek. This wasn't fair to Jill. Not fair at any level. He shouldn't be here, shouldn't be playing with her emotions this way. He never should have reentered her life.

But it wasn't Archie that had sought her out this time. It had been Joey—the fiend, the juvenile deviant, just aching to get his hands on Archie's little girl.

"Joey, What's the matter?" Now she looked scared, confused. He needed to end this quickly, needed to put some distance between them before Joey regained predominance.

"Your dad loved you, Jill," he said in a quick and urgent tone. "He wanted to come around more but didn't because he was trying to avoid conflict with your mother. You meant everything to him. Everything. You've got to believe that. Do you understand?"

She nodded, confused and likely shocked.

"Good," said Archie. "Now never come near me again." Not allowing her to respond, he pulled her into a tight hug, and then, releasing her, raced into the darkness. It was upon him already, the white, closing in, perhaps permanently this time. He could hear Jill calling for him as he raced into the street, nearly running into a stationary Ford before skidding right and continuing south, his feet slipping, not gaining traction.

She was chasing him now, calling after him.

"Jill! Stay away! Don't come near," he cried. But his words were garbled, not entirely his. The white sought control. He could feel it holding him back, inhibiting him, even attempting to force him to stumble. "Jill, run! Run, Jillie! Away! Please! Just run!"

He fell to the snow-covered asphalt, shaking and twisting, cursing at the invisible tentacles that pulled him deeper, deeper until all was white.

Chapter Forty-Two

Archie found himself in the Burke's backyard, near the pool. It was apparently early spring, perhaps March or early April. Flowers were budding, the trees turning green, sparrows fluttering and chirping. The blue pool water glistened and beckoned, though it was still too chilly for a swim. Joey was there, wearing black. Always black. The boy glanced at Archie and nodded; his expression serious, no youth or vigor in the eyes. "You need to see this," he said. "Exactly the way it happened."

The boy turned toward Archie, a cat cradled in his arms, white and black, barely more than a kitten judging by the size. "Mom!" he yelled. "Come out here. I want you to see something."

"Not now, Joey. I'm busy." It was Esther's voice coming through the open kitchen window.

"Too bad," said Joey. "I thought you'd want to say goodbye to Tickles." Facing the window, the boy withdrew a knife from a sheath at his hip and held the blade to the cat's neck. He wanted Esther to see this.

There was the clunk of Esther slamming something on the counter. "What do you mean say goodbye to Tickles?" She appeared in the window, her expression of annoyance changing to one of alarm. "Joey! Put her down!"

Joey smiled and poked the cat with the blade. It squirmed and hissed, but he had a solid grip on the little animal.

Esther was through the door and approaching Joey in only seconds, the cat meowed, its green eyes seeming to plead to the frightened woman. "Put her down this instant," she demanded. "What do you think you're doing?"

Joey smiled a broad smile. "Getting your attention." With a quick swipe he drew the blade across the cat's neck. The animal screeched and clawed causing Joey to drop it to the concrete pool deck where it squirmed for only a moment before gasping its final breath. Already, blood pooled beneath the tiny body.

Esther raced toward the boy, whether to punish Joey or to snatch her fallen pet, Archie didn't know, but Joey stepped forward, blade extended, causing her to stop in fear of her own son. "Nah, don't try nothing. Time to talk."

"What is wrong with you?" she screamed through tears. "Why do you do these things?" Already, she seemed entirely unhinged.

"I know things, mom. I've seen things."

"You're deranged. You need help."

Joey stepped forward, the blade extended before him, his posture casual, his expression intense. "I need help? Me? What about you—slut?"

"Joey, what are you talking about?" Her voice quivered, her eyes averted his. It was clear she knew exactly what he was talking about.

"I saw you," said Joey, holding the knife up and rotating it slowly back and forth, watching the bloodied blade glint in the sunlight. "I've seen you a few times. You and Dr. Patel with your whips and handcuffs. I bet you've seen me watchin' too, but you're too afraid to say anything. It's easier to pretend you don't know that I know." Esther said nothing, so Joey continued. "You like it rough, don't you? Whip. Leather. Chains. And you call me deranged?"

"Joey. I don't know what you think you've seen, but..."

"I've seen a lot." He stepped closer, almost to within striking distance of Esther. "How much does Dad know?"

"Joey, stop!"

Though armed, the boy stepped back, startled at her blind fury. Where Esther had been frightened and confused, now anger and desperation overrode all other emotions.

"Greg doesn't know. Greg will not know. But, he is going to be told that you've got issues and that you need help."

She advanced on Joey as he stepped further back toward the pool. Despite his aggressive behavior, Joey was still a frightened child.

"Mom, stop it."

"Give me that knife."

"No."

"You need help, Joey. Give me the knife."

"I need help? Look at you. Look at you!"

She made a grab for the knife and he swiped at her, missing by only an inch. "I'm telling Dad. I don't care what you do to me, I'm telling Dad about you and Dr. Patel."

Esther lunged forward, again attempting to grab the knife. "If you tell your father, I'll have you institutionalized. No one will believe a brat like you. You're sick, Joey. Sick!"

"With a mom like you, yeah, I'm sick."

Both were crying, shouting, vying for position. They moved closer to the water's edge. Joey took a swipe at Esther. She dodged, lost her footing, and grabbed Joey as she tumbled into the pool. His final words before going under were, "I'm telling Dad."

At first, Archie couldn't tell who was holding who under. The blade was now at the bottom of the pool and they were still wrestling about. Water sloshed wildly; occasionally an elbow or a leg would surface only to submerge again within seconds. Archie fought the urge to intervene, but knew it would be a useless exercise. Besides, he wanted—he needed—to see how Joey came to drown.

Eventually, Esther managed to raise her head above water, but she held Joey by both shoulders, not allowing him to surface. He struggled and kicked, but she continued to hold him below. "Sick boy, sick boy," she muttered over and over. "Sick boy, sick boy."

Water sloshed and splashed. Joey's hand found Esther's face. He pushed, grabbed, but still she held him below. His left hand now, pulling her hair.

"Sick boy, sick boy."

A foot surfaced and then most of a leg, but Joey had no angle, no way to use the limb to his advantage.

"Such a sick boy."

First one hand and then the other went limp, plopping uselessly into the water. The leg slid silently below. Joey offered no further resistance. And it was then that Esther came back to herself, panicking, pulling Joey from below, attempting mouth-to-mouth resuscitation. Bug appeared then, racing through the fence gate, likely alerted by the commotion. There was a moment of stunned silence between the two as Bug took in the scene: the dead cat, the knife at the bottom of the pool, Joey's lifeless form. Did he understand what had just occurred? Surely he at least suspected.

"Justin," said Esther, in a voice hundreds of miles distant. "Your friend fell in the pool. He's not breathing. Help me lift him onto the deck. And then you'd better call 911."

*****

Archie came out of the white as the knife descended toward Esther's chest. Realization came too late for him to change the course of the strike, and the blade sunk deep and true, striking first bone and then skirting slightly left and then penetrating her heart. Her cobalt eyes flashed horror as a gasp rushed from between her lips. There were no words. No reprisals, no cries. She didn't try to say that she understood, or that she loved him, forgave him, or wished he'd burn in hell. She simply gazed forward in shock and horror, took two faltering steps, fell face down onto her bed, and then died without much commotion.

Archie backed away, two steps, three. "Oh, God," he said but it was only a gasp. "Joey, you bastard."

The boy had chickened out in the end, vacating the scene at the last, leaving Archie to strike the killing blow. No matter how twisted the kid was, he didn't have the balls to kill his own mother—not exactly. Joey had done this, all of it; he'd simply thrown Archie into the mix in a final act of cowardice.

Archie looked right and then left. Greg was nowhere to be seen. Was he at work in the garage, still blissfully oblivious to the fact that he'd just become a widower, or had Joey tended to him as well?

His next thought was, "Thank God." Not that Esther was dead, not that this had happened, but that it wasn't Jill laying there dead, a knife protruding from her form. For when Archie had last occupied reality, Jill had been only a few yards distant. What had happened since then? Obviously, Joey had returned home. He'd left Jill. She was safe.

For now.

She had to be.

This had all been about Esther, hadn't it? Everything about Esther. The young boy had not known how to process the sights he'd seen, the blatant betrayal of his mother against his father—and ultimately against him. His mother had killed him. Drowned him. Archie couldn't know for sure, but likely the other kills—they had to be kills, he knew this now—the missing girl, the missing school counselor, these were merely a means of gaining the courage to kill Bug's father and Joey's own mother. He could only hope that Greg, the unwitting enabler, had been excluded from Joey's wrath.

Archie gazed down at the still form before him. There was no life there, nothing to revive. The chest did not rise and fall, the blade did not quiver with the beat of a heart, the eyes stared glassy and soulless into eternity. And Archie knew what he must do.

Chapter Forty-Three

Another gruesome discovery. Greg's body on the kitchen floor. Bloodied. Glassy eyes staring into nowhere. Archie was numb. He could only offer a mouse-like whimper at the sight and couldn't even muster the strength to approach the body, to feel for a pulse. Not that there was any hope of that. There were multiple slashes about the chest, the neck was cocked at a nauseating angle, and the pool of blood on the floor was simply far too large to have left much in the body.

Why Greg? He hadn't been perfect—who was? —but he'd been a decent guy. He'd tried to be a good father to Joey. True, he'd fought his own demons, and yes, he'd blindly allowed Esther to continue in her deviant ways—and that was the true sin, wasn't it? —but in many ways he'd been as much a victim as Joey. At the very least, he'd meant well. He'd been ineffective and weak, but his heart had been true.

Archie turned away. These thoughts were useless. Why try to make sense of the motives of a mad person? All that could come of that was more madness.

For some reason the knife was again in hand. He was barely aware of pulling it from Esther's chest. Had that been Joey's decision or his own. He wasn't quite sure. But the knife was there, clutched in his right fist still wet with blood. Mechanically, he snatched Greg's keys from the kitchen counter and then exited quietly through the front door, knowing but not fully knowing his intent.

In the time Archie had been indoors the light flurry had progressed into a full-fledged blizzard. Snow poured in thick white curtains from the dark late-evening sky as he made his way to Greg's pickup truck, whirling around in the wind, biting through Archie's flesh. If he'd waited any longer, he probably would have had to dig the vehicle out before driving away.

He turned the ignition, glanced over his left shoulder, put the truck into reverse, and then backed out of the driveway. He cut left, straightened the wheel, and then fully extended his too-short leg to press the accelerator. Archie caught a glimpse of movement and slammed the breaks causing the vehicle to slide precariously on the slippery surface. He'd nearly struck the slender figure before him.

Jill stood in the street. Gusts of wind buffeted her gentle face and her long hair flopped about in the unseasonably cold wind as she hugged herself tightly in an attempt to conserve body heat.

No, no, no, no. She couldn't be here. Not now, not when he was in such a volatile state. No. Not Jill. Not Jill. Archie rolled down the driver's side window. "Get out of the street," he hollered above the gusts. "Go! Leave!"

Jill shook her head. "I was worried about you. I wanted to make sure you're alright." He could barely hear her voice above the howling wind.

White flickered about the pickup. Archie squinted and trembled, trying to maintain his elusive hold on this reality. "Jillie-bean, you've got to leave."

Jill stepped forward, coming alongside the open window. Her eyes widened at the sight of him. "Whose blood is that?"

White flickered like a strobe light as Archie fought Joey for control of the form. Everything was in stop-action, herky-jerky movements.

When finally he gained some feeble control, he found that he was out of the truck, pitching about on the snow like a salmon in a boat. Jill, bless her heart, rushed to him, concerned for his wellbeing. She might have even thought the blood was his own, that he'd intentionally injured himself. Clearly, she wasn't thinking about her own safety.

"Joey! Are you alright? What's happening? What are you doing with that knife?"

Archie scrambled to his feet, still clutching the offending blade. "Get away from me!" He screamed. A harsh gust of wind buffeted his face, stinging his eyes.

"I don't understand." Jill appeared horrified at the sight of his bloodied clothing, but still she didn't run. Brave girl. Foolish girl.

He needed to get away from this place before he killed her. "You won't understand," he said. "Just, trust me. I've got to go."

He threw the knife off to his left. He couldn't have it with him, not with Jill in such close proximity.

"You're right, Joey. I don't understand. Tell me what's happening. I'm your friend." Her voice was pleading. There were tears in her eyes now.

"There's no time. Can't you see that?"

Straining to walk against a particularly harsh gust of wind, Archie made a move toward the pickup.

Jill blocked his way.

The white flickered bright and then brighter. Archie sensed movement, but it was all a rush, a jumble. Who was in control? Him? Joey? Neither? Both? He couldn't know. Not in those moments. When finally he was again aware of his surroundings, Jill was beneath him, pinned to the ground, the knife had somehow once again found its way into his grip.

He tumbled off of her with a horrified shriek. "Oh, my God. Jill are you alright? Did I hurt you? Jill!" His voice cracked with this last. He couldn't have killed her. He couldn't.

Jill rose slowly. Gasped for breath. Her neck was red. Had he been trying to strangle her? "Joey! What's happening to you?" Her voice was barely a croak.

The white flickered.

Still clutching the knife, Archie rose to pace in circles. "I'm dangerous, Jill. Run. Just run."

"I'm not leaving until you tell me what this is about. What's happening, Joey? The truth!" Why wouldn't she run? He'd obviously attacked her. But she just stood there demanding answers.

"The truth? God, Jill. Please, I can't hold Joey back much longer. Run. Just please run."

Snow whipped around mingling with the flickering white that only Archie could see. He clutched the knife as he gazed at his daughter. So wonderful. So brave. Look at her, standing in the midst of a blizzard facing down a lunatic that held a bloodied knife.

A lunatic that just happened to be her father.

"Joey! Tell me the truth! Please!"

Archie howled in frustration, cursing the sky, his horrific shout of agony swept almost silently away by the rushing wind.

"Joey! Talk to me. Okay? Just talk."

"Alright. The truth. The real truth. That's what you want." He stopped pacing to stare up into the storm and threw the knife far to the right. Flakes covered his face, flicked into his eyes and mouth. After a moment he lowered his head to meet Jill's gaze. "I'm not Joey."

"Don't be stupid. What do you mean?"

Archie stomped his foot attempting to scatter the gathering white. "Like I said, I'm not Joey."

"That doesn't make any sense. Who are you then?"

An agonized groan, and then, "I'm the guy who runs to a strip club the day he finds out he has cancer because the only way he can find sympathy is to pay for the affections of a stranger. I'm the guy who came home to find that his wife and daughter had left without so much as an explanation. I'm the guy who steals a child's body. The guy who lets that child run rampant. I'm the guy whose only daughter thinks he's a lush and a sleaze. And she's right. You know that? You're right to hate me, Jill. You're right!"

"What are you talking about?" The words were a scream choked off by tears.

White flickered and pulsed all about Archie. He could see a shadow within, not fully formed, but it was Joey. Who else could it be but Joey? And he would gain control. Archie knew this just as he now realized that there had always been only one way that this could end. Focusing on his daughter, he stepped forward, meeting her gaze, wishing with every fiber of his soul that he could be there to see her grow into the amazing young woman that she was certain to become, wishing he could see her marry and give him grandchildren, wishing he could buy her her first car. So many wishes and no genie. "I know this doesn't make any sense to you," he said. "But the only way for you to be safe is if I'm no longer living. I love you, Jillie. I'll always love you."

He leaned forward, almost as if to hug her and then abruptly pushed Jill to the snow-covered ground. Archie bolted for the pickup, slamming and locking the door, and shoving the key into the ignition while Jill was still scrambling to her feet. Archie threw the truck into gear, and sped away as Jill chased on foot, screaming after the boy who was her father. A quick glance in the rear-view mirror, and this was the last Archie would ever see of Jill.

Visibility was nearly zero as Archie sped south down the narrow winding road and toward the woods to the south of town.

Fumbling with the truck's Bluetooth, Archie dialed Colin's number.

"Hello? Mr., Mrs. Burke?"

"Colin. It's me."

"Archie, are you well? You sound tense."

Tense. Is that what you call it? "Colin, you need to listen to me. It's all come apart. Joey's asserting control. There's been… Things have happened. Irreversible things. It's all going to come down on you. I'm sorry. I didn't mean for you to take a fall for me."

Wind buffeted the truck. Thick sheets of snow blew horizontally before the windshield. Visibility was no more than fifty feet. Archie's hands shook as he drove. Not from the near zero temperature, but from something else.

The white.

Creeping, clawing, calling to him.

He blinked, attempting to maintain his vision as his world slipped to white. He shook his head and howled the cry of the damned. His vision cleared.

"Colin? Are you there?"

"Dear God, what's going on, son? Tell me what's happened."

Son? Archie couldn't remember the last time— if ever—Colin had called him son. "Joey took over. He killed Esther and Greg and… one other, probably more."

"Dear God."

Two calls to God in as many seconds. Apparently Colin wasn't quite so agnostic as he'd claimed.

"Colin. He wants Jill. He's already gone to her once that I know of."

"Is she…?"

"She's safe, Colin. For now. And after another minute, forever."

White again.

Another shake. The truck swerved. Archie somehow maintained control as he fishtailed down the road, nearly taking out a signpost. He was out of the residential district now, meeting up with the narrow highway leading toward the Gowon Institute.

"What was that, Colin? I didn't hear you."

"Come to the institute. Diana and I have studied your charts. We think we may have a solution."

"Too late for solutions, Colin. I'm only calling to give you fair warning."

"Archie, none of this is your fault. None…"

Archie disconnected the line.

He could see the bridge in the distance, the one that crossed Plummer's Creek. It would do. It would have to do.

"Joey!" he screamed. "Joey, you hear me?"

The phone buzzed. It was Colin. Archie ignored the call.

The white sought to intrude, but Archie blinked, concentrating on the slippery road before him.

"No you don't, Joey. We do this one on my terms."

White.

Everywhere, white.

But only for a second. Utilizing every scrap of mental energy he could produce, Archie pulled himself back into reality.

"You took it too far kid. I can't risk you ever having control again."

Archie accelerated, causing the truck to fishtail. He was coming upon the narrow bridge.

Somewhere off in the depths of his mind, he heard Joey scream as the boy finally realized what Archie intended to do. *"Why?"* screamed Joey. *"Why?"*

"For Jill," said Archie. "You'll never get my little girl."

The truck broke through the flimsy guardrail and seemed to hang suspended in space for several seconds before angling nose first into the frozen creek. Archie felt the sudden jolt of impact, the smothering thud of the airbag as it smacked against his face, and the ice-strewn water racing in through every crevice. Barely conscious, Archie found the two switches on the hand rest and lowered the windows, allowing the frigid water to flow uninhibited, to embrace him in its chilling grip. Far at the edge of consciousness, he heard Joey's frantic pleas. *"No! Not drowning. Not again. Not drowning—please!"* And then, as the truck lulled sideways and then slipped beneath the surface amidst a symphony of bubbling gurgles, Archie closed his eyes, said a silent farewell to Jill, and knew nothing ever again.

Epilogue

"James T. Roswell coming to you on The Flame, northwest Indiana's own source for news of the extraordinary. Today, we have a story originating right here in Ephesus. Mind infusions. That's right, people. The infusing of one person's consciousness, soul, his very being, onto the brain of another. Now, we addressed this issue some weeks ago to the skepticism and outrage of small-minded simpletons. But due to my perseverance, an investigation has been opened into the goings on at the Gowon Institute. Doctors Colin Lambert and Diana Mortonson have been subpoenaed to appear at the Lake County Court House in Crown Point later this month. Both have declined comment. But, having met with Dr. Lambert during the midst of these happenings, I have the inside scoop, and let me tell you it's spectacular. I'd be surprised if Lambert and Mortonson don't both lose their licenses. In truth, they'll likely both face criminal charges leading to imprisonment. But, first pygmy teleportation, fact or fiction…"

*****

There was fresh snow on the ground adding to the already existing twenty-six inches. School had been called off and most of the neighborhood kids were taking full advantage of the opportunity, breaking out sleds and ice skates, and, aside from the entrepreneurial among them, generally avoiding shovels and driveways at all costs.

Jill opened the door, peered out, nodded, and then stepped onto the porch. She wore a heavy wool sweater but still cradled herself in her arms as she watched her breath swirl in the wind. "Hi," she said.

"Hi," said Bug.

They stared at one another, each unsure of what to say. Finally, Bug spoke. "Not many people know what really happened, but you know, right?"

Jill nodded. "My mom told me, after Dr. Lambert told her."

They stood staring at one another for several moments. Bug withdrew something from his jacket pocket. It was a photograph, the one of Archie and Jill that Archie had carried with him throughout his time as Joey. It was bent, and crinkled, but still intact. Archie had shoved it into Bug's pocket during their final encounter. Bug handed it to Jill. "I think your dad wanted me to give you this," he said. "There's a note for you on the back."

Jill stared at the picture, studying the faces, the smiles, the apparent warmth and bonding shared between the two subjects. Finally she turned it over and read the words.

Jill, you may not know this, or even believe it, but you are the most important person in my life. I'm sorry I didn't see you more while there was still time. I should have been braver. I should have fought for our time together. It's amazing how easy it is to neglect what's really important until it's much too late. I love you.

Dad

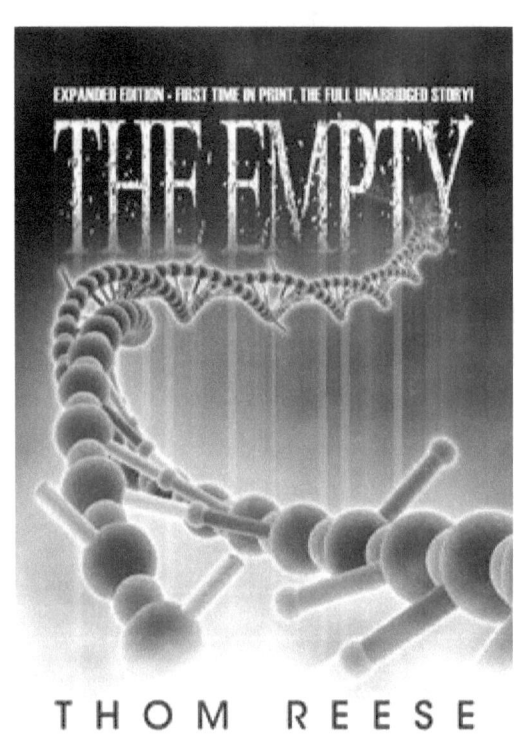

Visit us at: www.speakingvolumes.us

FROM THE AUTHOR OF
DEAD MAN'S FIRE: A MARC HUNTINGTON ADVENTURE

The Demon Baqach

by
THOM REESE

Published by SpeakingVolumes

Visit us at: www.speakingvolumes.us

Visit us at: www.speakingvolumes.us

Sign up for free and bargain books

Join the Speaking Volumes mailing list

Text

ILOVEBOOKS

to 22828 to get started.

Message and data rates may apply